Praise for the Re

"One of the all-time great characters in one of the all-time great series."   —Lee Child, *New York Times*
bestselling author of *Worth Dying For*

"Clearly this is a Repairman Jack moment. He's contacted, he arrives, he sorts things out for the deserving Munir—and readers will love the take-no-prisoners way he does it."

—*Kirkus Reviews* on *Fatal Error*

"With *Fatal Error*'s primary focus on Jack, and with the action almost nonstop, readers will find themselves so engrossed in this tale that they will be unable to put the book down. *Fatal Error* is, without a doubt, one of the most captivating releases in the Repairman Jack series of novels."   —*Horror World*

"[A] riveting supernatural thriller. Wilson gives his multi-layered plot an invigorating aura of cosmic creepiness as he deftly weaves together subplots and themes that have been snaking their way through the past dozen novels. Abounds with ingenuity and surprises."

—*Publishers Weekly* on *Fatal Error*

"One of the things that makes the Repairman Jack series stand out from the supernatural pack is that even though there are fantastical things going on, the stories, and Jack himself, are still grounded in reality. The books are about an ordinary guy doing whatever it takes to protect the innocent, and that's a story that always has resonance."

—*Chicago Sun Times* on *By the Sword*

ALSO BY F. PAUL WILSON

REPAIRMAN JACK*
The Tomb
Legacies
Conspiracies
All the Rage
Hosts
The Haunted Air
Gateways
Crisscross
Infernal
Harbingers
Bloodline
By the Sword
Ground Zero

YOUNG ADULT*
Jack: Secret Histories
Jack: Secret Circles
Jack: Secret Vengeance

THE ADVERSARY CYCLE*
The Keep
The Tomb
The Touch
Reborn
Reprisal
Nightworld

OTHER NOVELS
Healer
Wheels Within Wheels
An Enemy of the State
*Black Wind**
Dydeetown World
The Tery
*Sibs**
The Select
Virgin
Implant
Deep as the Marrow
Mirage
    (with Matthew J. Costello)
Nightkill
    (with Steven Spruill)
Masque
    (with Matthew J. Costello)
The Christmas Thingy
Sims
The Fifth Harmonic
Midnight Mass

SHORT FICTION
Soft and Others
*The Barrens and Others**
*Aftershock and Others**
The Peabody-Ozymandias
    Traveling Circus &
    *Oddity Emporium**

EDITOR
Freak Show
Diagnosis: Terminal

*See "The Secret History of the World" (page 389).

F. PAUL WILSON

FATAL ERROR

A REPAIRMAN JACK NOVEL

TOR®

A TOM DOHERTY ASSOCIATES BOOK
NEW YORK

This is a work of fiction. All of the characters, organizations, and events portrayed in this novel are either products of the author's imagination or are used fictitiously.

FATAL ERROR: A REPAIRMAN JACK NOVEL

A Tor Book
Published by Tom Doherty Associates, LLC
175 Fifth Avenue
New York, NY 10010

www.tor-forge.com

Tor® is a registered trademark of Tom Doherty Associates, LLC.

ISBN 978-0-7653-6280-3

First Edition: October 2010
First Mass Market Edition: November 2011

Printed in the United States of America

0 9 8 7 6 5 4 3 2 1

ACKNOWLEDGMENTS

Thanks to the usual crew for their efforts: my wife, Mary; David Hartwell, Becky Maines, and Stacy Hague-Hill at the publisher; Steven Spruill; and my agent, Albert Zuckerman.

Special thanks to Christopher Corbett—a reader known as Fenian1916 on the repairmanjack.com forum—for the title.

And special thanks to my cyberconsultants: Clint Collins, Ronald P. Crowe, Jr., Scott Garrett, Paul Hewitt, and Jason Tabor.

AUTHOR'S NOTE

The penultimate Repairman Jack novel.

As mentioned in the past few books, I'm ending the series with number fifteen (though Jack will be a major player in *Nightworld*).

I've always said this would be a closed-end series, that I would not run Jack into the ground, that I had a big story to tell and would lower the curtain after telling it.

The end of that story is just around the corner.

Fatal Error picks up in the winter following *Ground Zero,* and its finale coincides with that of *Reprisal.* If/when you read *Reprisal*, you'll understand what happened between Glaeken and Rasalom in North Carolina. (See "The Secret History of the World" at the end of this book for how everything fits together.) As with the last couple of novels, *Fatal Error* doesn't tie up as neatly as we'd all like, but it sets the stage for an ass-kicking finale to the series.

One more Repairman Jack novel remains. Working title: *The Dark at the End.* Appropriate, I think, considering it ends just before *Nightworld* begins.

In *Nightworld,* the Adversary Cycle and Repairman Jack saga will merge and . . . close. The Secret History concludes with *Nightworld*. More stories remain to be told, but the timeline stops there.

Hang in there, folks. It's been a long ride, and we've still got a lot of wonder, terror, and tragedy ahead. I promise you'll be glad you made the trip.

—F. Paul Wilson
the Jersey Shore

MONDAY

1. Munir stood on the curb, facing Fifth Avenue with Central Park behind him. He unzipped his fly and tugged himself free. His reluctant member shriveled at the cold slap of the winter wind, as if shrinking from the sight of all these passing strangers.

At least he hoped they were strangers.

Please let no one who knows me pass by. Or, Allah forbid, a policeman.

He stretched its flabby length and urged his bladder to empty. That was what the madman had demanded of him, so that was what he had to do. He'd drunk two quarts of Gatorade in the past hour to ensure he'd be full to bursting, but he couldn't go. His sphincter was clamped shut as tightly as his jaw.

Off to his right the light at the corner turned red and the traffic slowed to a stop. A woman in a cab glanced at him through her window and started when she saw how he was exposing himself. Her lips tightened and she shook her head in disgust as she turned away. He could almost read her mind: *A guy in a suit exposing himself on Fifth Avenue—the world's going to hell even faster than they say.*

But it has *become* hell for me, Munir thought.

He saw her pull out a cell phone and punch in three numbers. That could only mean she was calling 911. But he had to stay and do this.

He closed his eyes to shut out the line of cars idling before him, tried to block out the tapping, scuffing footsteps of the shoppers and strollers on the sidewalk behind him as they hurried to and fro. But a child's voice broke through.

"Look, Mommy. What's that man—?"

"Don't look, honey," said a woman's voice. "It's just someone who's not right in the head."

Tears became a pressure behind Munir's sealed eyelids. He bit back a sob of humiliation and tried to imagine himself in a private place, in his own bathroom, standing over the toilet. He forced himself to relax, and soon it came. As the warm liquid streamed out of him, the waiting sob burst free, propelled equally by shame and relief.

He did not have to shut off the flow. When he opened his eyes and saw the glistening, steaming puddle before him on the asphalt, saw the drivers and passengers and passersby staring, the stream dried up on its own.

I hope that is enough, he thought. Please let that be enough.

But he was not dealing with a sane man, and he had to please him. Please him or else . . .

He looked up and saw a young blond woman staring down at him from a third-floor window in a building across the street. Her repulsed expression mirrored his own feelings. Averting his eyes, he zipped up and fled down the sidewalk, all but tripping over his own feet as he ran.

2.   "Gross," Dawn said, turning away from the window to pace the consultation room. "What is it with people?"

"Pardon?" Dr. Landsman looked up from where he sat behind his desk, scribbling in her chart. "Did you say something?"

Dawn Pickering didn't want to talk about some creep

peeing in the street, she wanted to talk about herself and her baby. She ran her hands over her swollen belly, bulging like a watermelon beneath her maternity top.

"Can't you . . . like . . . induce me or something?"

She'd been reading up on labor and delivery lately, and was so not looking forward to it. A cesarean would be totally better—knock her out and cut her open. She wouldn't feel a thing, but then she'd have a scar. Well, a scar was a small price to pay for simply waking up and having it all over.

Dr. Landsman shook his head. "The baby's not ready yet."

A balding, fiftyish guy, he'd just done a pelvic exam, followed by her umpteenth ultrasound. Then he'd left her and waited here in his office for her to dress and join him.

"Isn't the ultrasound supposed to give you a clue?"

"It is, and it says he's not ready yet. But it won't be long. Your cervix is soft. Your body's getting ready to deliver."

"But I was totally due in January and here it is February." She rubbed her cold hands together. "Something's wrong. You can tell me."

"Ten months is unusual, yes, but nothing's wrong."

"Then why won't you ever let me see the ultrasounds?"

He did the scans himself instead of his tech, and never allowed anyone else in the room except Mr. Osala, her self-appointed guardian. The doctor had started giving her appointments on Mondays and Thursdays. Why? He had no office hours and no staff at all those days. Was that what he wanted? And during the ultrasounds, he always kept the monitor screen turned away from her. For some reason, he never seemed to tire of looking at her baby.

"You wouldn't understand what you were seeing."

She resented that. She might be only eighteen—turning nineteen next month—but she was no dummy. She'd been accepted to Colgate and would be there right now if she hadn't screwed up her life.

"You could point things out to me."

"The baby is fine. You feel him moving, don't you?"

"Like crazy."

Some days she felt like she had a soccer camp inside her.

"Well then, I've told you he's a boy and you know he's healthy. What more do you need?"

"I need to see him."

"I'm not sure I understand your eagerness to see a baby you're giving up for adoption upon delivery. A baby you tried to abort, if I remember correctly."

She had nothing to say to that. She'd totally changed her mind about the abortion, but she was so not ready to raise a child—especially this child, considering who the father was. Someone else would give him a good home and raise him better than she ever could. No way she was ready for motherhood.

He pulled out an old-fashioned pocket watch and popped the lid.

"Your friend, Mister Osala, should be calling soon."

"He's not my friend."

"Well, he's very concerned about you and your baby."

Maybe too concerned.

The design on the lid of his watch caught her eye. Following the lines made her eyes cross.

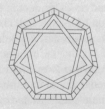

"That looks old."

He smiled. "It's been in the family for almost two hundred years."

"What's that design? It's weird."

"Hmm?" He glanced at it, then quickly pocketed it. "Oh, that. Just a geometric curiosity."

A phone rang. He dug out his cell and checked the display, then glanced up at her. "It's him. Excuse me."

"Sure." She knew who it was. "Don't forget to ask him how high."

He gave her a puzzled look, like he didn't get it.

"Jump," she said. "How high you should jump."

He still didn't get it. For such a supposedly top-notch OB man, he could be so dense at times.

Osala hadn't been around much lately. He used to come to all her appointments but now he was involved in some project down south that kept him away a lot. But he stayed in close touch with Dr. Landsman.

She felt the baby kick and shook her head. Sure felt like he wanted out. And she wanted him out. Not like she had back in the summer, when she'd tried to end the pregnancy. She'd been determined to get an abortion, and then Mr. Osala had told her, *You want this child . . . You will do anything to assure its well-being,* and everything changed, just like that. She couldn't believe now that she'd wanted to kill her baby.

But that was totally different from wanting the pregnancy over and done with. She simply wanted to be back to normal size. She'd never been skinny, but this was ridiculous. She couldn't seem to find a comfortable position anywhere, even in bed. She'd give anything for a full night's sleep.

And once her pregnancy was over and the baby born, maybe Mr. Osala would let her leave his home. She'd been a virtual prisoner there since last spring—almost her entire pregnancy. Could she complain about a Fifth Avenue duplex penthouse where she wanted for nothing? Yeah, she could, because although she could have anything material, she couldn't have what she wanted most: contact with the outside world. Because Mr. Osala feared that might lead the baby's father to her. That was the last thing she wanted, too, but it seemed to her Mr. Osala had taken precautions to the extreme.

She wanted a *life*.

"Yes, I know it's overdue," she heard Dr. Landsman say. "I was just discussing that with Dawn when you called. But the baby's healthy and, frankly, how do we know this isn't perfectly normal? It's not as if we have any precedents to follow."

Those kinds of comments popped out every so often and never failed to sour her stomach. She'd learned not to ask about them, because Dr. Landsman only stonewalled her.

But she was convinced something was wrong with her baby. Dr. Landsman could tell her it was healthy till he was blue in the face, but that look in his eyes when he watched the ultrasound screen said he was looking at something he didn't see every day.

And then there was the thing about the ultrasound images—Mr. Osala made the doctor delete them after every session. And when he wasn't here, his driver Georges made sure they were history. Georges was almost as scary as his boss.

What was so different about her baby that no one else could know?

3.   The phone was ringing when Munir opened the door to his apartment. He hit the RECORD button on his answering machine as he snatched up the receiver and jammed it against his ear.

"Yes!"

"Pretty disappointing, Mooo-neeer," said the now familiar electronically distorted voice. *"Are all you Ay-rabs such mosquito dicks?"*

"I did as you asked! Just as you asked!"

"That wasn't much of a pee, Mooo-neeer."

"It was all I could do! Please let them go now."

He glanced down at the caller ID. A number had formed in the LCD window. A 212 area code, just like all the previous calls. But the seven digits following were a new combination, unlike any of the others. And when Munir called it back, he was sure it would be a public phone. Just like all the rest.

"Are they all right? Let me speak to my wife."

Munir didn't know why he said that. He knew the caller couldn't drag Barbara and Robby to a pay phone.

"She can't come to the phone right now. She's, uh . . . all tied up at the moment."

Munir ground his teeth as the horse laugh brayed through the phone.

"Please. I must know if she is all right."

"You'll have to take my word for it, Mooo-neeer."

"She may be dead." Allah forbid! "You may have killed her and Robby already."

"Hey. Ain't I been sendin' you pichers? Don't you like my pretty pichers?"

"No!" Munir cried, fighting a wave of nausea . . . those pictures—those horrible, sickening photos. "They aren't enough. You could have taken all of them at once and then killed them."

The voice on the other end lowered to a sinister, nasty growl.

"You callin' me a liar, you lousy, greasy, two-bit Ay-rab? Don't you ever doubt a word I tell you. Don't even think about doubtin' me. Or I'll show you who's alive. I'll prove your white bitch and mongrel brat are alive by sending you a new piece of them every so often. A little bit of each, every day, by Express Mail, so it's nice and fresh. You keep on doubtin' me, Mooo-neeer, and pretty soon you'll get your wife and kid back, all of them. But

you'll have to figure out which part goes where. Like the model kits say: Some assembly required."

Munir bit back a scream as the caller brayed again.

"No—no. Please don't hurt them anymore. I'll do anything you want. What do you want me to do?"

"There. That's more like it. I'll let your little faux pas pass this time. A lot more generous than you'd ever be— ain't that right, Mooo-neeer. And sure as shit more generous than your Ay-rab buddies were when they killed my sister on nine/eleven."

"Yes. Yes, whatever you say. What else do you want me to do? Just tell me."

"I ain't decided yet, Mooo-neeer. I'm gonna have to think on that one. But in the meantime, I'm gonna look kindly on you and bestow your request. Yessir, I'm gonna send you proof positive that your wife and kid are still alive."

Munir's stomach plummeted. The man was insane, a monster. This couldn't be good.

"No! Please! I believe you! I believe!"

"I reckon you do, Mooo-neeer. But believin' just ain't enough sometimes, is it? I mean, you believe in Allah, don't you? Don't you?"

"Yes. Yes, of course I believe in Allah."

"And look at what you did on Friday. Just think back and meditate on what you did."

Munir hung his head in shame and said nothing.

"So you can see where I'm comin' from when I say believin' ain't enough. 'Cause if you believe, you can also have doubt. And I don't want you havin' no doubts, Mooo-neeer. I don't want you havin' the slightest twinge of doubt about how important it is for you to do exactly what I tell you. 'Cause if you start thinking it really don't matter to your bitch and little rat-faced kid, that they're probably dead already and you can tell me to shove it, that's not gonna be good for them. So I'm gonna have to prove to you just how alive and well they are."

"No!" He was going to be sick. "Please don't!"

"Just remember. You asked for proof."

Munir's voice edged toward a scream. "PLEASE!"

The line clicked and went dead.

Munir dropped the phone and buried his face in his hands. The caller was mad, crazy, brutally insane, and for some reason he hated Munir with a depth and breadth Munir found incomprehensible and profoundly horrifying. Whoever he was, he seemed capable of anything, and he had Barbara and Robby hidden away somewhere in the city.

Helplessness overwhelmed him and he broke down. Only a few sobs had escaped when he heard a pounding on his door.

"Hey. What's going on in there? Munir, you okay?"

Munir stiffened as he recognized Russ's voice. He straightened in his chair but said nothing. Monday. He'd forgotten about Russ coming over for their weekly brainstorming session. He should have called and canceled, but Russ had been the last thing on his mind. He couldn't let him know anything was wrong.

"Hey!" Russ said, banging on the door again. "I know someone's in there. You don't open up I'm gonna assume something's wrong and call the emergency squad."

The last thing Munir needed was a bunch of EMTs swarming around his apartment. The police would be with them and only Allah knew what that crazy man would do if he saw them.

He cleared his throat. "I'm all right, Russ."

"The hell you are." He rattled the doorknob. "You didn't sound all right when you screamed a moment ago and you don't sound all right now. Just open up so I can—"

The door swung open, revealing Russ Tuit—a pear-shaped guy dressed in a beat-up Starter jacket and faded jeans—looking as shocked as Munir felt.

In his haste to answer the phone, Munir had forgotten

to latch the door behind him. Quickly, he wiped his eyes and rose.

"Jesus, Munir, you look like hell. What's the matter?"

"Nothing."

"Hey, don't shit me. I heard you. Sounded like someone was stepping on your soul."

"I'm okay. Really."

"Yeah, right. You in trouble? Anything I can do? Can't help you much with money, but anything else . . ."

Munir was touched by the offer. If only he *could* help. But no one could help him.

"No. It's okay."

"Is it Barbara or Robby? Something happen to—?" Munir realized it must have shown on his face. Russ stepped inside and closed the door behind him. "Hey, what's going on? Are they all right?"

"Please, Russ. I can't talk about it. And you mustn't talk about it either. Just let it be. I'm handling it."

"Is it a police thing?"

"No! *Not* the police! Please don't say anything to the police. I was warned"—in sickeningly graphic detail—"about going to the police."

Russ leaned back against the door and stared at him.

"Jesus . . . is this as bad as I think it is?"

Munir could do no more than nod.

Russ jabbed a finger at him. "I know somebody who might be able to help."

"No one can help me."

"This guy's good people. I've done some work for him—he's a real four-oh-four when it comes to computers, but he's got a solid rep when it comes to fixing things."

What was Russ talking about?

"Fixing?"

"Situations. He solves problems, know what I'm saying?"

"I . . . I can't risk it."

"Yeah, you can. He's a guy you go to when you run out of options. He deals with stuff that nobody wants anybody knowing about. That's his specialty. He's not a detective, he's not a cop—in fact, if the cops are involved, this guy's smoke, because he doesn't get along with cops. He's just a guy. But I'll warn you up front, he's expensive."

No police . . . that was good. And money? What did money matter where Barbara and Robby were concerned? Maybe a man like this was what he needed, an ally who could deal with the monster that had invaded his life.

"This man . . . he's fierce?"

Russ nodded. "Never seen it, and you'd never know it to look at him, but I hear when the going gets ugly, he gets uglier."

"How do I contact him?"

"I'll give you a number. Just leave a message. If he doesn't get back to you, let me know. Jack's gotten kind of distracted these days and picky about what he takes on. I'll talk to him for you if necessary."

"Give me the number."

Perhaps this was what he needed: a fierce man.

4. I'm running out of space, Jack thought as he stood in the front room of his apartment and looked for an empty spot to display his latest treasure.

His Sky King Magni-Glow Writing Ring had just arrived from his connection in southeast Missouri. It contained a Mysterious Glo-signaler (*"Gives a strange green light! You can send blinker signals with it!"*). The plastic ruby unfolded into three sections, revealing a Secret Compartment that contained a Flying Crown Brand (*"For sealing messages!"*); the middle section was a Detecto-Scope Magnifying Glass (*"For detecting fingerprints or decoding messages!"*); and the outermost section was a Secret

Stratospheric Pen (*"Writes at any altitude, or under water, in red ink!"*).

Neat. Incredibly neat. The neatest ring in Jack's collection. Far more complex than his Buck Rogers Ring of Saturn, or his Shadow ring, or even his Kix Atomic Bomb Ring. It deserved auspicious display. But where? His front room was already jammed with radio premiums, cereal giveaways, comic strip tie-ins—crassly commercial tchotchkes from a time before he was born. He wasn't sure why he collected them, but knew when and where the addiction had started: in his teens when he'd worked at a store that specialized in junk. But he didn't know why. After years of accumulating his hoard, Jack still hadn't found the answer. So he kept buying. And buying.

Old goodies and oddities littered every flat surface on the mismatched array of Victorian golden oak furniture crowding the room. Certificates proclaiming him an official member of The Shadow Society, the Doc Savage Club, the Nick Carter Club, Friends of the Phantom, the Green Hornet GJM Club, and other august organizations papered the walls.

At least the place was his again. Weezy had moved out after Thanksgiving. She'd finally accepted that no one was looking for her anymore, and had found a sublet a few blocks away in a new high-rise. Still, she'd insisted on renting it under an assumed name.

Jack glanced at the Shmoo clock on the wall above the hutch. Time for a brew or two. He placed the Sky King Magni-Glo Writing Ring next to his Captain Midnight radio decoder, pulled a worn red Lands' End Windbreaker over his flannel shirt, and headed for the door.

Outside in the frigid darkness, he hurried through the Upper West Side, feeling kind of bummed that Gia and Vicky were leaving for Iowa tomorrow. Out of the blue she'd come up with this idea to visit her folks back home.

She went back a couple of times a year to keep Vicky in touch with her grandparents—the little girl's paternal family, the Westphalens, had been scoured from the face of the Earth—but usually in warmer weather. If it was this cold in Manhattan, what the hell was it like in Ottumwa, Iowa?

Didn't make sense, but since when did family need to make sense?

He passed trendy boutiques and eateries that catered to the local yuppies and dinks. The economic downturn that started back in '09 had caused a few to close, but the effect here had been mere decimation rather than the holocaust elsewhere. They were coming back already.

No recession at Julio's. Even on a Monday night, the drinkers stood three deep around the bar, two-hundred-dollar shirts and three-hundred-dollar sweaters wedged next to grease-monkey overalls. Julio's had somehow managed to hang on to its old clientele despite the invasion of the Ralph Lauren, Armani, and Donna Karan set. The yups and dinks had discovered Julio's a while back. Thought it had "rugged charm," found the bar food "authentic," and loved its "unpretentious atmosphere."

They drove Julio up the wall.

Julio stood behind the bar, under the FREE BEER TOMORROW . . . sign. Jack waved to let him know he was here. As Jack wandered the length of the bar he passed a blond dink in a gray Armani cashmere sweater that had to cost north of a grand. He must have been here before because he was pointing out the dead succulents and asparagus ferns hanging in the windows to a couple who were apparently newcomers.

"Aren't they just fabulous?" he said between quaffs from a mug of draft beer.

"Why doesn't he just get fresh ones?" the woman beside him asked.

She was sipping white wine from a smudged tumbler. She grimaced as she swallowed. Julio made a point of stocking the sourest Chardonnay on the market.

"I think he's making a statement," the guy said.

"About what?"

"I haven't the faintest. But don't you just love them?"

Jack knew what the statement was: Callusless people go home. But they didn't see it. Julio was purposely rude to them, and he'd instructed his help to follow his lead, but it didn't work. The dinks thought it was a put-on, part of the ambience. They ate it up.

Jack stepped over the length of rope that closed off the back half of the seating area and dropped into his usual booth in the darkened rear. As Julio came out from behind the bar, the blond dink flagged him down.

"Can we get a table back there?"

"No," Julio said.

The muscular little man brushed by him and nodded to Jack on his way to bus the empty glasses. Jack signaled for a Yuengling.

"Hey, Jack."

Jack looked up to see Russ Tuit stepping over the cord and approaching.

"Russ," he said, shaking his hand. "A little far from home, aren't you?" He lived over on Second Avenue.

"Need to talk to you."

Jack had his back against the wall and indicated a chair opposite him.

"Looking for work?"

Russ was Jack's go-to guy for all things cyber–legal or not so legal. He'd done time for hacking a bank and was still on probation.

He smiled. "Believe it or not, I'm gainfully employed. Full time too. And you'll never guess by who."

"The feds."

Russ's face fell. "How . . . how . . . ?"

Jack had to laugh. "Well, you said I'd never guess, so I figured the least likely people to hire a federal felon would be the feds. What've they got you doing—hacking citizens?"

"Close. This branch of the NRO hired—"

"What's NRO?"

"National Reconnaissance Office. They run all the satellites. Their research wing put me together with a bunch of other hackers to help tighten up their security. Seems their computers are under constant attack, especially from the Chinese. So what we do is pretty cool. One team sets up a security system, and the other team tries to break through it. If we get through, then we switch sides, shore up the breach, and now it's their turn to try to break through. We keep going back and forth, switching sides, and let me tell you, it's working. We've been building firewalls that are higher, wider, and smarter than anything else out there."

Jack's mind wandered as Russ went on about viruses and worms and trojans. He noticed the blond guy in the sweater stopping Julio again as he returned to the bar. He pointed toward Jack and Russ.

"How come they get to sit over there and we don't?"

Julio swung on him and got in his face. He was a good head shorter than the blond guy but he was thickly muscled and had that air of barely restrained violence. He went into his Soup Nazi act.

"You ask me one more time about those tables, meng, and you outta here. You hear me? You *out* and you never come back!"

Julio loved to use "meng" whenever he could, especially with the yups and dinks.

As Julio strutted away, the blond guy turned to his companions, grinning.

"I just *love* this place."

"So all in all," Russ was saying, "a pretty cool gig."

"Sounds utterly fascinating."

Russ grinned. "I can tell you'd rather stick pins in your eyes."

"Not pins. Nails. Glowing, red-hot nails."

"Hey, it's not bad being a white hat. It pays and they may go to bat for me and get me back on the Net." One of the terms of Russ's probation was banishment from the Internet, cruel and unusual for a guy like him. Of course, he'd found numerous ways around that. "But that's not why I'm here. Got a friend in trouble."

"This 'friend' wouldn't be named Russ, would he?"

"No. This is a buddy. We've been working on an MMO game hack—"

"NRO . . . MMO . . . I don't speak acronymese."

"Sorry. A massively multiplayer online game."

"Sounds like bad English."

"It's a big deal these days. WoW—I mean, *Warcraft*—has eleven million players, *Habbo*'s got eight, and people average between twenty and thirty hours a week at it."

Jack shook his head. He got game playing, but didn't get Russ. "And you want to hack it? Don't you ever learn?"

He laughed. "Hack's an umbrella term. Me and Munir are working on a way to make MMOs play faster. If it works out the way we hope it will, we'll patent it and be sitting pretty."

"And this Munir's got trouble? What kind?"

Russ shrugged. "Don't know. Won't tell me. I think it involves his wife and kid."

Jack remembered a voice mail that said, *Jack, please save my family!* He'd decided not to call back.

"And he can't go to the cops," Russ added. "You thinking what I'm thinking?"

A kidnap, most likely. One of Jack's rules was to avoid kidnappings. They were the latest crime fad these days, usually over drugs. They attracted feds and Jack had less use for feds than he had for local cops.

"Yeah." He leaned forward. "Look, Russ, kidnapping is best left to the big boys. They've got assets and manpower and teams specially trained—"

"He's scared shitless to make that call. I told him I knew a guy who could look into it and keep it outside the system."

"Sorry, Russ. No way."

5. *"Drexler, I have a task for you."*

Ernst straightened in his chair as he recognized the voice: the One.

His office seemed to shrink around him. Contact with the One never failed to make him feel like a frightened child. He grabbed a pen and poised it over the legal pad before him.

"Yes, sir."

"Do you remember the woman who created such a nuisance last summer?"

"Louise Myers? The woman posting on the nine/eleven sites?"

"Yes. Her."

Everyone Ernst had sent against that woman had ended up dead. A bit more than a nuisance. Quite a bit more.

"Did you ever find her?"

"No, sir. We gave up on the search some months ago. She's stopped posting and there didn't seem much hope—"

"Resume the search. Widen it. Find her."

"Is there something I should know?"

"Merely a contingency plan. She has a book I may have use for. She's in the city. I could find her myself if I were there, but I am in the middle of something else at the moment."

"I'll get on it right away."

"Also, a package shall be arriving for your safekeeping. As for the woman, remember this: I want no contact. Locate her, but do not contact her."

"No contact? But—"

He was gone.

The One had said to widen the search. Ernst assumed that meant mobilizing more than just the Order. He called his right-hand man, Kristof Szeto, and told him to fax a copy of her picture to the head of security for the Dormentalists—their Grand Paladin—as well as get it out to the members of the Order.

"The Myers woman," Szeto said in Eastern Europe–flavored English. *"Yes, this is good. This time we will find her. I have score to settle—"*

"No settling anything." Ernst knew he was still bridling from losing so many men to her. "No contact."

"But—"

"A personal directive from the One."

A pause, then, *"Well, in that case . . ."*

Hank Thompson had strolled in—as usual, without knocking—toward the end of the conversation.

"Her again?" he said when Ernst hung up. He was tall and trim, with a dark, shaggy mane. "Didn't you track her to Wyoming?"

Ernst nodded. "We did. But that was as close as we came. It turned out to be a dead end."

"I thought we gave up on her."

"The One, apparently, has not."

He dropped his lanky form into a chair. "He says 'boo' and your bosses drop everything, right?"

Ernst sighed. "The Ancient Fraternal Septimus Order—"

"Is this where you remind me once more that you and your Order have loaned this building to me and my guys? I know that. And we're grateful."

Thompson's posturing could be entertaining at times, tiring at others.

"The Order is devoted to the One's cause. I am an Actuator for the Order. It is my duty to carry out his wishes. It is to your benefit to do the same."

"Says who?"

"The One." Ernst pointed to the corner behind Thompson. "Why don't you ask him yourself."

It gave him enormous satisfaction to watch the color drain from the man's face as he did a slow turn, then flush with anger when he realized he'd been had.

"You son of a bitch!"

Ernst allowed a smile. Thompson was an odd case. A combustible farrago of intelligence and animal cunning. An ex-con who'd had the drive to write an internationally bestselling . . . how to classify his book? *Kick* was a manifesto and a memoir and a call to arms. A *Mein Kampf* without the racism. His call to kick down the doors that penned you in and evolve into something new cut through racial, religious, and ethnic barriers.

It is time to separate yourselves from the herd. You know who you are. You know who I'm talking to. You don't belong with the herd. Come out of hiding. Step away from the crowd. Let the dissimilation begin!

People everywhere—mostly males, an unusually high percentage of whom came with criminal records— answered the call and began thinking of themselves as "Kickers," even going so far as to have the Kicker Man, the symbol of what Thompson called "the Kicker Evolution," tattooed on their hands.

The strange thing was, Thompson had gathered this huge, worldwide following that cut across all national and cultural boundaries, with no idea of what to do with them.

Ernst had solved that problem, but the key was to let Thompson think it was all his idea.

"Speaking of sons of bitches and looking for people," Thompson said, "what about that guy we were after?"

Although Ernst knew exactly who he meant, he said, "And what 'guy' would that be?"

"The one who tasered us."

"Oh, him. I've gotten past that."

True, at least as far as being tasered. But he hadn't gotten past what the man had said to him. He'd known things he shouldn't have. And something about him had been hauntingly familiar.

"Well, I haven't. Shave off that beard and I bet he'd have been the same guy who stole the *Compendium* from me." His hands knotted into fists. "If I ever get hold of that fuck . . ."

Another thing about Thompson, he held grudges. Ernst couldn't resist rubbing salt in the wound.

"Ironic that he was within reach so many times, right under your nose here in the Lodge, posing as one of your followers. Why, you might even have spoken to him on occasion."

Thompson spoke through his teeth. "Don't think I haven't thought about that." He shook himself. "What's the latest on the virus?"

Thompson appeared to want a change of subject.

"The virus is perfected, but we're working on adding one last feature to the payload."

Thompson grunted. "You've been working on this since last summer. When are we going to get it done?"

Valez was in charge of a crucial feature of the virus that everyone hoped would complete the coding, but he was experiencing odd delays.

"Good question. I'll make a call right now."

He punched in Valez's number. The man picked up right away.

"Yes, Mister D."

"Where are we with the code?"

"As I mentioned earlier, I had trouble with the, um, setup, but everything is in line now."

"How long?"

"Two days, tops."

"Very good." Ernst ended the call and looked at Thompson. "Two days. Then we have to incorporate it into the virus and make sure it works the way we wish. Then we release the virus. It should take it only a couple of days to replicate and spread globally."

"So we're talking the weekend." He rubbed his hands together. "About fucking time."

"What did you expect? Bringing down the Internet is hardly child's play."

6. Jack was feeling a little annoyed with himself as he knocked on the door to Munir Habib's apartment in the Turtle Bay high-rise. He'd pulled on a pair of thin leather gloves downstairs, worn his Mets cap with the brim low over his face, and had kept his head down in the foyer and during the elevator ride. Good chance this mess was going to end up in the hands of officialdom and he didn't want to leave behind anything that belonged to him, not fingerprints, and especially not a face on a security camera.

Still didn't know how he'd let Russ talk him into this. Had to hand it to the guy, he was persistent. Pulled out all the stops:

Munir was one of his few friends, a good guy who didn't deserve this and was an emotional wreck over it, and had Russ ever asked Jack for a favor, no, and hadn't he always come through every time Jack needed something, yes, so couldn't Jack do this for him, because he wasn't asking for a freebie, the guy would pay, just go and listen to him, please-please-please?

Jack had agreed, just to shut him up.

He'd called, but Russ's pal wouldn't discuss it on the phone. Too scared. Had to be face-to-face. Normally Jack would never do a first meet in the customer's place, but Russ had vouched for him, so . . .

The door was opened by a short, stocky, fortyish man with milk-chocolate skin, a square face, and bright eyes as black as the stiff, straight hair on his head. His clothes were badly wrinkled, like he'd slept in them, and he looked halfway to zombie.

"You're the one who called?" he said in barely accented English.

Jack nodded and extended his hand. "Mister Habib, I assume."

They shook, followed by a few beats of silence as he stared at Jack. Jack knew that look.

Here it comes . . . here it comes . . .

"I was expecting . . ."

"Someone different? You and everybody else."

They all expected someone bigger, someone darker, someone meaner looking. Not the deliberately average-looking Joe before them.

"I'm sorry."

"Yeah, well, this is the guy you get. Mind if I come in?"

Habib stuck his head out the door and cast furtive looks up and down the hall.

"Don't worry," Jack said. "No one's seen me. And I took the elevator up an extra two floors and walked down. But if you keep me standing out here, pretty soon—"

"Yes-yes. Come in. Please."

Jack stepped inside and let Habib close the door behind him.

"You've got the down payment?"

He nodded. "Yes. I was afraid I could not get so much cash on such short notice."

"Keep it for now. I haven't decided yet whether we'll

be doing business. What's the story? Russ thinks your wife and son have been kidnapped. Is that it?"

The man broke down and sobbed. "Save my family. Please save my family."

Jack's throat constricted. The pain in those words . . .

He tried to imagine how he'd feel if Gia and Vicky were being held for ransom. Couldn't.

"Take it easy. Let's sit down and you tell me about it."

He led Jack past a small, cluttered kitchen, past a room with an inflatable fighter jet hanging from the ceiling and a New York Giants banner tacked to the wall—his son's, no doubt—ending in an office that had probably started out as a third bedroom but was crammed with computers and monitors.

"This where you and Russ play MMO games?" Jack said, trying to sound knowledgeable.

"What? Oh, yes."

He sat at the desk, Jack pulled up a straight-backed chair.

"It's true: My wife and son have been kidnapped and are being held hostage."

Jack noted that he didn't say "ransom."

Russ had sworn the guy hadn't called the cops. Said he was too scared by the kidnapper's threats. Jack believed Russ, but didn't know if he could believe Habib.

"Why not call the cops? I know it's SOP for kidnappers to tell you not to, but . . ."

Habib reached inside his jacket and pulled out some photos. His hand trembled as he passed them over.

"This is why."

The first showed an attractive blond woman, thirty or so, dressed in a white blouse and a dark skirt, gagged and bound to a chair in front of a blank, unpainted wall. A red plastic funnel had been inserted through the gag into her mouth. A can of Drano lay propped in her lap. Her eyes held Jack for a moment—pale blue and utterly terrified.

Caution: Contains lye was block printed across the bottom of the photo.

Jack grimaced and moved to the next. At first he wasn't sure what he was looking at, like one of those pictures you get when the camera accidentally goes off in your hand. A big meat cleaver took up most of the frame, but the rest was—

He bit the inside of his cheek when he recognized the bare lower belly of a little boy, his hairless pubes, his little penis laid out on the chopping block, the cleaver next to it, ominously close.

Okay. Habib hadn't called the cops.

Jack handed them back.

"How much do they want?"

"I don't believe it is a 'they.' I think it is a 'he.' And he does not seem to want money. At least not yet."

"Psycho?"

"I think so. He seems to hate Arabs—all Arabs—and has picked on me." Habib's features knotted as his voice cracked. "Why me?"

Jack realized how close this guy was to tumbling over the edge. He didn't want him to start blubbering again.

"Easy," he said softly. "Easy."

Habib rubbed his hands over his face, and when next he looked at Jack, his features were blotchy but composed.

"Yes. I must remain calm. I must not lose control. For Barbara. And Robby."

Jack had another nightmare flash of Gia and Vicky in the hands of some of the psychos he'd had to deal with and knew at that moment he wanted to work with Habib. The guy was okay.

"An Arab hater. One of Kahane's old crew, maybe?"

"No. Not a Jew. At least not that I can tell. He keeps referring to a sister who was killed in the Twin Towers. I've told him that I'm an American citizen just like him.

But he says I'm from Saudi Arabia, and Saudis brought down the Towers and an Arab's an Arab as far as he's concerned."

Jack stiffened. The Towers again? Last summer he'd become embroiled in the intrigue and paranoia surrounding their fall. The consequences were still reverberating through his life.

"Start at the beginning," he said. "Any hint this was coming?"

"Nothing. Everything in our lives has been going normally."

"How about someone from the old country?"

"I have no 'old country.' I've spent more of my life in America than in Saudi Arabia. My father was on long-term assignment here with Saud Petroleum. I grew up in New York. I was in college here when he was transferred back. I spent two months in the land of my birth and realized that my homeland was here. I made my hajj, then returned to New York. I finished school and became a citizen—much to the dismay of my father, I might add."

"Still could be someone from over there behind it. I mean, your wife doesn't look like she's from that part of the world."

"Barbara was born and raised in Westchester."

That surprised Jack. "Not Muslim? I'd have thought that would be against the Koran or something."

"It's against the law for Muslim women to marry infidel men, but not the other way around. If there's a pre-nup that the infidel woman will convert to Islam, it's okay."

"So she converted?"

He shook his head. "No. She's an atheist. Thinks religion's silly."

"Well, there you go. Sounds to me like your marrying someone like that drove one of these fundamentalist nut-cases—"

"No. Positively not." Habib's face hardened. Absolute conviction steeled his voice. "A true Muslim would never do what this man has done to me."

"Don't be so sure."

"He made me . . . he made me eat . . ." The rest of the sentence seemed to be lodged in Habib's throat. ". . . pork. And made me drink alcohol with it. *Pork!*"

Jack shook his head. "I take it you're still a believer then?"

He shrugged. "I don't pray six times a day or go to mosque, but some cultural proscriptions are so ingrained . . ."

But still, what was the big deal? Jack could think of things a whole lot worse he could have been forced to do.

"What'd you have to do—eat a ham on rye?"

"No. Ribs. He told me to go to a certain restaurant on Forty-seventh Street this past Friday at noon and buy a rack of baby back ribs. Then he wanted me to stand outside on the sidewalk to eat them and wash them down with a bottle of beer."

"Did you?"

Habib bowed his head. "Yes."

Jack was tempted to ask if he liked the taste but stifled the question. Some folks took this stuff very seriously. He'd never been able to fathom how otherwise intelligent people allowed their dietary habits to be controlled by something written in a book thousands of years ago by someone who didn't have indoor plumbing. But then he didn't understand a lot of things about a lot of people. He freely admitted that. And what they ate or didn't eat, for whatever reasons, was the least of those mysteries.

"So you ate pork and drank a beer to save your wife and child. Nobody's going to issue a fatwa for that. Or are they?"

"He made me choose between Allah and my family," Habib said. "I chose my family."

Jack figured if you had a god who couldn't forgive you for that, it was time to reassess that relationship, maybe the whole god thing. But he offered a more circumspect response.

"Well, I doubt if Allah or any sane person would forgive you if you hadn't."

"But don't you see? He made me do it at noon on Friday."

"So?"

"That is when I should have been in my mosque, praying. It is one of the five duties. No follower of Islam would make a fellow Muslim do that. He is not a Muslim, I tell you. You need only listen to the recording to know that."

"What recording?"

"I've been using my answering machine to record the monster's calls."

"Great. We'll get to that in a minute. Okay, so he's not Muslim. What about enemies? Got any?"

"No. We lead a quiet life. I run the IT department at Saud Petrol. I have no enemies. Not many friends to speak of except Russ. Barbara and I keep very much to ourselves."

If that was true—and Jack had learned the hard way over the years never to take what the customer said at face value—then Habib was indeed the victim of a psycho. And Jack hated dealing with psychos. They didn't follow the rules. They tended to have their own queer logic. Anything could happen. Anything.

"All right. Let's start at the beginning. When did you first realize something was wrong?"

"When I came home from work Thursday night and found our apartment empty. I checked the answering machine and heard a distorted voice telling me he had my wife and son and that they'd be fine if I did as I was told and didn't go to the police. And if I had any thought of going to the police in spite of what he'd said, I should look on the dresser in our bedroom. The photographs were there."

Habib rubbed a hand across his eyes. "I sat up all night waiting for the phone to ring. He finally called me Friday morning."

"You recorded that?"

"No. I didn't think about it till later. He would tell me nothing about Barbara and Robby except that they were alive and well and were hoping I wouldn't 'screw up' and not do as I was told."

"Which was eating the pork?"

He nodded. "I did as I was told, then hurried home and tried to vomit it up. He called and said I'd 'done good.' He said he'd call me again to tell me the next trick he was going to make me do. He said he was going to 'put me through the wringer but good.'"

"And the next trick was . . . ?"

"I was to steal a woman's pocketbook in broad daylight, knock her down, and run with it. And I was *not* to get caught. He said the photos I had were 'Before.' If I was caught, he would send me 'After.'"

"So you became a purse-snatcher for a day. A successful one, I gather."

Habib lowered his head. "I'm so ashamed . . . that poor woman." His features hardened. "And then he sent the other photo."

"Yeah? Let's see it."

Habib suddenly seemed flustered. "It's—it's at my office."

He was lying. Why?

"Bull. Let me see it."

"No. I'd rather you didn't—"

"I need to know everything if I'm going to help you." Jack thrust out his hand. "Give."

With obvious reluctance, Habib reached into his coat and passed across another still. Jack immediately understood his hesitance.

He saw the same blond woman from the first photo, only this time she was nude, tied spread-eagle on a mattress, her dark pubic triangle toward the camera, her eyes bright with tears of humiliation; an equally naked dark-haired boy crouched in terror next to her.

And I thought she was a natural blond was written across the bottom.

Jack's jaw began to ache from clenching. He handed back the photo.

"And what about yesterday?"

"He called in the morning and said Sunday was a day of rest. That all I'd have to do was go to Saint Patrick's and receive communion. He said he'd be watching."

"And did you?"

"Of course. After that, I received no further word all day. I was going crazy. Then he called this morning and said I had to urinate—'take a piss,' in his words—in the street on Fifth Avenue at midafternoon."

"Swell," Jack said, shaking his head. "Stop-and-go-traffic."

"Correct. But I would do it all again if it would free Barbara and Robby."

"You might have to do worse. In fact, I'm sure you're going to have to do worse. I think this guy's looking for your limit. He wants to see how far he can push you, wants to see how far you'll go."

"But where will it end?"

"Maybe with you killing somebody."

"Him? Gladly! I—"

"No. Somebody else. A stranger. Or worse—somebody you know."

Habib blanched. "No. Surely you can't be . . ." His voice trailed off.

"Why not? He's got you by the balls. That sort of power can make a well man sick and a sick man sicker."

He watched Habib's face, dismay tugging at his features as he stared at his desktop. "What'll you do?"

A pause while Habib returned from somewhere far away. "What?"

"When the time comes. When he says you've got to choose between the lives of your wife and son, and the life of someone else, what'll you do?"

Habib didn't flinch. "Do the killing, of course."

"And the next innocent victim? And the one after that, and the one after that? What if Russ is one? When do you say enough, no more, *finis*?"

Habib flinched. "I . . . I don't know."

Tough question. Jack wondered how he'd answer if Gia and Vicky were captives. How many innocent people would die before he stopped? What was the magic number? Jack hoped he never had to find out. The Son of Sam might end up looking like a piker.

"Let's hear what he sounds like."

Maybe listening to this creep would help him get a read on him.

Habib slid a combo phone/answering machine across his desk and hit a button. The voice on the recording was electronically distorted. Two possible reasons for that. One: obviously to prevent voiceprint analysis. But he also could be worried that Habib would recognize him. Jack listened to the snarling southern accent. He couldn't tell through the electronic buzz if it was authentic or not, but no question about the sincerity of the raw hate snaking through the phone line. He closed his eyes and concentrated on the voice.

Something there . . . something off-key about this guy . . . a picture was forming . . .

7. "What is *that*?" Kewan said.

Hank smiled to himself. He'd asked the same question yesterday when he'd first seen the thing.

"It's a ray gun. We're going to try it out tonight."

Kewan toyed with one of his dreadlocks as he stared at the three-foot oblong box with a parabolic reflector attached to one end and a wire coming from another. "Don't look like no ray gun I ever seen."

Pretty much overnight, Kewan Lyford had moved from nowhere in Kickerdom to one of Hank's most trusted men. Sort of the new Darryl. Except Kewan was black and in better health. Looked like he'd had a tough time with acne as a teen, but he had an infectious smile and an easy way with people. He got along with almost everyone. Hank needed someone like that to deal with the everyday Kickers.

He'd first come to Hank's attention after the mess last July. Darryl was gone and Hank had been tasered into Jell-O by some bearded guy. He and Drexler had put together a composite drawing of the guy and started passing it around. Kewan had recognized him immediately as "Johnny," an okay guy who'd been into Dormie bashing and always generous with his cigarettes. That had been a little embarrassing—a Kicker. Or maybe not. He'd reminded Hank of a guy who'd posed as "John Tyleski" and roughed him up and stolen a very special book from him last spring. The same? He couldn't be sure.

Kewan had proved useful in a lot of ways since then.

Hank pointed to the third man in the room—Nelson Ferron, a balding Dormentalist with a Santa Claus beard and belly. They had the cellar of the Lodge to themselves for this strategy meeting.

"It's a portable EMP generator."

Kewan grinned. "I don't need no help generating pee. I do fine all by myself."

Ferron didn't smile. "E . . . M . . . P. It stands for electromagnetic pulse. An EMP is poison for microcircuitry."

"What's it do to humans?"

"Nothing, unless you've got a pacemaker."

"So it's like a microwave?"

Ferron shook his head. "No. Microwaves only *confuse* a pacemaker. An EMP will *toast* it."

"Then I guess we should make sure nobody coming along tonight has a pacemaker. How's it work?"

"Just plug it in—"

"Plug it in?"

Ferron grinned. "You wouldn't like carrying the battery necessary to power this. That's the beauty part of what you're doing. You use the company's own electric power to do the job. Plug it in, aim it at the servers and routers, and they're toast."

Ferron seemed to relish that word.

Kewan turned to Hank. "This is gonna make people unhappy."

"We're not in the business of making people happy. We're here to make it easier for them to dissimilate."

Hank had spent the last six months locating and casing Internet exchange points and major data centers. He'd started arranging regular Kicker protests outside them. The protests had been peaceful up till now. Because they'd all been window dressing.

Tonight's would be different. But even this would be misdirection. Get them looking the wrong way.

The real targets would be hit at the end of the week. Hank and the Kickers had been ready to go for months. Now all that they needed was for Drexler to hold up his end.

8. Weezy took a break from her seemingly endless study of the *Compendium of Srem* to gaze out her eighth-floor window. She could see the triangle where Broadway angled across Amsterdam at 72nd Street, and found the perpetual snarl of trucks, buses, and cars fascinating. Only in the wee hours of the morning did traffic flow smoothly there.

She loved her apartment. To a decorator it might appear depressingly bare, but she had all she needed for comfort. Every material thing she'd owned had been reduced to ash last summer, and she couldn't see the point in accumulating more stuff. Jack loved clutter. She'd lived with too much of it for too long.

Her cell phone rang. She checked the caller ID and recognized the number.

Eddie? How had her brother—?

Then she remembered Jack had given her one of his TracFones and Eddie had the number.

She didn't want to speak to him. She'd broken all contact with him since learning he was a member of the Septimus Order. He'd finally stopped calling her—for good, she hoped. So why now, after all these months?

Maybe it was important. Maybe something was wrong.

She hit the talk button.

"What is it, Eddie?"

"Weezy? I'm so glad you answered. I wasn't sure—"

"Why are you calling?"

"We need to talk."

"I'm listening."

"I mean, face-to-face."

"Not going to happen."

She winced at how harsh that sounded. This was her younger brother. They'd never been terribly close, but still . . . he was her only living relative.

But he'd joined the Order, damn it. The group that last summer had hunted her down and tried to abduct her, razed her house, tried to kill her. And if not for Jack, they'd have succeeded. How could he be a part of that?

He sighed. *"Okay. Well, the Order is looking for you."*

She felt a chill in her blood.

"How . . . how do you know?"

"I got a fax with your face on it. If I see you or know your whereabouts, I'm to call it in."

"When did it come?"

"Minutes ago."

Her throat felt dry.

"Why are you telling me?"

"Because this isn't right. I've always thought you were paranoid about them, but why would they be looking for you?"

"They were looking for me last summer. I didn't know it was them at first, but I—"

"I'm beginning to wonder if you might be right about them."

Finally! Eddie finally sees the light. Maybe he's salvageable.

"I am. I know I am."

"I'm going to look into this."

Weezy almost dropped the phone.

"No! Say nothing! Do nothing!"

"Can't do that, Weez. They're looking for my sister and I damn well want to know why. I'll call you when I find out."

"Eddie, please! You can't—"

The phone went dead.

She called him back but he didn't pick up. The tables had turned. Now he wasn't taking her calls.

Was he crazy? What was he trying to prove? They'd eat him alive.

She left voice mail begging him to leave it alone. That she was safe and they'd never find her.

But was that true? And why the sudden renewed interest? She'd kept a low profile since the summer—no profile at all, in fact. How had she once again become a person of interest to the Order?

9.　Munir found it difficult to focus on the recording. After all, he had listened to that hated voice over and over until he knew by heart every filthy word, every nuance of expression. So he studied this stranger across the table from him instead.

This man was most unimpressive. True, he was taller than Munir, perhaps five-eleven, with a slim, wiry physique. Nothing at all special about his appearance. Brown hair, and such mild brown eyes; out on the street he would be almost invisible. Munir had expected a heroic figure— if not physically prepossessing, at least sharp, swift, and viper deadly. This man had none of those qualities. How was he going to wrest Barbara and Robby from their tormentor's grasp? It hardly seemed possible.

And yet, as he watched him listening to the recording with his eyes closed, stopping it here and there to rewind and hear again a sentence or phrase, he became aware of the man's quiet confidence, of a hint of furnace-hot intensity roaring beneath his ordinary surface. And Munir began to see that perhaps there was a purpose behind Jack's manner of dress, his whole demeanor being slanted toward unobtrusiveness. He realized that this man could dog your steps all day and you would never notice him.

Munir's thoughts wandered to the question that had dogged him for days: *Why me?*

He wasn't rich. He wasn't important. He kept to himself.

He did not write insulting blogs. He had no public or on-line identity. Because Arabs and Islam were viewed with suspicion in America, he kept a low profile. He was almost as invisible as Jack.

Why me?

Unless it was Allah's doing. Munir admitted that he had not been an observant Muslim. Worse, he, Barbara, and Robby celebrated Christmas these past few years. Not because of Barbara, who was an infidel as far as any religion was concerned, but because of Robby. They celebrated the secular aspects of Christmas, with the tree and the gifts and the Santa Claus fantasy. They were all Americans, and Christmas was an American holiday.

Had that drawn Allah's wrath? The Koran said that any man who renounces Islam must be killed. He had not renounced his faith, but he had certainly ignored it for many years. Was that why he was being tortured rather than killed?

The recording ended then. Jack pressed the stop button and stared at the phone.

"Something screwy here," he said finally.

"What do you mean?"

"He hates you."

"Yes, I know. He hates all Arabs. He's said so, many times."

"No. He hates *you*."

"Of course. I'm an Arab."

What was he getting at?

"But this almost seems personal. I get a feeling there's more going on here than just nine/eleven or you being an Arab or any of the bullshit he's been handing you."

Personal? No. It wasn't possible. He had never met anyone, had never been even remotely acquainted with a person who would do this to him and his family.

"I do not believe it." His voice sounded hoarse. "It cannot be."

Jack leaned forward, his voice low. "Think about it. In the space of a few days this guy has made you offend your God, offend other people, humiliate yourself, and who knows what next? There's real nastiness here, Munir. Cold, calculated malice. Especially this business of making you eat pork and drink beer at noon on Friday when a good Muslim is supposed to be at the mosque. I didn't know you had to pray on Fridays at noon, but he did. That tells me he knows more than a little about your religion—studying up on it, most likely. He's not playing this by ear. He's got a plan. He's not putting you through this 'wringer' of his just for the hell of it."

"What can he possibly gain from tormenting me?"

"Torment, hell. This guy's out to *destroy* you. And as for gain, I'm guessing on revenge."

"For what?" This was so maddening. "I fear you are getting off course with this idea that somehow I know this insane man."

"Maybe. But something he said during your last conversation doesn't sit right. He said he was being 'a lot more generous than you'd ever be.' That's not a remark a stranger would make. And then he said 'faux pas' a little while after. He's trying to sound like a redneck but I don't know too many rednecks with *faux pas* in their vocabulary."

"But that doesn't necessarily mean he knows me personally."

"You said you run a department in this oil company."

"Yes. Saud Petrol. I told you: I'm head of IT."

"Which means you've got to hire and fire, I imagine."

"Of course." Munir felt a chill. "A Saud employee?"

"That's my guess," Jack said. "Look in your personnel records. That's where you'll find this kook. He's the proverbial Disgruntled Employee. Or Former Employee. Or Almost Employee. Someone you fired, someone you didn't hire, or someone you passed over for promotion. I'd go with the first—some people get very personal about being fired."

Munir searched his past for any confrontations with members of his department. He could think of only one and that was so minor—

Jack was pushing the phone across the desk.

"Call the cops," he said.

Fear wrapped thick fingers around Munir's throat and squeezed. "No! He'll find out! He'll—"

"I'd like to help you, pal, but it wouldn't be fair. You need more than I can give you. You need officialdom. You need a squad of paper shufflers doing background checks on the people past and present in your department. I'm a one-man shop. No staff, no access to fingerprint files. You need all of that and more if you're going to get your family through this. The FBI's good at this stuff. They can stay out of sight, work in the background while you deal with this guy up front."

"But—"

He rose and clapped a hand on Munir's shoulder.

"I'd like to catch this guy for you, really I would, because he sounds like scum. I'd like to tie him up in a room and leave you alone with him. But I sense time growing short and I'm not the guy to find him before he does something really nasty to you, your wife, or boy. You need help with staff. That's not me. So I'm going to do you a favor."

"What?"

"I'm going to walk out that door and let you call the feds. They're what you need, not me."

And then he walked out of the room and out of the apartment.

He was right, Munir knew that, but still he wanted to cry.

10.   The number on the fax had had a 212 area code, which put it in Manhattan. So Eddie had called the Order's New York headquarters—a private number, members only. The man who answered the phone had tried to get out of meeting in person, but Eddie had insisted. Whoever was looking for Weezy had a face and Eddie wanted to see it. He was given the address of an "administrative office" in a medium-rise building in midtown where he found an elderly woman at a reception desk. The familiar seal of the Ancient Fraternal Septimus Order had been painted on the wall behind her.

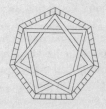

She'd led him to a room and told him that someone would be with him shortly. Shortly turned out to be almost immediately.

"Brother Connell?" said a voice behind him. "I am Claude Fournier."

Eddie's pulse jumped as he turned. He hadn't heard the door open. A tall, fiftyish man, painfully thin and dressed in a brown leather coat and dark slacks stepped toward him. He looked as if he had just come in off the street. He extended a long-fingered hand.

Eddie surreptitiously wiped his sweaty palm on his thigh before shaking the proffered hand. The man reeked of tobacco smoke.

"Yes, my name is Connell, but you're not the man I spoke to."

A blue-black mole sat dead center in Fournier's chin. Eddie tried to keep his eyes off it.

"No. He is busy. We are all busy. What can you tell us about Louise Myers? Do you know where she is?"

"No."

He frowned. "Then why this insistence on a face-to-face meeting?"

"The woman you're looking for is my sister."

Fournier's gray eyes narrowed as he hesitated. "This . . . this is true?"

Eddie had figured this would be the best way to go. If he tried to hide his relationship, it might backfire. He was pretty sure they didn't know that the woman they were looking for had a brother in the Order, but they might know that her maiden name was Connell. If so, and he lied about the relationship, he'd be screwed.

Screwed . . . the term had many levels. Screwed as in kicked out of the Order for lying . . . what he might expect. Or, in Weezy's world, screwed as in killed.

Not that he believed that for a second.

The Order . . . if anyone had ever told him as a kid that he'd someday be a member of the mysterious and secretive Ancient Fraternal Septimus Order, he'd have thought they were on drugs. One didn't apply to the Order; membership was by invitation only, and who would ever invite Eddie Connell? But six years ago a call had come from someone for whom he'd done some consulting. Would he be interested in joining? He'd been flabbergasted, flummoxed, and, well, flattered.

When he recovered from his shock, he said he was interested. Although the Order jealously guarded its membership rolls, highly influential people from around the world were rumored to belong. The networking opportunities would be good for business.

But saying he was interested didn't make him a member. Few were called and fewer were chosen. A rigorous vetting process began, involving interviews and stacks of paperwork. They wanted to know all about his lineage. It wasn't like the DAR or anything like that. Your parents' social standing or whether or not an ancestor arrived on the *Mayflower* didn't matter. The Lodge accepted people from all races and walks of life. They seemed to be looking for something else, though they'd never said what. They'd told Eddie he'd find out as he "matured" through the Order. That was what they called it: *maturing*. They'd also promised he'd learn other things . . . the way the world worked, and how he could turn that knowledge to his benefit.

Whatever criteria they had, Eddie passed and was accepted as a member. Part of that acceptance involved being branded with the sigil of the Order. It had all been very civilized, with local anesthesia and sterile conditions, but it had not been an option. If you accepted membership, you accepted the brand.

So far, Eddie's experience in the Order didn't seem much different from being an Elk or a Moose: meetings, dinners, networking. Weezy had been convinced since her teens that members of the Order were the guardians of the Secret History of the World. Well, after nearly six years as a member, he'd been made privy to no arcana. But he'd made tons of contacts that had proven immensely helpful in his business.

He hadn't expended much effort toward maturing in the Order—that involved going on special retreats to remote locations around the globe. Who had time? Eddie's actuarial business was flourishing and all his efforts went into growing that. He was never pressured to move up or take a more active role. Others he met at the meetings he attended felt the same way: The Order was good for business.

All of this had served only to bolster his opinion that Weezy was wrong—had always been wrong—about the Order. It was a perfectly benign organization that just happened to keep a close lid on its inner workings. Not unlike the Masons.

But then . . . today's shocking fax.

That changed everything. Last summer Weezy had said the Order was out to get her, but had offered not a shred of proof. Now this flier appeared out of the blue, asking the membership to report if they'd seen her.

He'd always been able to write off Weezy's suspicions as part of her mental instability—after all, she'd been on one psychoactive medication after another since her teens. She saw a conspiracy in every coincidence. And the Order, so secretive about everything—its origins, its membership, its holdings around the world—had always been a ripe target for her paranoia.

No more. The fax drew a line between his sister and the Order—or at least someone high up in the Order. Still, that didn't mean they were out to kill her.

"I can't see any reason why I'd make it up," Eddie said.

"You say she is your sister but you do not know where she is?"

"We haven't been on the best terms lately. But she's still my sister and I'm concerned that the Order is sending out a fax with her picture to the membership. Why do you want her? What interest is she to you?"

Fournier shrugged and pursed his lips. "That I do not know. Word comes from on high to find this woman, so that is what we try to do in the best way we know how."

"How high?"

Another shrug. "Very high, I suppose. The Council of Seven, I would think."

The thought of the High Council looking for Weezy caused an ache in Eddie's gut. What possible reason . . . ?

"May I ask what your instructions are once you find her?"

He held his breath as he awaited the answer.

"Right now our instructions are to locate her and nothing else. No contact. Simply find out where she is."

Eddie wasn't sure he could believe that, but the man seemed to be telling the truth. He gave off no hint of a personal interest in finding Weezy; he'd been given a job and was simply carrying it through.

Fournier was studying him. "As a brother of the Order, are you willing to help us find her?"

"I am." A lie. If Weezy wanted to stay off their radar, he'd leave her that way. "But I have a condition: I want to know why you're looking for her."

"I have told you—"

"Yes, you don't know. But you can find me someone who does. I need that question answered before I can help."

Fournier nodded. "I can understand that. I will make inquiries."

Eddie felt his bunched neck muscles relax. He'd done it. He'd taken the first step toward proving Weezy right or wrong, toward deciding whether or not he'd made a mistake in joining the Order. And proving to her that no matter what, she could trust her brother to do the right thing.

11. After a sip of water, Kewan raised the bullhorn to his lips and started the chants again. His throat felt raw from the shouting, but he'd checked the time while he'd sipped and knew he had only a few minutes to go before he could shut up.

Because that was when they'd make their move.

"Two-four-six-eight! Why can't folks dissimilate?"

The two dozen sign-carrying Kickers dutifully shouted their reply: "The Internet! The Internet!"

Round and round they marched in a rough oval outside the entrance to a brick-faced office building in Chelsea. Four heavy-duty glass doors, stacked side by side, separated the chilled marchers from the warm atrium within. Getting everyone through those fast enough to shock and awe security before they called the cops posed a problem. But the boss had solved that.

Taking over the atrium was only the first step. The data center occupied the whole fourth floor and you couldn't get there without a swipe card. But a Kicker on the inside had solved that problem.

"Why are we here?"

"The Internet!"

"And how do we want the Internet?"

"Dead!"

"Two-four—"

"Excuse me, sir," someone said close behind his right ear, accompanying the words with a tap on his shoulder.

Aw, hell, Kewan thought as he turned. If this was a cop it would ruin everything. But instead he found a sandy-haired white guy in an overcoat.

He put on his best scowl. "I'm busy here."

The guy smiled. "I'm Lonnie Pelham from WCBS Eight-Eighty News." He held up the digital voice recorder in his hand. "I'd like to ask you a couple of questions if I may."

Always cooperate with the media.

The boss had said that time and time again. Always cooperate, always treat them with respect, always mention the boss's book when talking about the Kicker Evolution. This was how to grow the Kicker numbers.

"What time is it?"

Pelham checked his watch. "Almost eleven."

"Exact time."

He checked again. "Ten fifty-three."

"Then I can give you seven minutes." He motioned Antoine out of the picket line and handed him the horn. "Take over while I talk to this gentleman."

Gentleman . . . hear that, boss? I'm doing like you said.

As Antoine restarted the chants, Kewan led the reporter half a block down to a corner where they could stand on the side street, away from the noise and out of the wind whipping along Eighth Avenue. Time for a friendly smile.

"I think I heard you a couple times on the radio, man. I ain't much for news stations, but I tune you guys in for weather and stuff. What you wanna ask me?"

Pelham thumbed a button on the recorder and held it between them. His breath steamed in the cold air.

"First off, what's your name?"

"Kick."

"No, your name."

"That *is* my name to people outside the Evolution. Other Kickers know me by a different name, but I'm just 'Kick' to the assimilated world."

This was a new policy instituted by the boss: Don't let outsiders know your name. A good policy, considering what they had planned for a few minutes from now.

"Very well then, Kick, how long have you been a Kicker?"

He smiled and gave the stock answer. "All my life. I just didn't know it until I read Hank Thompson's *Kick* last year." There: plug done. "After that, I knew I had to dissimilate and join the Kicker Evolution."

"Just in case there are a few people who haven't heard it explained by now, what exactly does it mean to dissimilate?"

Kewan had been coached on how to answer FAQs about Kickers, and this was one of them.

"It's Hank Thompson's own word for the opposite of *assimilate*. As everybody grows up, they're pushed into being absorbed by the society or culture or religion or just the plain old herd around them. But when you're an adult, it's time to break free, to throw off the chains of assimilation and *dis*similate."

"But critics say that by joining the Kicker Evolution you've simply traded one group for another."

"To anyone still assimilated, it might look like that, but you can't understand dissimilation until you've experienced it."

"But—"

"I ain't here to argue."

"I understand. What did you do before you were . . . before you dissimilated?"

"Life before dissimilation doesn't matter. Whatever you did, whoever you were, it's all irrelevant. As we like to say, 'You get a clean slate when you dissimilate.'" He spread the web between his right thumb and forefinger. "You also get one of these."

Pelham squinted at the black tattoo on the dark brown skin. "Oh, yes. That's certainly a familiar figure."

Should be, Kewan thought. It's been spray-painted all over town.

But he laughed and said, "Maybe I should get mine outlined in white."

"That would be . . . different." Pelham cleared his throat. "All right then, let's get to the here and now: Why are dozens of Kickers out here on this chilly winter night picketing a closed building?"

Kewan winked. "Well, for one, football season is over."

Pelham laughed. "Seriously."

"What time you got?"

A glance at his watch. "Ten fifty-eight."

Okay. Two minutes left—*if* the car was on time.

Kewan stepped back around the corner and pointed to the building.

"A major Internet data center hides on the fourth floor there. Big fat fiber-optic cables run in and out of it, feeding the World Wide Web in this country and crossing the Atlantic. We want that stopped."

"But why?"

"Because the Internet is the biggest assimilator of all. It sucks people in and won't let them out. So many more people would be able to dissimilate if not for the Internet. That's why we protest."

"But on a Monday night?"

"Why not? The Internet runs twenty-four/seven, and so does the Kicker Evolution."

And . . . that's when building security is at its lowest.

He eyed the marchers. They'd moved away from the doors and laid down their signs. He heard a roar of a car engine and saw a beat-up old Chevy speeding up Eighth Avenue from Greenwich Village. Its tires squealed as it braked into a hard left turn mid block, jumped the curb, and barreled across the sidewalk to smash through the glass doors.

Right on time.

"Oops!" Kewan broke into a run. "Gotta go."

The marchers had the car open by the time he got there. Most were hauling long- and short-handle sledgehammers, pry bars, and axes from the trunk; a few others who'd been trained in their use were easing the three EMP generators from the backseat. Kewan grabbed a long splitting maul and charged into the glass-littered lobby where a red-faced security guard was being tied to his chair with plastic fasteners.

The rest of the Kickers crammed into the two elevators. Kewan pulled out the insider's security card and swiped it through the scanner, then pressed *4*. He jumped out, then entered the second elevator with the EMP crew and repeated the process.

"Remember," he said as they rose. "No hesitation. Soon as we arrive, we open the doors and go after them. Only a few nerdy techs inside this time of night, so don't worry about resistance. Take the routers and servers down hard and the nerds down gentle. The boss don't want nobody hurt. It's bad press."

One of the guys with an EMP gun snickered. "Yeah, we'll get enough of that when nobody around here can check their Facebook or MySpace tonight."

Another laughed. "Kicker Man will be defriended all over town."

The Kicker Man had his own MySpace page with a strange assortment of friends. Yeah, a lot of people would be pissed, but that was the whole idea—gather them together to split them apart.

"And remember: Don't cut the cables, hammer them."

A cut cable was easy to fix. Hammering fractured the fibers inside with no clue as to where they were broken.

The car slowed and dinged for the fourth floor. The doors opened, revealing the first group massed and waiting outside the steel doors to the data center. Kewan swiped the card again and the doors opened.

He stayed back with the EMP guys while the others charged into the center. He pulled a sheet of paper from his back pocket and unfolded it to reveal a map of the center. Their insider had sketched it out for tonight's visit.

The commotion drew some nerdy-looking guys to the

front. One look at the invaders and they fled toward the rear.

"Okay, everybody! You know what to do! You see anyone on a phone, stop 'em!"

He led one of the EMP guys along the course laid out for him. The place was nothing like what he'd expected. In the movies computer centers were always brightly lit, high-tech palaces. This was dingy and dusty and not much more than stacks of black boxes on racks.

He headed for the routers that fed the high-capacity fiber-optic backbone cable that snaked across the floor of the Atlantic to England. He'd been briefed on what he'd find and given all sorts of names and abbreviations for the equipment, but he'd stopped listening after a while.

All he needed to know was that the equipment in the room in question had to be destroyed. His fellow Kickers would be smashing or frying every router and server and hammering every cable they could find, but Kewan had been assigned to the heart of the beast. His job was to pierce that heart and stop its beat.

TUESDAY

I. "What are they thinking?" Jack said as he stared at the headline of the *Post*.

KICK 'EM
IN JAIL!

Abe shrugged. "I should know? I should explain the doings of *meshuga* Kickers?"

Jack leaned on the customer side of the scarred counter at the rear of the Isher Sports Shop. Abe Grossman perched his egg-shaped body on the stool across from him, perusing his array of morning newspapers as he munched one of the bialys Jack had brought. Bits of onion decorated his white shirt and shiny black pants.

"It was rhetorical."

"Rhetorical implies you know the answer already."

"Whatever. I don't know much about the Internet, but I do know it's redundant as all hell. You can't bring it down by attacking a data center."

"But you can cause much *tsuris* for those who depend on that center. They still haven't restored service. They've had effects overseas as well, on the far end of that transatlantic cable they damaged."

"But they *will* get it up and running again—the TV says by the end of the day if not earlier. So what have they accomplished?"

"Annoyance, bad press." Abe looked over his reading glasses at Jack. "You've met Hank Thompson. You've dealt with him. He's a *shmegegi*?"

"Anything but."

Jack knew Thompson's felonious history—a high school dropout into grand theft auto. Might be uneducated, but he was no dummy. He'd sat down and written a bestseller that had induced a horde of people to hail him as their fearless leader.

"I should think there's no method to his madness? The papers say EMP generators were used. That is a little scary."

Jack had read the papers' explanations of the effects of electromagnetic pulse on delicate circuitry. He didn't understand why or how those waves could do their damage, but he believed. Like he believed in gravity and Britney Spears.

"I guess if they build one big enough, they'll simply have to drive by a data center and screw it up from outside."

Abe shook his head. "I don't think that's practical—it would have to be enormous. Better they should use a nuclear explosion."

"Let's not go there. I prefer Kickers limiting themselves to something more conventional—like a Tomahawk missile."

Abe stuffed the rest of the bialy in his mouth and spoke around it. "The question is, why such a problem with the Internet? It's blamed already for fragmenting families and relationships."

Families . . . Munir Habib's words echoed through Jack's skull . . .

Save my family!

Abe was saying, "Instead of playing baseball out in the sun with their friends, kids are sitting alone before their monitors. Instead of neighbors shmoozing over a back fence, they're on their computers watching a sit-com episode they missed. Sounds to me already like the Internet is doing Thompson's dissimilating for him."

Jack tried to visualize Abe leaning on a backyard fence gabbing with a neighbor. But first he had to picture Abe with a backyard. He failed.

"Yeah. That's what doesn't make sense."

"Unless he's telling the truth about the attack being perpetrated by non-Kickers trying to make his movement look bad."

Jack shook his head. "Uh-uh. Those were the real deal."

"You're so sure how?"

"They showed a clip from a bystander's cell phone on the morning news."

Abe's turn to shake his head. "A cell phone. Does nothing go unrecorded these days? Privacy is dying."

"It's dead and buried. People just don't know it yet. Anyway, I recognized one of the players."

"From your days in the group?"

Kewan had bummed more than his share of cigarettes off Jack last summer when he'd been posing as a Kicker.

Jack nodded. "Yeah. And that means it was an official Kicker operation. They don't do anything without Thompson's say-so. Which brings us back to the original question: What's he thinking?"

"Maybe it was simply a test run, to see how the EMP gadgets worked."

"You could go out and buy a server or a router or whatever they were after and test it on that without exposing your plans."

Abe drummed his fingers. "Maybe he was testing data center vulnerability."

"Okay. He found that one vulnerable, but that's only going to make other centers beef up their security. Sounds counterproductive to me."

Abe brushed at the onion bits but succeeded only in

smearing them. "To have real success against the Internet, he would need to attack almost every data center and Internet exchange point in the world—and even he, despite his large following, does not have the numbers or resources for that."

"But even then it would only be temporary, and he'd be in jail and no one would want to dissimilate after that because his name would be mud." Jack pushed the paper away. "I'll think about it later."

"Something's chewing your *guderim*. What?"

He told him about Munir and what he was going through, and how he'd turned him down.

"You should feel bad about that? Already you helped him. You pointed him toward his company."

"Yeah, but if he doesn't bring the feds in on it, that's not going to help. He needs lots of eyeballs searching employment records."

"Which you can't give him, so guilt you shouldn't feel."

"You're right. A hundred percent right. So why do I feel like I let him down?"

"Because you've been *farblondjet* lately."

If so, Jack figured Gia and Vicky's trip was contributing to it. He glanced at his watch. Almost time for the gathering.

"Gotta run."

"Where?"

"Meeting with the old folks."

Abe nodded. "Methuselah and his mother. And your old girlfriend too, I suppose."

"She was never my girlfriend."

He and Weezy held irregular meetings with the Lady and Veilleur, and one was scheduled for this morning. Maybe they could figure out what the Kickers were up to.

2. Munir snatched up the phone on the third ring. The hated voice grated in his ear.

"You had me a little worried this morning, Mooo-neeer."

"What? What do you mean?"

"When you left. Thought you might have been sneaking off to meet someone."

He must be watching me.

"I did not!"

He'd left the apartment for food and newspapers. But he had no appetite and hadn't been able to concentrate long enough to make sense of a single paragraph in the paper. He'd spent his time wandering from room to room, waiting to hear from the monster, wondering what his next demand would be. And all the while his promise of sending proof that Barbara and Robby were still alive gnawed at him. The way he'd said it . . . even the voice distorter couldn't obscure the obscene glee slithering through his tone.

"I know that. But it got me to thinking how you might be talking about your situation through email. That's a no-no."

"I swear I have not!"

"So you say, but I don't trust you. So I sent you an email. You will open it on both your home computer and your laptop."

"I don't understand."

"The email contains a rootkit that will allow me to monitor your activity."

A rootkit would allow the monster more than that—it would take over his computers.

Without thinking, Munir blurted, "I can't!"

"You what?"

"Wait-wait-wait. I didn't mean that. It's just that the laptop has proprietary data belonging to my company."

"Are you refusing?"

Panic squeezed his throat. "No, I don't care about the company. I—"

"Have you any idea of the consequences?"

He jumped from his chair and started for his home office.

"I-I-I'm going to the computer right now. I'll open your email immediately."

"You've really crossed the line now, you Arab twinkie. You know that proof you wanted about your whore and brat being alive? It's on the way."

He hung up.

Munir repressed a scream. He wanted to smash the phone into a thousand pieces but repressed that as well.

Jack's idea about it being a Saud employee, past or present, ran through his head. A rootkit would allow the monster to take control of his computer and use his passcodes to hack into the company's system. Why would he want to do that unless he was connected to the company? Jack's theory was looking better and better.

He reached his home computer and checked his mail. There . . . *911avenger* . . . that had to be him. Munir clicked it open and found a message.

Leave them running. If anything is encrypted, send the decryption key now.

With shaking fingers, he complied immediately. Maybe if he showed no hesitation the monster would show mercy. Munir had a terrible feeling about the "proof" that was on the way.

3.   Claude Fournier met him across the street from the Order's Lodge in Lower Manhattan.

Eddie had arrived early and had been dismayed by the number of scurvy types dawdling on or about the front steps, smoking in the chill air. Over the years he'd attended a number of meetings in that venerable, granite-block building. Now it looked like some sort of halfway house.

"What is going on here?" he said as Fournier stopped next to him.

The man removed the cigarette that had been dangling from his lips and gazed across the street. He didn't look happy at what he saw.

"Kickers. Didn't you know?"

"I'd heard talk, but . . ."

Fournier was nodding. "Yes. I know. A scruffy bunch."

Outsiders in one of the Lodges. It wasn't supposed to happen. And yet, here they were.

"Whose idea was this?"

"Word came from the High Council last year to give them the run of the place. The High Council would not make that decision lightly. It must see them as useful in some way."

"Useful how?"

He gave a typically Gallic shrug. "They have not yet deigned to inform me."

Eddie was surprised at how offended he felt. And chagrined at how deeply he'd bought into being a brother in the Order.

"We're not meeting with one of them, are we?"

"Hardly. An Actuator maintains an office there. It's him we are meeting." He gestured across the street. "Shall we?"

Actuator? Eddie thought as he followed Fournier. Why does that sound familiar?

They crossed the street and headed up the stone steps. The lounging Kickers gave them curious stares but no one challenged them until they stepped through the heavy front doors into the large open foyer.

"Can I help you guys?" said a bearded heavyset fellow who looked like a biker.

"We have a meeting."

"Who with?"

Appalled by the spectacle of brothers of the Order explaining their presence in a Lodge to an outsider, Eddie wandered deeper into the foyer and stared at the bas relief sigil on the rear wall.

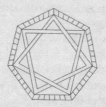

As a kid, whenever he'd seen it over the door of the Lodge in his hometown, he'd found the pattern vaguely confusing, like an optical illusion. Now he was so used to it—hell, it was seared into the skin on his back—that he found the Möbius-strip quality almost comforting . . . a promise of eternity . . . or infinity.

He noticed a dark smudge or smear on the edge at about seven o'clock. It looked like something had been wiped off. He wondered what.

Fournier appeared at his shoulder. "The Actuator is in a meeting that is running late. He will see you as soon as he is free. Come with me."

He led Eddie to a small room furnished with a couple of chairs and nothing else. Their footsteps echoed on the bare hardwood floor.

"Wait here. It won't be long."

Eddie walked to the window as Fournier left. He stared out at the street for a moment. Nothing interesting there, so he sat in one of the chairs and tilted it back against the wall. He began rehearsing what he'd planned to say when he noticed a murmur of voices. He looked around and saw the door was closed. So where—?

A ventilation grille was set in the wall just above the baseboard a few feet away. He leaned closer. That was the source. But where from? Curious, and with nothing else to do, he dropped to a knee and tried to listen.

4. Nelson Ferron's grin shone through his thick white beard as he turned off the network broadcast he'd recorded. The attack on the data center was all over the news.

"Hear that? My babies worked like a charm."

Hank nodded and decided the fat Dormentalist deserved some props.

"Yeah. Those guns made crispy critters of the servers. You did good."

And what was better, their use of EMP had really shaken things up. All the on-air experts were wringing their hands at the "dire implications" of this sort of attack.

"Yes," Drexler said from the far end of the table. "Excellent work."

"What about me?" said Kewan, the fourth attendee around the basement table. "I'm the guy who ran the show. I took out that transatlantic cable."

"You surely did," Hank said. "But you got yourself caught on that cell phone. Not good."

He rolled his eyes. "Can't help that. If y'gonna be on the street, there's always that chance. Everybody got phones." He turned to Ferron. "Hey, can't you make a bigger EMP thing?"

Ferron shrugged. "Of course. How big?"

"One big enough so we don't have to show our faces or risk getting nabbed. Something that can fry those circuits from a distance, or zap the whole city in one shot."

"Not possible—at least with existing technology. That would take a nuclear explosion."

"I didn't say blow the place up—"

Hank had heard this before but he didn't mind listening again. The subject fascinated him.

"You wouldn't have to," Ferron said. "You'd detonate the bomb outside the atmosphere. In fact, the higher the better. Set one off thirty miles above Lebanon, Kansas, and you—"

"Why there?" Kewan said.

"It's the belly button of the lower forty-eight. Right smack in the center. Explode a nuke thirty miles over that and you toast all the circuitry in the Midwest. Set it off *three hundred* miles up, and you take out all of North and most of Central America."

Kewan's eyes lit. "You mean the whole country would be an Internet-free zone? Let's do it!"

Hank shook his head. That had been his own reaction. Then he'd learned that more than the Internet would be affected. "We'd also be cell phone–free and car-free, plus—"

"Wait. What you mean, car and phone free?"

"Well, cell phones use the same kind of chips as computers, and all modern cars have onboard computers."

"Right," Ferron said. "If you had a vintage car with original equipment, you might keep that going, but you'd have trouble finding a working gas pump because there'd be no electricity."

Kewan frowned. "Why not?"

"Because the EMP would also toast the power grid." Ferron snapped his fingers. "Like *that* we'd be back in the eighteenth century."

"Okaaaay," Kewan said slowly. "Let's *not* do that."

Hank knew that the Change was coming soon, bringing the Others back to this world, and he'd been doing his best to prepare the way for them—hopefully guaranteeing himself better treatment when they took over. But he didn't want to go back to burning wood for heat until they showed up.

"Right," he told Kewan. "Let's just limit our target to the Internet."

Kewan nodded. "We're gonna need more of those guns, then—lots more."

"Wrong. The data centers and exchanges aren't the real targets. We just want people thinking they are."

He looked offended. "You mean last night was all for show?"

"Yes. And you put on an excellent show. Too excellent, perhaps."

"What that mean?"

Drexler spoke up. "Your image was captured on that cell phone, Mister Lyford, and shown on national TV. You must leave the city."

"I ain't leaving. This where I live."

Hank leaned toward him. "It's okay, Kewan. You're being transferred to one of the field groups."

"What's that? I never hearda no field groups."

"That's where the real work's going to be done. They're getting set to move. And when they do, it won't be for show." He glanced at Drexler. "Any word from your man on that final piece of code?"

Drexler nodded. "He guarantees sometime today."

"About time. And if it lives up to its press, when can we expect Jihad to be ready?"

"Jihad?" said Kewan. "What's this Jihad talk? We dealin' with Arabs?"

Hank caught Drexler's furious look. He shouldn't have mentioned that in front of Kewan and Ferron. Until his slip just now, he'd been the only Kicker in on the virus. Top-tier Dormentalists knew, but Ferron wasn't one of those.

Drexler composed his features. "Just a figure of speech,

Mister Lyford. Jihad is a holy war, and we're leading a holy war against the Internet."

"You mentioned 'code,'" Ferron said. "Are we talking virus here?"

Shit.

"Another kind of code," Hank said quickly. "One we need to break."

But Ferron was right. Jihad—its official designation would be Jihad4/20—was one hell of a virus. If all went according to plan, it would be spread across the globe by the end of the week.

5.   "The Internet is not their real target," the Lady said.

Jack studied her. She looked better than she had last summer right after Rasalom and his boys in the Kickers and the Order damn near killed her. Against all odds, despite the *Fhinntmanchca*, the mythic killing force that had zeroed in on her, she'd survived. But just barely.

Jack first met her when he was a kid. She'd appeared then as an eccentric old woman with a three-legged dog. Over the ensuing years she'd stepped in and out of his life as females of varying ages, always with some sort of dog at her side.

The dog was gone now—it hadn't survived the assault—but she persevered. But only as an old Lady. Used to be she could change her looks, but she seemed to have lost that ability. Used to be she could shift her presence to anywhere on Earth, but no more. She never left this apartment.

"Sorry," Weezy said as she stepped into the room, late as usual.

She'd shed some weight since popping back into Jack's life last summer. Instead of the baggy sweat suits she'd worn then, she was now dressed in fitted jeans and a long-sleeved black sweater under a ski vest. She'd let her dark hair grow and had it tied back in a simple ponytail. Her pale face was makeup free, a far cry from the heavy gothesque eyeliner she'd worn as a teen. She carried the *Compendium of Srem* under her arm.

The group—Jack had started calling it the Ally's Gang of Four—was now complete. They'd been meeting a couple of times a month, sometimes more often, to discuss the goings-on in the world and which of those might be related to Rasalom or those doing his bidding. And also to learn what Weezy had gleaned from her ongoing study of the *Compendium*.

But that was all they did: Talk. And it was driving Jack nuts.

The meeting place was always the same: the Lady's apartment in the building on Central Park West owned by Glaeken, who had adopted the identity of Gaston Veilleur and insisted on being addressed as "Veilleur." As usual, he sat at one end of the heavy oblong table, the Lady at the other. Jack and Weezy occupied the flanks.

Jack shook his head. The Gang of Four . . . a former immortal, a woman who wasn't really a woman—or even human—and a pair of thirty-something humans . . . all that stood between humanity and the Otherness.

Pretty pathetic. A kind of cosmic joke. But the cosmic shadow war raging behind the scenes was anything but a joke. Two nameless, unimaginable forces vying for control of the sentient realities across the multiverse. Earth was one of those. Just one of many. Not the golden prize, simply another marble in the pouch. But only the sentient marbles were valuable; the non-sentient were brushed aside.

Earth was currently the possession of a force people had come to call the Ally—not really an ally, and in no way benign; more like indifferent. The Otherness, however, was unquestionably inimical, and had been vying for millennia to make Earth its own. Rasalom led its forces here. Veilleur, as Glaeken, used to lead the Ally's, but had been released and allowed to age. He was now as mortal as Jack and Weezy.

"Then what *is* their target?" Weezy said.

The Lady waited for her to take her seat opposite Jack before speaking.

"I am."

"Because the Internet feeds the noosphere?" Veilleur said in his rumbling voice. A broad-shouldered man with a scarred face, a gray beard, and a dominating presence—not unexpected, considering he'd been born thousands of years ago in the First Age.

The Lady nodded. "And the noosphere feeds me."

The noosphere again. Jack had first heard the term last summer; Weezy had bandied it around a lot back then, but not much since. He hadn't quite grasped it then, and most of what he'd learned had slipped away over the ensuing months. He'd had other things on his mind.

"Can you give me a refresher on that?"

Weezy said, "Where are you fuzzy?"

"Around the edges . . . and all through the middle."

She smiled. "Okay. Capsule version: Back in the nineteenth century a Jesuit named Pierre Teilhard de Chardin had a theory that the growth of human numbers and interactions would create a separate consciousness called the noosphere. Turned out he was right. It's real, and it's fed by every thought, every interaction between every sentient being on the planet. It's not cyberspace, though cyberspace adds to it. Every email, every Twitter tweet, every MySpace or Facebook add or app or comment, every chat-room quip, every blog entry or comment, every text message or eBay bid—billions upon billions of interactions every hour, all between sentient beings, and all adding to the noosphere."

"I should have been destroyed by the *Fhinntmanchca*," the Lady said. "The noosphere suffered devastating damage and, under different circumstances, would not have been able to support my existence. In fact, for a few heartbeats, I ceased to exist . . . was, in fact, dead. Again."

"Again?" Weezy said.

"The first death occurred in Florida. The *Fhinntmanchca* caused the second. A third time and I will be gone."

Weezy looked shocked. "Where does it say that?"

The Lady gestured toward the *Compendium*. "You will find it somewhere in your book. After the third death I will be resorbed into the noosphere."

"And that's it?"

"I will eventually reemerge, but as a child. And in the interval, my beacon will be extinguished. That nearly happened this time, but because the Internet has made the noosphere so much stronger than the One or anyone else realized, I was able to return almost immediately, albeit without my companion."

Yeah. Her dog . . . Jack kind of missed him.

"I think it was more than just the noosphere," Veilleur said.

Weezy turned to him. "You think the Ally stepped in?"

He shook his head. "No. The Ally has minimal presence in this sphere. I sense that something else was involved in bringing you back. By all tradition, the *Fhinntmanchca* should have completely crippled the noosphere and blasted you into nothingness."

Weezy said, "Another player? Please don't tell me you think there's a fourth force at work here."

Jack didn't want another player either, but . . .

"Fourth?"

"We've got three now." She ticked off on her fingers. "The Ally, the Otherness, us."

"Us? I could see you saying the noosphere, but—"

"The noosphere *is* us—humanity. We created it, and it can't exist without us. It's not fighting for us, it's humanity fighting for itself." She looked at Veilleur. "You're not suggesting divine intervention or anything like that, are you?"

He shook his head. "Of course not. I think the Lady herself might have had something to do with her own return."

She frowned. "I don't see how that is possible. I am no one. I am simply a projection, an avatar of the noosphere."

That might be true, but Jack couldn't help thinking of the Lady as a person. She was all that stood between humanity and a takeover by the Otherness. She was a beacon, announcing to the multiverse that this place was inhabited by sentient beings. If she were snuffed out, the Ally would discard the Earth as worthless, leaving the Otherness to reshape this reality to its liking—a hell for humanity.

"No one?" Veilleur smiled. "No, my dear, I think you are someone. I think you are more than you realize."

She shook her head. "I know what I am and am not. I am no one. Without a healthy noosphere, I cannot exist."

"But the noosphere *isn't* healthy. You expected to be getting back to your old self by now, but that hasn't happened."

"True. It is taking more time than I anticipated for the noosphere to heal itself. Imagine the noosphere as a mountain lake, fed by many streams. It has had a sidewall blown away and much of its water has flowed downhill— and will continue to leak away until the breach is repaired. The Internet is one of the lake's major feeder tributaries."

Jack said, "So the One's crew must think if they bring down the Net, they'll empty the noosphere to a point where it won't be able to sustain you."

She nodded. "If the Internet is cut off before the breach is healed, the noosphere will dry up . . . and I with it."

"If that's really their purpose," Weezy said, "I don't think we have much to worry about. The Internet's infrastructure is too spread out and too redundant."

"What about a huge EMP?" Jack said.

She blinked. "You mean a high-altitude nuke? If they had that, they wouldn't be messing around with portable EMP generators in data centers. And even if they detonated one over the U.S., high enough to take out the whole country, there's still the rest of the world up and running."

"Maybe they've got a bunch of nukes."

She shook her head. "The Kickers and Dormentalists like to tell the world that they're everywhere, but they're not. They're all over, yes, but not everywhere. They can't launch nukes all over the world to knock out the entire Net. They simply can't."

Jack wished he could be so confident.

"Hank Thompson isn't stupid, Weezy, and he's hooked up with Drexler, who's definitely not stupid. They're all working together. And that tells me that last night's attack on that data center means something. They didn't build EMP guns and go to all that trouble for nothing. They've targeted the Internet."

Weezy leaned back and tapped her fingers on the table. "Maybe it's just Thompson. He could be acting on his own. You know he's got a thing against the Internet. He was very up front about that in his book."

Jack banged a fist on the table—not too hard, just enough to vent some frustration. "Too bad I'm not inside anymore. Might be able to pick up something. At least I was *doing* something then."

But Jack had managed to make himself persona non grata at the Lodge, both with and without a beard.

"We have Eddie inside the Order."

"But he's like a social member, with no access to the inner circles and their agenda. And besides, you aren't talking to him."

"He called me yesterday."

Weezy told him about Eddie's call and how he was going to "look into" the Order's renewed search for her. The news sent bolts of alarm through Jack.

"Did you tell him not to?"

She looked offended. "Of course I did, but he wasn't having any of it. I'm worried about him."

"So am I. I'll give him a call and warn him off. Eddie's not cut out for that kind of stuff."

As a kid he'd always been the loose lip of their trio, the one most likely to blow a secret.

"So . . . what are we going to do about this Internet plot?"

Veilleur shrugged. "What else can we do besides watchful waiting until—"

"Damn!" Jack said. "That's all we do! Watch and wait. Which is the equivalent of doing nothing. Why do we even bother with these meetings? To find more things we can't or won't do anything about?"

He saw Weezy roll her eyes.

"Don't do that, Weez."

She shrugged. "Sorry. But we seem to be having this argument every time we meet lately."

Frustration burned in Jack's gut. "Because all we do is sit around and talk and let the One and his toadies do whatever the hell they want. I'm sick of it."

"But your alternative is too risky."

"I disagree."

Veilleur spoke up. "Remember your promise."

"I remember. I want you to release me from it."

Veilleur shook his head. "I'm afraid I can't."

"Why the hell not? The One is human, right? Flesh and blood like you and me, right?"

"Not quite like us. He has tremendous healing ability." He sighed. "Like I used to have."

"So you've said, and a few other tricks that make him something more than human. But he's not invulnerable and invincible, right?"

"No. Not either."

"That means he can be taken down."

"Only with an enormous amount of deadly force."

"I can bring that. Cut me loose."

Veilleur shook his head again. "You might never find him."

"At least I'd be doing something."

The constant passivity of waiting for the other side to make a move . . . that lay at the heart of Jack's frustration. Defense wasn't how he solved problems.

"And even if you did find him, and even if you brought this deadly force to bear, what if you failed?"

"Then I'd try again."

"But then he'd be on to you. He pays no attention to you now. But he would then. And through you he'd find me. And then he'd know that I'm simply an old man who is no longer a threat to him. He must never learn that. The consequences would be catastrophic."

Veilleur had presented this argument to Jack last year. It had made sense then, but less and less sense since. He bitterly regretted his promise then to keep away from Rasalom.

"As I've said before and I'll say again: I think the potential benefit outweighs the risk."

He caught Weezy staring at him with that look. He wasn't sure what "that look" meant, but he'd glanced up and seen it often enough when she'd been staying at his place. She seemed to be looking through his skin, seeing his core. It made him a bit uncomfortable.

He checked his watch. Almost one o'clock. Where did the day go? He bottled his frustration. "Gotta run."

Nearing the time to pick up Gia and Vicky and hustle them out to the airport.

One more reason to hate LaGuardia.

6. Eddie hadn't gleaned much from his eavesdropping—or would that be ventdropping? The sounds of conversation had been muffled and distorted. He'd picked up a word here and there, but nothing of any consequence except "jihad." He'd caught it twice, and was pretty sure he had that right, but without context it was meaningless.

He was back in his chair when Fournier returned.

"Come," he said, standing in the doorway. "The Actuator will see you now."

A few doorways down he was ushered into a high-ceilinged office where a man in a white suit sat behind a desk, scribbling in a notebook.

"Mister Drexler," Fournier said. "Brother Connell is here."

As the man looked up, Eddie froze in the doorway. His saliva vanished and he was suddenly a pudgy teenager again. Drexler's slicked-back hair had streaks of gray in the black, and time had added a few wrinkles to his face, but the hawk nose, the cold blue eyes, and the white suit were the same.

"Is something the matter?" he said in a lightly accented voice.

Eddie struggled for words, found them. "Mister Drexler?"

"Yes. Have we met?"

"Y—" He would *not* stammer. "Yes. In Johnson, New Jersey, way back in the eighties."

"Ah, yes. The summer-fall of eighty-three. A problem at

the local Lodge." He frowned. "Connell . . . that does ring a bell." He snapped his fingers. "I recall a rather impertinent girl with that name. She caused more than her share of trouble."

Eddie had to smile. "That would be Weezy."

Drexler pursed his lips. "An odd name."

"It's from Louise." From Eddie himself, really, who'd mispronounced her name so often as a toddler that it had stuck.

"I recall a male friend who was equal trouble."

Another smile. "Yeah. That would be Jack."

Immediately he wished he hadn't said anything, because the name seemed to spark something in Drexler.

"Ah, yes. The Lodge's groundskeeper for a while. What is Jack doing these days?"

Eddie fought to maintain a neutral expression. According to Weezy, Jack had killed maybe half a dozen men who had been after her last summer. She swore they were members of the Order, but Eddie wasn't convinced—yet. But if she was right . . .

"I hear he's some sort of repairman."

"Interesting. He did appear to like working with his hands, but I'd have expected more from him." He steepled his fingers and fixed Eddie with his sharp blue gaze. "So then, you are telling us that the Louise Myers we seek is actually your sister, Louise Connell. Am I correct?"

"If the drawing on the fax is accurate, yes."

"It is quite accurate. Brother Fournier says you are unaware of her whereabouts."

"As I told him, we haven't been on the best terms since she learned I'm a member of the Order."

Drexler's thin lips curved into a small, tight smile. "Does she still believe that we stole some petty artifact from her?"

We both know you did, Eddie thought.

But that wasn't important.

"Weezy never forgets. Anything."

"Be that as it may, I understand you are willing to help us find her."

Eddie took a breath. Now the hard part: defying the Order, setting conditions and laying them out for Drexler, of all people.

"*If* I know why you're looking for her."

Drexler leaned back. "I can't answer that because I don't know. Word came from . . . on high to locate her."

"I need to know that you mean her no harm."

Another thin smile. "The Order is not in the business of hurting people."

Eddie wished he could be as sure of that now as he had been a year ago.

"That doesn't answer the question of why you're looking for her. Get me a satisfactory answer to that, and I'll help you find her. And I'm sure I can find her. If not, you're on your own."

"But you're a brother of the Order. You have an obligation—"

"I'm a brother to my sister. I have a bigger obligation there." Now for the ultimate defiance: He turned his back on Drexler and headed for the door. "I'll be waiting to hear from you."

He hurried down the hall, through the foyer, and out to the steps. As the cold air hit him he realized he was drenched with sweat.

7.   As soon as Connell left, Ernst signaled to Fournier. "Get Szeto."

A moment later Kristof Szeto stepped into the room. He was dark, with short black hair; he always appeared to have five-o'clock shadow, even when he'd just shaved, and he liked black leather. Szeto couldn't be present during the meeting because he had already met Connell in the Myers woman's hospital room last summer.

"Did you hear?"

Szeto nodded but said nothing.

"Do you believe him?"

"Not a word," he said in his accented English.

Ernst leaned back. "Neither do I. But what's his purpose, do you think?"

Szeto shrugged. "Perhaps no more than he says: He receives fax with sister's picture and wants to know why Order is looking for her."

"But there's got to be more to it than that, don't you think?"

"Why? He had thorough backgrounding done before he was allowed in, and that showed nothing. Yesterday I go over his record in Order as soon as I receive his call, and it is completely ordinary: typical outer-circle member who pays dues on time and attends meetings."

"But his sister is the woman who caused us so much trouble last year, the one who stirred up all those nine/eleven groups."

Szeto's face darkened. "And killed good men, some my friends."

Ernst shook his head. Once they learned her maiden name yesterday they'd been able to fill in the gaps in her history, but could find nothing in her life that would imbue her with the skills necessary to kill Szeto's men.

"We're sure now it wasn't her, but rather that mystery man she hired as a bodyguard."

Szeto ground a fist into his palm. "She will know where to find him."

"Obviously. But you will not be asking her. The instructions are clear: Find her, mark her location, and do nothing. Is that clear? *Nothing.*"

"Yes. Clear."

"Good. You are following Brother Connell?"

"Of course."

Ernst rubbed his eyes. He did not like the way this had circled back on him. The woman he had hunted unsuccessfully last year turned out to have crossed his path as an adolescent. Her brother turned out to be a member of the Order—invited in. Paths kept circling back to that nothing town on the edge of the Jersey Pine Barrens, which just so happened to play home to the Order's oldest existing Lodge on this continent.

Circles . . . Ernst didn't trust circles unless he created them. Was something else at work here?

And what of the woman's childhood friend, Jack? Ernst had never met anyone so ripe with the taint. And yet now he was . . . what? Connell had said he was a repairman of sorts. A waste of potential.

He turned to Szeto. "Send someone to the Johnson Lodge and see if there are any records on a groundskeeper named Jack. I forget his last name. It would be late in 1983. Track him down. Find out where he is."

"He is involved?"

"I have no idea. But he's a cipher now, and I don't like ciphers. He shares a past with the woman and her brother and I want to make sure he's not circling through the present with them."

"And what about finding woman?"

"We'll find her. Last time we had only members of the Order looking for her. We've expanded the search exponentially. By now every brother in the Order, every Kicker, and every Dormentalist has seen her picture. Someone will recognize her or spot her. Not to worry. We'll find her."

8. Munir sipped orange juice and wished he drank alcohol. He could pour it into the juice and not taste it. The oblivion it offered would blot out this constant, aching fear, quell the frustration at being so *helpless.*

In a sudden fit of rage he hurled his glass across the kitchen. It smashed against the wall, sending glass shards flying.

Now why had he done that? He'd have to clean up the mess before Barbara . . .

. . . came home.

He sobbed.

Oh, God.

Barbara . . . he'd always known she was strong, but never realized till now how much strength he drew from her on a daily basis. It had taken courage to marry an Arab after 9/11. Maybe she'd latched on to him at first as an in-your-face gesture to the world, but they'd developed deep feelings for each other. She was funny and self-aware and very much her own person. So unlike the Islamic women his family shoved at him. They were all about dowries and pleasing the man, and Barbara was more like *How about you pleasing me as much as I please you . . . or maybe more?*

He'd had to have her. No one else would do. They bonded. No, they *fused.* And when it came time to make their fusion official, neither family was enthralled.

His family was dismayed but accepting as long as she converted to Islam and the children were raised in the faith. Munir did not tell them that clerics would be shaving their beards and singing "Hava Nagila" before that happened.

Her family—from outside Atlanta—had been aghast at her choice, but not terribly surprised. Apparently she'd been a rebel all her life. A devout atheist, she adamantly refused a church service and only reluctantly agreed to a reception. What a surreal scene that had been . . . with his imported family occupying one table and hers eight, his people not dancing and not drinking, hers carousing like New Year's Eve.

He and Barbara would probably have had little or no further contact with her family if not for her pregnancy. The birth of a grandson caused a dramatic thaw in her folks. They didn't see Robby often, but when they did, they doted on him.

Looking back, maybe it hadn't taken courage on Barbara's part. Maybe all it took was being Barbara. She was her own person and didn't care what people thought. She didn't let the opinions of others—family, friends, whoever—sway her. Maybe that was why they'd become such a self-contained unit.

Robby had inherited her strength. He needed it with a name like Habib in a New York public school—he was a constant target for bullies wanting to know if he was an Islamic terrorist. But Robby had learned to stand up to them, admitting only to being an American and giving as good as he got.

He thought back to their last exchange before he'd left the house Thursday morning. Barbara had bought a new outfit the day before and had modeled it for him. She had her own style—a tailored look she wore year in and year out, despite the vagaries of fashion. If he really truly disliked something, he supposed she would take it back, but that had yet to happen. He doubted it ever would—she'd look beautiful in a burqa.

The modelings had become a ritual with its own litany. She knew she had a good figure, but the litany demanded she ask . . .

Does it make me look fat?
Hmmm . . . what did it cost?
Nine hundred dollars.

Honestly, honey, I think it adds about ten pounds, especially to your butt.

Oh, wait—it was on sale for ninety.

Skinny Minny!

And they'd laughed as they always did . . .

And he hadn't seen her since. Except in photos from that monster.

To see her tied down, spread-eagle, naked . . . a proud, proud woman humiliated like that . . . it made him—

The sound of the intercom startled him. Someone buzzing from downstairs. Could it be—?

He leaped to the speaker and pressed the button.

"Yes?"

A gruff voice said, *"Package for ya."*

"Who is this?"

"Leavin' it here."

"Who—?" But the speaker was dead.

A package? His heartbeat stumbled, missed a beat, then began racing.

The "proof" the monster had promised?

Munir plunged into the hallway and dashed for the stairwell. The elevator was too slow. He could be down in the vestibule by the time it reached his floor. He almost tripped on the stairs in his haste, and forced himself to slow his pace. If he wound up in the hospital, who knew what the monster would do to Barbara and Robby?

He reached the vestibule and found a yellow padded envelope leaning against the wall under the bank of buzzer buttons. Grabbing it, he checked the address box. Three words were hand-printed with thick black pen: *the raghead bastard.* In the return address box, two more words: *Trade Towers.*

The envelope nearly slipped from his fingers. The monster! Had he been here? Had he delivered it himself? Munir stepped outside and looked around. No one in sight. In nicer weather, mothers would be walking their young children or pushing strollers. But now, in the dead of winter, no one.

As he stepped back inside he saw the elevator standing open and waiting. He hopped in, pressed his floor number, and was fumbling with the tab of the opening strip before the doors closed. Finally he got a grip on it and ripped it across the top. He looked inside. Empty except for shadows. No. It couldn't be. He felt a bulge, a thickness within. He upended it.

A photograph slipped out and fluttered to the floor.

Munir dropped to a squat and snatched it up. He groaned as he saw Barbara—naked, gagged, bound spread-eagle on the bed as before, but alone this time. Something white was draped across her midsection. Munir looked closer.

A newspaper. A tabloid. The *Post*. The headline was the same he'd seen on the newsstand this morning. And Barbara was staring at the camera. No tears this time. Alert. Angry. *Alive*.

Munir wanted to cry. He pressed the photo against his chest and sobbed once, then looked at it again to make sure there was no trickery. No, if this had been Photoshopped, it was expert work.

At the bottom was another one of the monster's hateful inscriptions: *She watched*.

Barbara watched? Watched what? What did that mean?

The elevator stopped on his floor then. As the doors slid open, he heard a phone ringing. His phone. He'd left his door open. He tore down the hall, leaped inside, and grabbed the receiver before the answering machine picked up. He pressed the RECORD button as soon as he recognized the distorted voice.

"Finished barfing yet, Mooo-neeer?"

"I—I don't know what you mean. But I thank you for this photo. I'm terribly relieved to know my wife is still alive. Thank you."

He wanted to scream that he ached for the day when he could meet him face-to-face and flay him alive, but said nothing. Barbara and Robby could only be hurt by his angering this madman.

" 'Thank you'?" The voice on the phone sounded baffled. "Whatta you mean, 'thank you'? Didn't you see the rest?"

Munir went cold all over. He tried to speak but words would not come. It felt as if something were stuck in his throat. Finally, he found his voice.

"Rest? What rest?"

"I think you'd better take another look in that envelope, Mooo-neeer. Take a real good look before you think about thankin' me. I'll call you back later."

"No—!"

The line went dead.

Panic exploded within as he hung up and looked around for the envelope. Where was it? Had he dropped it in the elevator?

He ran back into the hall and spotted it on the floor.

Didn't you see the rest?

What rest? Please, Allah, what did he mean? What was he saying?

He snatched up the stiff envelope and felt it as he hurried back to the apartment. Yes, something still in it. A bulge at the bottom, wedged into the corner. He closed the apartment door behind him and smacked the open end of the envelope against the top of the slim hallway table.

Once. Twice.

Something tumbled out. Something in a small Ziploc bag.

Short. Cylindrical. A pale, dusky pink. Bloody red at the ragged end.

Munir jammed the back of his wrist against his mouth. To hold back the screams. To hold back the vomit.

And the inscription on Barbara's photograph came back to him.

She watched.

The phone began to ring.

9. "I wish you weren't going," Jack said, meaning it more than ever now that they were at the airport.

They'd just checked her bag at the American Airlines counter and were ambling toward the security check area. Gia was swathed in a down coat and had her short blond hair hidden under a Life Is Good knit cap. Vicky scouted ahead, looking for a Cinnabon stand.

Gia gave him a wan smile. "I wish I weren't either."

"Then don't."

"I've got to. Vicky needs to see her grandparents every so often, otherwise they're just voices on the telephone."

"Then have them come here. I'll pay for the tickets."

"That's kind, but my dad's back makes travel a real problem." She tilted her head and pierced him with her blue gaze. "We go for visits regularly. This is the first time you've made such a fuss. What's up?"

Jack hesitated, not sure of what to say, or if he should say anything. No, he had to say something. He'd had vague forebodings for a while, but this morning's news had crystallized things.

"Something's in the air. I don't know what it is, but something's going to happen and I want you nearby when it does."

Unease twisted her features. "What's going to happen?"

"I don't know." He felt his gut knotting. "Those Kicker kooks using EMPs last night . . . it scares me. If they do damage the Internet, it'll disrupt travel and communications. You could be trapped in the Midwest."

"At least I'd have a safe place to stay."

Yeah, Jack thought, but will it stay safe? Never know what some people will do if they think no one is watching.

"So . . . can't you put the trip off?"

She shook her head. "No."

"Why not?"

Tears rimmed along her lids. "For the same reason. Something bad's going to happen."

Jack threw up his hands. "That's a reason *not* to go!"

"But don't you see? I have this feeling that if I don't go now I'll never see them again."

Jack felt his shoulders slump. "The coma vision?"

She nodded.

When Gia was in a coma a year ago she'd seen the future and it didn't go beyond this spring. Nothing but featureless blackness after that. Jack wouldn't have given it much credence, but Gia wasn't the only one. A dead guy Jack knew, and spoke to now and again, had told him the same thing. According to these visions the world ended in a few months.

"Then I guess you've got to go."

She nodded, biting her upper lip. "I do. I've just got to see them. But I'll be back Sunday. I promise."

What could he say? All he could do was let her go and hope for the best.

"Okay, but you call me from O'Hare, and again when you land in Des Moines, and then again when you reach your folks' place. Got it?"

Jeez, I sound like a nervous mother.

Well, he *was* nervous. Couldn't help it. That feeling of growing menace in the air . . . and these were the two most important people left in his life.

She smiled and wiped away a tear. "Got it."

He walked her to the security check line, kissed her and Vicky good-bye, then watched until they were passed through and headed for their gate.

He avoided the baggage claim area on his way out, but

memories rose like ghosts . . . red memories . . . blood . . . his father in a pool of it . . .

He'd have to face it when Gia and Vicky returned, but for now—

His phone rang. Eddie? He'd called but got no answer so he'd left a voice mail to call him back.

But this wasn't Eddie.

"My boy!" cried a male voice. *"H-h-he cut off—"* He broke into sobs.

"Munir?"

"Please . . . I have no one else to call. He's hurt Robby! He's hurt my boy! Please help me, I beg you!"

"But what—?"

"PLEASE!"

"Okay. I'll get there as soon as I can."

What the hell?

10.   The woman coming her way along Columbus Avenue looked familiar.

Aveline Lesueur had been trundling along, wishing she were about fifty pounds lighter and that it weren't so cold. Her down coat hid her RT uniform. She was proud of the yellow tunic and what it represented—it gave her instant respect in the Dormentalist temple—but it was sleeveless and this wasn't sleeveless weather. Not by a very long shot.

She enjoyed her job as a Reveille Tech. It paid some of her expenses at the temple, but didn't put food on the table. So she was on her way to her second job as a restaurant hostess when she caught sight of this dark-haired woman in her midthirties coming the other way. She was sure she didn't know her but her face—

The BOLO!

She'd found a Be-on-the-Lookout flier on her desk this

morning and was sure this was the same woman. Her hair was longer, her face a bit thinner, but the resemblance was remarkable.

She stepped to the side and stopped, fishing the flier from her coat pocket. She unfolded it and checked the drawing as the woman passed.

Yes. No question. The same woman: Louise Myers.

Aveline did an about-face and followed her. She felt like some sort of secret agent. Well, in a way she was—an agent for the Dormentalist Church. She had no idea why the Church was interested in this woman, but her place was not to question, simply to obey on her road to Fusion.

After a few blocks on Columbus Louise Myers turned onto a side street. She carried a North Face backpack over one shoulder with something bulky and heavy looking within. As she approached a high-rise apartment building she slipped a plastic card from her pocket. Aveline came up close as the card swiped through the slot—just like in the temple—and slipped into the vestibule right behind her. She followed her to the elevator and joined her in the cab.

Her heart thumped in her chest. This was so exciting.

She noticed the Myers woman had pressed the seventh floor, so she pressed a button at random—the eighth.

What to do now? She hadn't thought this out. Couldn't follow her to her apartment—too obvious. Besides, she'd already pressed another floor. How to prove this was the woman when she returned to the temple? If only she had some sort of mini spy camera, she could—

Her phone!

She pulled out her cell and flipped it open.

"Don't get your hopes up," the woman said.

Aveline froze. She looked up, half expecting to see a gun pointed at her. But instead the woman's finger was pointed at her phone.

"What?"

"No signal in the elevator," the woman said.

Right. Aveline's screen showed no bars.

"My—my phone's pretty good."

She thumbed the camera, framed Louise Myers in the screen, then pressed ok. No click like a regular camera and *yes*! A bit blurry due to her shaking hand, but it would do. She saved it and snapped the phone closed.

"You're right. 'No carrier.' "

The doors slid open and Louise Myers stepped out. "See ya."

"Yeah."

The doors closed and Aveline sagged against the rear wall of the cab.

I did it. I really did it.

She couldn't wait to get back to the temple and show her photo to one of the paladins.

11. "Take it easy, guy," Jack said to the sobbing man slumped before him. "It's going to be all right."

Jack didn't believe that, and he doubted Munir did either, but he didn't know what else to say. Hard enough to deal with a sobbing woman. What do you say to a blubbering man?

Munir had been so glad to see him, so grateful to him for coming back, that Jack practically had to peel him off.

He helped him to the kitchen where he noticed a heavy meat cleaver lying on the table. Several deep gouges, fresh ones, marred the tabletop. Jack finally got him calmed down.

"Where is it?"

"There." He pointed to the upper section of the refrigerator. "I thought if maybe I kept it cold . . ."

Munir slumped forward on the table, facedown, resting his forehead on his crossed arms. Jack opened the freezer compartment and pulled out the plastic bag.

A finger. A kid's. The left pinkie. Rock hard from the freezer. Cleanly chopped off. Probably with the cleaver he'd seen yesterday in the photo of a more delicate portion of Robby's anatomy.

The son of a bitch.

And then the photograph of the boy's mother. And the inscription.

Jack felt a surge of blackness from the abyss within him. He willed it back. He couldn't get involved in this, couldn't let it get personal. He turned to look back at the kitchen table and found Munir staring at him.

"Do you see?" Munir said, wiping the tears from his cheeks. "Do you see what he has done to my boy?"

Jack quickly stuffed the finger back into the freezer.

"Look, I'm really sorry about this but nothing's changed. You still need more help than one guy can offer. You need the cops."

Munir shook his head violently. "No! You haven't heard his latest demand! The police can*not* help me with this! Only you can! Please, come listen."

Jack followed him down a hall to the office again where he waited while Munir's trembling fingers fumbled with the answerphone controls. Finally he got it playing. Jack barely recognized Munir's voice as he spewed his grief and rage at the caller. Then the other voice laughed.

VOICE: *Well, well. I guess you got my little present.*

MUNIR: You vile, filthy, perverted—

VOICE: *Hey-hey, Mooo-neeer. Let's not get too personal here. This ain't between you'n me. This here's a matter of international diplomacy.*

MUNIR: How . . . [a choking sound] how could you?

VOICE: *Easy, Mooo-neeer. I just think about how your people blew my sister to bits and it becomes real easy. Might be a real good idea for you to keep that in mind from here on in.*

MUNIR: Let them go and take me. I'll be your prisoner.
You can . . . you can cut me to pieces if you
wish. But let them go, I beg you!

VOICE: [laughs] *Cut you to pieces! Mooo-neeer, you
must be psychic or something. That's what I've
been thinking too! Ain't that amazing?*

MUNIR: You mean you'll let them go?

VOICE: *Someday—when you're all the way through the
wringer. But let's not change the subject here.
You in pieces—now that's a thought. Only I'm
not going to do it. You are.*

MUNIR: What do you mean?

VOICE: *Just what I said, Mooo-neeer. I want a piece of
you. One of your fingers. I'll leave it to you to
decide which one. But I want you to chop it off
and have it ready to send to me by tomorrow
morning.*

MUNIR: Surely you can't be serious!

VOICE: *Oh, I'm serious, all right.* Deadly *serious. You
can count on that.*

MUNIR: But how? I can't!

VOICE: *You'd better find a way, Mooo-neeer. Or the
next package you get will be a bit bigger. It'll
be a whole hand.* [laughs] *Well, maybe not a
whole* hand. *One of the fingers will already be
missing.*

MUNIR: No! Please! There must be—

VOICE: *I'll call in the mornin' t'tell you how to deliver it.
And don't even think about goin' to the cops.
You do and the next package you get'll be a lot
bigger. Like a head. Chop-chop, Mooo-neeer.*

He switched off the machine and turned to Jack.
"You see now why I need your help?"
"No. I'm telling you again the police and the feds can
do a better job of tracking this guy."

"But will the police help me cut off my finger?"

"Forget it!" Jack said, swallowing hard. "No way."

"But I can't do it myself. I've tried but I can't make my hand hold still. I want to but I just can't do it myself." Munir looked him in the eyes. "Please. You're my only hope. You must."

"Don't pull that on me." Jack wanted out of here. Now. "Get this: Just because you need me doesn't mean you own me. Just because I *can* doesn't mean I *must*. And in this case I honestly doubt that I can. So keep all of your fingers and dial nine-one-one to get some help."

"No!" Anger overcame the fear and anguish in Munir's face. "I will not risk their lives!"

He strode back to the kitchen and picked up the cleaver. Jack was suddenly on guard. The guy was nearing the end of his rope. No telling what he'd do.

"I wasn't man enough to do it before," he said, hefting the cleaver. "But I can see I'll be getting no help from you or anyone else. So I'll have to take care of this all by myself!"

Jack stood back and watched as Munir slammed his left palm down on the tabletop, splayed the fingers, and angled the hand around so the thumb was pointing somewhere past his left flank.

Jack didn't move to stop him. Munir was doing what he thought he had to do.

He raised the cleaver above his head. It hovered there a moment, wavering like a cliff diver with second thoughts, then with a whimper of fear and dismay, Munir drove the cleaver into his hand.

Or rather into the tabletop where his hand had been.

Weeping, he collapsed into the chair then, and his sobs of anguish and self-loathing were terrible to hear.

"All right, goddammit," Jack said. He knew this was going to be nothing but trouble, but he'd seen and heard all he could stand. He kicked the nearest wall. "I'll do it."

12. Dawn had carried her lunch salad up to the top floor of the penthouse. She sat in one of the poolside chairs and gazed through the green-tinted glass walls at Central Park below. Not nearly as pretty now as in the summer when the trees were in full leaf. The bare branches and winter-brown grass were totally ugly. Shadows from the buildings along Central Park West were stretching her way, edging onto the frozen surface of Jackie O Lake. On the far side of the park, the setting sun peeked between the towers of the El Dorado building.

She sighed.

So damn lonely. She could have eaten downstairs with Gilda bustling about, but being around Gilda was worse than being alone. She'd had a thing against Dawn ever since Henry got the sack, or whatever happened to him. A lot of that was Dawn's fault, yeah, but Henry had gone along with it.

Anyway, she was sure Gilda would have totally poisoned her food long before now if not for her boss. "The Master," as she called him, kept Dawn locked away here for her protection. Supposedly. If anything hap—

She cried out and doubled over, sending her plate flying as a sharp pain ripped through her lower belly.

The plate shattered and the flying pieces hadn't settled before the pain was gone.

Dawn straightened and took a breath.

What was that? The start of labor?

Tensing, she waited for the next shot but it didn't come. After ten minutes of nothing happening, she rose and headed for her room, leaving the broken plate and scattered lettuce behind. Let Gilda clean it up. If it had been anyone else, Dawn would have picked up the pieces as best she could, but not for Gilda.

She stepped carefully, not wanting that pain to hit again while she was on her feet. But she reached her room without even a tiny pang. She lay down on her bed and waited.

13. "Ready?"

Munir's left hand was lashed to the tabletop. Jack had loaded him with every painkiller in the medicine cabinet—Tylenol, Advil, Bufferin, Anacin 3, Nuprin. Some of them were duplicates. Jack didn't care. He wanted Munir's pain center deadened as much as possible. He wished the guy drank. He'd have much preferred doing this to someone who was dead drunk. Or doped up. Jack could have scored a bunch of Dilaudids for him. But Munir had said no to both. No booze. No dope.

Tight-ass.

Jack had never cut off a finger. He wanted to do this right. The first time. No misses. Half an inch too far to the right and Munir would lose only a piece of his pinkie; half an inch too far to the left and he'd be missing the ring finger as well. So Jack had made himself a guide. He'd found a plastic cutting board, a quarter-inch thick, and notched one of its edges. Now he was holding the board upright with the notch clamped over the base of Munir's pinkie; the rest of his hand was safe behind the board. All Jack had to do was chop down as hard as he could along the vertical surface.

That was all.

Easy.

Right.

"I am ready," Munir said.

He was dripping sweat. His dark eyes looked up at Jack, then he nodded, stuffed a dishrag in his mouth, and turned his head away.

Swell, Jack thought. Glad you're ready. How about me?

Now or never.

He steadied the cutting board, raised the cleaver. He couldn't do this.

Got to.

He took a deep breath, tightened his grip—

—and drove the cleaver into the wall.

Munir jumped, turned, pulled the dishrag from his mouth.

"What? Why—?"

"This isn't going to work." Jack let the plastic cutting board drop and began to pace the kitchen. "Got to be another way. He's got us on the run. We're playing this whole thing by his rules."

"There aren't any others."

"Yeah, there are."

Jack continued pacing. One thing he'd learned over the years was not to let the other guy deal all the cards. Let him *think* he had control of the deck while you changed the order.

Munir wriggled his fingers. "Please. I cannot risk angering this madman."

Jack swung to face him. An idea was taking shape.

"You want me in on this?"

"Yes, of course."

"Then we do it my way. All of it. First thing we do is untie you." He began working at the knots that bound Munir's arm to the table. "Then we make some phone calls."

14.   Munir understood none of this. He sat in a daze, sipping milk to ease a stomach that quaked from fear and burned from too many pills. Jack was on the phone, but his words made no sense.

"Yeah, Ron. It's me. Jack . . . Right. That Jack. Look,

I need a piece of your wares . . . small piece. Easy thing . . . Right. I'll get that to you in an hour or two. Thing is, I need it by morning. Can you deliver? . . . Great. Be by later. By the way—how much? . . . Make that two and you got a deal . . . All right. See you."

Then he hung up, took the glass from Munir's hands. Munir found himself taken by the upper arm and pulled toward the door.

"Can you get us into your office?"

Munir nodded. "I'll need my ID card and keys, but yes, security will let me in."

"Great. There a back way out of here?"

Munir led him down the elevator to the parking garage and out the rear door. Night was falling. They caught a cruising gypsy cab and rode downtown to a hardware store on Bleecker Street. Jack told the cabbie to wait, then grabbed Munir's arm.

"Let's go."

"I can stay with the cab."

"No way. This won't work without you."

Munir followed him inside to where a painfully thin man with sallow skin and no hair whatsoever, not even eyebrows, stood behind the counter.

"Hey, Jack," he said.

"How's it going, Teddy? How're you feeling?"

"Like warmed-over shit. This chemo sucks the big one."

Munir noticed a pack of cigarettes in the breast pocket of Teddy's shirt and made a tentative diagnosis. And yet he was still smoking? He didn't understand some people.

He followed Jack to the paint department at the rear of the store. They stopped at the display of color cards. Jack pulled a group from the brown section and turned to him.

"Give me your hand."

Baffled, Munir watched as Jack placed one of the color cards against the back of his hand, then tossed it away. And again. One after another until—

"Here we go. Perfect match."

"We're buying *paint*?"

"No. We're buying flesh—specifically, flesh with Golden Mocha number one-sixty-nine skin. Let's go."

And then they were moving again. Jack slapped a ten-dollar bill on the counter as he passed.

"What's that for?" Teddy said.

"Your trouble. Hang in there, Teddy."

"Like I got a choice."

And then they were back in the cab. Jack directed the driver to the East Side now, up First Avenue to Thirty-first Street—Bellevue Hospital. He ran inside with the color card, then came out and jumped back into the cab empty-handed.

"Okay. Next stop is your office."

"My office? Why?"

"Because we've got hours to kill and we might as well use them to look up everyone you fired in the past year."

Munir thought this was futile but he had given himself into Jack's hands. He had to trust him. And as exhausted as he was, sleep was out of the question.

He gave the driver the address of the Saud Petrol offices.

15.   Kris Szeto knocked on the door of apartment 7C and waited. He'd already checked A and B, so now it was C's turn. Best to search in an orderly fashion. Much less apt to miss something.

The photo of the woman had come attached to an email from the Grand Paladin of the Dormentalist temple on Lexington Avenue. A Dormentalist woman had spotted someone who looked like Louise Myers—Drexler had begun referring to her as Louise Connell, but she would always be Louise Myers to Kris.

Because he hated Louise Myers.

To the Dormentalist's credit, she had followed the woman to her apartment, even knew her floor, and somehow had managed to take a picture of her.

It all sounded perfect, but the resultant photo was blurry and the lighting poor. The woman in the photo did resemble Louise Myers, but Kris saw enough differences to make him wonder. Last year they had tracked her to Wyoming through her debit card.

Since he was the only one left alive who had seen Louise Myers in the flesh, it had fallen to him to follow her there. But the trail had dried up. Now she was back in the city. Couldn't stay away, apparently. Not that he blamed her. He blamed her for many things, but he'd been to Wyoming and wouldn't want to stay there either.

And since he was the only one left alive who could recognize her, he was here to make certain this was the woman they sought.

The only one left alive . . .

He ground his teeth at the good men he had sent after her who had never come back . . . at least not alive. Shot to death, one and all. Drexler said it couldn't have been her, but Kris wasn't so sure.

When Kris had seen her she'd been comatose in a hospital bed. Was that why he was still alive? Because she'd been unconscious.

A woman's voice spoke through the door.

"Can I help you?"

"Yes, please. I live on fifth floor and I am looking for my dog."

"Sorry. I haven't seen any dogs."

Wasn't she going to open the damn door?

"Please?"

He took one of the fliers he had brought along and held it up to the peephole. He'd found a picture of something called a shih chon—a sickeningly cute cross between a shih tzu and a bichon—and had printed a close-up of its face on the flier. He figured it would be irresistible.

"I haven't seen a single dog on this floor."

Still the door remained closed.

"I did not think you would. He got off leash outside. Would you please keep watch for him?"

Locks clicked and the door opened a few inches. Kris noticed a chain pulled tight across the opening. A woman's face appeared.

Despite his training and experience, he couldn't help a short, sharp intake of breath.

Louise Myers.

Thinner, longer hair, but her. No question. His first instinct was to kick down the door and strangle her.

"Are you all right?" she said.

"Yes. I mean, no. My wife and I are very attached to our Binky."

She smiled and seemed to relax. *"Binky?"*

He forced a smile. "Yes. A long story. But if you see him about, that is name he will answer to. Grab him if you can—he is friendly—but if you cannot, just follow him and call that number. We are offering five-thousand-dollar reward."

He passed the flier through the opening and she took it.

So easy to grab her wrist and yank it through. Then he'd—

"I'll keep my eyes open."

"Thank you. Thank you so much."

The door closed and he walked away.

Mission accomplished.

Drexler wanted only her address, nothing else. Not even observation. Simply a location.

But Kris wanted so much more.

16. Ohio, Kewan thought as he trudged through the dark up a rise behind a guy he'd met only a few hours ago. The fuck am I doing in Ohio?

He'd been ushered into a car right after this morning's meeting and driven out to the middle of nowhere. He'd been met by this white guy named Clinton Bridger who'd be putting him up and showing him the ropes. Exactly what ropes, no one was saying.

He thought it had been cold in the city, but here was much worse. The wind—damn, it cut like a razor. Even with his hooded parka and heavy pants, he was freezing his nuts off. Bridger didn't seem to mind. Maybe it was that thick biker mustache, or maybe he was wearing long johns.

Better question: The fuck am I doing in Ohio freezing my ass off near midnight in the middle of open country?

When they reached the top of the rise, Bridger pointed to a brightly lit building about a quarter mile away.

"There you go," he said.

Kewan was puffing. "Looks like a warehouse."

"It's not. It's the McVicker IXP."

Kewan knew what that meant: Internet exchange point.

"Oh, like a super data center."

"More like data center to the nth power. An IXP is where all sorts of ISPs crisscross and share information. Take that out and a shitload of people don't have Internet."

"So that's our next target?"

"Lemme tell you about that place, friend."

They weren't friends, but Kewan let it pass.

"They chose this spot because we don't get earthquakes, tornadoes, hurricanes, or floods around here. It's got two electric supplies from two separate substations, plus its own generators. The walls are foot-thick reinforced concrete with Kevlar lining. What few small windows it's got are bomb-resistant laminated glass. And the air handlers inside can be set to recirculate in case of a gas attack. See those planters ringing the place? They're really bollards. Plus they've got two staggered sets of retractable bollards at the gate. Only two ways into the building—the front door and the loading dock. The fire doors are exit only. Security cameras are everywhere. And even if you get inside, there are more layers of security within."

Kewan stared at the place. "So you're telling me getting in's a bitch."

"More than a bitch. Nigh on impossible."

"So what do we do?"

He started back down the rise and waved for Kewan to follow.

They got into his pickup truck—still holding a little warmth since when they left it—and drove about a mile along a four-lane county road, where Bridger stopped on the shoulder. He pulled some sort of crowbar from behind his seat and hopped out.

"Come on."

Back into the cold. Damn.

He joined Bridger by the rear of the truck where he stood watching the traffic. Wasn't much. Just one set of lights coming their way from the left.

"Where we going?" Kewan said, rubbing his gloved hands and shivering.

Bridger pointed across the road with the bar. "There."

"Why don't we just drive over there?"

"No." He pointed again. *"There."*

Kewan saw now that the bar wasn't pointing across the street, but *at* the street—at a manhole cover.

"What?"

As soon as the lone car passed, Bridger walked to the middle of the road, stuck the end of the bar through a hole in the manhole cover, and levered it free. He pushed it aside and gestured to the opening.

"In you go."

"Like hell."

Bridger dropped the bar inside, then slipped through, disappearing through the hole. A flashlight beam speared up from the opening.

"Hurry your ass down here before a car comes!"

Well, okay, Kewan thought. Long as you're in there first.

He eased down. His feet landed in about an inch of water as he found himself in a concrete pipe about four feet high.

Shit!

He crouched as Bridger popped his head and an arm back through the hole and used the bar to maneuver the cover back into place.

"What the fuck we doing here?"

Bridger flashed his beam along the collection of wires and thick cables running along the side of the pipe.

"Some of these are fiber-optic cables—OC-twenty-four and forty-eight—running to the IXP I just showed you. You've got other OC cables running into it from other directions, but almost all of them are as easy to access as these."

Kewan saw what was going on.

"You're kidding. They're this easy to get to?"

Bridger nodded, grinning. "Yep. They go to all that trouble to protect the IXP building, but the lines feeding into it are sitting ducks. We've got brother Kickers inside lots of these places, and they feed us the cable layouts, tell us which are the important ones."

"So all we've got to do is take a hammer and—"

"Hammer? My friend, we've got something a lot better than hammers at our disposal."

"Like what?"

"You'll see."

WEDNESDAY

1. At first Dawn thought it was just another of the backaches that had totally plagued her the past two months. But they'd never bothered her in bed before. Usually the ache stopped once she got herself horizontal. But this one had awakened her. Not that she slept much anyway these days. But she'd finally managed to doze off.

She checked the bedside clock: 3:22. Another long, lonely night.

The pain eased. Maybe she'd twisted in her sleep and set off a spasm, because this had seemed like more of a clenching than an ache. She closed her eyes and tried to find sleep again. So hard these days. She tried counting backward. That sometimes—

There, starting in the back again, only this time reaching forward into her lower abdomen, almost like a period cramp, except it couldn't be. She was—

The baby? Was this a contraction? Was she going into labor?

Oh, God, she'd been totally waiting for this moment, hungering for it, because it meant the end of this eternal pregnancy. And yet she'd totally dreaded it as well, because it meant pain. How was this baby ever going to pass out of her? No way it could fit.

No. She could do it. She'd have to. Countless women through the ages had done it. So could she.

But she was so scared. All through the pregnancy she'd

had no one to talk to about it. She wished her mother were here. Mom would tell her how it would go, talk her through it. But Mom was gone, murdered by that—

Wait. There. It eased off.

Shouldn't she time the contractions? She'd read about that in her pregnancy books. She noted the time on the clock, and waited . . . and waited. And then, eight minutes later, it came again.

No question about it, she was in labor.

She pressed the call button next to her headboard. A minute later, just as the contraction was subsiding, Gilda knocked and stepped into the room.

"Yes, Miss?" she said in her vague, East European accent.

She'd tucked her gray hair up inside some sort of old-fashioned sleep cap and wrapped herself in a bulky, flower-print robe. Her eyes were puffy slits and she looked anything but happy to be called to Dawn's room.

"I think it's started."

The slitted lids parted halfway. "What has started?"

Dawn wished she and Gilda had been getting along better. She could use some help now but didn't know how much Gilda would be willing to give. Dawn had asked forgiveness for what had happened to Henry, but Gilda didn't seem to have much of that in her.

"Labor! I think the baby's coming."

The older woman's eyes popped wide open. "Yes? This is true?"

"I think so. I've had three now."

The woman's face creased as she smiled and clapped her hands. "I must call the Master!"

"Never mind him! Call Doctor Landsman!"

"No-no-no!" she said, bustling out. "The Master must know first!"

Mr. Osala was in North Carolina or someplace like that. What could he do?

Dawn punched her pillow. She'd call Dr. Landsman herself if she had a phone. But she didn't, and didn't know the passcode for the few the duplex contained.

So she watched the clock and waited. Twelve minutes and still counting when Gilda returned, looking uncertain.

"He is not answering and he has not responded to my messages."

"Maybe just as well," Dawn said. "It seems to have stopped. Maybe it was just, you know, false labor."

"Perhaps."

"Do you have any children?"

Her expression hardened into the stony look Dawn had grown accustomed to. "Yes."

"How many?"

"One."

"A boy or a girl?"

"A boy."

This was totally like pulling teeth.

"What's his name?"

"Kristof."

"What was delivering him like?"

Her eyes glittered and her lips curved into a smile. "Terrible. I was your age. The worst pain I ever have had. I will never forget it."

Dawn's stomach lurched. What a mean bitch. "You're just saying that. You're just saying that to scare me."

Gilda shook her head slowly back and forth, right, then left, once each way. "No, it is truth. But in end I had my Kristof."

"Does he work for Mister Osala too?"

A single nod. "In a way."

"Does—?"

And then a contraction hit, harder than before. She writhed on the bed.

"It's back! Call Doctor Landsman. Now!"

Gilda hurried out, leaving Dawn to deal with the pain.

This one was lasting longer than the others. It seemed to go on forever.

Gilda popped back holding a terry-cloth robe, usually reserved for the pool area.

"The doctor says to come right away."

Dawn struggled from her bed and started for her closet. She'd been wearing an oversized Giants T-shirt to bed these days.

"I need to get dressed first."

"No-no-no! He says baby will come very quickly when it begins." She held up the robe by its shoulders and shook it. "Come-come. Georges awaits to drive you."

Dawn hesitated, then turned and slipped her arms into the sleeves. She'd be changing into a hospital gown as soon as she got there anyway.

Gilda hustled her out into the hall where Georges waited like a bad portent. A liveried block of granite, with about as much emotion. Without a word—he rarely spoke—he led her to the penthouse's elevator. Dawn was praying she wouldn't get hit with another contraction before the hospital. She didn't want to double over in front of Georges.

Not like he gave off a creepy vibe or anything. He gave off no vibe, and that was sort of creepy in itself. He looked relaxed and wide awake in his fresh, uncreased suit. Didn't he ever sleep?

She realized the insides of her thighs felt wet. She looked down and saw thin fluid running down her legs into the Crocs she'd slipped on. Her gut clenched. She knew what that meant.

"My water broke!"

Georges looked down, looked at her, then pulled out his cell phone and pressed a button. After a few seconds he said, "Gilda? Mess in elevator."

The door slid open into the building's front hall. Georges led the way to the front doors.

"Which hospital are we going to?" she said as she sloshed along in her shoes.

"No hospital."

She stopped. "What? What are you talking about?"

"Doctor Landsman has a clinic. Your baby, he is much too special for hospital."

2. "This guy looks promising," Jack said, handing Munir a file. "Remember him?"

Until tonight, Munir never had realized how many people his department had let go—"downsized" was the euphemism—in the course of the past year. He was amazed.

And exhausted. They had been at this for hours, checking names against an online list of victims of the Trade Tower attacks. No hits so far. That didn't rule anyone out, because the madman's sister could have been married, and therefore wouldn't necessarily carry the same name.

Munir had slept in fitful naps since Wednesday and could barely keep his eyes open. But he opened the file and blinked the text into focus.

Richard Hollander. The name didn't catch until he read the man's performance report.

"Not him. Anyone but him."

"Yeah? Why not?"

"Because he was so . . ." As Munir searched for the right word, he pulled out all he remembered about Hollander, and it wasn't much. The man hadn't been with the company long, and had been pretty much a nonentity during his stay. Then he found the word he was looking for. "Ineffectual."

"Yeah?"

"Yes. He never got anything done. Every assignment, every report was either late or incomplete. He had a wonderful academic record—good grades from a good school, that sort of thing—but he proved incapable of putting any of his learning into practice. That was why he was let go."

"Any reaction? You know, shouting, yelling, threats?"

"No." Munir remembered giving Hollander his notice. The man had merely nodded and begun emptying his desk. He hadn't even asked for an explanation. "He knew he'd been screwing up. I think he was expecting it. Besides, he had no southern accent."

For the sake of completeness, he checked the 9/11 list, but no Hollander.

Munir passed the folder back. "It's not him."

Instead of putting it away, Jack opened it and glanced through it again.

"Wouldn't be too sure about that. Accents can be faked. And if I was going to pick the type who'd go nuts for revenge, this guy would be it. Look: He's unmarried, lives alone—"

"Where does it say he lives alone?"

"It doesn't. But his emergency contact is his mother in Massachusetts. If he had a lover or even a roomie, he'd list them, wouldn't you think? 'No moderating influences,' as the head docs like to say. And look at his favorite sports: swimming and jogging. This guy's a loner from the git-go."

"That does not make him a psychopath. I imagine you are a loner, too, and you . . ."

The words dribbled away as Munir's mind followed the thought to its conclusion.

Jack grinned. "Right, Munir. Think about that."

He reached for the phone and punched in a number. After a moment he spoke in a deep, authoritative voice: "Please pick up. This is an emergency. Please pick up."

A moment later he hung up and began writing on a notepad.

"I'm going to take down this guy's address for future reference. It's almost three A.M. and Mr. Hollander isn't home. His answering machine is on, but even if he's screening his calls, I think he'd have responded to my little emergency message, don't you?"

Munir nodded. "Most certainly. But what if he doesn't live there anymore? Or is visiting his mother?"

"Always a possibility." Jack glanced at his watch. "But right now I've got to go pick up a package. You sit tight and stay by the phone here. I'll call you when I've got it."

Before Munir could protest, Jack was gone, leaving him alone in his office, staring at the gallery of family photos arrayed on his desk. He began to sob.

3. "Fully dilated and effaced," Dr. Landsman announced to all present.

For what seemed like the millionth time in the past hour, he had his gloved hand in her vagina, checking her cervix. She lay on the delivery table with her knees up, her crotch totally exposed to anyone who cared to look. And there seemed to be a lot of potential lookers—potential only, since no one seemed interested.

Why so many people for a simple delivery? What were they all doing here? And where exactly was *here*? Why wasn't she at a hospital instead of this private surgicenter somewhere in Queens?

She'd think about that later. Right now all she wanted was for the pains to stop.

"Is that good?"

He nodded. "Very good."

"Then why isn't he coming out?"

"He's trying. You've got to help him a little more."

"But what if he's too big to fit?"

"No worry about CPD—you've got a perfect pelvis for childbearing."

"Yeah, but—unnnngh!"

Another contraction. They were coming closer and harder. This was the worst yet.

"Breathe like I showed you," said the nameless nurse in scrubs by the head of the bed.

Dawn started panting through pursed lips, blowing hard. It helped, but not much.

"Make it stop!" she groaned. "I can't take much more of this."

Another woman in scrubs appeared at her bedside. "We're going to take care of that right now."

When the contraction subsided she was rolled onto her side and her lower back was swabbed with something cold.

"What are you doing?"

"It's epidural time."

She'd read about that—injecting anesthetic into the fluid around the spinal cord. But it involved sticking a needle into the spinal canal. Scary, but if it worked . . . anything to stop these pains.

She was ready for the stick when it came.

"Okay, we're in," the woman said. "Now the anesthetic. This will be like money from home."

She felt a new contraction coming on, building. "Better hurry. I've got another . . ."

And then the pain faded. They did some taping and then eased her onto her back again. She looked at the woman—doctor, nurse, she couldn't tell, and didn't care—and loved her.

"If you were a man, I'd kiss you."

She smiled. "I've heard that before."

Another man in surgical scrubs, tall and fair-haired with a round, cherubic face, walked into the room.

"Who's that?"

"That's Doctor Heinze."

"*Another* doctor?"

He must have heard because he stepped forward and smiled down at her.

"I'm a pediatrician. I'm here to examine your baby after he's born."

Wow. Mr. Osala was sure going all out for this baby. He'd totally thought of everything.

"All right!" Dr. Landsman said, rubbing his gloved hands together. "Let's deliver us a baby!"

Dawn flowed through a blur of pushing and then not pushing and then pushing again and again and again until . . .

Dawn felt a great pressure relieved, heard a high-pitched wail, and then someone said, "We have a baby!"

Joy, relief, and fear roiled within her. It was over, she had a baby, but what was she going to do with a baby? Oh, right. He was already adopted.

"Is he all right?"

"He's . . ."

Dr. Landsman seemed at a loss for words. She could see his head framed between her raised thighs. He was gazing down at the baby in his arms, well below Dawn's line of sight, with the same fascinated expression she'd seen during the ultrasounds.

The nurse and the anesthetist flanked him, each looking over a shoulder. Their expressions reflected different emotions. A certain fascination, yes, but tinged with something else. Revulsion?

"He's what?"

Dr. Landsman shook himself and looked at her, then looked down again. "He's stopped breathing! Quick! We'll need to suction him!"

As he shot to his feet, cradling the baby, Dawn caught a glimpse of her child.

And screamed.

He had hair—a full head of black hair and a dark

down covering his skin. But what were those things under his arms? They—

Snakes!

Two baby snakes, maybe four inches long, had sunk their fangs into his armpits and were writhing—

No! Tendrils! That's what they were. No—tentacles! Two smooth, twisting, coiling tentacles. No suckers like an octopus. Flesh colored . . . looked like rattails.

Dawn screamed again as Dr. Landsman rushed away with the baby. Her little boy's eyes opened and he looked at her with a black gaze. As she screamed again she saw the anesthetist injecting something into her IV line.

"You've done your job," she said softly. "Now rest."

Something warm in her arm, and then the world faded to white . . .

4. The phone startled Munir out of a light doze. Confusion jerked him upright. What was he doing in his office? He should be home . . .

Then he remembered.

Jack was on the line: "Meet me downstairs."

Out on the street, in the pale, predawn light, two figures waited. One was Jack, the other a stranger—a thin man of Munir's height with light, shoulder-length hair and a goatee. Jack made no introductions. Instead he led them around a corner to the front of a small all-night coffee shop. He stared through the window at the lights inside.

"This looks bright enough," Jack said.

Inside he ordered two coffees and two cheese Danish and carried them to the rearmost booth in the narrow, deserted store. Jack and the stranger slid into one side, Munir the other, facing them. Still no introductions.

"Okay, Munir," Jack said. "Put your hand on the table."

Munir complied, placing his left hand palm down, wondering what this was about.

"Now let's see the merchandise," Jack said to the stranger.

The thin man pulled a small, oblong package from his pocket. It appeared to be wrapped in brown paper hand towels. He unrolled the towels and placed the object next to Munir's hand.

It looked like a finger. Not Robby's. Different. Adult size.

Munir pulled his hand back onto his lap and stared.

"Come on, Munir," Jack said. "We've got to do a color check."

Munir slipped his hand back onto the table next to the gruesome object, regarding it obliquely. So real looking.

"It's too long and that's only a fair color match," Jack said. "After all this time I thought you'd do better."

"Hey," the stranger said, "I have to be careful. I not only gotta find the right shade, the boarder's gotta be a John Doe, and one that's headed for the oven or med school real soon."

Jack shook his head. "Still . . ."

"It's close enough. Pretty damn good on such short notice, I'd say."

"I guess it'll have to do." Jack handed him an envelope. "Here you go."

The goateed stranger took it and stuffed it inside his shirt without opening it, then left without saying good-bye.

Munir stared at the finger. The grisly flesh on the stump end, the detail over the knuckles and around the fingernail—even down to the dirt under the nail—was amazing. It almost looked real.

"This won't work," he said. "I don't care how real this looks, when he finds out it's a fake—"

"Fake?" Jack said, stirring sugar into his coffee. "Who said it's a fake?"

Munir snatched his hand away and pushed himself
back. He wanted to sink into the vinyl of the booth seat,
wanted to pass through to the other side and run from
this man and the loathsome object on the table between
them. He fixed his eyes on the seat beside him and managed to force a few words past his rising gorge.

"Where . . . ?"

"He works at the city morgue."

"Please . . . take . . . that . . . away."

He heard the soft crinkle and scrape of paper being
folded and dragged across the tabletop, then Jack's voice:

"Okay, Cinderella. You can look now. It's gone."

Munir kept his eyes averted. What had he got himself
into? In order to save his family from one ruthless madman he was forced to deal with another. What sort of
world was this?

He felt a sob build in his throat. Until last week, he
couldn't remember crying once since his boyhood. For
the past few days it seemed he wanted to cry all the time.
Or scream. Or both.

He saw Jack's hand pushing a cup of coffee into his
field of vision.

"Here. Drink this. Lots of it. You're going to need to
stay alert."

An insane hope rose in Munir.

"Do you think . . . do you think the man on the phone
did the same thing? With Robby's finger? Maybe he went
to a morgue and . . ."

Jack shook his head slowly, as if the movement pained
him. For an instant he saw through the wall around Jack.
Saw pity there.

"Don't torture yourself."

Yes, Munir thought. The madman on the phone was
already doing too good a job of that.

"It's not going to work," he said, fighting the blackness

of despair. "He's going to realize he's been tricked and then he's going to take it out on my boy."

"No matter what you do, he's going to find an excuse to do something nasty to your boy. Or your wife. That's the whole idea behind this gig—make you suffer. But his latest wrinkle with the fingers gives us a chance to find out who he is and where he's holed up."

"How?"

"He wants your finger. How's he going to get it? He can't very well give us an address to mail it to. So there's going to have to be a drop—someplace where you leave it and he picks it up. And that's where we nab him and make him tell us where he's got your family stashed."

"What if he refuses to tell us?"

Jack's voice was soft, his nod almost imperceptible.

"Oh . . . he'll tell us."

Munir shuddered at what he saw flashing through Jack's eyes in that instant.

"He thinks I won't do it," he said, looking at his fingers—all ten of them. "He thinks I'm a coward because he thinks all Arabs are cowards. He's said so. And he was right. I couldn't do it."

"Hell," Jack said, "I couldn't do it either, and it wasn't even my hand. But I'm sure you'd have done it eventually if I hadn't come up with an alternative."

Would I? Munir thought. *Could* I have done it?

Maybe he'd have done it just to demonstrate his courage to the madman on the phone. Over the years Munir had seen the Western world's image of the Arab male distorted beyond recognition by terrorism: The Arab strapped bombs to women and children to blow up school buses; the Arab videotaped the beheading of helpless hostages; Arab manhood aimed its weapons from behind the skirts of unarmed civilian women and children.

"If something goes wrong because of this, because of

my calling on you to help me, I . . . I will never forgive myself."

"Don't think like that. It gets you nothing. And you've got to face it: No matter what you do—cut off one finger, two fingers, your left leg, kill somebody, blow up Manhattan—it's never going to be enough. He's going to keep escalating until you're dead. You've got to stop him now, before it goes any further. Understand?"

Munir nodded. "But I'm so afraid. Poor Robby . . . his terrible pain, his fear. And Barbara . . ."

"Exactly. And if you don't want that to go on indefinitely, you've got to take the offensive. Now. So let's get back to your place and see how he wants to take delivery on your finger."

5. Dawn blinked in the dimness. Where was she? This wasn't her bed. She—

The baby!

It all rushed back at her—the labor, the delivery, the glimpse of her baby and his . . . tentacles?

No, that couldn't be. It had to be a dream. Had to be . . .

She looked around and realized she wasn't in her room in the penthouse. Some sort of hospital room. The shade was pulled on the single window but daylight seeped around the edges. She pushed herself up to a sitting position and hung on to the bed rails as the room spun. They'd doped her with something last night, injected it into—

She looked at her arm and saw the IV was still running into her.

"Hello?" she called. "Is anybody here?"

Almost immediately a woman in green scrubs scurried in.

"You're awake. Oh, good."

As the nurse busied herself taking her blood pressure, Dawn said, "Where's my baby?"

The nurse concentrated on the blood pressure cuff's dial. "Doctor Landsman will discuss that with you."

A twinge of alarm fluttered through her. "Discuss? What's to discuss?"

"He'll tell you. He's down the hall. I'll get him."

She rushed out before Dawn could ask anything more. Minutes later Dr. Landsman appeared with the nurse in tow.

"How are you feeling, Dawn?" he said as he reached the bedside. "You did really well. No episiotomy or repairs necessary." He reached over the rail and gripped her hand. "Any pain?"

Dr. Landsman holding her hand? Something had to be wrong.

"Never mind me, where's my baby?"

He squeezed her hand. "I'm sorry, Dawn."

Her chest clenched inside. "Sorry? Sorry for what?"

"He had neurological birth defects, I'm afraid, ones that didn't show up on the ultrasounds. And they turned out to be incompatible with life."

"'Incompatible with life'? What does that mean?"

His smile was sad. "An old medical term referring to fatal, uncorrectable birth defects."

"You mean his tentacles?"

Dr. Landsman's eyebrows rose, then fell. "Tentacles? Where did you get the idea he had tentacles?"

"I saw them. I—"

He patted her hand. "You were distraught. You'd just gone through an arduous delivery and suddenly your baby stopped breathing. Your eyes played tricks on you. Your baby had birth defects, yes, but I assure you he did not have tentacles."

"I want to see him."

"He's . . . dead, Dawn. Do you really think that's a good idea?"

Dawn wasn't sure what she was feeling—panic or anger.

"I have a right to see him, and I want to see him *now!*"

Dr. Landsman released her hand. "I'm afraid that's impossible. The baby's remains were sent to the city morgue."

"What?"

"It's the law. The baby was full term. His death is reportable."

"But I'm his mother!"

"Not officially. You gave him up for adoption upon birth, remember? I'm terribly sorry. I thought it was for the best. I've notified the adoptive parents. They're crushed, of course, but they said they'd take care of cremation expenses."

"Cremation! But I should be able to *see* him at least once!"

Dr. Landsman shook his head. "I wish I'd known you'd feel this way. But since you'd put him up for adoption, and did try to abort—"

"Stop throwing that in my face!"

He patted her hand. "There, there. I know you're upset."

Upset? Upset didn't come close to how she was feeling.

But why? All she'd wanted all these months was to be free of that baby, and now she was. But she hadn't wanted him dead—at least, not anymore.

She couldn't explain this terrible sense of *loss*.

Wait.

She'd seen tentacles, or things that looked like tentacles. She hadn't imagined them. Were those what had so fascinated Dr. Landsman on the ultrasounds? Was that why he'd never allowed her even a peek? He'd said nothing was wrong, that there was nothing to see, but he'd lied. And if he'd lied about that—

"I don't believe you," she said.

"Trust me, my dear, he had no—"

"I don't believe you about the tentacles. I don't even believe he's dead. I think you've hidden him away."

He loosed a strangled laugh. "Why would I want to do that?"

"I don't know." The words seemed to form on their own and poured from her in a torrent. "But I do know there's been a lot of strange stuff going on with this baby. Jerry wanted him, then Jerry's brother stopped me from having an abortion. Those crazy monks wanted him—or at least I think they did—and then Mister Osala came along, and he wouldn't let me have an abortion. He had a reason for that—supposedly for my own protection—and it sounded good, at least in theory, but I wonder, because the outcome of it all was to keep me pregnant with this baby, not let anything happen to the baby. The baby, the baby, the baby! What's so damn important about my baby? The tentacles?" She heard her voice rising in pitch and volume but couldn't help it. "What? Somebody tell me! Somebody stop lying to me for just half a fucking minute and tell me!"

By the end she was screaming.

Dr. Landsman turned to the nurse and nodded. Dawn saw a syringe in her hand, saw her plunge it into the IV tubing and empty it. She reached over to rip out the line but Dr. Landsman grabbed her wrist and held it.

"Relax, Dawn. You're hysterical. It's a postpartum mood disorder. You're imagining things. This will relax you."

She struggled, but the strength seemed to leak out of her. A moment later she had to lie back. She fought to keep her eyes open but they refused to obey. She heard Dr. Landsman saying something to the nurse but his voice was too far away to understand . . .

6. "Mister Tuit?" someone called as Russ stepped off the elevator.

He mispronounced it as *Too-it*. Most people did.

"It's 'Tweet,'" he said. "Like that thing you do on Twitter."

The guy gave him a blank look. Under his topcoat he was thin as a memory board and looked like he had a black BB embedded in the middle of his chin.

Then he blinked and said, "Sorry, Mister . . . Tuit." This time he got it right. He extended a hand. "My name's Belgiovene. I'm with the Operation."

That was how they referred to the project—the Operation—and it involved some of the most satisfying work he had ever done. The National Reconnaissance Office, manned by DoD and CIA personnel, operated the nation's reconnaissance satellites. As such it was under constant attack by foreign hackers. It had secretly gathered a group of veteran hackers—Russ among them—to do some white-hat work, challenging them to push the hacking envelope, to take the most vicious worms and trojans hurled against the NRO's computers and make them worse. Then find defenses against them. And then develop a virus to breach those defenses. And then a firewall to block that attack. And on and on.

But as for this guy really being with the NRO, Russ wasn't so sure.

"How do I know that?"

The guy pulled out an ID folder and flipped it open to reveal his NRO ID. It looked good, but Russ still wasn't satisfied.

"How come you're meeting me out here and not in there?" he said, jerking his thumb down the hall to where the security teams worked.

The NRO had installed them on the sixth floor of this

office building on West Houston. To earn their salary, the teams were required to put in eight-to-five days, but they often stayed late—sometimes all night if things were rolling. Russ appreciated the generous income, but the potential bonus he'd been offered meant more than money.

"Because the Operation is closing down and your team will be finishing up without you."

Russ felt like he'd just been shoved into a black hole.

"Like hell!"

He started for the office door.

"Wait!" Belgiovene called out behind him. "It's not what you think."

Russ ignored him. Something wrong here. He'd done primo work for the Operation, given it his all. They couldn't—

He was halfway to the door when it opened and Hart, overseer of the teams, stepped out.

"Oh, Russ. I see you've met Belgiovene. Good news, eh?"

"Good news? I'm being canned and you call that good news?"

Hart looked flabbergasted. "Canned? Who said anything about—?"

"A misunderstanding, I'm afraid," Belgiovene said, joining them. He put a hand on Russ's arm. "We're moving you to a different project."

"Yeah," Hart said. "This one's done. Just a matter of tying up loose ends. You're too valuable to waste on scut work."

The praise shot a blast of relief through Russ.

Belgiovene said, "We're very impressed with your work. And . . . there's another matter I need to discuss with you."

"What?"

"The terms of your parole?"

Relief morphed into exhilaration. Was he finally going to stop paying for that bank hack?

"You mean—?"

Belgiovene raised a hand. "Not here."

"What? Oh, right. Sure. Where?"

"It's best we talk in private. We will have to meet with people. It is a delicate procedure. Judicial egos are involved—not local, but federal. We keep our promises. You've delivered your end, so we'll deliver ours. We'll get this done."

Russ followed him toward the elevator, feeling lighter than air.

7. "I'm falling apart," Munir said.

They sat in his kitchen while they waited for the phone to ring, and he did feel as if he were crumbling, physically as well as emotionally.

"You're under unimaginable stress," Jack said as he bandaged Munir's hand in thick layers of gauze to make it look injured. "You've got a guy out there trying to break you."

"Well, he's succeeding."

"You can't let him win. You've got to hold on. You've got a wife and child somewhere out there depending on you."

He sensed Jack was not comfortable in the cheerleader role. And he shouldn't have been. He wasn't very good. Motivational speaking would not be a good alternate career choice.

"But what good am I to them? I'm not good for anything. This has made me realize how isolated the three of us have become. We became a self-sustaining unit: Barbara, Robby, and me. And now they're gone and I'm useless without them. You're all that's holding me together."

"I didn't sign on to hold anyone together," he said. "That's your responsibility."

After finishing the bandage, Jack rose and went to the refrigerator where he removed the bag with the amputated finger.

"Where are you going?" Munir said.

"The bathroom, to give this a little wash. We want this to be as convincing as possible, and you don't strike me as the type to have dirty fingernails."

Munir shook his head. Jack thought of everything.

When the call finally came, he ground his teeth at the sound of the hated voice. Jack stayed beside him, gripping his arm, steadying him as he listened through an earphone he had plugged into the answering machine. He had told Munir what to say, and had coached him on how to say it, how to sound.

"Well, Mooo-neeer. You got that finger for me?"

"Yes," he said in the choked voice he had rehearsed. "I have it."

The caller paused, as if surprised by the response.

"You did it? You really did it?"

"Yes. You gave me no choice."

"Well, I'll be damned. Hey, how come your voice sounds so funny?"

"Codeine. For the pain."

"Yeah. I'll bet that smarts. But that's okay. Pain's good for you. And just think: Your kid got through it without codeine."

Jack's grip on his arm tightened as Munir stiffened and began to rise. Jack pulled him back to a sitting position.

"Please don't hurt Robby anymore," Munir said, and this time he did not have to feign a choking voice. "I did what you asked me. Now please let them go."

"Not so fast, Mooo-neeer. How do I know you really cut that finger off? You wouldn't be bullshitting me now, would you?"

"Oh, please. I would not lie about something as important as this."

Yet I *am* lying, he thought. Forgive me, my son, if this goes wrong.

"Well, we'll just have to see about that, won't we? Here's what you do: Put your offering in a brown paper lunch bag and head downtown. Go to the mailbox on the corner of Lafayette and Astor. Leave the bag on top of the mailbox, then disappear. Got it?"

"Yes. Yes, I think so."

"Of course you do. Even a bonehead like you should be able to handle those instructions."

"But when should I do this?"

"Ten A.M."

"This morning?" He glanced at his watch. "But it is almost nine-thirty!"

"Aaaay! And he can tell time too! What an intellect! Yeah, that's right, Mooo-neeer. And don't be late or I'll have to think you're lying to me. And we know what'll happen then, don't we."

"But what if—?"

"See you soon, Mooo-neeer."

The line went dead. His heart pounding, Munir fumbled the receiver back onto its cradle and turned to Jack.

"We must hurry! We have no time to waste!"

Jack nodded. "This guy's no dummy. He's not giving us a chance to set anything up."

"I'll need the . . . finger," Munir said. Even now, long after the shock of learning it was real, the thought of touching it made him queasy. "Could you please put it in the bag for me?"

Jack nodded. Munir led him to the kitchen and gave him a brown lunch bag. Jack dropped the finger inside and handed the sack back to him.

"You've got to arrive alone, so you go first. I'll go out the back way and follow a few minutes from now. If you don't see me around, don't worry. I'll be there. And whatever you do, follow his instructions—nothing else. Understand? *Nothing else.* I'll do the ad-libbing. Now get moving."

Munir fairly ran for the street, praying to Allah that it wouldn't take too long to find a taxi.

8. "Gentlemen, I have an announcement," Ernst said when Thompson and Szeto had seated themselves on the far side of his desk. "Valez has delivered the goods."

Thompson muttered, "About time."

Szeto simply nodded.

Ernst hadn't expected cheers, but had thought he'd see a little more enthusiasm than this.

"Come, come, gentlemen. This is excellent news."

Szeto said, "Not until we test code and see if it lives up to expectations."

Ernst couldn't help smiling. "But we have. And it does."

Szeto straightened in his seat. "So soon?"

"Valez delivered it yesterday and our people have been testing it all night. It lives up to its advance press. It does everything we hoped and more. It's a work of genius, and it's all ours."

"And you have incorporated into Jihad?" Szeto said.

"Yes, and Jihad can slip past any firewall in existence."

Szeto pumped a fist. "Then we are set."

Ernst nodded. "We are testing and retesting, but I am assured that Jihad4/20 will be ready tonight."

Szeto sighed. "A big step. The High Council is sure this will speed Opus Omega?"

This was the story being fed to all lower echelon members of the Order working on Jihad. Like them, Szeto knew nothing about the Change. He was high enough to know about the One, but believed that bringing the One to power would simply put the Order in charge of his dominion, not end the world as he knew it.

"Of course they do." He quickly shifted the subject. "The Connell woman's brother. What do we do about him? Let him know we've found her, or keep him in the dark?"

"I have been thinking about that. Why do we not take photo we have and see what he says when we show to him?"

"Excellent idea. A sort of loyalty test. I like that. He's met Fournier. Use him. But right now, go make sure our Lebanese brother is on schedule with the video."

Nodding, Szeto rose and left.

Ernst glanced at Thompson who sat staring at his hands, strangely silent. "Mister Thompson . . . have you nothing to say?"

Was he worried that his Kickers would not be able to carry out their part of the plan?

"This is it, then?" he said, looking up. "We pull this off, the Others return?"

Thompson's late father had imparted a warped version of reality to his young son, and Thompson still clung to it. He believed that certain powerful beings—the Others—had been booted off the Earth and were trying to return, and would reward those who helped them regain their former status here. Its simplicity made it easy to grasp, but the truth was more nebulous. The Otherness was not a discrete being but rather a consciousness, a state of being.

"Not right away," Ernst said. "This will, in a sense, clear the path to a doorway which the One will open."

Thompson was the only one among all the Kickers who knew that bringing down the Internet was a means rather than an end. And among members of the Order, only the Inner Circles knew of the organization's connection to the One and to the Secret History.

"Big step," Thompson said.

"You're having second thoughts?"

He squared his shoulders. "Me? Hell no. It's just . . .

we don't really know what happens after, do we. We've
been told stuff—your people supposedly have all sorts of
secret writings—but at this point it's all just jawboning."

"It's ancient lore, Mister Thompson."

"Yeah, that's all well and good, but my point is: It's
never happened before. We're stepping through a doorway into a place no one's ever been. And once we set that
virus loose, there's no calling it back. There's no time-out
or reset button. Once it starts doing its business, there's
no stopping it."

"That is the whole point. That is why we have spent so
much time and treasure developing this virus—so that no
one could stop it, and that includes us."

"Hey, I'm still with you. It's just that, like I said, it's a
big step, you know?"

"Oh, I know. I know very well. But it is our time, Mister Thompson. Can't you feel it?"

Thompson shook his head. "Not really."

Ernst felt it. Everything was going smoothly, everything falling into place. Take the final code, for instance.
It had been slightly delayed, but Valez had delivered it,
and it worked perfectly. The Jihad virus had been perfected. Even the search for the Myers woman—or rather,
the Connell woman—had gone swimmingly. The One
had asked him to find her, and what happened? A strolling Dormentalist spotted her just one day after the notice
had gone out.

Everything was going the One's way . . . everything.
He'd been pleased when Ernst had given him the location, and he had reiterated that he wanted the Order to
have nothing more to do with her.

"Well, feel it or not, our time has come. As has your
niece's. I have good news."

"Like what?"

"I have been informed that in the early hours of this
morning you became an uncle."

For the life of him Ernst could not read Thompson's expression.

After a long pause, Thompson said, "Where is he?"

"I know nothing beyond that. I found a message on my office voice mail. I've heard nothing more."

Again, that same strange expression.

"When do you release Jihad?"

"As soon as I hear from the One and receive the go-ahead. I expect him to call tonight. Trust me, Mister Thompson. It is our time."

9. Somehow Jack's cab made it down to the East Village before Munir's. He had a bad moment when he couldn't find him. Then a taxi screeched to a halt and Munir jumped out. Jack watched as he hurried to the mailbox and placed the brown paper bag atop it. Jack stepped into the huge Starbucks on the corner of Lafayette and scanned the area through a window wall. While Munir strode down toward the Astor Place Theater and passed a Blue Man Group poster, Jack kept an eye on the mailbox as he began an animated conversation with no one on his cell phone.

Midmorning in the East Village. Layered against the cold, the neighborhood's homeless brigade was out in force, either shuffling aimlessly along, as if dazed by the bright morning sun, or huddled like discarded rag piles around the huge cube in the traffic island. The nut could be among them. Easy to hide within layers of grime and ratty clothes. But not so easy to hide a purpose in life. Jack hunted for someone who looked like he had somewhere to go.

Hollander . . . he wished there'd been a photo in his personnel file. Jack was sure he was the bad guy here. If only he'd been able to get over to his apartment before now. Maybe he'd have found—

And then Jack spotted him. A tall bearded guy traveling westward along Eighth Street, weaving his way through the loitering horde. He was squeezed into a filthy, undersized army fatigue jacket. The cuffs of at least three of the multiple shirts he wore under the coat protruded from the too-short sleeves. The neck of a pint bottle of Mad Dog stuck up like a periscope from the frayed edge of one of the pockets; the torn knees of his green work pants revealed threadbare jeans beneath. Blue eyes peered out from under a navy watch cap.

The sicko? Maybe. Maybe not. One thing was sure: This guy wasn't wandering; he had someplace to go.

And he was heading directly for the mailbox.

When he reached it he stopped and looked over his shoulder, back along the way he'd come, then grabbed the brown paper bag. He reached inside, pulled out the paper towel–wrapped contents, and began to unwrap.

Suddenly he let out a strangled cry and tossed the finger into the street. It rolled in an arc and came to rest in the debris matted against the curb. He glanced over his shoulder again and began a stumbling run in the other direction, toward Jack.

"*Shit!*" Jack said aloud, working the word into his one-way conversation, making it an argument, all the while pretending not to notice the doings at the mailbox.

Something tricky going down. But what? Had the sicko sent a patsy? Jack had known the guy was sly, but figured he'd have wanted to see the finger up close and personal, just to be sure it was real.

Unless of course the sicko was playing the wino and he'd done just that a few seconds ago.

The guy was almost up to the Starbucks now. Keeping his cell to his ear and continuing his argument, Jack stepped outside as if looking for better reception. The only option was to follow him. Give him a good lead and—

He heard pounding footsteps. Munir coming this way— *running* this way, sprinting across the pavement, teeth bared, eyes wild, reaching for the tall guy. Jack repressed an impulse to get between the two of them. Wouldn't do any good. Munir was out of control and had built up too much momentum. Besides, no use in tipping off his own part in this.

Munir grabbed the taller man by the elbow and spun him around.

"Where are they?" he screeched. His face was flushed; tiny bubbles of saliva collected at the corners of his mouth. "Tell me, you swine!"

Swine? Maybe that was a heavy-duty insult in Muslim-ville but it was pabulum around here.

The tall guy jerked back, trying to pull free. His open mouth revealed gapped rows of rotting teeth.

"Hey, man—!"

"Tell me or I'll kill you!" Munir shouted, grabbing his upper arms and shaking his lanky frame.

"Lemme go, man," he said as his head snapped back and forth like a guy in a car that had just been rear-ended. Munir was going to give him whiplash in a few seconds. "Don't know whatcha talking about!"

"You do! You went right to the package. You've seen the finger—now tell me where they are!"

"Hey, look, man, I don't know nothin' 'bout whatcher sayin'. Dude stopped me down the street and told me to go check out the bag on top the mailbox. Gave me five to do it. Told me to hold up whatever was inside it."

"Who?" Munir said, releasing the guy and turning to look back down Eighth. "Where is he?"

"Gone now."

Munir grabbed the guy again, this time by the front of his fatigue jacket.

"What did he look like?"

"I dunno. Just a guy. Whatta you want from me anyway, man? I didn't do nothin'. And I don't want nothin' to do with no dead fingers. Now getcher hands offa me!"

Jack had heard enough. Keeping the phone clapped to his ear, he approached the pair.

"Let him go," he said, raising his voice while still pretending to talk into the phone.

Munir gave him a baffled look. "No. He can tell us—"

"He can't tell us anything we need to know. Let him go and get back to your apartment. You've done enough damage already."

Munir blanched and loosened his grip. The guy stumbled back a couple of steps, then turned and ran down Lafayette. Munir looked around and saw that every rheumy eye in the area was on him. He stared down at his hands—the free right and the bandaged left—as if they were traitors.

"You don't think—?"

"Get home." Jack turned away and gestured into the air, as if angry with what he was hearing. "He'll be calling you. And so will I."

Facing the window glass, he watched Munir's reflection move away toward the Bowery like a sleepwalker. Jack talked and gesticulated for another minute or so, then closed the phone and stepped back into the Starbucks. Might as well get a coffee.

What a mess. The nut had pulled a fast one. Got some wino to make the pickup. But how could a guy that kinked be satisfied with seeing Munir's finger from afar? He seemed the type to want to hold it in his grubby little hand.

But maybe he didn't care. Because maybe it didn't matter.

Jack pulled out the slip of paper on which he'd written Richard Hollander's address. Time to pay Saud Petrol's ex-employee a visit.

10. Eddie's direct line was ringing. He picked it up and immediately recognized the voice.

"Brother Connell, I need a word with you."

"How did you—? Never mind." He was going to ask how Fournier had found his office number, but realized what a ridiculous question that was. "About my sister?"

"Yes. We have a photo."

His gut coiled. Already?

"You've found her?"

"We need you to look at the photo. I am outside on the street. Shall I come up?"

"No, I'll come down."

He threw on his coat and took the stairs—he needed the exercise. All the way down he debated what to say if the photo showed Weezy. If he told the truth, they'd have her—and for what purpose, he still didn't know. If he lied, he might be found out later. What were the consequences of that?

Maybe he should have kept his damn mouth shut. Well, too late for that. Had to see this through.

He found Fournier standing to the side of the office building entrance, smoking with the secretaries on their cigarette break. He stepped away from them as Eddie walked over to him.

"Take a look," Fournier said, handing him a three-by-five photo. "Is this her?"

Not wanting to give anything away, Eddie set his features before looking. He felt a sinking sensation as he recognized the blurred face. She'd lost weight since he'd last seen her, but no question: Weezy.

So soon? They'd sent out the fax only yesterday.

He tried to guess where they'd taken it—on a street, in a restaurant?—but it was so closely cropped he couldn't tell.

What to do? How about stonewalling?

"I'm not saying. Because the Order still hasn't explained its interest in her."

Fournier shrugged as he took back the photo. "That is not my decision." He held up the photo. "So . . . you are saying this is not your sister?"

"Keep looking." Eddie was ready to turn away when something occurred to him. "Oh, by the way . . . as I was waiting around at the Lodge, I overhead a couple of people talking about 'Jihad.' I thought that an odd thing for a couple of Kickers to be discussing."

Fournier frowned. "Jihad? I have not heard any talk of this. Just chatter, I am sure. I know of no Muslims who are Kickers. I do not think they would be allowed in."

"Well, no one can know everything about every Kicker."

"No." He looked Eddie in the eye. "No one can know everything about anyone, *n'est-ce pas*?"

11.   Munir paced his apartment, going from room to room, cursing himself. Such a fool! Such an idiot! But he couldn't help it. He'd lost control. When he'd looked back and seen that man walk up to the paper bag and reach inside it, all rationality had fled. The only thing left in his mind had been the sight of Robby's little finger tumbling out of that envelope last night.

After that, everything was a blur.

The phone began to ring.

Oh, no! It's him. Please, Allah, let him be satisfied. Grant him mercifulness.

He lifted the receiver and heard the voice.

"Quite a show you put on there, Mooo-neeer."

"Please. I was upset. You've seen my severed finger. Now will you let my family go?"

"Now just hold on there a minute, Mooo-neeer. I saw

a *finger go flying through the air, but I don't know for sure if it was* your *finger."*

Munir froze with the receiver jammed against his ear.

"Wh-what do you mean?"

"I mean, how do I know that was a real finger? How do I know it wasn't one of those fake rubber things you buy in the five-and-dime?"

"It was real! I swear it! You saw how your man re-acted!"

"He was just a wino, Mooo-neeer. Scared of his own shadow. What's he know?"

"Oh, please! You must believe me!"

"Well, I would, Mooo-neeer. Really, I would. Except for the way you grabbed him afterward. Now it's bad enough you went after him, but I'm willing to overlook that. I'm far more generous about forgiving mistakes than you are, Mooo-neeer. But what bothers me is the way *you grabbed him. You used both your hands the same."*

Munir felt his blood congealing, sludging through his arteries and veins.

"What do you mean?"

"Well, I got a problem with seeing a man who just chopped off one of his fingers doing that, Mooo-neeer. I mean, you grabbed him like you had two good hands. And that bothers me, Mooo-neeer. Sorely *bothers me."*

"Please. I swear—"

"Swearing ain't good enough, I'm afraid. Seeing is believing. And I believe I saw a man with two good hands out there this morning."

"No. Really . . ."

"So I'm gonna have to send you another package, Mooo-neeer."

"Oh, no! Don't—"

"Yep. A little memento from your wife."

"Please, no."

He told Munir what that memento would be, then he clicked off.

"No!"

Munir jammed his knuckles into his mouth and screamed into his fist.

"NOOOOO!"

12. Jack stood outside Richard Hollander's door.

No sweat getting into the building. The address in the personnel file had led Jack to a rundown walk-up in the far west Forties. He'd checked the mailboxes in the dingy vestibule and found R. HOLLANDER listed for 3B. A few quick strokes with the notched credit card Jack kept handy, and he was in.

He knocked—not quite pounding, but with enough urgency to bring even the most cautious resident to the peephole.

Three tries, no answer. Jack pulled out his bump key set and checked out the deadbolt. A Quickset. He found a Quickset bumper and inserted it. These were so much better than the standard rake-and-tension-bar method he'd learned as a kid. He was rusty at that anyway. Might have taken him up to a minute that way, and a minute was a long time when you were standing in an open hallway fiddling with someone's lock—the closest a fully clothed man could come to feeling naked in public.

He took off his shoe, gave the bump key a gentle tap as he twisted, and the cylinder turned. He drew his Kel-Tec backup and entered in a crouch.

Quiet. Didn't take long to check out the one-bedroom apartment. Empty. He started to toss the place.

Neat. The bed was made, the furniture dusted, clothes folded in the bureau drawers, no dirty dishes in the sink.

Hollander either had a maid or was a neatnik. People who could afford maids didn't live in this building; that made him a neatnik. Not what Jack had expected from a guy who got fired because he couldn't get the job done.

He checked the bookshelves. A few novels and short story collections—literary stuff, mostly—salted in among the business texts. And in the far right corner, three books on Islam with titles like *Understanding Islam* and *An Introduction to Islam*.

Not an indictment by itself. Hollander might have bought them for reference when he'd been hired by Saud Petrol.

And he might have bought them *after* he was fired.

Jack was willing to bet on the latter. He had a gut feeling about this guy.

On the desk was a picture of an older woman. Hollander's mother maybe?

He went through the drawers and found a black ledger, a checkbook, and a pile of bills. Looked like he'd been dipping into his savings. Paying only the minimum on his MasterCard. A lot of late payment notices, and a couple of bad-news letters from employment agencies. Luck wasn't running his way, and maybe Mr. Richard Hollander was looking for someone to blame.

Folded between the back cover and the last page of the ledger was a receipt from the Brickell Real Estate Agency for a cash security deposit and first month's rental of Loft #629. Dated last month. Made out to Sean McCabe.

Loft #629. Where the hell was that? And why did Richard Hollander have someone else's cash receipt? Unless it wasn't someone else's. Had he rented loft #629 under a phony name? That would explain using cash. But why would a guy who was almost broke rent a loft?

Unless he was looking for a place to do something too risky to do in his own apartment.

Like holding hostages.

Jack copied down the Brickell agency's phone number. Might need that later. Then he called Munir.

Hysteria on the phone. Sobbing, moaning, the guy was almost incoherent.

"Calm down, dammit! What exactly did he tell you?"

"He's going to cut her . . . he's going to cut her . . . he's going to cut her . . ."

He sounded like a stuck record player. If Munir had been within reach Jack would have whacked him alongside the head to unstick him.

"Cut her what?"

"Cut her nipple off!"

"Oh, jeez. Stay there. I'll call you right back."

Jack retrieved the receipt for the loft and dialed the number of the rental agent. As the phone began to ring, he realized he hadn't figured out an angle to pry out the address. They wouldn't give it to just anybody. But maybe a cop . . .

He hoped he was right as a pleasant female voice answered on the third ring. "Brickell Agency."

Jack put a harsh Brooklynese edge on his voice.

"Yeah. This is Lieutenant Adams of the Twelfth Precinct. Who's in charge there?"

"I am." Her voice had cooled. "Esther Brickell. This is my agency."

"Good. Here's the story. We've got a suspect in a mutilation murder but we don't know his whereabouts. However, we did find a cash receipt among his effects. Your name was on it."

"The Brickell Agency?"

"Big as life. Down payment of some sort on loft number six-two-nine. Sound familiar?"

"Not offhand. We're computerized. We access all our rental accounts by number."

"Fine. Then it'll only take you a coupla seconds to get me the address of this place."

"I'm afraid I can't do that. I have a strict policy of never giving out information about my clients. Especially over the phone. All my dealings with them are strictly confidential. I'm sure you can understand."

Swell, Jack thought. She thinks she's a priest or a reporter.

"What I understand," he said, "is that I've got a crazy perp out there and you think you've got privileged information. Well, listen, sweetie, that kinda thing don't include Realtors. I need the address of your six-two-nine loft rented to"—he glanced at the name on the receipt—"Sean McCabe. Not later. Now. *Capice*?"

"Sorry," she said. "I can't do that. Good day, Lieutenant—if indeed you are a lieutenant."

Shit! But Jack wasn't giving up. He *had* to get this address.

"Oh, I'm a lieutenant, all right. And believe me, sweetie, you don't come across with that address here and now, you've got trouble. You make me waste my time tracking down a judge to swear out a search warrant, make me come out to your dinky little office to get this one crummy address, I'm gonna do it up big. I'm gonna bring uniforms and squad cars and we're gonna do a thorough search. And I do mean *thorough*. We'll go through *all* your files. But we won't do it there. We'll confiscate all your computers and storage devices and take them down to the one-two and keep them for a while, just to be sure we didn't miss anything. And maybe you'll get them back next Christmas. Maybe. And maybe when you do some information'll be missing. And maybe an obstruction of justice charge as a kicker. How's that sound?"

"Just a minute," she said.

Jack waited, hoping she hadn't gone to another phone to call her lawyer and check on his empty threats, or call the Twelfth to check on a particularly obnoxious lieutenant named Adams.

"It's on White Street," she said suddenly in cold, clipped tones. "One-thirty-seven. Two-D."

"Thank—"

She hung up on him. Fine. He had what he needed.

White Street. That was in Tribeca—a trendy triangle below Canal Street. Lots of lofts down there.

He punched in Munir's number.

"One-thirty-seven White," he said without preamble. "Get down there now."

No time for explanations. He hung up and ran for the door.

13. *"The Order may have found you."*

Weezy felt her chest tighten at Eddie's words.

"What—what do you mean?"

"They have a photo but weren't sure it was you. I told them to keep looking."

"I'm confused. You're saying they found me but may not be sure it's me?"

"Right."

"What does it all mean?"

"I don't know, but maybe you should think of moving back in with—"

"Can't do that," she said, cutting him off before he could mention Jack's name. Who knew who might be listening? "He needs his space and I need mine. Besides, I've caused him enough trouble. And you as well. Please drop this, Eddie."

"I can't. Not till I find out why the Order is interested in you."

She begged, he refused, they argued, but Eddie wasn't budging. Finally they ended the conversation.

Weezy wandered her apartment, rubbing her suddenly cold hands. A photo of her—how? Where? When? Had they followed her home? She'd seen a number of new faces lately. The girl on the elevator yesterday . . . the guy looking for his dog . . .

But the building was new and half empty and new people were moving in all the time.

She went to the window to watch the Broadway traffic, then backed away. Someone could be watching her from an apartment across the street. She pulled the curtains, darkening the room.

She hated this. She'd been so comfortable here, able to concentrate on the *Compendium*. All the disparate pieces were fitting together into a cohesive picture of the First Age and its secrets. And maybe . . . just maybe a way to stop Rasalom, referred to in the *Compendium* only as "the One."

She heard noise outside and hurried to her door. Through the peephole she saw men in overalls angling a new mattress through the door across the hall. That apartment had been empty since she'd moved in. Looked like someone had rented or bought it.

The Order gets a photo of her and then someone moves in across the hall. For some reason, that didn't sit right.

She'd have to keep a careful watch.

14. The building looked like a deserted factory. Probably was. Four stories with no windows on the first floor. Maybe an old sweatshop. A NOW RENTING sign next to the front door. The place looked empty. Had the Brickell lady stiffed him with the wrong address?

With his trusty credit card in his gloved hand, Jack hopped out of the cab and ran for the door—a steel leftover from the building's factory days. An anti-jimmy plate had been welded over the latch area. Jack pocketed the plastic and inspected the lock: a heavy-duty Schlage. A tough pick, even with a bump key. Here on the sidewalk, with the clock ticking, in full view of the passing cars and pedestrians . . . no go.

He ran along the front of the building and took the alley around to the back. Another door there, this one with a big red alarm warning posted front and center.

Two-D . . . that meant the second floor had been subdivided into at least four mini lofts. If Hollander was here at all, he'd be renting the cheapest. Usually the lower letters meant up front with a view of the street; further down the alphabet you got relegated to the rear with an alley view.

Jack stepped back and looked up. The second-floor windows to his left were bare and empty. The ones on the right were draped with what looked like bedsheets.

And running right smack between those windows was a downspout.

Jack tested the pipe. Not some flimsy aluminum tube that collapsed like a beer can, this was good old-fashioned galvanized steel. He pulled on the fittings. They wiggled in their sockets.

Not good, but he'd have to risk it.

He began to climb, shimmying up the pipe, vising it with his knees and elbows as he sought toeholds and fingerholds on the fittings. It shuddered, it groaned, and halfway up it settled a couple of inches with a jolt, but it held. Moments later he was perched outside the shrouded second-floor windows.

Now what?

Sometimes the direct approach was the best. He knocked on the nearest pane—two feet high, three feet wide, and filthy. After a few seconds, he knocked again. Finally a corner of one of the sheets lifted hesitantly and a man stared out at him. Dark, buzz-cut hair, wide dark eyes behind thick glasses, pale face in need of a shave. The eyes got wider and the face faded a few shades paler when he saw Jack.

Jack smiled and gave him a friendly wave. He raised his voice to be heard through the glass.

"Good morning. I'd like to have a word with Mrs. Habib, if you don't mind."

The corner of the sheet dropped and the guy disappeared. Which confirmed that he'd found Richard Hollander. Anybody else would have asked him what the hell he was doing out there and who the hell was Mrs. Habib?

Had to move quickly now. No telling what this gutless creep might do before he scuttled off.

Bracing his hands on the pipe, Jack planted one foot on the three-inch windowsill and aimed a kick at the bottom pane.

Suddenly the three glass panes above it exploded outward as a rusty steel L-bar smashed through, narrowly missing Jack's face and showering him with glittering shards.

Jack swung back onto the pipe and around to the windows on the other side. The bar retreated through the holes it had punched in the sheet and the glass. As Jack shifted his weight to the opposite sill, he realized that from inside he was silhouetted on the sheet. Too late. The bar came crashing through the pane level with Jack's groin, catching him in the leg. He grunted with pain as the corner of the bar tore through his jeans and gouged the flesh across the front of his thigh. In a sudden burst of rage, he grabbed the bar and pulled.

The sheet came down and draped over Hollander. He fought it off with panicky swipes, letting go of the bar in the process. Jack pulled it the rest of the way through the window and dropped it into the alley below. Then he kicked the remaining glass out of the pane and swung inside.

Hollander was dashing for the door, something in his right hand—gloved hand.

Jack started after him, his mind registering strobe-flash images as he moved: a big empty space, a card table, two chairs, three mattresses on the floor, the first empty, a boy tied to the second, a naked woman tied to the third, blood on her right breast.

Jack picked up speed and caught him as he reached the door. He grabbed the collar of Hollander's T-shirt and yanked him back. As the fabric ripped, Hollander spun and swung a meat cleaver at Jack's head. Jack ducked, grabbed the wrist with his left hand—Hollander was wearing latex gloves—and smashed his right fist into the pale face. The leather glove cushioned the blow a little, but not much. The glasses went flying, the cleaver fell to the floor, and Hollander dropped to his knees.

"I give up." He coughed and spat blood. "It's over."

"No." Jack hauled him to his feet. The darkness was welling up in him now, whispering, taking control. "It's not."

" 'Not'?" The wide blue eyes darted about in confusion. "Not what?"

"Over."

Jack drove a left into his gut, then caught him with an uppercut as he doubled over, slamming him back against the door.

Hollander retched and groaned as he sank to the floor again.

"You can't do this," he moaned. "I've surrendered."

"And you think that does it? You've played dirty for days and now that things aren't going your way anymore, that's it? Finsies? Uncle? Tilt? Game over? I don't think so. I *don't* think so."

"No. You've got to read me my rights and take me in."

"Oh, I get it," Jack said. "You think I'm a cop."

Hollander looked up at him in dazed confusion. He

pursed his lips, beginning a question that died before it was asked.

"I'm not." Jack grinned. "Mooo-neeer sent me."

He waited a few heartbeats as Hollander glanced over to where Munir's naked wife and mutilated child were trussed up, watched the sick horror grow in his eyes. When it filled them, when Jack was sure he was tasting a crumb of what he'd been putting Munir through for days, he rammed the heel of his hand against the creep's nose in a spray of blood, slamming the back of his head against the door.

He wanted to do it again, and again, keep on doing it until the gutless wonder's skull was bone confetti, but he fought the urge, pulled back as Hollander's eyes rolled up in his head and he collapsed the rest of the way to the floor.

He went first to the woman. She looked up at him with terrified eyes.

"Don't worry," he said. "Munir's on his way. It's all over."

She closed her eyes and began to sob through her gag.

As Jack fumbled with the knots on her wrists, he checked out the fresh blood on her left breast. The nipple was still there. An inch-long cut ran along its outer margin. A bloody straight razor lay on the mattress beside her.

If he'd tapped on that window a few minutes later . . .

As soon as her hands were free she sat up and tore the gag from her mouth. She looked at him with tear-flooded eyes but seemed unable to speak. Sobbing, she went to work on her ankle bonds. Jack stepped over to where the fallen sheet lay crumpled on the floor and draped it over her.

"That man, that . . . animal," she said. "He told us Munir didn't care about us, that he wouldn't cooperate, wouldn't do anything he was told."

Jack glanced over at Hollander's unconscious form. Was there no limit?

"He lied to you. Munir's been going crazy doing everything the guy told him."

"Did he really cut off his . . . ?"

"No. But he would have if I hadn't stopped him."

"Who are you?"

"Nobody."

He went to the boy. The kid's eyes were bleary. He looked flushed and his skin was hot. Fever. A wad of bloody gauze encased his left hand. Jack pulled the gag from his mouth.

"Where's my dad?" he said hoarsely. Not *Who are you?* or *What's going on?* Just worried about his dad. Jack wished for a son like that someday.

"On his way."

He began untying the boy's wrists. Soon he had help from Barbara. A moment later, mother and son were crying in each other's arms. He found their clothing and handed it to them.

While they were dressing, Jack dragged Hollander over to Barbara's mattress and stuffed her gag in his mouth. As he finished tying him down with her ropes, he heard someone pounding on the downstairs door. He ushered the woman and the boy out to the landing. His thigh throbbed as he went down and found Munir frantic on the sidewalk.

"Where—?"

"Upstairs," Jack said.

"Are they—?"

Jack nodded.

He stepped aside to allow Munir past, then waited outside awhile to give them all a chance to be alone together. Five minutes, then he returned upstairs. It wasn't over yet.

He found them huddled on the landing in a group hug. Now came the tough part. He was in a bad position here.

"Okay. Decision time." They looked up. "Robby needs a doctor. But there's not an ER in the city that won't be phoning in a child abuse complaint as soon as they see that hand."

"He *was* abused." Barbara's eyes blazed. "But not by us."

"I know a doctor who won't say anything to anybody."

Because he couldn't. Doc Hargus's license had been on permanent suspension for years.

"But can he reattach Robby's finger?" she said.

Jack shook his head. "That's beyond him, I'm afraid."

Beyond anyone, Jack thought.

He'd read somewhere that the last thing you wanted to do with a severed anything was freeze it. Keep it cold, yes, but freezing killed the cells. The finger was most likely already a goner by the time Munir received it. He thought he'd done the right thing, but sticking it in his freezer had been the coup de grâce.

Jack couldn't tell these people that. They wouldn't believe it, wouldn't want to hear it, needed to give their boy every chance at a full complement of fingers.

Munir straightened. "He needs a hospital, the best surgeons. And now I'm free to tell the police everything."

And that would start officialdom down a road that might lead them to Jack. He clenched his jaw. This was why he stayed the hell away from kidnappings.

"Except about me, okay? I don't exist. You've got two victims who can testify against him, you have the recordings of his threats—an airtight case against the bastard. You don't need me."

Munir nodded. "I owe you . . . everything. Without you—"

"But that's taken care of. Now your so-called justice system goes to work. It doesn't know about me. I'd like to keep things that way."

"Of course. Anything you say. I am forever in your debt." He looked back at the closed door of 2D. "I still cannot understand it. Richard Hollander . . . how could he do this to me? To anybody? I never hurt him."

"You fired him," Jack said. "He's probably been loony tunes for years, on the verge of a breakdown, walking the line. Losing his job just pushed him over the edge."

"But people lose their jobs every day. They don't kidnap and torture—"

"I guess he was ready to blow. You just happened to be the unlucky one. He had to blame somebody—anybody but himself—and get even for it. He chose you. Don't look for logic. The guy's crazy."

"But the depth of his cruelty . . ."

"Maybe you could have been gentler with him when you fired him," Barbara said.

The words sent a chill through Jack, bringing back Munir's plea from his first telephone call.

Please save my family!

Jack wondered if that was possible, if anyone could save Munir's family now.

It had begun to unravel as soon as Barbara and Robby were kidnapped. It still had been salvageable then, up to the point when the cleaver had cut through Robby's finger. That was probably the deathblow. Even if nothing worse had happened from there on in, that missing finger was going to be a permanent reminder of the nightmare, and somehow it would be Munir's fault. If he'd already gone to the police, it would be because of that; since he hadn't, it would be his fault for *not* going to the police. Or for firing Hollander in the first place. Munir would always blame himself; and deep in her heart Barbara would blame him too. Later on, maybe years from now, Robby might blame him too.

Because there'd always be one too few fingers on Robby's left hand, always that scar along the margin of Barbara's nipple, always the vagrant thought, sneaking through the night, that Munir hadn't done all he could, that if he'd only been a little more considerate before the kidnapping, had been just a little more cooperative after, Robby still would have ten fingers.

Sure, they were together now, and they'd been hugging and crying and kissing, but later on Barbara would start asking questions: Couldn't you have done more? Why *didn't* you cut your finger off when he told you to?

Even now, Barbara was edging into the possibility that Munir could have been gentler when he'd fired Hollander. The natural progression from that was to: Maybe if you had, none of this would have happened.

The individual members might still be alive, but Munir's family as a viable unit was still under the gun.

And that saddened Jack. It meant that Hollander might still win.

Barbara hugged Robby against her side. "We need to get to the hospital. Now."

Jack said, "You can flag a cab on the street."

As they started for the stairwell, Munir held back.

"I must speak to him. I have to ask him why."

Jack wondered if talk was all he had in mind.

"Sure. Go ahead. We'll hold the cab for you."

Jack led Barbara and Robby down to the steel front door. He grabbed a takeout menu flier from the floor, wadded it up, and stuffed it in the door's latch hole.

Might want to give the place a once-over before the cops arrived.

Took a couple of minutes, but finally a cab cruised by and he flagged it. As Barbara and Robby slid into the rear, Munir stumbled from the building looking dazed.

Had Hollander escaped?

"What's wrong?"

"That is not Richard Hollander."

"Then who is he?"

"I have never seen that man before in my life."

15. Dawn stepped off the private elevator into Mr. Osala's duplex. She felt totally dazed and knew she looked like some sort of mental patient in her bathrobe and borrowed scrubs from the surgicenter. After she'd come to a couple of hours ago, they'd checked her over to see if she was all right, then stuck her in a cab. Lucky the doorman, Mack, recognized her and keyed her up in the elevator, or she'd never have been able to return.

She felt totally awful and weird. She'd been trying to get out of this place for like nine months, and now that she had her chance to take off, she didn't. She'd never thought she'd look at this place as home, but that was what it felt like at the moment.

She passed a stack of cardboard boxes as she stumbled down the hall to her room, but stopped at the door when she found Gilda within. The older woman was scooping clothes out of her drawers and dumping them into a cardboard box, just like the ones in the hall.

"What do you think you're doing?"

She started—so intent on what she was doing she hadn't heard Dawn arrive. She straightened and gave her a cold smile.

"I am packing your things."

"Why?"

The smile became harder, colder. "You are moving out."

The words shocked her. Moving out? No. No way.

"You're crazy!"

"Oh, no. Not me. The Master has called and told me to pack up your things. You leave tomorrow."

"Like hell!"

The woman stepped closer. "Yes. He is kicking you out. And good riddance, I say. You have been nothing but trouble since you set foot in this house. No more will I have to listen to your whining and complaining. I cannot wait till you are gone. Then there will be peace."

"You're lying."

"We will see. The Master will be here tomorrow to personally throw you out on the street."

No . . . he couldn't. Not now.

"Get out," Dawn said.

"I will not! The Master told me to—"

Despite feeling she might collapse at any minute, Dawn grabbed the older woman by the front of her blouse and swung her around, then shoved her toward the door.

"Get *out!*"

Gilda stumbled backward through the doorway and almost fell. She steadied herself at the last instant just as Dawn slammed the door and locked it. Feeling too exhausted, too totally rotten to deal with any of this now, Dawn pulled back the covers on her unmade bed and slipped under them.

Sleep . . . she needed sleep . . . she'd be able to deal with this once she got some sleep.

16.   Jack peeked through the tiny glass pane set in the emergency exit door. Outside in the alley, Abe stood next to the open rear doors of his dark blue panel truck. He looked edgy, repeatedly glancing toward the street.

The mystery man hung over Jack's shoulder. Trussed head to foot in duct tape and wrapped in a sheet, he'd struggled at first. But the bouncing trip down the stairs had taken some of the fight out of him. Jack's shoulder nestled in his gut and he had to be sore by now. The guy was heavier than he looked.

Jack kicked the door to get Abe's attention.

"Get behind the wheel," he shouted when Abe looked up.

Abe nodded and bustled away toward the front of the truck. Jack gave him thirty seconds, then pushed the door open. An alarm bell began clanging, just as the sign on the door had promised.

Jack dumped the guy into the back of the truck, hopped in, and closed the door behind him.

"Go!"

Abe hit the gas and they lurched into motion, out of the alley, onto the street, and into the traffic—a nondescript panel truck in a stampeding herd of other nondescript panel trucks.

"Where to now?"

Jack was slipping into a pair of work gloves Abe had had lying about. "Let's just drive around while this fellow and I get better acquainted."

Before sending Munir and his family off in the cab, Jack had pulled him aside and told him to hold off as long as possible giving the address where his wife and boy had been held. None of this was making sense and he wanted a little time with the mystery man.

But back upstairs he spotted a familiar scar through the tear in the guy's shirt and realized the situation had suddenly become complicated. He called Abe and asked him to bring his truck downtown.

He peeled back the sheet to free the guy's bloodied, blindfolded face, then yanked the tape off his mouth.

"Help!" he screamed as he started slamming his feet against the truck floor. "Help!"

"No tumel!" Abe shouted from up front.

Jack gave him a backhand slap across the face.

"Don't waste your breath. You're in a truck with no rear windows in the middle of downtown traffic."

"Just turn me in."

Jack shook his head. "Not gonna happen. Who are you?"

"Richard Hollander."

"Nah. You went to a lot of trouble to make people

think that, did everything to make this look personal—
fooled me on that one—but Munir has met Hollander and
he says you're not him."

His face twisted. "You believe a lying sand nigger
over—"

Jack backhanded him again.

"None of that," he said as he wiped the blood off his
glove onto the man's shirt.

"You're pretty brave with me tied up."

Feeling the darkness struggle to get loose within him,
Jack leaned closer and spoke through his teeth.

"Do you have any idea what I want to do to you? You
mutilated a little boy! And you made his mother watch!
People like you—"

"Worthless mongrel," he muttered.

Jack hit him again.

The guy clenched his teeth. "Be a man. Untie me and
we'll see—"

"What? See you running away like you did when I
came through the window—even though you had a meat
cleaver? If I hadn't grabbed the back of your shirt, you'd've
been gone. But I'm glad it happened that way, otherwise
I'd never have seen the brand."

"What are you talking about?"

"How long have you been a member of the Septimus
Order?"

"I'm not—"

Jack poked the guy's chest and he flinched.

"Uh-uh. I know the brand."

"So, you know the brand. Big deal."

"Is the Order behind this?"

"Of course not."

"What's the Order got against Munir?"

"Absolutely nothing. This is personal."

"Where's the real Richard Hollander?"

"You're looking at him."

Jack shook his head again. "You left all the evidence where it could be easily found, so that when this was over, everything would point to Hollander. Where is he?"

And then, in a strobing epiphany, it all became clear. Jack sat back, stunned.

"Hollander is dead."

"Ridiculous." But his voice carried no conviction, no sense that he'd be believed.

"I just realized . . . you weren't wearing a mask when I broke in. Barbara and the boy knew your face. But you didn't care if they could recognize you, because you were planning all along to kill them. Hollander would get the blame, but Hollander wouldn't be able to defend himself because you killed him first and probably disposed of his body. The cops will be looking for someone they'll never find while you roam about free as can be."

"You're obviously on drugs."

Jack stared at him. "Why?"

The man's face twisted into a snarl. "Because he's a no-good Arab piece of shit!"

No act there. The naked rage in his eyes said he was speaking what he felt.

"But why this particular Arab?"

The face went slack. Not going there. Hiding something.

"An Arab's an Arab," he said.

Jack couldn't buy that. Something else going on here. Very good possibility the Order was involved. And if that was the case, then Jack needed to be involved.

As he slapped the tape back over the guy's mouth, he began twisting and kicking and making frantic noises.

"What's that? Take off the tape?"

The guy nodded.

"Why? You're not telling me anything. I think we'll let you marinate awhile. Maybe you'll be feeling more loquacious in a few hours."

As the guy made all sorts of protesting sounds, Jack slipped the sheet back over his face.

Needed to find a way to make him open up.

He'd come up with something.

17.   "Christ, it's cold," Russ said, hugging his arms around him as the wind off the water cut through his coat.

He was surprised he could feel cold at all after all he'd had to drink.

This Belgiovene guy was all right. This morning he'd explained all the intricacies of getting his parole modified to allow him back online. Cruel and unusual punishment, banning him from the Internet for ten years after his release. Russ didn't tell him he was already online under various identities. He'd be FUBAR without the Net, but the risk of discovery hung over him like the sword of Damocles. If word got back to his parole officer, some hard-ass judge could lock him up again. Yeah, it might be federal soft time, but time was time. Outsiders called them country clubs. Screw them. The two years he'd spent inside had sucked. Royally. He'd come *this close* to offing himself.

Belgiovene had dropped him off home and then picked him up later for dinner. They wound up at Peter Luger's in Williamsburg for the best porterhouse he'd ever had— and more wine than he usually drank in a month.

Then they'd come here, to the Chelsea Piers.

They weren't really piers anymore. Everything but. Huge warehouselike structures housed shops, restaurants, dining halls, tennis courts, nightclubs—anything that might entertain or distract anyone at any time.

Belgiovene said, "As I told you, we're to meet the U.S. attorney outside here, and then we'll go up to the space we've rented for the next project."

Russ stood at the water's edge and stared at the lights of New Jersey across the Hudson. What was he looking at? Hoboken? Jersey City? He knew they were over there somewhere, but they were just names. Who cared which was where? They were in Jersey.

"Do we have to meet him right on the waterfront? There's gotta be a place that's out of the wind. I mean, like, is all this secrecy necessary?"

"It was his request. It's a touchy thing, messing with a federal judge's ruling. We should accommodate him, don't you think?"

"I suppose."

Belgiovene pointed down at the rippling surface of the river. "Look. Lights underwater."

Russ didn't see anything, so he leaned forward. He felt a hand press against his back and then he was falling. He hit the water and went under.

Cold—colder than any cold he could ever imagine. Colder than interstellar space.

He fought to the surface and saw Belgiovene standing above him, watching.

"Help! Help me!"

The guy did nothing. Just stared.

Panic lanced through him. What was going on here? Was he crazy?

Well, Russ would show him. He could swim. He'd been a pretty damn good swimmer in his day.

But his clothes were dragging him down. And the cold was paralyzing his muscles. He sank and clawed back to the surface. After gulping air, he tried to shed his coat but went down again as he struggled with it. This time, despite his best effort, despite the panic adrenaline coursing through his arteries, he couldn't make it back to the surface. His arms felt like lead. Legs too. Wouldn't respond.

A great lethargy came over him, and with it, a strange

sort of peace. His oxygen-starved brain kept asking the same question, over and over.

Why?

With a sob he exhaled what he knew was his last breath.

18. "Are we ready?"

Ernst dropped his glass of water. It shattered in the sink. He turned, knowing who he would find. He knew that voice. But the kitchen was empty. He stepped into the living room/dining room area of his apartment.

The One stood in the far corner. He looked relaxed, his hands loosely clasped before him.

Ernst felt sweat break out all over his body. These unannounced appearances always rattled him. The man—well, he was something more than a man—had an unsettling ability to enter and leave rooms without warning, without a sound.

"Yes, sir. We are."

The One clasped his hands behind him and began to wander the living room at a leisurely pace . . . like a shark in a tank. He was dressed in his usual dark business suit. He had adopted his current, somewhat Hispanic appearance last summer: slim frame, soft features, darkened skin tones, mustache. He had never honored Ernst with an explanation, probably never would. Whatever the reason, he'd maintained the look. He stopped pacing and fixed Ernst with his abysmally dark eyes.

"Will it work?"

The dreaded question.

"I believe it will bring down the Internet."

"And that will extinguish the Lady?"

"The lore says she must be slain three times. The first death was accomplished by another hand."

The One's eyes gleamed. "Yes. That upstart mutant in

Florida unknowingly aided us. She might have proven to be an asset, but she was impossible to control."

Ernst knew little of this, had gleaned only bits from passing references to the incident. Now was not the time to ask for more.

"I understand those circumstances were unique. Since they were not reproducible, we turned to the *Fhinntman-chca*."

"Yes. But that failed."

Ernst wanted to shout that it *didn't* fail—not completely—but held his tongue.

"Only because the noosphere was too strong."

"Will this succeed?"

"Yes, I believe so, yes."

"You do not sound terribly confident. And as I recall, this was all your idea."

Another wave of nervous perspiration seeped from his pores.

"Yes . . . yes it was. But we are in uncharted territory here. First, no one has crippled the Internet before, but I believe we have the best chance ever. The final piece was acquired just yesterday and we are set to begin."

"Whether the Internet is down or up is of little interest to me. I want the Lady extinguished—nothing more, nothing less."

"Yes, of course. That is what we all want. But as I explained last year when we embarked on this mission, I believe the reason the *Fhinntmanchca* failed to extinguish her—"

"She *did* cease to exist for an instant."

"Yes. And even though that was only her second death, she should not have returned. The noosphere should have been too weakened by the *Fhinntmanchca* to permit it. But she did return. The damaged noosphere was able to revive her almost immediately. That possibility was never addressed in our lore, because it was inconceivable. But the Internet, with its myriad human interactions, was also inconceivable in the First Age. It has energized and strengthened the noosphere to a level far beyond what anyone ever dreamed possible. After the failure of the *Fhinntmanchca* I theorized that if we removed that input, the still-damaged noosphere would be unable to maintain the Lady. It would have to re-create her from scratch, as originally hoped, giving you the window you need to allow the Otherness to achieve dominance."

"And I have allowed you a chance to prove your theory."

Ernst bowed. "For which I am honored. Still I must stress that it is but a theory. I have no means to test it, other than to crash the Internet."

"It has taken you quite some time to reach this point."

"Yes, even with the combined aid of the Kickers and the Dormentalists, it has been a massive, time-consuming undertaking. But it is the only means we have left to us."

"There is, perhaps, another way," the One said as he began pacing again.

Ernst swallowed. Another way? "What might that be, if I may ask?"

"You may not. The means have only just recently become available. I am preparing contingencies in case your grand scheme fails."

Ernst felt a sudden pain in his gut. It *couldn't* fail.

"I was hoping you had more confidence—"

The One's expression darkened. "After the failure of the *Fhinntmanchca*—not your fault, I realize—I cannot afford to take anything for granted. I've been so close for so long—"

He cut himself off.

Ernst realized they had both waited their entire adult lives for the advent of the Otherness, but the One had lived for millennia. By comparison, Ernst's wait was a mere eye blink.

The One said, "When do you put your plan into motion?"

"As soon as you say so."

"Then I say so. Why did you wait?"

"Why . . ." Ernst was surprised at the question. "As a courtesy. To be sure the execution date fit with your plans."

"My plans?"

"Well, you told me you were engaged in a project . . ."

The One had been away for months, appearing only occasionally. All he would say was that he was "down south" engaged in "a personal matter."

"Yes. That is in its final stage. In fact, I expect to have it wrapped up by the weekend."

"Then shall we set the execution date for Saturday night? If we release the virus now, we will be more than ready by then."

The One's eyebrows lifted. "It will spread that quickly?"

"We calculate global saturation within less than forty-eight hours of release."

"I am impressed."

"We have had the best computer minds in the world working on it for months. Jihad4/20 is so unlike previous viruses that no existing AV software will recognize it. We will introduce it to random email addresses. All the recipient need do is open the email. No link to click in the mail. Simply opening it will allow the virus in."

"And then what?"

"Well, it's what is known as a rootkit—"

The One waved a hand. "Never mind technological terms. Those sort of details mean little to me."

"It will access the address book and send email to all of the contacts listed, thereby entering all those computers where it will do the same, time and again, on and on, spreading itself across the globe in a geometric progression. But it will do more than merely propagate itself. It will take over each computer, turning it into what is known as a zombie—a machine that will do what the virus tells it to do, independent of what its owner wishes."

"But neither is anything new."

"True. And as the virus spreads, it will create a network of zombies—a so-called 'botnet'—which, again, is nothing new. But the pervasiveness and penetration of Jihad's botnet will be unprecedented, as will what the virus will tell its network of zombies to do on Saturday night."

Ernst felt a swell of pride as he thought about that. He'd come up with the idea himself. And it was brilliant—not because it was arcane and esoteric, but because it was so obvious, and so elegant in its simplicity.

"All I care is that it gets the job done. And it had better."

The implied threat doused Ernst's inner glow. "I have every confidence that the Internet cannot stand against it."

"Good. I trust the package I sent arrived?"

"Yes." A mysterious, locked, oblong box, three feet long. "It is safe."

"Then I shall leave you to your task."

He turned and started for the door.

"Oh, I assume you've heard about the baby," Ernst said.

The One did not break stride. "Of course."

"Why is the baby—?"

"None of that is your concern."

And then he was out the door and gone.

Ernst stood a moment, letting the tension seep out of him. He couldn't help thinking of the Oscar Wilde remark about how some people bring happiness wherever they go, and others whenever they go. The One fell squarely in the latter category. The room seemed brighter without him.

He picked up his phone to call Szeto and give him the go-ahead. But his thumb stalled over the speed-dial button as Hank Thompson's words came back to him.

We're stepping through a doorway into a place no one's

ever been. And once we set that virus loose, there's no calling it back. There's no time-out or reset button. Once it starts doing its business, there's no stopping it.

True. Once this djinn was out of the bottle, there would be no ordering it back. When the Lady was extinguished, this world would be perceived as non-sentient. The Enemy would abandon it, leaving the Otherness an open field.

What would happen then?

The Order's ancient lore spoke of a Great Change, but was vague on what form that change would take. The Otherness would make alterations that would be terrifying and painful for the masses of humanity. The elite few who aided the One in bringing about the Change, however, would be rewarded, but the lore was even more vague as to what form that reward would take. Ernst assumed it meant insulation from the Change or perhaps even a way to adapt to it.

The lore also stated that those who had been active participants in aiding the Otherness—he and the Council of Seven and other high-ups in the Order, and perhaps even Hank Thompson—would be awarded positions of power. But "power" was such a nebulous term.

He smiled at the parallels between what was about to happen and the Christian myths of the Rapture and the Tribulation. But then, leaks from the Order's lore over the millennia were what had sparked those myths.

Taking a breath, he pushed the button. Time to take the big step: Tell Szeto to set Jihad4/20's activation time for Saturday night and unleash it on the Internet.

No turning back now.

THURSDAY

1. Jack stopped outside a dirty white doorway next to an equally dirty white roll-up garage door in the West Thirties. He looked around. A few pedestrians uphill toward Ninth Avenue. The bulk of the Javits Center squatted down by the Hudson River to the west. Not many people out and about at this hour on a frigid morning.

He rested his coffee cup atop a nearby standpipe and stuck a key into the door lock. After another glance around—no one looking—he pulled his Glock from the small of his back. He held it ready under his jacket as he pushed the door open and stepped inside. He'd left the single overhead incandescent bulb on overnight. Abe's dirty blue van sat directly under it. The garage occupied half the ground floor of an old dilapidated former tenement. Abe rented it to store his delivery truck and other sundries he had no room for at the store.

Jack had left the van's rear doors closed and they remained that way. He stepped up and pulled one open.

There, with taped head, hands, feet, arms, and legs, lay the blindfolded mystery man. Jack and Abe had decided to let him stew overnight. To keep him in place, they'd snaked bungee cords around him and hooked them into the rings in the floor panels. Gulliver might have looked like this if the Lilliputians had had duct tape and bungees.

Jack retrieved his coffee from outside, locked the door behind him, and returned to the van.

"Restful night?" he said through the door as he sipped his coffee.

The guy tried to speak through the tape across his mouth.

"A bit chilly, I'll bet."

The garage wasn't heated but it was warmer than outside. By now the mystery man had to be cold, hungry, and exhausted.

"Ready to talk?"

More tape-muffled squawking.

Jack slipped inside. He pulled off the blindfold and grabbed an edge of the piece of tape covering his mouth.

"No yelling or this goes back on, *capice*?"

The guy nodded. Jack ripped off the tape. The guy glared at him as he puffed, mouth-breathing for the first time in about a dozen hours. He noticed a pungent odor.

"What's that—?" He spotted a wet stain around the guy's crotch. "Uh-oh. I see you peed your pants during the night. That's gotta be *reeeeal* uncomfortable."

Another glare.

Jack held up his blue-and-white container. "You drink coffee?"

The guy nodded vigorously.

"Good. I'll run out and get you a cup as soon as we've had a little Q and A. First Q: Who are you?"

Silence.

Jack prodded him with his boot. "This is where you give the A."

The guy glared at him. "Why do you give a shit?"

"I have an inquiring mind."

"Yeah? Then who are *you*?"

"If this were a B movie, I'd say something like, 'Your worst nightmare.' Truth is, I am no one."

"So am I."

Jack hadn't been able to find any ID on the guy or in the loft, and hadn't any contacts among the cops to run prints for him. He decided to come back to the name later.

"Okay . . . why Munir?"

"Told you: He's an Arab."

"But why that particular Arab?"

"He was convenient."

"I don't believe you, pal. I might if it weren't for that Septimus brand on your back. What's their interest in Munir?"

"Nothing. The Order's never even heard of him."

That could be true. This guy could be a psycho who just happened to be a member, but Jack's gut wasn't buying. He drained his coffee, tossed the container out the back door, and picked up the fourteen-inch bolt cutter lying nearby. Jack had brought it along from the loft. The coffee soured in his stomach as he looked at the bloodstains along the pincer edges.

"You cut off a little boy's finger with this. How does a grown man do that to a child?"

The guy smirked. "When he has Arab blood? Easy. I picture the Trade Towers collapsing. I picture Daniel Pearl being beheaded and hear his gurgling cries."

"But the kid wasn't even born when the Towers went down. And he's never hurt anyone."

"Neither did Daniel Pearl. Neither did the people in the Towers."

"How about I start lopping off your fingers until I get some answers?"

The guy looked him in the eyes and said, "I don't think you've got it in you."

Jack stared back. In a way, he was right. He'd cooled down since yesterday. Under different circumstances— say, if Gia and Vicky were at risk—he'd have no problem getting medieval. But here, now?

No. He wanted to know why this creep had put Munir through "the wringer," as he'd put it, and whether or not the Septimus Order had anything to do with it, but not enough to assume the role of torturer. They'd have to remain one of life's mysteries. Jack could go on without knowing . . .

But what about Munir?

Yeah. This was personal for Munir . . . about as personal as it got.

"Yeah, you're right. I'm not in a fingernail-ripping mood at the moment, but I bet I know someone who is."

He pulled out his cell phone and made a call.

"Munir?" he said when he answered.

"Yes?"

"How's Robby?"

His voice thickened. *"His finger could not be saved. I should not have frozen it. I didn't know. It's all my fault."*

"No, not your fault. Not your fault at all. In fact, I'm sitting with the man who's really to blame."

"The one who—?"

"Yeah. Mister Non-Hollander. He's reluctant to explain why he did all this to you and your family. I thought you might want to persuade him."

A brief pause, then, *"I'll be right over. Where are you?"*

"Hang on a minute." Jack slipped out of the van and pointed to the mystery man. "Stay put."

He walked outside to the street, well out of earshot of the garage, and gave Munir the address. Then he returned to the van.

"I'm afraid you're going to have to deal with a guy who's got a bit of a chip on his shoulder where you're concerned."

The guy smirked again. "Who? Mooneeer?"

"Yeah. He's on his way over to get sharia on your ass."

"Not likely. The guy's a wimp. Probably faint if he saw blood."

Jack eyed the bolt cutter . . . looking pretty good right now.

No . . . not ready to go there yet.

"You seem to know a lot about him. Almost like you did some real in-depth research."

"I heard him whining and blubbering on the phone. That was all the research I need. Typical Arab wimp."

The cutter . . . looking better and better.

"And what's that make you? If he's such a wimp, why didn't you have the cojones to go mano-a-mano with him?"

He looked away. "I'm through talking to you."

"In that case, keep quiet till Munir gets here, or the tape goes back on."

"Moooneeer . . . what a joke."

Jack slammed the doors and found a crate to sit on while he waited for Munir.

2.   Finally! Jack thought as a buzzer echoed through the garage. Where's he been?

He stepped over to the door and used the peephole. Not Munir . . . a woman.

What the hell?

And then he recognized her.

"Mrs. Habib?" he said as he pulled open the door.

She stepped inside, rubbing her hands against the cold wind that followed her. She wore a parka and a large shoulder bag.

"Call me Barbara, please."

"All right . . . Barbara." He stuck his head out the door and checked the street. No sign of Munir. "I was expecting your husband."

He closed the door against the cold and turned to her. Her face was pale in the dim light of the single bulb. Her eyelids were dusky from lack of sleep, but a hard, fierce light glinted in the eyes behind them.

"I came in his place."

Jack cleared his throat. "Well, what I had in mind was some rather intense interrogation and—"

"Munir is a decent man with a gentle soul. He would not be good for this. He's better off staying with Robby."

Was she saying the mystery man's "wimp" remark hadn't been so far off the mark?

Jack watched her closely. "Am I to infer that your soul is not so gentle?"

"Robby's finger cannot be saved. He will go through life maimed, mutilated. He will be fine, physically—a missing pinky is mildly disfiguring but will not be a handicap. But psychologically . . . I don't see him ever getting over the trauma of being strapped down, fully awake and alert, while a stranger cut off his finger. The memory of the pain will fade, but his helplessness, and the cold-blooded cruelty of what was done to him . . . those will remain with him forever. He will need therapy . . . years and years of it."

"Do you think you feel worse about this than Munir?"

She nodded. "Because he was not there."

Jack remembered the photo of her that had accompanied the severed finger, and its inscription.

"You watched?"

She shook her head. "He wanted me to. He tied Robby down with his hand just inches from my face, but he had no way to keep my eyes open. He demanded that I watch but I couldn't."

"Of course not."

"But I heard the crunch of his little bone, and I heard his screams through his gag. Munir heard none of that. And he was not tied down and prevented from comforting her poor terrified baby when he needed her after it was done." She looked at Jack with tear-filled eyes. "I'm pretty sure I'm going to need years of therapy too."

"I'm sorry."

"But it will help me to know why this . . . creature did this to us."

"He said it's because Munir is an Arab."

She shook her head. "He hates Arabs. The way he raged about the attack on the Towers . . . that was real. But I cannot help but feel there was some other reason."

The Septimus Order's seven-pointed sigil flashed in Jack's brain.

"I'm with you." He glanced at the van. "But you don't have to dirty your hands with him. I'll—"

"No. He mutilated my son. I need to find out why."

"I'll find out why and tell you."

She set her jaw. "I must do this myself. I *need* to do this. It will be the start of my therapy."

Jack thought about it . . . setting a mother loose on the man who'd maimed her child . . .

He sort of liked that. Something almost poetic there.

"All right, but first . . . wait here."

He opened one of the van's rear doors and hopped inside. The mystery man gave him a puzzled look as Jack checked to make sure none of the tape or bungees was loose.

"I guess he finally got the nerve to show up, huh? Making sure I don't get loose and hurt him?"

"He couldn't make it."

"Bullshit. I heard you talking. He's afraid of me. Even all trussed up like this, I scare the hell out of him."

"He stayed with his son. Someone else came in his place."

Jack pushed open the other rear door to reveal Barbara.

The guy's eyes did the closest Jack had ever seen to a real-life Bob Clampett bug-out.

"No! Wait!" His voice kept rising. "Not her! You can't!"

Jack found the mouth tape and slapped it back across his face.

"Keep it down."

He began twisting and writhing, but the bungees held him in place. As Jack slid out and helped Barbara in, the guy's struggles became even more frantic. High-pitched, panicky squeals leaked through the tape. It looked like a fresh wet stain was spreading across his crotch.

The guy knew he was about to be repaid in kind and Jack savored his terror. What had gone around was about to come around.

Sweet.

"Thank you," she said. "Now please close the door."

Jack hesitated. "I don't know. He might—"

"He's secure. And I need privacy for this."

"All right. But I'll be right outside. Yell if you need me."

"I will. Thank you."

As Jack pushed the doors closed he saw Barbara remove a paper sack from her shoulder bag. It read "Ace Hardware."

Hoo boy.

Nor hell a fury like a woman scorned popped into his head, and he thought how a scorned woman's fury couldn't hold a candle to that of the mother of a brutalized child.

3.   Dawn was dressed and waiting when Gilda opened the door. Her belly still bulged some, and she could have worn one of her maternity tops, but she totally refused. She was so done with maternity clothes. She'd opted for a loose sweat suit. The opposite of stylish, but until she lost these pregnancy pounds, she'd opt for comfort over style.

She'd expected a knock first, but apparently the old bat didn't think Dawn deserved the courtesy. Because she was staying and Dawn was going.

Well, not if Dawn had anything to say about it. Not yet.

"The Master wants to see you in his office."

Without so much as a glance at her, Dawn stood and walked into the hall. She stopped before Mr. Osala's door at the far end. For a second she considered popping in like Gilda had done to her, then reconsidered. Why get down on her level? And why piss off a guy she wanted on her side.

So she knocked.

"Come," said a voice on the other side.

Come? Was he kidding?

She entered and found him sitting behind his desk. She still wasn't used to his appearance. When he'd taken her in last spring he'd looked taller, paler, broader. More WASPish. As the months went by he'd seemed to become darker and more delicate. And he'd grown a thin little mustache. She hadn't seen him much at all since the summer. Working on some "demolition project" down South.

"Have a seat," he said, pointing to a chair on the far side of his desk.

Nothing had changed here since she'd sneaked a peek last summer. Same glaring overhead fluorescents and bare white walls. No paintings, photos, degrees, or knickknacks. Just the big mahogany desk, its computer monitor, and a filing cabinet. Totally devoid of personality. Just like its occupant.

She closed the door—didn't want Gilda the bitch eavesdropping—and eased onto the chair. She was still sore from the delivery, but definitely better than yesterday.

"You wanted to see me?"

"Yes. We need to discuss your future."

Dawn couldn't help blurting, "Gilda says you're kicking me out."

He looked troubled. "Oh, I wouldn't put it that way. You should look at it as being freed to live your life."

Then it was true. She was history here.

"Comes down to the same thing, doesn't it? I'm being put out on the street."

He smiled. "I'd hardly call being moved into a two-bedroom Upper West Side apartment 'on the street.'"

"What are you talking about?"

"I'm talking about you moving on. This episode of your life is past. It's time to start a new chapter. And moving on requires moving out."

She couldn't believe how totally devastated she felt. She'd so not wanted to stay and now she didn't want to leave. She'd grown used to the place. Out there was . . . uncertainty.

And Jerry Bethlehem . . . the baby's father . . . *her*—

Couldn't think about that.

Jerry was the reason Mr. Osala had hidden her away here, making her a virtual prisoner.

"What about Jerry?"

"Not a problem."

"You've been telling me all along I was safe from him as long as I was pregnant with the baby, and if I aborted it, he'd kill me. Well, guess what? The baby's dead—"

"And so is Jerry."

The words struck her like a blow, catapulting her to her feet.

"*What?* Why didn't you tell me?"

"I only recently found out."

"I don't believe you!"

He spread his hands. "Believe what you wish. I double and triple checked. Jerry died under a different, assumed name, so the news never reached me until a few days ago."

She eased herself back into the chair.

Jerry . . . dead. It seemed almost impossible.

"How did he die?"

"In a most mundane way: a motor vehicle accident. But no matter the manner, it's the result that counts. He's dead, and that means the threat to you has been eliminated. I promised your mother I would protect you from Jerry Bethlehem, and I have. I am free of my obligation and you are free to go."

Free . . . she'd thought she'd never be free. But where—?

"What did you say about an apartment?"

"I've found you a nice one and paid the rent in advance for six months. The lease will be up then, and you can decide to renew or find another place."

He might have given her a little warning. And he might have given her a little say in where she lived, but still . . .

"That's awfully generous."

"Money is not a problem. Your status with the law, however, is. You cannot move into your old home—"

She shook her head so violently it hurt. "No way. I couldn't."

Mom had been murdered there.

"Just as well. You remain a fugitive. Not that the police are actively pursuing you now, but you are, as they say, 'a person of interest' in your mother's death."

"Oh, God."

How could that be? How could they even think . . . ?

"Your temporary accommodations will serve as a base from which you may begin to extricate yourself from your legal predicament."

"But what about—?"

"Money? When I found you, you had a quarter of a million dollars in cash in your car. I deposited that in a small, secure bank with conservative investment policies that insulated it from the vagaries of the financial markets. Your money is safe. In fact you have more now than when you arrived."

Dawn could only shake her head. "You . . . why have you done all this?"

He shrugged. "Why not?" He pulled a large manila

envelope from the top drawer and slid it toward her across the desktop. "Here's a copy of the lease, the keys to the apartment, and a debit card linked to your account in the bank."

She stared at it, afraid to take it.

"I've . . . never been on my own."

He smiled. "You've got wings, but you'll never learn how to fly until you use them."

Oh, spare me, shot through her mind. The last thing she needed now were tired clichés. She was scared. But she kept her expression neutral.

"I guess so."

He rose. "Georges is waiting to take you to your new quarters. Your belongings have been moved in."

"Already?"

It was like he could so not wait to get her out of here. She knew she'd been something of a pain, but had she been that bad?

"Yes." He extended his hand across the desk. "Your life awaits. Good luck with it."

She pushed herself up from the seat. He was trying to make it sound inviting, yet she was totally scared out of her wits.

She shook his cool, dry hand. "Thank you."

She took the envelope, turned toward the door, then turned back. One more thing before she left . . .

"About the baby—"

"Yes, unfortunate."

"I don't believe he's dead."

He looked surprised. "What makes you think that?"

"They're not telling me the truth."

"Why should anyone lie about this?"

"Because he's abnormal."

She shuddered. Considering the identity of his father, maybe she should have been surprised if the baby had had *no* birth defects.

"Then all the more reason for its failure to survive."

"But why wouldn't they let me see him? Maybe they're keeping him to experiment on or something."

"Are you listening to yourself?"

Yeah, she knew it sounded totally crazy, but she couldn't get it out of her head that Dr. Landsman had been lying.

"I know."

"This is the baby you could not wait to be rid of. Well, now you have your wish. No one is lying to you. No one is experimenting on your baby. It died and you are unencumbered." He made a shooing motion. "Go. Georges is waiting for you."

Unencumbered . . . that was good, she guessed. She was so not ready for motherhood. But still . . . that baby had grown and kicked and turned and *lived* inside her . . . she'd gone through a lot of pain giving birth to him . . . perfectly natural to feel connected.

She stepped out into the hall and saw Georges waiting by the elevator. A large suitcase sat at his feet.

She gestured back down the hall toward her room. "I have a few things left—"

"All here," he said, pointing to the bag.

"Are you sure?"

"Yes, he is sure," said Gilda's voice from behind her.

Dawn turned and saw her standing outside the room, grinning.

She must have swept through the room as soon as Dawn stepped into Mr. Osala's office.

She started toward Georges and the elevator. Scary as hell to be on her own, but better than spending another minute under the same roof with that old bitch.

4.   Jack jumped at the sound of the buzzer.

He'd been listening to the thumping sounds from the van. A couple of times it rocked on its springs and he thought of the old bumper sticker, *When the van is a-rockin', don't come a-knockin'*, but figured that was the last thing that might be happening. A couple times he'd approached and asked if everything was all right, and Barbara had told him it was.

The buzzer couldn't be Abe. He had a key. A quick peek through the peephole revealed Munir. Jack let him in.

"Is Barbara here?"

"Yeah, she—"

"Oh, no," he said, squeezing his eyes closed.

Uh-oh.

"You mean you didn't know?"

"Where is she?" he said, starting forward.

Jack pushed him back. "Wait-wait-wait. What's going on?"

"I told her about your call. She said she needed to stop at the apartment first, that I should wait with Robby until she got back. But she didn't come back and when I called her, her phone was turned off. And then I noticed the paper I'd written this address on was missing."

Oh, hell. Barbara had given the impression Munir had sent her.

"So you had no idea?"

"None. When I found the address missing, I knew where she was. I can't let her—"

One of the van's rear doors swung open and Barbara eased herself out. She looked pale, shaken. She wore latex gloves—bloody ones.

Munir ran to her and threw his arms around her. "Barbara! What—?"

"Where's Robby?" she said.

"Sound asleep at the hospital. You know how the pain-killers knock him out. Why did you—?"

"I had to, Munir. I had to know. I had to make him tell me—myself."

Jack peeked in the back and saw the mystery man where he'd left him. No surprise there. He wasn't moving but he was breathing. A bloody mass of gauze swathed his right hand.

"He tell you who he is?"

"He said his name is James Valez."

Jack closed the door. "Why'd he do all this?"

She looked at her husband. "For a piece of computer code."

Munir looked stunned. "Code? What code? He never once mentioned anything about—" He stopped and frowned.

"What?"

"The other morning—what is today? I've lost track."

"Thursday."

"Then it was Tuesday morning. He made me admit a virus into both my computers. He said it was so he could track my emails, to make sure I wasn't communicating with the police."

"Did you let him?" Barbara said.

"Of course. I thought it strange at the time that he wanted the key to my encrypted files, but now it makes sense. He was going through all my files looking for this piece of code. But what—?"

Barbara sobbed. "Tuesday morning? That's when . . . even though you did what he asked, he still cut off Rob-by's finger."

Jack shook his head. "And told Munir he had to cut off one of his own. Even though he probably already had the code. Sick bastard."

Munir's expression remained incredulous. "But what do I have that he wants?"

"Something to do with the online game program you've been working on," she said.

He pressed his hands against the sides of his head. "The game? The MMO? What could he possibly—?"

"What's it do?" Jack said.

"It speeds up play. Russ and I—"

"Russ!" Barbara said. "He mentioned Russ!"

Jack shook his head. "I can't believe Russ would be involved in anything like this."

"He's not," Barbara said. "But Valez told me that Russ was shooting his mouth off about the wonders of this software."

"Then why didn't he go to Russ?"

Munir sighed. "Because I store all the code."

"But didn't he have a copy?"

Munir shook his head. "I have—or at least *had*—the more secure system. Russ calls me 'Mister Encryption.' But still . . ." He frowned. "He would have gone to Russ first."

Jack remembered something. "Maybe he did. Maybe he got in through the guy next door. Russ gets online by poaching his neighbor's Wi-Fi."

Munir closed his eyes as if in pain. "Oh, that makes it so easy. He found out Russ didn't have it, so he came after me."

"And he couldn't get into your system—"

"Even if he did, I use two-fifty-six-bit AES encryption."

"So he attacked you through your family and made it look like crazy racism when all he really wanted was a bit of code."

Munir turned to Barbara. "Did he say why?"

She shook her head.

"Or who he was working for?" Jack asked.

Another shake. "It was hard enough extracting what I did. Once I learned that it was neither random nor personal, but just for a chunk of innocent computer code, I . . .

I was so sickened I couldn't bear to be near him anymore." She closed her eyes and tears squeezed between her lids as she sobbed. "He cut off my little boy's finger for a string of letters and numbers!"

Murnir threw his arms around her. "I'm so sorry."

As Jack gave them a moment, he thought about how it was pretty near a sure thing that certain strings of letters and numbers out there could change the world. But code for an online game? To use the online lingua franca: WTF?

"What happened to his hand?"

Still sobbing, Barbara reached into her coat pocket. She pulled out a clear plastic bag and handed it to him. Jack checked it out.

A human thumb.

Munir gasped.

Jack said, "What are you going to do with it?"

"See to it that he and it are never rejoined."

Jack pocketed it. "I'll take care of that."

He'd noticed a rat hole in the rear wall of the garage. Maybe he'd treat them to a midday snack.

"But we've a bigger problem: What do we do with the rest of him?"

Munir looked at him. "What do you mean?"

Might as well slap it on the table: "If I were in your shoes, I'd get rid of him as well."

Barbara's eyes widened. "You mean kill him?"

"Think about it. He knows who you are, knows where to find you. He snatched you and Robby once. What's going to keep him from doing it again? His plan was to kill you—"

"You don't know that," she said.

"Why else would he allow you to see his face? When I mentioned it to him yesterday he didn't deny it."

Barbara pressed herself against her husband. "You're talking cold-blooded murder."

"Sure sounds like it."

"No," Munir said, shaking his head. "I won't allow it. I . . . I can't."

" 'Allow'? I wasn't talking about Barbara doing it."

He looked confused. "No, I meant you. Monster that he is, I don't think I can be a party to something like that."

Now Jack saw the problem.

"Whoa. We've got our signals crossed here. I'm not a contract killer. I don't do that. Remember, I said, 'If I were in your shoes.' I'm talking about *you* offing him."

Their eyes widened simultaneously as they spoke in unison. *"No!"*

"Better give that a little more thought. He started cutting off your wife's nipple when the only thing he had against her was she married you. Now how do you think he feels about her?"

Munir swallowed. "There must be another way."

"Not that I can see. He's a ticking time bomb."

"The police . . . we can press charges."

"Sure, but that might not go the way you hope." He looked at Barbara. "He was wearing surgical gloves when I broke in—"

"He wore them the entire time."

Jack nodded. "No prints left behind. And he's set the real Hollander up as a fall guy. I'm pretty sure Hollander is dead, so he won't be able to deny his involvement."

"But *we* can all identify him."

"What about his thumb? How do you explain that? He's established reasonable doubt, while you've cut him up. In this system, with the kind of judges we have in this city, he could walk while Barbara ends up behind bars."

Munir shook his head. "No, that can't happen."

"It damn well can. I'm not saying it will, but it *can*. You want to take that risk?"

Jack wouldn't. If this were personal—if Gia and Vicky were at risk—James Valez would not see sunset. Hell, he wouldn't see noon. But this wasn't personal. This was Munir and Barbara's problem. They had to make the choice and do the deed.

Munir seemed lost in thought.

Barbara said, "Oh, Munir . . . you can't be considering . . ."

He looked at her. "What do *you* say? He kidnapped you, he cut you, he hurt Robby in front of you. I will go along with whatever you choose."

She closed her eyes. "I've hurt him back. If he had a heart attack now I would not try to save him. The world would be a better place without him, but I don't want any more of his blood on my hands, and I don't want it on yours." She turned to Jack and shook her head. "No. We can't."

Jack sighed. "I didn't think you could."

He understood. They were regular citizens. They hadn't walked in Jack's shoes, or made the mistakes he'd made—like allowing a killer with a grudge to walk away. Someone had died because of that. He'd never make that mistake again.

"Then we'll have to let him go."

He could tell from their expressions they were frightened, and well they should be.

Munir tightened his arm around his wife. "What can we do to protect ourselves?"

"Arm yourselves and hire someone to teach you defensive tactics. Meanwhile, take off. I'll deal with him."

"How?"

"Let me worry about that. I'll be expecting the rest of my fee tomorrow."

Munir nodded. "Absolutely."

When they were gone, Jack climbed back into the back of the van. He'd noticed the door ajar earlier. He hoped Valez had heard his conversation with the Habibs. He lay there with his eyes closed. The bandage on his hand was completely red now.

Jack yanked the tape off his mouth.

"You awake?"

Valez moaned. "My hand . . ." His voice was hoarse, gravelly. "Killing me. Need a doctor."

Jack had to laugh. "You're kidding, right? You're lucky you're still alive. Up to me you'd be rat meat. Like your thumb."

He groaned.

"Okay," Jack said. "Here's the deal: You live to see another day. Just how many more days depends on you. I know who you are and I know where you live."

He opened his eyes. "No you don't. The first thing you asked me this morning was my name."

"Had a cop buddy trace your prints last night." I wish, he thought. "You weren't easy to find, but he found you."

"Bullshit. Don't have a record."

"Amazing how many people think that means something. But just because you've never been arrested doesn't mean your prints aren't on file somewhere. Anyway, my buddy matched yours, James Valez. And the reason I asked you your name this morning is because an interrogator should always know the answer to at least one question he's asking. How else you gonna know if the interrogatee— that'd be you—is telling the truth?"

Sounded good for something Jack had just made up on the spot.

"Anyway, here's the deal: I dump you somewhere and you find your own way to a doctor. After that, you leave the Habibs alone. You bother them again, or they get even a hint that you're sniffing around, I'm back in the picture. Despite what the wife did to you—be thankful she wasn't working on your crotch—they're gentle people. I, on the other hand, have impulse issues. I'll come back and shoot off your kneecaps and smash your elbows. It's part of my warranty. I guarantee my work. So the bottom line is, you're out of their lives forever. Got it?"

Valez said nothing, so Jack kicked his wounded hand. "Got it?"

He howled. "Yes! Yes!"

Jack hoped the message had penetrated.

"Now, a couple more questions."

"Please . . ."

"Why did you want that code?"

"Don't know."

Jack stared at the wounded hand. "You gonna let this turn ugly?"

Jack wanted to avoid that almost as much as he guessed Valez did, but he couldn't let on.

Valez followed his stare. "No, please, I swear. I was only supposed to get into his hard drive and find the code. I don't know what for. I swear on my mother's life I don't."

Could be telling the truth. No way to know for sure.

"Who put you up to it? And don't hold back. You *are* going to tell me, so why don't we save me a little time and you a lot of pain by spilling? You don't even have to speak. Just nod. The Order put you up to it, right?"

He hesitated, then closed his eyes and nodded.

Well, well, well . . . Barbara had broken him.

"Why?"

"Didn't say. Not high enough to know."

That had a ring of truth as well. From what he'd learned about the Order, it was layered, with only the top echelons privy to the real agenda.

Jack wanted to ask if Drexler was involved but didn't want to give away how much he knew about the group.

"Was it the Order's idea to have you torture the Habibs and mutilate their boy?"

He shook his head. "Mine."

"Why?"

His answer surprised Jack.

5. Georges placed Dawn's suitcase on the floor inside the front door of the apartment and handed her the door keys.

"Unlike Gilda," he said, smiling at her from the doorway, "I bear you no ill will. In fact, I wish you well. Had you been better behaved, I would not hold my current position."

He pulled the door closed, leaving her alone in her new place. Boxes of her belongings littered the floors, waiting to be unpacked.

Alone . . . when was the last time she'd been alone anywhere?

Her shoes clicked on the hardwood floor as she checked out the front room, dining area, and kitchen. Then to the two bedrooms. All furnished in a minimalist way. Although she couldn't imagine him bothering, the furniture totally looked like something Mr. Osala would pick out: no personality.

Well, so what? Not like she'd be throwing parties, or even having company. All the kids she'd hung with in high school were in college now. She'd been headed for Colgate before Jerry . . . and the baby . . . and Mom's death . . .

Suddenly overwhelmed, she dropped into a chair. The world had been her oyster, waiting for her to pry it open and grab the pearl. She'd done an expert job of screwing up her life and her mother's. If she hadn't fallen for Jerry's line . . .

She felt her throat tighten but she was *not* going to break down. She was on her own now and was going to have to stop acting like a baby.

She noticed her hands trembling. Nerves? She felt like crap. Her stomach growled. When was the last time she'd eaten? She thought back. Had to be Tuesday afternoon—

almost two days ago. She tended to get low blood sugar if she didn't eat.

She pushed herself up from the chair and almost fell back as the room did a 360. Had to get some food into her.

She staggered to the kitchen, all but bouncing off a wall along the way. She yanked open the refrigerator door and stared at empty shelves. Mr. Osala had taken care of everything but stocking the fridge.

She totally needed food. She'd spotted a coffee shop across the street. She could grab a sandwich and some milk, get her bearings, then do some grocery shopping.

Sounded like a plan.

She fumbled around, found the envelope Mr. Osala had given her, grabbed the apartment key, and stepped out into the hall. As she closed the door behind her, the hallway undulated like a snake. She sagged against the wall as she broke out in a sweat and her legs turned to Twizzlers.

She was sliding toward the floor when she heard a door open nearby.

"Are you all right?" said a woman's voice.

Dawn conquered an urge to say she was fine and always acted this way.

"Low blood sugar."

"Are you a diabetic?"

She shook her head. "Just need something to eat."

Hands gripped her under the arms, lifted her to standing, and the two of them stumbled into the neighbor woman's apartment. She was guided to a chair and she gratefully dropped into it.

"Stay there. I'll get you some juice."

But instead of heading straight for the kitchen, the woman closed and locked the door. Dawn got a look at her then: midthirties, straight dark hair, no makeup, medium build.

She disappeared into the kitchen, then reappeared with

a glass of orange juice. As Dawn gulped it down, the woman went back to the kitchen and returned with a couple of cheese sticks.

"Here," she said, unwrapping one. "Eat these. The protein will give you a more sustained blood sugar."

"Are you a doctor?"

She smiled. Nice smile. "Hardly."

"My name's Dawn. I just moved—"

"Yeah, I gathered you were my new neighbor. My name's Louise, but people call me Weezy."

6.   One of the things Abe stored in his garage was a stock of defunct license plates Jack had acquired from Sal Vituolo, a former customer who owned a Staten Island junkyard. A set of those plates—from Mississippi—adorned Abe's van now.

He'd driven downtown to Allen Street, then turned onto the Lodge's block. Valez was blindfolded, gagged, and wrapped in a sheet in the back. He had no idea of what Abe or the van looked like, or the location of the garage, and Jack planned to keep it that way. Jack wore an oversized cap with the brim riding his eyebrows, and big sunglasses.

A few car lengths upstream from the Lodge, he double-parked, freed Valez from the bungees, and dragged him out the back door. He left him between two parked cars. The cold kept sidewalk traffic lean and the few people around paid him little heed.

As he drove off, he called the Lodge. He knew the number of the phone in the foyer.

When someone answered, he asked for "the Lodge guy." After multiple requests and clarification to "someone from the Septimus Order," Drexler came to the phone.

Good. Finding him there was hit or miss.

"Hello? Who is this?"

"Just dropped one of your goons off by the curb—the guy who kidnapped Munir Habib's wife and kid. Do you know he cut off the kid's finger just for kicks—I mean after he broke into the computer and got the code. Nice buncha people you got in the Order."

"What are you talking about. Who—?"

"Yeah, he told me all about the game code and what you want it for. You jerks are sicker than I thought."

He broke the connection and turned off the phone.

There . . . that ought to rattle some cages.

7. This is a disaster, Ernst thought as he stared across his desk at Valez.

The man was a disheveled mess—bruised, battered, and missing his right thumb. All bad enough, but the phone call.

"Tell me again what happened."

"I already—"

"Tell. Me."

Valez sighed. "I was attacked. It was a case of mistaken identity. They thought I was someone else . . . thought I had information about something I knew nothing about. They tortured me until they realized they had the wrong man."

An absurd story, obviously concocted on the spot. Apparently he hadn't had time to make up something more credible.

"So . . . this had nothing to do with acquiring the code from Habib's computer?"

"No. Absolutely not. I'd already secured the code and released his wife and child."

"But not before amputating the child's finger."

Watching the blood drain from Valez's face, Ernst

knew the caller had been telling the truth. It took all his will to restrain his fury.

"That's . . ." Valez's mouth worked in silence for a heartbeat or two.

Ernst forced a calm tone. "Don't bother denying it."

"How do—?"

"How do I know? That does not concern you. What I do not know is why you deviated from the plan. Your mission was to extract the code from Habib's computer without him knowing it. You were provided a scapegoat and a covering motive. I don't remember any mention in the plan of mutilating a child. Explain."

"I went a little crazy, I guess."

"You guess?"

"If he hadn't been an Arab, I would have been fine. But—"

"What does being an Arab have to do with anything? We have many Arab brothers in the Order."

Valez looked away. "But it's my *sister* I'm talking about. A flesh-and-blood sister who worked at Cantor Fitzgerald in the Trade Center. She'd been on the job just six weeks on nine/eleven when the jets hit. She was twenty-four years old. Since then I can't look at an Arab without wanting to kill him. So you can see why I went a little crazy."

Ernst repressed a scream of rage. "I see nothing of the sort. You were given a task—"

He looked up. "Which I successfully completed."

"Do *not* interrupt me!" Control . . . control. "Ever."

"Yes, sir."

"Tell me everything. I want a day-by-day account of every event as it transpired."

As Valez spoke, Ernst could not escape the crushing irony of the situation. James Valez, a member of the Ancient Fraternal Septimus Order, had quite possibly sabotaged the most important project in the Order's millennia-long history because of his hatred of Arabs as the culprits behind the fall of the Trade Towers. The irony? He was not a high-enough ranking brother to know that the Order itself had guided the Arabs who had guided those fatal jets.

Ernst might not have learned any of this if Habib had not hired some sort of detective to help him. As a result, Habib, his wife, the detective, the police, and who knew how many others were aware that Habib's game code had been the object.

But they could not know why . . . because Valez did not know.

Ernst gathered his thoughts. How to deal with this?

He could see only one path open to him.

"At the first inkling that you were becoming emotionally involved, you should have informed us and we would have replaced you."

"I know that now. I'm sorry. I swear to you, this will never happen again."

How right you are, Ernst thought.

"I believe you, and I accept your apology. You need medical attention, but we can't risk a hospital. Wait outside. Szeto will take you to a doctor who's a brother and will guarantee discretion."

Szeto came in right after Valez left.

"Is it as bad as you thought?"

Ernst nodded. "Yes and no. He could not have made a worse mess of it, unless he had failed to acquire the code. But he succeeded there, and Jihad has been set free and is spreading around the globe. So our plans remain unchanged."

"So, he suffers no repercussions?"

"Of course he does. He thinks you'll be taking him to a doctor. I do not wish him seen by a doctor, or anyone else, for that matter. See to it that he's never seen again. By anyone."

He smiled. "Consider it done."

"But before he disappears for good, remove the rest of his fingers. One by one."

The smile broadened . . . "Consider it done" . . . then faded . . . "We may have another problem."

"Nothing serious, I hope."

"Could be."

Ernst closed his eyes. "What now?"

"Connell. He met with Fournier yesterday and mentioned 'Jihad.' "

Ernst felt a lead weight plummet into his stomach. This couldn't be happening. Not now. He could not allow Jihad to be connected in any way to the Order. If the virus was successful, it would not matter. But should it fail . . .

"How could he possibly . . . ?"

"I don't know. But that may have been his real purpose all along—to spy on us."

"But for whom?"

"If you want my opinion—his sister."

Far-fetched but not impossible, though Szeto's opinions regarding that woman were automatically suspect.

"Round him up and find out what he knows, and who he's told."

A light glinted in Szeto's eyes. "His sister too?"

Ernst jabbed a finger at him. "What was the One's directive regarding that woman?"

The glint faded and he looked away. "No contact of any sort."

"Then why did you suggest picking her up?"

"I just thought—"

"Is there confusion on your part as to the meaning of 'no' being something less than an absolute?"

"None at all."

"Then banish that woman from your thoughts. We will not mention her ever again unless we are instructed otherwise."

If the One wanted her left alone, then left alone she would be. With the Great Change imminent, this was no time to jeopardize his store of goodwill with the One.

"As you wish. Since Connell has seen me, I will have to involve someone else in picking him up."

"Fournier will do. Did he take care of that hacker?"

"Last night."

"No links to us?"

"You know Fournier—very clean. But what of the remains of these two brothers?"

"The usual—q'qr them both. And I don't want them found."

Again, none of that would matter if Jihad succeeded and paved the way for the Change.

8. Jack idled the van next to a fire hydrant upstream from the Lodge as he waited for Valez to reappear. He figured they eventually had to find him some medical care.

Or maybe they wouldn't. The Order couldn't be happy with him after what Jack had told them.

Between periodic glances in the rearview to check for a passing patrol car—didn't want a ticket for parking here—he watched Kickers straggling in and out. One of those glances revealed Hank Thompson himself walking down the sidewalk. To further hide his face in case the hat and shades weren't enough, Jack scratched his cheek as Thompson passed. Thompson knew him as the guy who did a smash and grab on his *Compendium of Srem* almost a year ago. Things would get ugly if he recognized Jack. But he passed without glancing inside.

A little later, a vaguely familiar figure appeared—swarthy, dark-haired, with a unibrow and perpetual five-o'clock shadow, wearing a chrome-studded black leather jacket. Took Jack a few seconds to place him. He didn't know who he was, but he'd shown up in Weezy's hospital room last year, pretending to be a good Samaritan. What had he called himself? Bob Garvey. Yeah, right. Like a guy with a Czech or Polish accent would be named Bob Garvey. He'd tried to pump Jack and Eddie for information about Weezy.

Garvey walked off in the other direction.

Still no sign of Valez.

Shortly after that, a car pulled up ahead of him and double-parked, idling like Jack.

The so-called Garvey sat behind the wheel.

Interesting.

Then a big black Lincoln Town Car pulled up in front of the old stone Lodge. Less than a minute later Valez came limping down the steps and got in.

About time.

Jack put the van in gear and pulled out to follow, but Garvey had the same idea.

Even more interesting.

So Jack followed Garvey.

A mini caravan.

Why was Valez in one car and Garvey following? Didn't make sense. Or maybe it did. Maybe the Order had plans for him other than medical care. Jack knew from personal experience how murderous the Order became when it felt threatened. Was it equally murderous with members who displeased it? In Valez's case, he hoped so. If not, Jack would follow Valez to the hospital or wherever, then follow him home. He wanted to know where he lived so he could look him up should the need arise.

9. Eddie's private line rang in his office. He picked it up. Weezy maybe?

"Brother Connell?"

He recognized Fournier's voice.

"Yes."

"The Actuator wishes to meet with you."

Didn't they ever refer to Drexler by name?

"Sure. When?"

"Immediately."

"I'm in the middle of—"

"I am on my way over with a car to pick you up. I will be out front in three minutes."

He had an urge to tell him what Drexler could do with his car, but hesitated. Maybe he had some information on Weezy and why the Order was so interested in her.

"Okay. Meet you out front."

He saved the file he'd been working on, threw on his coat, and headed out. When he arrived down on Sixth Avenue, he found the car waiting for him. Fournier stood outside and pulled open the rear door as Eddie approached.

"I'm riding in the back?"

"It seems I am a chauffeur of sorts for the day."

Eddie thought this royal treatment a bit odd, but didn't see much choice but to go along. As he slid into the rear he noticed another man sitting at the far end of the seat. He looked disheveled and had a bloody bandage on his right hand.

"Meet Brother Valez. He had an accident. We are taking him for medical care, then going to Mister Drexler."

The man nodded to him distractedly. Eddie nodded back and hid his annoyance. Fournier had made it sound as if Drexler were in a rush to see him, but here they were, making a side trip.

As the car slid into motion, the door locks clicked shut.

The sound made him uneasy. But some cars locked automatically. He tried the door handle but it didn't work.

He was seated directly behind Fournier so he tapped him on the shoulder.

"What's going on with the doors? Why won't they open?"

Fournier shrugged. "Child-guard locks, I suppose. I do not know why they are engaged. Are you claustrophobic? Do you want me to stop and undo them?"

Eddie suddenly felt foolish. Yes, he was a bit claustrophobic—not so much as when he'd been a kid—but he could handle this.

"No, of course not. Just curious."

None of this seemed to bother Brother Valez. He sat to Eddie's right, brooding and clutching the wrist of his injured hand. So why let it bother him?

10. Jack hunched over the steering wheel of the van and stared in shock as the Lincoln pulled away . . . with Eddie inside and Garvey, or whoever he was, following.

Garvey's staying out of sight made sense now. Eddie would remember him from the hospital. And if Eddie connected him to the Order, he'd know something was up. But why follow at all unless . . .

. . . Eddie was headed for the same fate as Valez?

Jack hit the gas. He had to get Eddie out of the car.

But how? Under other circumstances he might approach them, acting all innocent and asking for directions. But both Garvey and Valez knew him, and even if they didn't, Eddie might give it away.

An idea began to form . . . one that involved a much more direct approach.

Jack hated direct approaches.

As they headed uptown, he pulled the van ahead of

Garvey and settled beside the Lincoln, pacing it, looking for some indication that it might be getting ready to turn. It pulled to the far left and stopped at a light with its turn signal blinking.

Jack stopped a little ahead and to its right, checking out the driver through the windshield. No one he'd seen before. Valez slumped on the rear passenger side, looking a little dazed. Eddie, seated behind the driver, wasn't visible from this angle.

As the light for crosstown traffic turned yellow, Jack jumped the green, darting around the Lincoln and beating it onto the cross street. The Town Car honked its annoyance. Jack took his time along the block, slowing enough to make sure he was first at the stop line when the next light turned red.

He put it in park and pulled on a pair of driving gloves. He unlatched the driver door, then lay back on the front seat bench, drew up his knees, and poised the soles of his boots toward the door, ready to kick.

Things were about to get ugly.

11.   Fournier muttered something that sounded like a curse and leaned on the horn. Eddie shifted his gaze from people watching on the sidewalk to straight ahead.

"What's wrong?"

"That damn van won't move!" He hit the horn again. "Is he asleep?"

True enough—the traffic light had turned green and the truck wasn't budging.

"Maybe he stalled."

"No," Valez said, speaking for the first time since Eddie had entered the car. "His tailpipe is smoking."

Fournier grabbed his cell phone and speed dialed someone. "I don't know what's wrong with him. Do you want me to go see?" He listened, then nodded and said, "Very well."

"Who was that?" Eddie said.

"No one."

Eddie was about to call him on that when he saw someone in a black leather biker jacket hurry past on his left and approach the van.

"Now we will see," Fournier said.

"Hey, that looks like Szeto," Valez said.

Eddie glanced over and saw a concerned, almost frightened look on his face.

"Who's that?"

"One of the Order's enforcers."

He said it like everyone knew.

"We have enforcers?"

Eddie watched as Szeto reached the van's door. Suddenly it exploded open, its edge catching him in the face and throwing him back against a parked car. Eddie jumped and leaned forward.

What the hell?

He got his first look at Szeto's face and realized he'd seen it before. But where?

He winced as the door caught Szeto twice more, slamming him against the parked car again and again. And each time Eddie saw booted feet kicking it open.

Then a man in a sweatshirt, baseball cap, and sunglasses jumped out and grabbed Szeto by the back of his head and slammed his face against the side of the truck, and once more on the roof of the parked car. He released Szeto and let him crumple to the pavement.

The bloodied face was barely recognizable now, but memory of it before all the damage sparked recognition.

Eddie cried, "He was in the hospital!" just as Valez said, "I know that guy!"

"Who?" Fournier shouted, reaching inside his coat.

The man from the van bent and pulled something from

inside Szeto's jacket, then sprinted their way. Eddie noticed he now carried a pistol in his gloved hand, then looked at his face and recognized him.

"Jack!"

What was he doing—?

"Who?" Fournier repeated.

Valez said, "Him!"

Eddie saw Fournier raise his right hand clutching something dark and oblong.

A gun! What? Why? To shoot Jack?

Eddie grabbed for it. He got a two-handed grip on the barrel and tried to yank it free. Flame erupted from its muzzle with a deafening blast. Valez's head exploded in a spray of red as the window behind him shattered.

Eddie recoiled in shock and revulsion and lost his grip on the pistol. As it swung toward him he grabbed Fournier's wrist but that only slowed the angling of the muzzle toward his face. The pistol went off again and Eddie felt what seemed like a blast of compressed air against his right cheek as a bullet whizzed past.

And then the driver's window exploded inward as two shots sounded from outside the car. Fournier's left eye erupted in a gush of red and he released the pistol as his face slammed against the top of the front seat, then slid from view. Eddie dropped the pistol and fought back a surge of vomit.

"You all right?" Jack shouted through the shattered window as he tried to open Eddie's door. His voice seemed far away, distorted by a high-pitched whine.

"It's locked," Eddie managed. His own voice echoed in his head. "I can't open it."

Jack opened the driver's door and hit a button. The lock popped up. He threw the pistol onto the front seat, then opened Eddie's door, grabbed his upper arm, and yanked him out.

"Into the van! Move!"

Jack shoved him away from the car and retrieved Fournier's gun from the backseat, then raced ahead of him back to the van. Szeto was stirring, raising himself off the pavement onto his elbows. Jack jumped on his back and used him as a step into the van.

Eddie found his way to the passenger door and hauled himself inside. Jack was already in the driver's seat. He threw the van into gear and gunned it into motion. Eddie hadn't closed his door yet. He leaned out and lost lunch in one hot, acidic gush.

"Jack!" he gasped as he pulled the door shut and wiped his mouth. "What the—?"

"You do know you were on a one-way trip, don't you?"

Eddie hadn't realized it then, but no argument now. Clear as day. Two men killed, right before his eyes, their heads blown open just inches away. He couldn't stop shaking.

"Why me? What did I do?"

"You screwed up. You got in over your head. You played boy detective and got caught."

Boy detective . . . he used to make fun of Jack with that when they were kids.

"But how . . . how did you wind up here?"

"Long story. Can't talk now. Gotta get this crate off the road. Strap in and hang on."

As Eddie complied and Jack started driving like a maniac, he spotted Fournier's gun on the seat between them.

"What are you going to do with that?"

"Wipe it down and get rid of it. It's lousy with your prints."

Was it? Yes, he guessed it was. How had Jack even thought of that? His mind must click through details like—

He hung on as the truck made a wild swerve around a slowing car. This wasn't the Jack he'd known as a kid. This was someone else. Weezy had mentioned this side of him but Eddie hadn't understood. He did now.

After he'd put a few blocks between themselves and

the shooting, Jack said, "Did you recognize the guy who got a faceful of door as the guy who called himself Garvey in Weezy's room at the hospital?"

"Yes. The other passenger—"

"Valez?"

"Yes." Was there anything Jack didn't know about this? "He said his name is Szeto. He's some kind of 'enforcer' for the Order."

"I believe it. He was carrying a Tokarev"—he pointed to the pistol between them—"just like this one."

"What's—?"

"A nine-millimeter pistol. Same kind carried by the guys who were gunning for Weezy last year. Now they're gunning for you."

"The Order wants me dead?" It was so unreal. *Anyone* wanting him dead was unreal. "It can't be."

"Get used to it. You must know something they don't want spread around."

"But I don't. All I did was say I'd help them find Weezy if they'd tell me why they were interested in her. You'll never guess who they brought me to."

"Drexler."

Eddie blinked. "Yes! How did—? Never mind."

He realized he'd have to stop being surprised by what Jack knew about all this.

"What did he tell you?"

"He said he didn't know but he'd find out."

"That's not enough to want you dead. Did you see or read or overhear something you shouldn't have?"

"No, I—wait. I overheard part of a conversation where 'jihad' was repeated a number of times."

"That could be it."

"It's just an Arabic word."

"The Order has had some dealings with Islamic nutcases in the past. Maybe they're dealing again. Weezy was uncovering the connection. That was why they were after

her. This 'jihad' could be something new along that line or
nothing." Jack glanced at him. "Do they know you know
about this 'jihad' thing? I mean, you didn't ask Drexler
what it meant, did you?"

"No." He hated to admit it . . . "But I did ask Fournier,
the guy who was driving."

"Jeez, Eddie. How could you be so—?" He waved a
hand. "Did he tell you?"

"No. But I guess he told Drexler."

"*If* that's it. Means nothing to me beyond holy war. But
whether it's this 'jihad' or something else, the fact remains you've got to disappear."

"Disappear? How?"

"Fall off the radar. I assume you've got a savings or
checking account?"

"Both."

"Good. Where?"

"Citi."

"First thing you do is empty them—*almost* empty them.
Now. Use your CrackBerry to find the nearest branch. I'll
drop you there. While I'm hiding this van, you go to the
nearest Duane's or department store and buy a duffel bag.
You empty those accounts and put the money in the
bag. I'll come by and pick you up and we'll start your
disappearing act."

Eddie felt a surge of panic.

"But I've got a business—"

Jack gave him a hard look. "Your business or your life.
Choose."

Eddie leaned back and stared through the windshield.
He'd worked so hard to build up his actuarial business.
Things were going so well. But none of that would matter
if the Order caught up with him.

He pulled out his BlackBerry and hunted up a Citi
branch.

12. Ernst stared at Szeto's swollen, bruised, stitched, bandaged face and shook his head in disgust. He wanted to scream but didn't want the Kickers wandering the Lodge's halls to hear.

"You have no idea who did this?"

"I had no chance. Door hit me in face before I get look at him. I see nothing after that."

"He took your pistol and used it to kill Fournier and Valez, then whisked Connell off to safety. Are you feeling a sense of déjà vu?"

Szeto nodded. "Max and Josef."

Though not exactly the same—Max's pistol had been stolen but not used to kill either him or Josef—both had died transporting another Connell . . . Edward's sister Louise.

Ernst steepled his fingers. "Do you think it's the same man?"

"I am sure. These Connells seem to have guardian angel."

"A deadly one." Ernst aimed a hard gaze at Szeto. "An angel with inside information."

Szeto frowned. "What do you mean?"

"How could he possibly know you were taking Connell anywhere? Connell had only minutes' warning that he was being picked up, no hint that he would be in danger, and even if so, no time to set up a tail."

"Only Fournier and I knew."

"And Fournier is conveniently dead."

Szeto's already swollen eyes narrowed further. "You can't think—"

"Odd, don't you think, that he would kill Valez and Fournier, but leave you alive?"

"I was down and no threat."

"Valez was no threat either."

"He might not have known that. You insult me."

Ernst had no doubts about Szeto's loyalty, but a hint that he might be under suspicion would keep him sharp.

"Just speculating. I am disturbed by someone's uncanny ability to be in the right place at the right time to rescue the Connell siblings. Could it have been the same man who abducted Valez?"

"Possible but not likely. If he wanted Valez dead, he could have killed him when he had him."

"Yes, I suppose that makes sense. But this incident . . . right on the street . . . you aren't a suspect?"

Szeto shook his head. "They think I am victim. I hide my holster under parked car. Police question me and I tell truth: I did not see man, his van is blue, and had Mississippi plates. I know nothing else. But I know how to find more."

He meant the woman, of course—Connell's sister—but knew better than to bring it up directly. Ernst decided to misinterpret his remark.

"Yes. Locate Brother Connell. If we are lucky, he will run to the police. If that happens, our brothers within the authorities will isolate him and interrogate him."

"What if he goes into hiding like sister?"

"We'll find him just like we found her."

"That was luck. We thought she was in Wyoming."

"But she came back. We weren't networking with the Dormentalists and Kickers then. Besides, I doubt he knows how to hide. But check his bank accounts and his credit and debit cards anyway. Track him that way."

The Order had members in all the large financial corporations and law enforcement agencies as well. No information was privileged.

"And when he is found?"

"When he is found, he shall lead us to his guardian angel. You will see to it that he cooperates. And then you shall have the pleasure of dealing with that one."

Instead of smiling, Szeto frowned. "We do not have much time. When Jihad brings down Internet, we will have difficulty tracing anything."

Ernst hadn't thought of that.

He was going to miss the Internet.

13. "Feeling better?" Weezy said, watching Dawn closely as she sat next to her on the couch.

Dawn nodded. "Much."

The juice and cheese had worked a mini miracle. She certainly looked better. A little color in her cheeks made a world of difference. But she looked disheveled. Her medium-length blond hair needed a brushing and her oversized blue sweat suit didn't do her figure any favors.

"Should I call your parents?"

Suddenly she looked as if she was about to burst into tears.

"Is something wrong?"

She nodded, biting her lip. Finally she said, "I don't have any. My mother . . . died . . ."

Weezy touched her knee. "I'm so sorry. Who are you staying with?"

"No one."

"You're living by yourself? Across the hall?"

She nodded.

But she looked so young.

"How old are you?"

"Nineteen next month."

A teenager . . . living alone in this building. The rent was reasonable for the location, but not cheap. How did she afford it? Unless she'd inherited it. Like Weezy.

"I'm an orphan too, if it makes you feel any better."

Lame! she thought.

Dawn offered a weak smile. "No offense, but it doesn't." Then she quaked with a sob. "I miss my mother so much!"

Weezy hesitated, then put an arm around her shoulders. "It's been years and years for me, but I still miss mine. How long for you?"

Another sob and she pressed her face against Weezy's shoulder. "Not even a year."

Still a fresh wound, she thought. For some odd reason she thought of a couple of girls she knew who had gotten pregnant during high school. Their children would be just about Dawn's age.

I'm old enough to be your mother.

What a thought.

Dawn gathered herself and pulled away. "Sorry."

"It's okay. Really, it's okay."

She was overweight like Weezy had been until a few months ago. As Dawn straightened her sweat suit top, Weezy noticed the bulge of her belly.

"Can I ask you a personal question?"

Dawn's face took on a guarded look. "Maybe."

"Are you pregnant?"

Weezy thought she was going to cry again, but she held it together.

"I was . . . until yesterday morning."

"You delivered yesterday? And now you're here alone?" She nodded.

No wonder she almost passed out.

"Where's your baby?"

The tears flowed again. "Gone. He died."

Oh no. The poor kid.

Weezy squeezed her hand. "That's terrible."

"They said he had birth defects but they wouldn't let me see him."

"You didn't see your baby?"

She shook her head. "Only a glimpse when they rushed him away because he'd stopped breathing."

That was hard to believe, but she didn't seem to be lying. She seemed genuinely upset.

Weezy gave her hand another squeeze. "I'm so sorry. I—"

A knock on her door startled her. If that guy looking for his dog was back, she wasn't answering. She looked through the peephole and saw Jack. She'd given him a swipe card for the downstairs door.

Always glad to see Jack. Sometimes too glad, because sometimes it hurt to spend time with a man she wanted and knew she could never have. He was so attached to Gia and Vicky—hermetically sealed was more like it. She'd never pry him free. Didn't know if she wanted to, really. For his sake. Gia made him happy, filled in the spaces where he was empty.

Weezy could do that too, she was sure of it. And the thing was, she'd known him first, and should have had first dibs. But that had been such a—literally—crazy time in her life that she hadn't realized what was sitting right in front of her.

If only she could go back in time. She'd follow him to New York and become his partner in all ways. What a life they'd have lived—would still be living. He'd have never met Gia and would be unable to imagine a single day without his dear, sweet, ever-loving Weezy.

Instead of solace, fantasies like that had made her miserable and forced her to move out of Jack's place and find her own.

And now, happy as she was to see Jack, she wasn't happy with his expression. He looked concerned.

She pulled the door open. "Hey."

"Hey." He took a step across the threshold. "We need to—"

He froze, wide-eyed, as he stared over her shoulder, then ducked back into the hallway and to the side.

"Jack?" she said, following him.

"Close the door," he whispered.

She couldn't do that—she'd be locked out—but she pulled it closed without latching it. She'd never seen Jack like this. He looked agitated . . . flabbergasted.

"What's wrong?"

"Where did you find *her*?"

"I didn't find her." She pointed to Dawn's door. "She just moved in."

His eyes widened further. "*There?* Across the hall?"

"Yes. What's wrong with that?"

"Everything! Get rid of her. Get her out of your apartment."

"I can't do that. She's not feeling well and—"

"We've got to talk—about Eddie and about her. And I can't let her see me."

"Why not?"

"Because she knows my face." He backed away toward the elevator. "I'll wait downstairs and check back with you in a few minutes."

Just then she felt a tug on the door. Dawn pulled it open.

"I should be going," she said.

Weezy noticed Jack turn away. He stopped at the elevator and stood with his back toward them.

Still off balance from Jack's strange reaction, Weezy studied Dawn. She appeared composed now, and steady on her feet.

"Do you think that's a good idea?"

"I'm much better now. I'm going to do a little food shopping."

"Do you need money?"

She smiled and started down the hall. "No, I'm good."

Weezy glanced past her and saw Jack still waiting for the elevator. She couldn't imagine what was going on between him and a nineteen-year-old girl, but was sure he had a good reason for not wanting her to see him.

"Wait. Let me give you my number in case you need anything."

She hurried inside and jotted it down on a sticky note. By the time she returned to the hall, Jack was gone.

She pressed the note into Dawn's hand, telling her she could call any time, then shooed her down the hall.

She couldn't wait to hear what this was all about.

14. "That's the girl I told you about," Jack said, pacing Weezy's front room like a caged tiger. "The one with the super oDNA baby that everyone's been looking for."

"Dawn Pickering?"

"Yes!"

Sometime last year he'd told her about oDNA, the Otherness-spawned genes hiding in the mass of junk DNA cluttering the human genome. Dawn's baby was the fourth generation of what someone had called "barnyard genetic engineering" aimed toward creating a child packed with oDNA. For what purpose, no one knew.

She pressed her palms against her temples. "She told me her name was Dawn and that she'd just had a baby . . . I should have put it together. But who'd ever guess?"

" 'Just' had a baby?"

"Yesterday morning, she said."

"Wait. That's not right. She was pregnant last April . . . ten months ago. But that's not important. Her moving in across the hall from you—*that's* important."

"I know it's a coincidence, and I know what the Lady told you about coincidences, but she's just a scared kid."

Jack remembered the Lady's words, spoken at Kate's graveside: *No more coincidences for you.*

"Things like that don't just happen. Someone—whether

working for the Otherness or the Ally, I can't tell anymore—put her there for a reason."

"But that would mean they know where I am."

Jack nodded. "Exactly. I'll bet that's why the Order was looking for you."

Weezy looked a little ill. "Eddie called me yesterday and said they had a photo of me."

Eddie . . . that was what he'd come here to discuss with her, but the shock of seeing Dawn had blasted it out of his head. He'd get to Eddie in a minute, but first . . .

"That clinches it. They found you."

"But he told them it wasn't me."

"They were testing him, I bet. And he flunked."

Another reason to want Eddie gone.

Weezy frowned. "But how could they have moved her so fast?"

"When did her furniture arrive?"

"Um . . . yesterday afternoon. I see what you mean. Still . . . awfully fast."

"Fast or not, the fact is she's here. And the only reason I can think of for that is to get to know you."

"No way," Weezy said with an emphatic shake of her head. "She wasn't faking. She was about to pass out. You can't fake green color and sweat."

"I'm not saying she knows, I'm saying she's being used."

"And you call me paranoid."

"Seriously, Weez. I think you should stay away from her. She says she had a baby just yesterday, so what is she doing here?"

"She said the baby died and—"

"Whoa. Died?"

"She said it had birth defects."

Jack thought about that. "Makes sense in a way. Maybe all that oDNA was too much for it . . . turned it into some awful mutant. No surprise, considering who its father was. Was it misshapen?"

"She said she never saw the body."

Jack held up a hand. "Wait-wait-wait. How can that be?"

"Yeah, I know. Weird. She said she'd had a glimpse before they whisked him away, but after that . . . 'They wouldn't let me see him.' Those were her exact words."

Jack knew as much about labor and delivery as about particle physics, but he figured every mother had a right to see her baby, even dead.

And then he knew.

"They lied to her. It's alive."

"Why would anyone—?"

"This is a unique child, a unique *being*. Somebody wants to keep its existence secret, even from its mother. Did she say where she's been staying until now?"

"No. She might have come around to mentioning it, but you knocked on the door. And I guess we'll never know if we're going to avoid her like she's Typhoid Mary."

Jack wanted to know . . . needed to know. But was that wise? Maybe that was why she had been put here—to make them seek out the answer to the question of the baby's purpose.

But which side would the answer benefit? That was the bigger question.

"Let's put Dawn aside for a moment and deal with a more immediate problem: Eddie seems to be on the Order's hit list."

Weezy shot from her seat, her hand against her mouth.

"Oh, no! Are you sure?"

He told her about the shoot-out.

"I think we have to assume he was on a one-way ride. And that means we have to disappear him like we did you."

"Eddie's going to be tougher."

Jack nodded. "A lot tougher."

Weezy had kept most of the considerable proceeds from her share of her parents' estate, swelled by her father's death benefit, under her maiden name. The Order had been looking for someone named Myers, so she'd had time to transfer them to a new identity. Eddie wouldn't have that luxury.

"Where is he?"

"He's stashed in Abe's garage, but he can't stay there very long. It's not meant for human habitation."

"He can move in with me. I've got a spare—"

Jack shook his head. "Not a good idea. We have to assume they know you're here. They may be out there watching for him, expecting him to run to his sister. You two have got to stay separate."

"But where—?"

"I'm going to take him over to Ernie, just like I did you. We'll get him some papers then start building him a new ID."

"If he needs money—"

"He's okay for now."

"Poor Eddie. He's losing everything . . . his home, his business . . . everything he's worked for."

Jack sensed guilt in her tone. Weezy hadn't had much of a life after her husband offed himself, rarely leaving her house, virtually no social contact except Eddie, so going into hiding hadn't been an appreciable change in lifestyle.

"I don't see any other way."

She wandered over to the window. "I warned him. Why wouldn't he listen?"

Jack shrugged. He understood. "He thought his sister might be in trouble so he got involved. Trouble is, he's a direct guy. He's not cut out for that sort of thing."

"Yeah, but now his life is ruined." Her voice thickened as she stared out at the city. "And it's all my fault."

"Bullshit. He's a grown man who made a choice—a noble one, I might add."

"But he'd never have had to make that choice if I'd kept my mouth shut and stayed out of the Order's business."

"You smelled something rotten and cried foul."

She turned to face him, her eyes red. Her words came in a rush.

"And did I change one damn thing? No. Life goes on just as before, with the same people pulling the same strings and everybody dancing to their tune while Eddie and I are both in hiding, which is better than dead, I guess, which is what we'd both be if not for you."

"Easy, Weezy. It'll be all right. We take it a day at a time. And who knows . . . I mean, who knows how much time we really have left?"

"You mean about everything ending in the spring?"

He nodded. "Yeah."

"We're losing, aren't we."

"We're not winning, that's for damn sure. And we'll never win as long as we let them keep us on the defensive."

She said, "We don't seem to have much choice."

"It only seems that way—because they have a center, a focal point, a *leader*. We don't."

"We have Veilleur."

Jack shook his head. . . . Glaeken. But Glaeken wasn't Glaeken anymore.

"Who won't let me go on the offensive. He's old, he's tired, he's fading. He's got only a few more years left and he knows it. He's ready to pack it in. But the One, the Adversary, R, or whatever we're calling him at the moment—he's immortal, he's got powers, and he smells blood. He's going for the kill."

"It's like those lines from 'The Second Coming' . . . 'The best lack all conviction, while the worst are full of passionate intensity.' "

"I guess it *is* a second coming of sorts. He lost out in the First Age, but now he's back to get it right. And he's got troops to help. The Otherness maintained an active infrastructure during the half millennium the One was imprisoned, while the Ally let its own deteriorate."

"And hasn't done much to rebuild it since the One's rebirth," she said. "Plus the other side's got something we don't: a specific goal."

Jack knew exactly what she meant. "Kill the Lady."

A bizarre errant thought popped into his head and he brushed it away before it could complete itself. Something must have shown in his expression.

"What?" Weezy said.

"Nothing."

"You just made a strange face. What? Maybe it's important."

"Oh, trust me, it's not important."

"Can I decide that?"

"Okay. Don't say I didn't warn you. For an insane instant I heard a strange little voice singing in my head. It went"—he did his best approximation of Elmer Fudd—*'I'm going to kill the Waaaaaady!'* " He watched Weezy's features go slack. "Warned you. Happy now?"

She stared at him a long moment. "You know . . . the way your mind indexes and references is a little disturbing."

"A *little*? You should be on this side of it."

"Not to mention inappropriate at times."

"Yeah, that too. But we're off topic. Let's get back to their goal of killing the Lady—which, by the way, brings us full circle: We're on defense again—or should I say, as usual."

Jack had been racking his brain but couldn't come up with any way of taking the battle to them outside of a direct assault.

Weezy said, "That's always the problem with the conservative position."

"Who's conservative?"

"Well, in the basic, non–political/philosophical meaning of the term, we are. We're trying to preserve the status quo, while they're the radicals, trying to undermine it."

Me . . . a conservative. What a kick in the head.

But when he thought about it . . .

"I've never been a fan of the status quo, but when you consider the alternative these creeps have got waiting in the wings . . ."

Weezy nodded. "The status quo we're protecting now is the Lady's existence. On our side is the fact that nothing of Earthly origin can harm her, including the One himself, since he's human. The only way to strike at her is indirectly—through the noosphere."

"And they seem to be trying to strike at that via the Internet."

"Right. By bringing it down."

Jack said, "But the Internet's already got a whole slew of governments protecting it, and it's so diffuse and redundant it's virtually impossible to bring down. So I don't see how we can be useful on that front."

"Speaking of the Internet, what was supposed to be in that email you sent me?"

"What email?"

"About an hour ago."

"I haven't been home since early this morning. I checked my email then but didn't send any. And you know I don't have a BlackBerry or anything like that. What did I say?"

"Nothing. It was blank." She frowned. "Ooh, I don't like that."

"What's wrong?"

"You may have picked up a virus."

"Show me the email."

He followed her to the laptop sitting on the kitchen counter. She wiggled the mouse, the screen came to life, she clicked around, then pointed to the screen.

"There. Empty subject line, empty body."

Jack didn't use email very often, and when he replied to strangers inquiring at repairmanjack.com, he used a pseudonymous remailer. The site used a webmail account on a different server from the Web site. Neither host knew him or his whereabouts, and didn't care so long as the money order for the annual fee arrived on time. This was from the Gmail account he used for the rare email he sent to even rarer friends.

"Come to think of it, I got a blank email from Abe this morning."

Weezy was clicking around again. "Damn. Three more emails with no subject line." More mousing. "All blank. I think we've got a virus running here. I could be infected too. Weird. My firewall should have stopped it."

He thought about Valez stealing Munir's code. Related? But Munir's code was for an online game.

"What do we do?"

"I'll check it out later." She straightened and looked at him. "Right now we need to figure out what we do about Dawn."

An idea had been growing. Not a battle plan so much as a path to explore.

"I'm going to look into this baby. See if it's really dead."

"How're you going to do that?"

Jack smiled. "A friend at the city morgue. Every dead newborn or even a stillborn past twenty weeks' gestation gets a death certificate."

"And you know this how?"

He felt his smile vanish. "Emma."

Weezy looked away, then back. "Oh. Right. Sorry."

"Anyway, if her baby's really dead, then that ends that trail. If not, then we do our damnedest to find out why they want it. If it's been spirited off, then I'm pretty sure whoever's behind it is connected to the One in one way or another. And if the baby's important to the One, it's important to us."

Weezy nodded. "Sounds logical. Find out where she's been hiding during her pregnancy and we'll have a good idea who's got the baby. But I can see only one way to learn that."

So did Jack and he didn't like it.

"Yeah. Ask her."

"And that means contact with her, which you think is a bad idea."

"Because it's pretty obvious that's why she was put here: to make contact with you."

"Well, let's fall for it. Except we won't be falling for it. We'll be going in with our eyes open. That way we might be able to turn the situation to our advantage."

Jack wasn't so sure. He had a feeling this kind of second-guessing could lead them in circles.

"First thing for me to do," he said, "is find out how many newborns died yesterday morning."

"And I'll start combing Craigslist for a sublet for Eddie."

"Good." That was how they'd found this sublet for Weezy. "If one of the dead newborns was Dawn's, we're back to square one. But if not . . ."

"Then we start looking for the baby."

Jack had a thought. "What if they want us to find the baby?"

"Well, then I think they'd have let Dawn keep it when they moved her in across the hall."

"Maybe they want us to work for it."

She gave him a sidelong look. "Are we overthinking here?"

"Could be. We could end up in a poisoned-cup debate."

She rolled her eyes. "*The Princess Bride*?"

"Sorry."

He couldn't escape the way his mind worked. And he couldn't escape the uneasy feeling that they were missing something.

15. Munir ignored the incessant rings from his inbox. A blizzard of emails was filling it. They seemed to be coming from everyone he knew and even some he didn't—or didn't recognize. And not just one from each, but multiples, all without a subject line, all blank. He had stopped opening them.

Somebody somewhere had a virus.

When the storm abated he'd delete them en masse. Right now he was more interested in the rootkit virus that Valez had forced him to allow into his computer. It had hijacked his system and refused to be removed.

It gave him something to do. Barbara was at the hospital at Robby's side—they were taking shifts—and Munir was supposed to be here at home resting. But he couldn't rest. Robby would be back in a day or two and they'd have to start dealing with the aftermath of all this horrendous trauma. This was a way of keeping his mind occupied.

He'd located the virus but it had integrated itself so deeply into his system that he could not pry it loose. Three times now he thought he had eradicated it, but it reappeared each time he rebooted his system.

And then he realized this wasn't the original rootkit. A second virus, introduced sometime since Tuesday, had overlaid the first.

He could see it now: This had to be related to the email assault. But what was the purpose? It wasn't even slowing down his machine. It was merely annoying.

He wished he could contact Russ. He'd been calling him all day, ever since Valez had said he'd heard of the game code from Russ. Munir couldn't believe he'd been involved in any way with what had befallen him and his family, but he needed to know the connection between the two. He also needed Russ's hacker expertise to help eradicate this virus.

Of course, Munir could simply wipe his hard drive clean and reinstall everything. A simple, effective solution, but he was loath to admit defeat.

After another half hour of tinkering, he finally managed to break into the rootkit's code.

What he found there sent him running to the phone to call Russ.

But once again Russ wasn't answering. So Munir called Jack.

16.   First thing Jack did when he got home was check his various email accounts. All had multiple blank letters with no subject line from seemingly everyone he'd ever emailed. Not a large number, since he preferred the ephemeral nature of a phone call to committing words to electronic blips that could conceivably exist forever in cyberspace.

Conspicuously absent from the in-box were Gia and Vicky. Gia liked to send him a link now and again, and he'd occasionally shoot Vicky a cartoon or joke he thought she'd like. But Gia was about twelve hundred miles away from her computer.

Weezy said he'd caught a virus. Where from? Abe's email? Did these other folks have it too? Whatever, he'd leave finding a solution to Weezy. The intricacies of the Net were a mystery to him and he was content to let them remain so.

He checked his voice mail and found a message from Munir saying he had to talk to him, immediately.

Yeah, in a minute. Someone else he had to talk to first.

He called Ron Clarkson for the second time in two

days. Ron worked at the city morgue in Bellevue. He'd probably think Jack was calling with a complaint about the color-matched finger he'd supplied for Munir, but Jack only needed him to answer a question this time.

"Hey," he said when he recognized Jack's voice. *"Figured you might be calling."*

"It's not about the merchandise," Jack said. "That was fine."

It had all been for nothing, but none of that was Ron's fault.

"Well, I'm glad to hear that, but I was talking about Russ."

"Russ who?"

"Tuit. Who else? I thought you was calling 'cause you'd heard the news."

Not something Jack wanted to hear from a morgue attendant.

"Aw jeez, you're not telling me—"

"Yeah. Fished him out of the Hudson this morning, poor guy. Looks like he drowned."

Jack couldn't speak for a moment. Russ . . . geeky, good-natured, harmless Russ. The feds listed him as a felon, but he was one of the least violent people Jack knew. His crime had been hacking a few banks and skimming a fraction of a cent off their transactions. For years he'd been Jack's go-to guy for all things cyber—to solve a problem or sometimes create one. When Jack had been looking for a contact in the morgue, Russ had put him in touch with Ron.

"Any signs of foul play?"

"I ain't the ME, but preliminary word is no."

Jack wasn't buying that for a second.

"Shit."

"Yeah. Good guy. Coulda knocked me over with a feather when I heard. But if you didn't call about Russ—?"

Jack told him about looking for a newborn who died Wednesday morning.

"Piece o' cake," Ron said. *"Lemme run a check on the computer and call you right back."*

Jack hung up and stared at his computer screen. Valez said they'd heard about Munir's game code from Russ. How? Bigger question: Why kill him?

Because Jack had no doubt Russ had been murdered. Drowned in the Hudson? No doubt true. No sign of foul play? Easy enough to do. Take a guy out on the river for a party or a girl or some weed, whatever, and push him over. The water out there in February is not much above freezing. No matter how good a swimmer he is, he can't last fifteen minutes, if that, before his muscles seize up and he sinks.

No sign of foul play . . . not one bit. And if you liquor him up a little beforehand, the ME's got all he needs to construct a neat little scenario: He got drunk and fell into the river.

Bastards.

Or maybe . . . maybe he *had* jumped or fallen. Maybe he'd been involved in what had happened to Munir and felt so guilty—

Not Russ. If he'd wanted the game code, he could have gotten it without all the drama that had gone down. All he'd have had to do was ask Munir for a copy.

No, Russ had not been involved. But for some reason, he had been murdered.

His cell rang and he recognized Ron's voice.

"That was fast."

"Told ya. Piece o' cake . . ."

17. Munir took Russ's death pretty hard.

Jack had figured he would. They'd been friends, working together on a freelance project. And the way Russ had gone to bat for Munir when he was in trouble said a lot about how close they were.

So that was one of the reasons Jack had come over for a face-to-face. The other was his naïveté about the world of computer viruses. He figured he'd understand better in person.

So the two of them sat in Munir's computer room. Jack watched him rub his teary eyes and struggle to get a grip. Finally he did.

"Do you really think it was an accident?" he said.

"Not saying it's impossible, but my gut says no."

"That leaves murder."

Jack nodded. "Yes, it does."

"If that is so, then it makes it more important than ever to find out who's behind this virus. Because if we find them, we find the people behind Valez and the ones who murdered Russ."

Jack had already come to that conclusion—and knew the answer—but how had Munir arrived at the same place?

"What makes you say that?"

"On Tuesday morning Valez sent me an email. Just opening it allowed a virus into my system. That isn't supposed to happen. Email programs were vulnerable to that back in the day, but the glitch was fixed. Nowadays no program allows an email to execute code just by being read or previewed. Usually you have to click on a link or do something to allow the virus in. But this one has some new workaround." He gave Jack a quizzical look. "Low-level binary data bursts on open ports, maybe?"

"You're asking *me*?"

"Sorry. Whatever they're doing, the upshot is the hijacking of your system."

"Like hijacking a car?"

"Exactly. It takes over the driver's seat. And what this one does is invade your email address books, cull all the addresses, and then send a blank email to everyone on your lists."

Jack nodded. "I got one this morning from an old friend."

"And you opened it?"

"Well, yeah."

"Of course you did. It's only natural. You recognize the sender so you open it. But each email the virus sends out contains a copy of itself. That email from your old friend's infected system infected your system as well, then emailed itself to everyone in your address book."

"Not many."

"It doesn't matter. Every computer you infected went on and sent infected mail to every computer in its address book, and then each of those did the same, and on and on. It's a geometric progression with an unfixed, ever expanding ratio. It must be creating a tidal wave of email around the globe."

Tidal wave . . . tidal waves destroy things.

"Around the globe? Wouldn't that take a while?"

Munir shook his head. "Not at all. A geometric progression can do astounding numbers in almost no time. There's an old story about a king paying a dowry for his daughter. The prince asked simply that he place a single grain of rice on one square of a chessboard, two grains on the next, four on the third, eight on the fourth, and so on, doubling on each square up to the final, sixty-fourth square."

"I can see how that might involve a lot of rice."

"A 'lot'? Try a little over one-point-eight times ten to the nineteenth power. That's eighteen quadrillion grains of rice. A quadrillion is a billion billions. The entire world produces only a fraction of that in a year."

Jack nodded. Impressive.

"So this virus—"

"If each infected computer infects just two new computers every minute—and we know it infects many times more because of all the email addresses people store—it will pass the two-billion mark in just over half an hour—thirty-two minutes, to be exact."

"And how many computers in the world?"

"We hit the billion mark in 2008. We may be nearing a billion and a half now. Of course, it can only infect those computers that open email. But how many computers don't have email? And it would have to wait through a twenty-four-hour cycle for people around the world to wake up and check their email. So, in a single day it's conceivable that it could have infected a billion computers—and that's a conservative estimate."

A *billion*?

"Could this bring down the Internet?"

He saw the Lady's imaginary mountain lake, its water spilling downhill through the damaged wall . . . saw its feeder tributary from the Internet choking off . . . the lake drying up . . . the Lady disappearing . . .

Munir shook his head. "Not even close. It's a spam tsunami, but the Internet can easily absorb it."

That was a relief, but then . . .

"What's the point?"

"Sometimes it's prankish maliciousness, simply to cause trouble. Other times there's a definite purpose—like creating a botnet. That's what I think we have here."

"Means nothing to me."

"All right. Let's see. My computer is now what can be called a zombie or a slave or a robot—it's under someone else's control. So is yours. So is everyone in our address books who opened email from us. If you link up all our zombie machines, you've got a robot network, or botnet, that you can force into coordinated efforts. A botnet can be used to assault another system with what's known as a DDoS attack—a distributed denial of service. It uses all the computers in its network to target a system and overwhelm it with a barrage of traffic and shut it down."

"So this virus is creating a *global* botnet."

Munir nodded. "I'm sure it already has, one that's still growing. I'm also sure that governments are already aware of it and looking for a way to stop it. Unfortunately, it's way too soon for the antiviral companies to have a fix."

"Then somebody needs to get the word out not to open any email with a blank subject line, especially if it's from someone they know."

Munir shook his head. "Too late for that."

Jack swallowed. "Could *this* bring down the Internet?"

"No. The Internet's too big, too resilient. Besides, bringing down the Internet is the last thing hackers want. That's where they live. It would be like burning down their own home."

"A psycho might burn down his own home."

"Yes, but this isn't one psycho. This is a well-organized, well-funded group. Trust me, they want to *use* the Internet, bend it to their will, not bring it down."

Well, Jack thought, he's right about the well-organized and well-funded part, but dead wrong about its purpose.

"But they stole the code you were using for that Magog game."

"The *MMO* game."

"Whatever." These acronyms were going to drive him nuts. "What's that got to do with this email virus?"

"I found a piece of my code in the virus. It's something I wrote for the gaming program to accelerate upload and download of video. It triples, quadruples video transfer speed, depending on your bandwidth."

"What good is that?"

"The only thing I can think of is that at some point they're going to send a video message throughout the botnet."

"To what? Sell Viagra?"

"No," he said in a grave tone. Probably thought Jack was serious. "It must be something bigger than that."

"Ya think?"

"It may be propaganda, or a religious message."

Jack couldn't see that. The Order operated behind the scenes. Coming out in a video fed to a zillion computers in a botnet didn't make sense. Had to be something more sinister.

"You're *sure* they couldn't use it to crash the Internet?"

Munir shook his head. "I am telling you, these people want to *use* the Internet, not bring it down."

Munir was refusing to get on board that train, so he wasn't going to be much help in building a scenario of how an Internet kill might work.

"Gotta go," Jack said, rising. "Meeting some people later."

"If we could get hold of Valez," Munir said, "we could wring the answer out of him."

Obviously he hadn't heard. How could he? The victims' names hadn't been released yet.

"Valez won't be telling anyone anything. He's dead."

He gave Munir the news account of the shooting: According to the police, both the driver and his passenger had been shot by the mystery man in the mystery van from Mississippi. Logical assumption. Ballistics would square that eventually, not that it mattered.

He looked horrified. "Who *are* these people? What kind of monsters are they?"

You don't want to know, Jack thought. You really don't.

He pointed to Munir. "As you said, well organized and well financed. And smart. Smart enough to keep any of their people on the lower rungs from knowing the big picture. Even if Valez were alive, I don't think he could help us. I think he knew he was supposed to acquire your game code and little else. He had no idea what it would be used for. But my guess is he went too far with you and paid the price. What I don't get is Russ . . . how'd he get involved?"

Munir leaned back and looked like he might puddle up again, but he held on.

"I've been thinking about that, and as I've been explaining this virus to you, the pieces began to fit. Do you know what Russ was involved with lately?"

Jack remembered him telling him something at Julio's . . .

"Some government project to foil hackers. Said he was a 'white hat' now."

Munir nodded. "Yes. A team of hackers, supposedly put together by the NRO."

" 'Supposedly'?"

"I don't believe the project had anything to do with national defense. I think they were put together to come up with this virus."

"He told me they were doing protection. Said they'd been building firewalls higher, wider, and smarter than anything else out there."

Munir looked at him. "And how do you test a firewall?"

Oh, crap. "You create bigger and better ways to breach it."

Munir jerked a thumb at his computer. "And if that was the case, neither the NRO nor any other agency would want their name connected. I think the one thing we can be certain of is that whoever hired Russ was not who they said they were. Maybe it was some other agency, or some group outside the government."

The latter, Jack thought. The Ancient Fraternal Septimus Order.

"You think Russ helped design that?"

"Yes. It's a very elegant virus, revolutionary, you could say. You would need a team of experienced hackers—just the sort of blue-ribbon team Russ was working with—to come up with something like that. I think in his conversations with the other hackers he must have mentioned the MMO game enhancer we were working on. He had been impressed with my video code and probably talked about it. The wrong person overheard, and I was targeted. But they couldn't have Russ around when they inserted my code. He'd recognize it. So . . ."

"So they killed him."

Munir slammed a fist on his desk. "They could simply have fired him!"

Yeah, they could have. But death seemed the Order's favorite way of dealing with problem people.

"Do you see any way of stopping this?"

Munir shook his head. "Until someone writes a program to kill it, you can stop the spread by not opening emails with no subject line. But the virus has too much of a head start. And once in your system, it's almost impossible to remove. It hides in multiple areas. You think you've gotten all of it, but if you've missed any, it immediately regenerates itself the next time you power up."

"Swell."

18. "A global botnet created by a virus built to download video," Weezy said with a slow shake of her head. "To what end?"

Jack, Weezy, Veilleur, and the Lady sat around the table in the Lady's apartment. With Weezy's help, Jack had explained as best he could what he'd learned from Munir. They seemed to understand.

"That's the big question," Jack said.

A wild scenario flashed through his brain.

"What if they plan to broadcast a never-ending loop of a hypnotic chant which, if repeated often enough by millions upon millions of people, would part the veil between the worlds and let the Otherness flood in. Or maybe show non-Euclidean designs that if enough people copy will alter geometry and have the same effect."

Veilleur and the Lady stared at him uncomprehendingly. Weezy gave him the same look as this afternoon after his Elmer Fudd remark.

"This isn't an H. P. Lovecraft story, Jack. This is serious business."

"I know that. But if their goal isn't an Internet crash, I've got to ask myself what else it can be. And this is what pops up."

She shook her head. "Your mind . . . the Order playing '*Cthulhu fhtagn*' over and over?"

"Well, not those exact words, I suppose. Okay. Dumb idea. I'm just throwing things out as they hit me. Here's something else that hit me on the way over: Could the release of this virus have anything to do with the birth of Dawn's baby?"

Weezy's eyes widened. "Did you find out about him? Is he alive?"

Jack nodded. "I can't say it's alive, but it wasn't reported dead. No death certificate filed on a newborn with Wednesday morning time of death."

"According to Dawn, the baby's a 'he,' not an 'it.' And I think we have to assume he's alive."

Veilleur said, "Is this the baby laden with the Taint?"

The term threw Jack for an instant, then he remembered that back in the First Age they called oDNA the Taint.

"That's the one."

After Jack explained the situation, Veilleur looked at Weezy.

"I don't like her moving in next to you. That cannot be an accident."

"Exactly," Jack said.

Weezy shrugged. "No argument. But that's the way it is, so we've got to deal with it."

Veilleur continued to stare at her. "She said nothing else about these so-called 'birth defects'?"

"She said she only got a glimpse of him before they whisked him away. Supposedly he'd stopped breathing."

Veilleur stroked his beard. "I'm interested in those birth defects. If you speak to her again, ask her what she saw. Any details at all."

"Why?" Jack said.

"Just . . . curious. A creature so rife with the Taint might have predictable deformities."

"Like what?" Jack said.

"Let's wait until you hear what the mother has to say."

Weezy looked offended. " 'Creature'? It's a child."

The Lady shook her head. "One so heavy with the Taint might not be quite human."

Weezy paled and said nothing.

Jack tried to steer the talk back to his original question.

"The baby was born yesterday morning. The virus shows up all over today, which means it was probably released yesterday. Connection?"

Weezy shrugged. "Maybe. But synchronicity doesn't signify a causal relationship."

"Thank you, Ms. Sting."

She offered a sour smile. "That's Ms. Sumner to you."

"I agree," Veilleur said. "But I think we must assume a connection. The people behind the virus could very well be the people who hid Dawn away during her pregnancy. My money is on the Order. So yes, there's a connection. But whether the baby's birth triggered the release of the virus, I can't say."

Jack said, "Fair enough. But I think the baby should be our focus now. It's the only lead we have. It's important to someone—important enough to hide its mother away during her pregnancy and then lie about it dying. So that, I think, makes it important to us."

"We have to consider that the baby might be dead and unreported," Weezy said. "There might have been something about his deformities, whatever they were, they didn't want made public."

Jack looked at her. "Do you buy that?"

"Not for a second, but it is a possibility."

Veilleur said, "The child is an enigma at this point. It had its origins in a crude plot conceived by Jonah Stevens to create a descendant richer in the Taint than any other living being. But you all know that."

Jack nodded along with the others. "But how did he know about the Taint?" He glanced at Weezy. "Or oDNA?"

"As a boy he lost his left eye in the Great Lower Mississippi Valley flood. After that he began to have visions in whatever was left of that eye."

Jack thought of Diana and her dad. "Sort of an Oculus for the Otherness."

"I suppose. Back in the spring of 1941, after I slew the One—at least his physical form—his essence, instead of dissipating, found a place to hide: the body of a unique human infant."

"Unique how?" Weezy said.

"I'll save that for another day. Suffice it to say that the Ally was unaware of this, and decided it didn't need me anymore, and so it freed me to grow old and die."

"After millennia of service?" Jack said. "Some reward."

Veilleur smiled. "After all those millennia of watching loved ones die while I went on . . . trust me, it was a magnificent boon. But the Otherness knew where the essence of its champion hid, and it brought in a protector: Jonah Stevens. The visions led Jonah to adopt that unique human infant—the 'vessel,' the One's unknowing host. The One was trapped within that helpless little body, a passive passenger, unable to exert any influence. Jonah's task was to guard the vessel until he grew to be a man who fathered a very special child."

"The One," Jack said.

Pieces were falling together.

"When was that?" Weezy said. "You've mentioned he'd been reborn a number of times, but when exactly was this?"

"I believe the exact date of his reconception was on or about February tenth, 1968, in the village of Monroe on Long Island. He was reborn November seventh in Hickory Hill, Arkansas."

Jack shook his head. "Eleven-seven. Supposed to be lucky numbers."

"Not so lucky. After the One's rebirth into a new body, to a new life devoted to the cause of the Otherness, Jonah stayed with him and his mother, guarding him as he grew. But I believe the part of him that made him uniquely suited for the guardian post also led to his eventual betrayal of his charge."

"That's why he's no longer with us," Jack said.

Veilleur nodded. "Exactly. For a while he took his job seriously, moving the child and his mother throughout the South to elude any Ally-influenced people who might try to harm him."

"So there was a movement to stop him?"

"Yes, but not terribly ambitious. It very nearly succeeded in Monroe, but fell apart after a horrific failure. I doubt that whatever iota of the Ally remains involved here considers him much of a threat. The One has been very circumspect, very cautious.

"But back to Jonah. As the One grew, so did his powers, and Jonah came to see a day coming soon when he would no longer be needed. From his visions he knew that he had been chosen as the guardian because of his bloodline, which we can assume meant he carried an abnormally high level of the Taint—supremely high. But he decided it could be higher. So he began his plan to concentrate it further, to create a child with a Taint so deep and so dark that it could replace the child he guarded and become the One. Then the One would be Jonah's progeny."

"Putting his bloodline in the catbird seat when the Otherness took over?" Jack said. "How was loading a child with the Taint going to accomplish that? I don't follow the logic."

Weezy shook her head. "Neither do I."

"It would not have worked," the Lady said.

Veilleur shrugged. "He may have known something we do not, or he may have misinterpreted some of his visions. But as it turned out, he never had a chance to find out. The One learned of the plot and, though occupying the body of a ten-year-old boy at the time, arranged a slow agonizing death for Jonah Stevens."

Weezy winced. "Do I want to know how?"

"Crushed in an elevator shaft. Took him hours to die."

"I could have lived without knowing that."

"Speaking of knowing," Jack said, "how'd you learn all this? I doubt you got it from the One."

Veilleur smiled. "I've become acquainted with the One's mother—I suppose I should say his most recent mother. He's had three."

Jack saw Weezy's jaw drop, then realized his own was gaping.

"He had a mother?"

The One's mother . . . the idea that that cold-blooded freak had had someone to nurture him when he was young and helpless . . . well, of course he did, but it boggled Jack's mind. If only she'd been careless . . . left the gate to the pool area open . . . something, anything . . .

He waved a hand in the air. "Never mind. Of course he did. Even you had a mother, I suppose."

"Naturally, though I remember nothing about her. The only one in this room who never had a mother is the Lady."

"The noosphere is my mother . . . and my father."

"Okay," Jack said. "But let's get back to this woman. You know the One's mother?"

Veilleur nodded. "We've become good friends. Quite a story she has, raising the One. She knew there was something very different about him, something wrong with him, but had no idea of the magnitude of his evil."

"I don't suppose he keeps in touch with her."

"Oh, right," Weezy said. "He really seems the kind to send Mother's Day cards."

"No contact. Ever. He left home at age fifteen with thirty million dollars and never looked back. As far as he was concerned, she was an incubator, nothing more."

"Can she help us find Dawn's baby?"

Veilleur shook his head. "She knows nothing of Dawn Pickering or her baby, or Dawn's relationship to Jonah Stevens. You're on your own, I'm afraid."

Jack looked across the table at Weezy. "I guess we'll have to invite Dawn over tomorrow for a chat. You make the tea, I'll bring the crumpets."

"You're going to let her see you? You said she knows you."

He smiled. "I'm ninety-nine percent sure she'll remember me. And I think I can make it a fond memory." Weezy gave him a puzzled look. "I'll explain tomorrow."

FRIDAY

I. "What is the state of your investigations?" Ernst said from the rear of his Bentley as it cruised the city.

He'd given his driver the day off and replaced him with Szeto. His usual driver knew nothing about Jihad4/20, and would live longer by remaining ignorant.

Szeto half turned his battered face to speak through the opening in the glass partition between them.

"Connell has not gone to police. Instead he made large withdrawals from bank accounts yesterday as soon as he escaped."

That wasn't good. It showed a cool head at work. Probably not Connell's. He was an actuary, a number cruncher, who had sat only inches from the cold-blooded murder of two men. His likely response was panic.

"I see the hand of the Connell guardian angel. I think we can assume our brother will not be going to the police. If he's carrying a large amount of cash, it's obvious he's going into hiding. We may have to resort to putting out a BOLO on him."

Szeto shook his head. "That will not help if he goes to Wyoming like sister."

"No, but if he's hiding, he's silent, and that will be a good thing."

If they didn't find him, it was not the end of the world. Ernst shook his head at the phrase. *End of the world* . . .

the end of the world, at least as anyone knew it, was just around the corner.

But he couldn't allow the imminence of the Change to lull him into complacency. So easy to slip into the attitude that the Change will make all these concerns irrelevant, so why bother?

"What about that other investigation?"

"The boy Jack from New Jersey?"

"That would be it."

Szeto said, "I find record of him in the town of Johnson, as you said, but little beyond that."

Ernst frowned. "Where is he now?"

A shrug. "He went to local high school, to state college but did not graduate. After that, nothing."

"*Nothing?* There's no such thing as *nothing* unless you're dead."

"Much bad luck in family. Parents and sister dead, brother missing, wanted by Philadelphia police and may be dead too. Perhaps your Jack from New Jersey is also dead."

"No. Connell told me he's some sort of repairman. His Social Security number will—"

"I could not find Social Security number."

"Ridiculous. Every American has one."

"Was not necessary when he was child. Maybe he never get."

How interesting. No SSN and working as a repairman. Thinking back on his encounters with the teen, he remembered how strong a Taint he had. And he'd sensed a deep independent streak coursing through him. Repairs were often paid for in cash. Yes, he could well imagine a grown-up Jack dodging taxes and—

Ernst stiffened in his seat.

And killing to protect his friends?

No.

He forced himself to relax.

Rich though he was with the Taint, Jack had exhibited no violent tendencies. But could something in his life have brought the Taint to the surface, changing him?

Possible . . .

But highly unlikely.

Szeto had described this guardian angel as highly skilled—a "ninja," he'd called him. That bespoke training. In real life the grown-up Jack was most likely just as he appeared on paper: a college dropout living off the books as a repairman.

Still . . . too many blank spaces in that picture. Ernst did not like blanks. And did not want another crossed path from that little town in New Jersey circling back on him.

"Keep after both of them," he told Szeto. "In the meantime . . ." He reached for the radio button. "Let's see what's going on in the world."

He scanned the channels until . . .

"*. . . and so far, beyond filling in-boxes with avalanches of blank emails, the virus appears to be more of a nuisance than a threat to the computers it has infected. And it has infected many. Experts estimate that more than half of the world's personal computers and networks have already been infected with this as yet unnamed virus, and the number is rapidly growing.*

"*If in the last forty-eight hours you've opened an email with no subject line and no content, you are probably infected. If you haven't, then it's very easy to avoid infection: Do not open any email with a blank subject line, no matter who it's from. Even if it's from your mother or your best friend—*especially *if it's from your mother or your best friend—DO NOT OPEN IT.*

"*Antivirus software companies are scrambling for a cure to release to their subscribers. Stay tuned here for the latest. We'll keep you posted on what you can do to clear this nuisance from your computer.*

"So far, no one has stepped forward to take credit—maybe we should say 'blame'—for the virus."

Ernst smiled as he turned off the radio. The world was aware of the virus. This was what he'd been waiting to hear.

"We'll remedy that right now. Has the video been uploaded?"

Szeto had been on his cell phone. He ended the call and said, "The video is up."

"Excellent."

He had obtained the number of Ellen Rifkin, one of the reporters for the ABC television network. He turned on a voice distorter and punched in the number. A woman answered.

"Rifkin."

"Ms. Rifkin," he said in a matter-of-fact tone. "I have news about the email virus."

"I'm listening," she said in a bored tone.

Ernst wondered how many of these calls the network was receiving.

"The virus is called Jihad four/twenty. To see a video with more details, search 'Jihad four/twenty' on YouTube."

He ended the call, then made similar calls to specific reporters at the *New York Times* and Fox News Network. That pretty much covered the political spectrum.

He opened the back of his prepaid phone and removed the battery. Then he pulled out the chip. He was carrying caution to an extreme, he knew, but it gave him comfort.

A Lebanese brother high in the Order had recorded the deliberately out-of-focus video just yesterday. He had recited the message in Arabic first, then repeated it in English.

Ernst turned the radio back on.

"It won't be long now."

2.   Jack arrived at Weezy's a little early. Dawn had accepted her invitation for coffee and Jack wanted to be there when she arrived.

He didn't get a chance to knock. As he raised his hand, the door swung open and Weezy grabbed his arm.

"Jack!" She pulled him in. "You've got to see this! It's all over the news."

"What is?"

He followed her to her computer where a YouTube video was running. She backed it up some and started it running again.

"Watch."

He saw some guy with his head and face wrapped in a patterned white keffiyeh babbling in a foreign language. What was this? Another al Qaeda slimeball with a threat against the world?

"What language is that? Arabic? You going to translate for me?"

He knew Arabic was one of the half dozen or so languages she spoke.

"I don't have to. He starts repeating it in English just about . . . now."

And sure enough, he broke into pretty decent English. He rambled on about Jihad4/20, the virus he'd released into the "Godless Internet," and how on April twentieth it would awaken and exorcise Satan and his demons from the world's computers by filling them with prayers of praise to Allah.

"So I was right," Jack said as the video ended. "The virus is some sort of prayer wheel. But instead of 'Cthulhu fhtagn,' it'll be 'Allah Akbar' or the like over and over."

She was staring at him.

"What?" he said.

"You're not serious."

He decided against putting her on any longer. She didn't seem in the mood. And besides . . . this wasn't funny.

"Of course not."

She looked relieved. "I never know with you."

"The video's bullshit."

She nodded as she glanced at her monitor. "Yes, it's bullshit. But remarkable bullshit. When I first watched it I thought of Eddie. You said he told you he'd overheard something about 'jihad' at the Lodge. This has to be it."

"And mentioning it to someone in the Order is most likely what earned him a death sentence."

"Poor Eddie," she said. "He had no idea what he was getting into."

"None of us did. Or do. What's this all about?"

"I don't think there can be any doubt: They're going to try to crash the Internet."

"But how? Not with prayers to Allah. And what's with the four/twenty? What's that mean?"

"April twentieth is Mohammed's birthday by the Gregorian calendar. At least it's supposed to be. I don't think anyone knows his exact birth date for sure. Happens to be Hitler's too, by the way. And the date of the Columbine massacre."

Anyone else and Jack would assume she'd Googled it before he came in, but he knew if he asked Weezy how she knew she'd just tell him she'd "read it somewhere."

"Well," he said, "the video with the Islamic angle is brilliant. It gives the virus a name, it gives the hacker a face—sort of—and makes praising Allah the motivation."

"Exactly. And so we all pigeonhole the group behind it as Islamic nuts and look no further."

Another angle hit him. "And maybe people don't look so hard for a cure because it's only going to be prayers, and they have a couple of months before anything happens."

"Do you believe that?"

He shook his head. "No way. If they've found a way to

crash the Internet with this virus, they're not going to wait until April twentieth. They'll go for it ASAP."

"Exactly."

"But *what* are they going to do?"

Weezy shrugged. "I have to assume it has something to do with Munir Habib's video transfer code, but how they intend to use it, I haven't the vaguest."

"Maybe his code is a red herring. Get the experts looking at that, thinking it'll be used to download the promised praise-Allah video, when all the while the virus is really aimed at something else."

"Like what?"

"Like wiping a zillion hard drives."

Weezy shook her head. "But that will affect only the infected computers, leaving the Internet up and running for the uninfected. And the fix for a wiped drive is a simple reinstall of software. Traffic would be back to normal in no time. The Internet itself has to be the target."

As he listened, a depressing thought took hold.

"Even if we knew what the Order was going to do, could we stop it?"

"Not unless we can convince everyone with an infected computer to turn it off and keep it off."

Jack made a face. "Oh, yeah. That'll happen."

"Even that might not work, because the virus could have the ability to turn on infected machines."

"So unless everyone unplugs their computer, we're screwed."

Weezy shrugged and looked down. "On that front, yes, considering the number of computers already infected. Plus we're a couple of nobodies against a global organization."

"Then we're back to finding Dawn's baby."

She nodded. "Speaking of which, she'll be here any minute."

3. Dawn arrived right on time.

Jack had managed only a brief glance at her yesterday—just long enough to recognize her face—but now he could see she'd put on a good twenty pounds since last summer. He rose as she entered the room.

"Dawn," Weezy said, "this is my friend, Jack."

Dawn frowned at him as they shook hands. "Do I know you? You look familiar."

"We met last spring in a bar in Queens . . . a place called Work."

A pause, and then her eyes widened and she stepped back. "You're that friend of Jerry's."

"I wouldn't say 'friend.' "

She took another backward step as she looked from Jack to Weezy. "Hey, what's going on here?"

"Just coffee and conversation," Weezy said. "Jack recognized you yesterday but wasn't sure you'd remember him."

"And I am *no* friend of Jerry's," he said. "Not by a long shot."

She stopped her retreat and pointed at him. "That's right! He went after you with a tire iron and you totally beat the crap out of him!"

That surprised him. He hadn't noticed her around at the time, but figured Jerry would have made up a story about being jumped or sucker punched. He hadn't known he'd had a witness. Jack had planned to tell her that he'd done that. Looked like he wouldn't have to.

"How nice," Weezy said.

"No, it was awesome! Like a jerk I felt sorry for Jerry then, but now I wish you'd whaled on him with his own tire iron."

"You saw that?"

"Yes! I was waiting in the car. But . . . but your name wasn't Jack, it was Joe something."

"Yeah. Joe Henry or something like that. I was, um, undercover."

"You're a cop?"

"No . . ." Here comes the hard part, the tough sell. "I was hired to check out Jerry Bethlehem. To dig up some dirt on him."

"That shouldn't have been too hard. He was a world-class creep. But who—?" Her already pale skin blanched a little further. "Oh, no. You're not going to tell me it was my mother."

"Afraid I am. She wanted something to use to drive a wedge between you two."

She looked shaky.

"Maybe you should sit down," Weezy said, stepping closer with a concerned look.

Dawn held up a hand. "No, I should go. Because you're lying to me."

"Hey, look," he said. "Maybe your mother could have handled it differently, but she was worried—"

"Oh, I know she hired someone. It just wasn't you."

Baffled, Jack looked for a way to respond.

"Um, yeah, it was," he said slowly. "When she approached me, she told me she needed to keep her daughter from making a terrible mistake. That sound familiar?"

He could tell by her expression that it did.

He related the details of what Christy Pickering had told him about how Jerry had insinuated himself into Dawn's life with the ploy of designing a video game together. He could see his words hitting home, but she still wasn't sold.

"Jerry could have told you that."

"Yeah, he could have, but he didn't." Time to start fudging the truth. "When I did a background check on him I couldn't learn anything about him—like he had no past. But eventually I found out he wasn't who he said he was."

"Who was he then?"

He didn't want to open *that* can of worms.

"A wanted criminal."

That didn't seem to faze her. "I'm so not surprised. Did you tell my mom?"

"I didn't get the chance. She was . . . gone before I could reach her."

He figured it best to keep the part about finding her body to himself.

She sat down, looking shaky again. "Then what?"

"I went looking for you but you dropped off the face of the Earth."

"I've been hiding from Jerry." Her tone had gone flat.

"All this time?"

She looked up. "I couldn't let him find me."

"But he's been dead since last spring."

Her eyes widened. "Last spring? I thought it was more recent."

"So you know?"

"I just heard. Mister Osala said Jerry died under a phony name, so nobody knew. He said—"

"Who's Mister Osala?"

"Why should I tell you anything about him?"

"Why not? Is it a secret?"

She shrugged. "I guess not. He was hiding me from Jerry. My mother hired him to investigate—"

"Two of us?" Jack said. "Does it seem logical that she'd hire two investigators?"

Jack didn't think of himself as a PI, but in this case he guessed he'd served as one.

"Totally not." She rubbed her temples. "I don't know . . . this is so not making sense. One of you has to be lying."

Jack pulled out his ace. He hoped it was enough.

"Remember that letter you received from Doctor Vecca?"

Her head snapped up. "How do you know about that?"

"It wasn't from her. I wrote it. I even delivered it to you personally—in a blond wig. Remember? It contained everything I'd learned about Jerry."

She stared at him, her eyes growing wider and wider. "Then you know . . . ?"

He nodded.

She looked up at Weezy. "You too?"

Weezy nodded.

Dawn buried her face in her hands. "Oh, God! I didn't want anyone else to know! Ever!"

Weezy put a hand on her shoulder. "No one blames you. You were the victim of a sick, sick man."

"And it's over," Jack said. "He's gone for good—out of your life, out of everyone's life."

"But I was so *stupid*!"

"You were young," Weezy said, squeezing her shoulder. "*That* was the problem."

Still young, Jack thought, leaning forward. "So who's this Mister Osala?"

"Jack," Weezy said with a warning tone. What was with the look she was giving him?

"What?"

"She's upset. Maybe later."

What was up with her? This was important.

"Just this one thing, okay?" Jack sat next to her. "Tell me about this Osala, Dawn."

She took a deep breath. "Well, he's very rich, lives in a duplex on Fifth Avenue overlooking the park. He said he'd made a promise to my mother to protect me and that's what he did."

"Why aren't you there now?"

She looked away. "He kicked me out. He said with Jerry dead, I was in no danger, so his obligation was up. He found me this apartment and—"

"*He* chose it for you?"

"Totally. Even paid the first six months' rent."

Jack couldn't help a glance at Weezy.

"What's wrong?" Dawn said.

"Weez, can you get me a pen and a piece of paper?"

"Right here."

She plucked a Sharpie and a yellow legal pad from the table. Jack took them and drew a crude figure. He held it up for her.

"Did you see anything like this around Mister Osala's house?"

She shook her head. "Never."

Damn.

"But," she added, "my obstetrician had something like that on his pocket watch."

Jack tensed. "And who set you up with the obstetrician?"

"Mister Osala."

He choked back a whoop. There was the connection: The Order had had its sights on the baby all along. They'd placed Dawn under the wing of a well-heeled member until she delivered, then they dumped her and spirited the baby away.

The question was, had they searched out Weezy just so

they could install Dawn across the hall? Seemed so. But to what end?

"What's that symbol mean?" Dawn said.

He didn't want to start in on the history of the Septimus Order. Weezy could handle that beautifully, but it wasn't where he wanted the conversation to go.

"Just a fraternal order . . . like the Masons."

Yeah, I wish.

"Enough of this," Weezy said from the kitchen. "Let's eat. I'm starving."

4. Dawn sipped coffee and nibbled on half of a sesame bagel with nothing on it. Weezy did the same, but was more aggressive with the coffee, draining cup after cup. Jack knew from the time they'd been apartment mates that she had an astounding capacity for caffeine.

Jack loaded his poppy-seed bagel with cream cheese and chomped.

"How are you feeling?" Weezy said.

They hadn't planned out a good-cop, bad-cop thing, but she seemed to be falling into the more touchy-feely role.

Dawn looked at her. "You never had a baby?"

Weezy shook her head.

"Well, then," Dawn said, "I'm sore. Not totally sore like I was yesterday, but sore."

Jack tried to imagine giving birth. Gave up. He'd tried many times while Gia was pregnant but his mind couldn't go there.

He wanted to ask Dawn about her baby but held back. He sensed Weezy tacking in that direction.

She tapped a finger against her temple. "How are you feeling up here?"

Dawn frowned. "What do you mean?"

"Emotionally. You've been living in somebody's house, now you're on your own. You were pregnant, now you're not. You just delivered a baby and . . ." Weezy shook her head. "That's got to get to you."

Jack could see Dawn withdrawing, shutting down. Weezy must have sensed it too. She reached out and touched her arm.

"I'm messing this up. What I'm trying to say is, if you're ever feeling down or lonely or just want to talk, I'm here all by myself too. I hardly ever go out, and sometimes I get lonely, so any time you want to talk or just come over to sit and read or watch TV with someone else around, feel free."

Jack thought Weezy might be laying it on a little thick, acting all mother hennish, which was not Weezy. Then it dawned on him that she wasn't playing good cop . . . this was genuine.

Dawn's voice was thick when she spoke. "Why do you care?"

Jack wanted the answer too.

Weezy looked flustered. "I . . . I'm not sure. You needed help yesterday, and you seem, I don't know . . . lost. I'm just offering to help until you find your bearings."

"Lost . . . yeah, you've got that right. I was headed for college, everything was going my way, but I screwed up *everything*." She looked like she might cry but got on top of it and turned to Jack. "What about you, Mister Thousand Questions? Why do you care?"

So many reasons . . . most he couldn't tell her.

But he knew one, as true as any of the others, that would mean something to her.

"Because I let your mother down."

Dawn blinked. "What? How?"

"I took too long getting the job done. In my defense, I didn't know a clock was ticking, and neither did she. She was gone before I could tell her I'd dug up something that would end your relationship with Jerry forever. She loved you fiercely, Dawn, and knew you'd be ruining your life with him."

"She had that so right. I just wish I'd seen it."

"She was ready to do anything to save you from him. Unfortunately she died not knowing she'd succeeded."

Dawn was staring at him. "So she didn't know about . . . ?"

Jack shook his head. "I was on my way to tell her. I figured it was news that needed to be delivered face-to-face, but I didn't get to her in time."

"So she died not knowing?"

He nodded.

She closed her eyes and let her head fall back. "Thank God!"

He glanced at Weezy and she gave him a small smile and an approving nod. Approving of what? Comforting her? Gaining her trust? Or both?

He cocked his head toward Dawn: *Your turn.*

"I'm sorry about your baby," Weezy said. "I won't pretend that I can imagine how that feels."

Dawn straightened and looked at her. "I'm not sure how it feels either. I totally didn't want the baby—"

"I can imagine why you wouldn't," Weezy said.

"I even tried to abort it. But now that they tell me he's dead . . ." She sighed. "You know, it wasn't his fault. He didn't, you know, ask to be conceived. He had nothing to do with it. He's totally an innocent bystander. But after he was born they told me he had neurological problems, 'incompatible with life' . . ."

Remembering Veilleur's request to find out about the birth defects, Jack said, "Weezy told me they didn't let you see him?"

"I got a peek." She made a face. "He looked hairy . . . black hair all over . . . kind of like a monkey, you know?"

Weezy said, "That could be lanugo. Some infants are born with a lot of body hair."

"I read about that while I was pregnant, but this seemed awfully thick. But that wasn't the weirdest . . ." She shook her head.

"What?" Weezy said.

"I thought he had . . . you're so not going to believe this."

"Try us," Jack said.

"Well, it looked . . . I only caught a glimpse . . . but it looked like he had . . . tentacles."

Jack felt queasy as he remembered how they'd been making Lovecraftian jokes about the Order's schemes, but this . . .

"You mean like an octopus?"

"No, they didn't have suckers or anything like that. They looked more like snakes . . . like slim little garter snakes."

"Instead of arms?"

"No, he had arms too, although his fingers looked kind of clawish. Two arms with a tentacle coming from . . . they looked like they were coming from his armpits."

Something stirred and rustled in the back of Jack's mind. Something long buried. He glanced at Weezy and saw she'd gone dead white.

He was about to ask her if she was all right when Dawn spoke again. She was staring straight ahead, oblivious to both of them.

"Maybe he's better off dead—*if* he's dead. I mean, they say he is, and I kind of wish I could believe them, but . . ."

Jack felt like he'd just stuck his finger in a live socket.

"Wait-wait-wait! You don't believe he's dead?"

She sighed. "I know it sounds totally paranoid, but you probably already think I'm crazy because of the tentacles, so I might as well go for the gold, right? No, I don't believe he's dead."

"And you base this on . . . ?"

She shrugged. "Mother's intuition? Or maybe the way they wouldn't let me see his body."

"What excuse did they give?"

"Well, he—Doctor Landsman—told me that since I'd already signed the adoption papers, he wasn't officially mine, and anyway, they'd already sent him to the morgue."

Jack glanced at Weezy. Some of her color was back but she didn't look right. What was upsetting her? Had she made a connection to something she'd read in the *Compendium*?

"Did you mention the tentacles?"

Dawn nodded. "He said I must have been hallucinating from all the stress of the delivery. Well, yeah, I was stressed, but not to the point where I was totally seeing things."

"But why do you think this doctor would lie to you?"

"Ready for more paranoia?"

Jack had to smile. "Bring it on. I eat it for breakfast, lunch, and dinner."

"Okay. Try this: Doctor Landsman always did the ultrasounds of the baby himself, never his tech, and he'd never let me see them. He'd show Mister Osala, but never me. I'm sure he knew about these deformities in advance, and so did Mister Osala. I've done some thinking. I think the adoption papers were fake. I think they've taken the baby themselves."

"Why?"

She shrugged. "I don't know. To experiment on? To put in a sideshow? I don't know. Call me paranoid if you want, but I just know they're lying to me. They are *so* lying to me."

Jack debated whether or not to tell her about his call to the morgue. As the mother, didn't she have a right to know?

"I don't think you're paranoid, Dawn. In fact, I'm pretty damn sure you're not."

She frowned. "What do you mean?"

"When Weezy told me how they wouldn't let you see your baby's body after he died, I had the same thought: No reason in the world they wouldn't show you unless they couldn't—because they had no body . . . because he wasn't dead. Now, granted, I've got a suspicious mind that sometimes leads me astray, but more often than not, it's on target."

Dawn straightened. "And this time?"

"Well, you tell me: No death certificate was filed for a newborn with a Wednesday morning time of death."

"I knew it!" She balled a fist. "I'm *not* crazy!" She looked at Jack and then Weezy. "But where is he? Where's my baby?"

"If I had to guess," Weezy said, "I'd say he's in this Mister Osala's house."

Dawn gasped. "No way! I was just—"

"Kicked out," Jack said, seeing the logic. "You had to go because he was expecting another guest." He ripped the top sheet off the legal pad and prepared to take notes. "First off, how do you spell his name?"

"O-s-a-l-a."

Jack printed that at the top of the sheet. Something about the name . . . but it wouldn't come.

"Okay, now tell me everything you know about Mister Osala and his place . . ."

5. "Jack," Weezy said as he followed Dawn out the door, "I need to talk to you about something."

He watched Dawn disappear into her apartment, then stepped back into Weezy's. The plan was for him to pay a visit to Osala's place and see if he could get in and find the baby, or evidence that a baby was living there.

"What's up?"

"Did Dawn's description of her baby stir up any memories?"

"Should it?"

He did remember a faint reaction, but it had been overshadowed by Dawn's belief that her baby was still alive.

"Covered with dark hair . . . clawlike hands . . . and tentacles? Ring any bells?"

"No."

"Back when we were teens . . . the basement of the Lodge . . . ?"

And then it hit.

"Oh, jeez!"

. . . the feeling of something coiling around his neck . . . black-furred paws scraping along concrete . . . a snakelike thing—maybe a tentacle—waving in the air . . .

No wonder she'd gone pale. He was probably looking a little pale himself right now.

"You don't think there's any connection, do you? I mean, how can there be?"

"Lately I've been catching references to q'qrs in the *Compendium*, so they're up front in my mind. Srem doesn't present a drawing of a q'qr—at least I haven't found one yet. Her references are always oblique because, like so many things in the *Compendium*, she assumes the reader is already familiar with what she's discussing. But that thing that chased us back in Johnson seems to fit what I've put together about q'qrs. And things that Dawn said about her baby fit too."

Jack was having trouble wrapping his mind around that one . . . or maybe his mind simply didn't want to go there.

"But q'qrs disappeared with the First Age, what, fifteen thousand years ago."

"Maybe not. Maybe some survived the cataclysm."

"But Dawn's baby?"

"Think about it: Q'qrs were created by the Otherness

back in the First Age. Maybe 'created' isn't the best word—genetically retrofitted or repurposed from human DNA is more like it. They became the source of the Taint, what we know as oDNA, which everyone carries to varying degrees. So, in a sense, they've never been away. They live on, right here in our genomes."

Lots of them lived on in Jack's genes, and he didn't like it. But he saw where Weezy was going.

"I get it. According to Veilleur, Jonah Stevens's plan was to produce a child—Dawn's—so packed with oDNA that it would be able to replace the One. You're thinking he wound up creating a q'qr instead."

"Not a real, one hundred percent q'qr, but something close."

"But what could the Order want with it?"

She shrugged. "Who knows? Maybe to use it as a mascot. Maybe they plan to supplant the One themselves."

He gave her a look. "What?"

"I don't believe that either. Just throwing things out. Whatever their reason, we should know it, don't you think?"

"Exactly. That's why I'm going to pay a visit to Mister Osala."

Her expression turned worried. "You'll be careful, please?"

"I'm always careful."

For some reason he had a feeling he should be especially careful with this Osala guy.

6. The lobby of Osala's building had an almost cathedral air about it. High-ceilinged but not that high. Maybe it was the wrought iron affixed to the entry door, or the dark wood and pointed arches within that gave it a gothic feel. Maybe it *was* a cathedral—consecrated to money and set in the ionospheric rent district.

He noticed two elevators opposite the entrance.

"Got a repair order for"—Jack squinted at the name scrawled on the work order—"the Osama elevator."

He carried a red steel toolbox and wore oil-smudged overalls.

"It's Osala," the doorman said, giving him a suspicious look. "Repair order from who?"

He had a small, thin frame and deep brown skin, with short gray hair and a matching beard. He wore a gray uniform with dark red piping and a brass name tag that read MACK. He looked sixtyish and like he'd been around the block a few times.

Jack shrugged. "From whoever manages this place. I just go where they send me."

He handed over the work order and Mack studied it.

"This says you're to fix a noise."

"That it do."

"It ain't making a noise. It works perfect."

Jack shrugged again. "Like I said: I don't write up the work orders, I just go where I'm sent."

Dawn had told him everything she knew about the place. She'd described the Osala duplex in impressive detail but was vague about the rest of the building. One elderly doorman during the day—that would be Mack here—two elevators, one for the exclusive use of Osala's penthouse. She said the building had been virtually deserted since the holidays, with most of the other tenants fleeing to warmer climes till spring. Even Osala had been "down south" a lot lately.

Jack liked the virtually deserted part because he might have to improvise. He hoped it wouldn't come to that because he hated to improvise. But in case it did, he'd applied a droopy mustache and shoved some cotton pledgets between his cheeks and upper gums to change the shape of his face.

Mack looked at him. "How the hell you gonna stop a noise that ain't there?"

"Well, why don't we put her in motion and see about that. If there's no noise, I'm outta here."

Mack gave him a long stare, then said, "Let's do that."

He led Jack to the elevator on the left, pressed a button, and the ornate doors parted, revealing a good-size elevator.

"This the one belongs to Osala?" Jack wanted to be sure he was in the right one.

Mack nodded. "This is it. No one uses it but him and his people. Runs from here to the penthouse. No stops in between."

Just like Glaeken's. Jack knew from Dawn that it had a DOWN button but no UP. It required a key to go up.

"This Osala . . . he got a first name?"

"Yeah. 'Mister.' "

"You don't sound like you like him much."

"Ain't paid to like people."

Mack stepped inside and moved to a rear corner where he folded his hands in front of him, looking like he was waiting for a train.

Jack held out his hand. "Key?"

Mack looked surprised. "Didn't the management give you one?"

"No. I was planning on using yours."

"I don't have one. Only Osala and his people have keys. Didn't they tell you?"

"No."

Dawn hadn't mentioned anything of the sort. Maybe she didn't know. They hadn't let her leave the place.

Damn.

Okay. Time to improvise. He looked at the lock: small keyhole, no brand name. He didn't have a bump key for this. These mini-locks could be a royal pain to pick because of their tiny pins. Then too, Mack could be lying.

He held out his hand. "Give me your keys."

Mack looked at him like he'd grown another head. "You on crack? I ain't giving you my keys."

Jack *really* didn't want to do this, but time was running out. He pulled the Glock from the small of his back and pointed it between Mack's eyes.

"Please?"

Mack pressed back into the corner. "Easy with that! I'm telling you I ain't got a key!"

"I'm not convinced. Hand them over."

Mack straightened, steely determination hardening his eyes and setting his jaw.

"No."

Jack couldn't believe this.

"In case you haven't noticed, there's a hollowpoint-loaded semiauto aimed at your head. You have any idea what one of these rounds will do to your brain?"

"Go ahead. Shoot. You're not getting my keys."

Aw no. He did *not* need this.

"Look. If, as you say, you don't have the key, then what's the harm in letting me check?"

Listen to me. *I've* got the gun, and *I'm* reasoning with *him*.

"Got the keys to other people's apartments on that ring. They trust me with them. I can't let you have them."

Jack bared his teeth and leaned closer, looking as tough as he could.

"Would they want you to *die* for that key ring?"

He shook his head. "Don't matter. This ain't about them. This is about me. You can't have it."

"What if you *don't* die? What if you just get your knee-caps blown off?"

Mack kept shaking his gray head. "I ain't giving it to you."

Jack wanted to break something. Of all the doormen in the city, he had to run into one with a sense of duty.

Jack pulled him from the wall and forced him down till he was face-first on the floor of the cab. Pinning him with a knee in the center of his back, he holstered the Glock and pulled out his lockpick gun. Using that and a small tension bar, it took him only a few seconds to turn the lock.

The doors closed and the elevator started up.

"Do you really not have the key?" Jack said, pulling Mack back to his feet.

He dusted off his uniform. "I told you I didn't."

Jack helped brush him off. "Sorry about the dirt. But you didn't answer the question. You got a key or not?"

"Yeah, I got a key. Fire regs say I gotta have one."

Jack inspected the ornate ceiling of the cab.

"They have video surveillance here?"

"Of course."

Of course. That meant someone could be watching them right now. Dawn had mentioned a big driver and all-around helper named Georges. Maybe him? Maybe Osala himself? Or maybe no one because no one knew the elevator was in operation.

The cab stopped and the doors opened into a tiled foyer. With one hand behind him on the grip of the Glock, Jack used the other to push Mack out ahead of him. He followed and glanced around.

Empty.

He looked for something to stick between the elevator doors to keep them from closing, but found nothing. The foyer was bare of furnishings. In fact . . .

"How many home right now?" Jack whispered as the elevator doors slid closed behind them.

"No one."

"You're sure?"

"Absolutely. They all moved out last night. The movers

finished hauling out the last of the furniture just before you showed up."

Shit.

"You could have told me."

Mack smiled, showing a gold tooth. "Would you have believed me?"

"Guess not."

"Besides, ain't none of your beeswax."

Jack suppressed a laugh. " 'Beeswax'? How old are you?"

"Older than you'll ever be."

Jack stared at him a moment. "You might be right about that, but let's hope not."

Jack wandered up and down the central hall. Not a stick of furniture anywhere. And it *felt* empty.

"Why the hell didn't you tell me?"

"You were supposed to be fixing an elevator. Didn't matter who was home. What do you want here anyway? You come here to kill someone?"

That surprised Jack. "What makes you think that?"

"Well, you're carrying."

"I always carry. You wouldn't have happened to notice a baby being taken in or out, would you?"

"Never." He stared at Jack. "You're not a cop. So what are you?"

"A nobody."

Mack pressed the elevator button and the door opened.

"Well, Mister Nobody," he said as they got in, "you gotta work on your tough-guy act."

Jack hid a smile. "Yeah? Where'd I fail?"

Mack hit the DOWN button.

"Shoulda bashed me with your gun the first time I said no. Real tough guy woulda dented my skull for that. When you didn't, I knew you was mostly show."

Jack shrugged. "Not many jollies in pistol-whipping a skinny old man just for doing his job."

"Ain't old."

"So . . . when you told me to go ahead and shoot, you knew I wouldn't."

His smile was sheepish. "You don't look like you have it in you, so I was pretty sure."

" 'Pretty sure'? Tell me the truth: Would you have taken a bullet for that key ring?"

"Don't know. I would've hoped whoever was on the other end of that gun wouldn't shoot."

"But you weren't going to give up that key ring."

He shook his head "Uh-uh."

Jack pressed him. "It's only a set of keys."

Mack held his gaze. "I think you know what I'm talking about."

"I think I do, Mack. I think I do."

He really liked this old guy.

"What's the 'Mack' stand for? I've got a feeling your mother didn't name you that."

"Yeah, she kind of did: McKinley's on my birth certificate."

"Last name?"

"First."

"Oh, right. Next you'll be telling me your last name's Morganfield."

He gave Jack a look. "You a blues hound?"

"Better believe it."

He smiled. "Well, the last name ain't Morganfield, but I *am* the Hoochie Coochie Man."

"That you are. No question about it."

The doors opened onto the lobby and they both stepped out.

"All right," Jack said. "Osala's gone, left the building for good. You've got no obligation to him anymore. So what can you tell me about him?"

Mack looked around the empty lobby, then shrugged.

"Ain't much to tell. Strange duck, I can tell you that. Not like I'd know from anything he ever said, because I don't think he ever spoke to me. Had his people do it for him. Usually his housekeeper, Gilda, did his talking. Lemme tell you, there's a lady with a face I wouldn't want to come home to every night. And if it's not her, it's his driver-gofer. Used to be a guy named Henry, but he quit or got fired last year. Liked him. Now it's Georges who's got this kinda French accent. Won't miss either of them. Come to think of it, I ain't sure Mister Osala's ever even *looked* at me. Not once."

"What's he do?"

"For a living? Damn if I know. Got lotsa money, that's for sure. Need a ton to own this place and have all that plastic surgery."

"Whoa-whoa-whoa! Plastic surgery?"

"Well, it's gotta be. His looks changed last year. He started off this lily-white guy somewhere like forty or so, and now he's darker, like a Latino or something, and younger. Even looks smaller, though I don't know how he did that."

"You mean he darkened his skin?"

"Yeah, though not as bad as Michael Jackson lightened his. Sort of like a good tan. And grew a mustache . . . like he was going for the Latin-lover look or something."

Dawn hadn't mentioned that. Maybe because she'd grown used to it.

"Where'd he go?"

Mack shrugged. "Never said."

"Well, he must have left a forwarding address."

"Not with me."

"What happens if a package arrives?"

"I don't know. I suppose he'll have Georges stop by now and then and pick it up."

Jack narrowed his eyes. "You sure?"

"Absolutely."

Jack pretended to reach behind him for the Glock. "Don't make me use this."

Mack waved a hand. "Yeah, yeah, yeah. Sure you will. I'd tell you if he left a number, but I wouldn't give it to you."

Jack laughed and offered the man his hand. "I don't know what these folks pay you, Mack, but it can't be enough."

Mack gave his hand a firm shake. "You got that right."

As Jack pushed through the door into the tiny vestibule before the sidewalk, he glanced at the directory of tenants, listed in order of their floor. He froze when he saw the top name.

MR OSALA

Again . . . something about it . . .

And then he knew.

"Holy shit!"

He turned and slammed back through the door and strode toward Mack. The man turned at his approach and backed up two steps when he saw him.

"Jesus God! What—?"

"Osala," Jack said. "You work for him?"

"N-no. I work for the building."

"And you don't have any idea where he's gone?"

"No, I told you. And I take back what I said about you." The remark surprised Jack.

"What?"

"About you not having it in you to kill someone. You do. What happened?"

"Why do you think something happened?"

"Your face. You look ready for murder."

Jack realized he was.

Mack stepped closer. "What set you off?"

"An anagram," Jack said. "A lousy goddamn anagram."

7. "You really think this is necessary?" Weezy said.

Despite the gravity of the situation, Jack had to suppress a smile. Weezy looked ridiculous in the oversize worn cloth coat, babushka, and huge sunglasses he'd picked up in a secondhand shop on his way over.

"You've been made, Weezy."

"You really think they're watching?"

"I didn't see anyone outside, but they could have someone parked in an apartment across the street keeping an eye on the front entrance. We can't risk leading them to Veilleur."

She distastefully inspected the rubber tips of the four-footed cane he'd picked up along with the clothes. "Why don't I just teleconference the meeting? I don't have to be there in person."

"You know we're not set up for that. And besides, I need you there with the *Compendium*."

"Gonna give me a hint of what it's about?"

"Has to do with the One. I'll explain the rest when we're all together."

"You looked upset when you showed up. Still do."

He'd been kicking himself for missing the anagram.

"You'll understand later—if we ever stop talking and get you out of here."

"Okay, okay. I'm ready. But . . ." She looked at the warning on the exit door before them. "It's alarmed."

He'd scouted her apartment building's rear before approaching her with the plan. They now stood before the exit door that opened onto an alley that led to the neighboring street.

"That's okay." He held up a rectangular metal wafer. "We have this."

"And that is . . . ?"

"A magnet. All I—"

"What kind?"

"NIB. I don't know what that stands for but—"

"Neodymium, iron, and boron. Those things are *powerful.*"

He stared at her. "How do you . . . ? Never mind."

She looked up at the magnetic contact on the door-frame. "You're assuming that's a closed circuit sensor."

He sighed. Was there anything she didn't know?

"It's too new not to be. I'm going to—"

"—slip it between the magnet and the sensor to keep the circuit closed. Cool. Let see."

He did just that and the NIB wafer snapped up against the sensor. Jack pushed on the door but it wouldn't budge.

Weezy pointed to the handle labeled PULL. "Another Midvale graduate, I see."

Jack sighed as he pulled on the handle. "Class of eighty-seven. We're everywhere." He opened the door an inch. When no alarm sounded he said, "Vy-oh-la."

"My hero."

A slew of memories peppered him.

"You used to say that to me when we were kids."

"I didn't mean it then."

Jack let that slide.

"Okay . . . time to get into character."

Weezy hunched her back, knocked her knees so she was flat-footed, then stepped through the door into the alley-way. Jack watched her wobble toward the other street, then closed the door and removed the magnet. She'd catch a cab while he went out the way he'd come in. They'd meet at the Lady's.

8. "I can't believe I didn't see it."

Mr. Osala . . . Rasalom.

Jack still hadn't forgiven himself for missing that anagram. Jerk.

Rasalom . . . the Adversary . . . the One . . . right under their collective noses.

"Neither did I," Weezy said. "Because we *weren't* seeing it. We were only hearing it."

"But I wrote it down."

"You only wrote 'Osala.' Kind of hard to scope out an anagram without all the letters present."

Veilleur spoke from the end of the table. "Failing to recognize the anagram is of little importance now. But its simple existence *is* important—and instructive."

Jack had called Veilleur and then Weezy as soon as he'd left Mack. They'd rushed to the Lady's apartment and settled into their usual positions around her big table.

"How so?" Jack said. "I thought using anagrams of his name was his MO."

"It has been. For millennia. In fact it was an anagram—Molasar—that allowed me to track him to Wallachia and eventually imprison him in the keep."

"He could name himself anything," Jack said. "Why's he so fixated on that one?"

Veilleur leaned back. "I guess you could say it's cultural. Names were important back in the First Age, especially to those serving the Otherness. He has three names. The first was given by his parents and that one is lost to antiquity. The other two he acquired when he was elevated to the Seven."

"I've read about the Seven," Weezy said, patting the ever-present *Compendium of Srem*. "They were sort of the Otherness's joint chiefs of staff."

Veilleur nodded. "Correct. But they were more than

that. They were rulers as well. They governed the land controlled by the forces of the Otherness. The man who later became the One was the last to join, and the others lived to rue the day they allowed him in."

"I also read about how he became known as the One," Weezy said. "Because of him, the Seven were eventually reduced to . . . One."

"Exactly. But when he was inducted he was allowed to choose a seven-character name by which the world would know him."

Jack said, "What's with all the sevens?"

Weezy patted the *Compendium* again. "According to this, I gather the Otherness uses a base-seven counting system."

"In an arcane ceremony," Veilleur said, "the Adversary was also given a name by the Otherness—again, seven characters. Each of the Seven had a similar name—their Other Name—composed of the same seven characters. That name was kept secret from the world and known only to the other members of the Seven."

"I see the hubris," Weezy said. "He can't use his Other Name because that one must remain secret. But the R-name is entwined with his identity as the One, so he refuses to drop it for another."

Veilleur smiled. "Exactly the way I see it. It's not that he can't break an old habit—he *won't* break it. Hubris is at work. And hubris is a very human failing."

"So?"

"So never forget that: He is human."

Jack remembered his encounter with Rasalom in Florida, and here in the city last winter.

"Well, he's the only human I know who can walk on water and float in the air."

"He can?" Weezy said with a shocked expression. "You never told—"

"I will. Later. Promise."

"He may be an extraordinary human," Veilleur said, "but he's still *human*, with all the faults and foibles of any other human. Just because he can measure his years in millennia—"

"As can you," Jack said.

"Ah, but I look my age, he doesn't. And never will. As a result, there's a tendency to think of him and react to him as some sort of demigod. But he has human faults. One of them is, as I said, hubris. Another is a certain pettiness of spirit."

Jack perked up. That sounded exploitable.

"How so?"

"He is incapable of letting go of a slight. If he has been injured, he must retaliate. Time will not lessen his need. He will bide his time and wait for the right moment to inflict the most pain. Then he will strike, and feast on that pain."

"How does that help us?"

Veilleur frowned. "I'm not sure yet. The doorman told you he'd changed his appearance?"

" 'Latin lover' was how he described it."

Veilleur nodded. "We can only guess why he'd do that. Not for anything to do with his mission for the Otherness, I'll bet. I believe it's personal. And I believe that is where he might be vulnerable."

Jack felt a tingle of anticipation. "You mean it may be coming time to make a move against him?"

Veilleur shook his head. "Sorry, Jack, but we can't risk any head-to-head confrontations. You know that."

Jack balled his fists under the table. No point in arguing. They'd been over this too many times already.

"Then what?"

"I don't know. But I'm going to investigate. Perhaps we can use your skills and ingenuity to make something backfire on him. Who is to say?"

Better than nothing, Jack guessed.

"He is also impatient," Veilleur added. "He was reborn in 1968 and has run into no opposition since. He senses that something is amiss on our side—"

"And he's right," Jack said.

Veilleur nodded. "Yes, he is right. But that very lack of opposition causes suspicion. He paid a terrible price for letting his guard down in the fifteenth century. He won't do that again. But that does not leaven his impatience. And his impatience may trump his caution . . . again, presenting us with an opening."

An opening for what? Jack wondered. An opportunity to sit on our hands some more?

"That's all fine and good," Weezy said, "but where does Dawn fit in?"

Jack wasn't following. "We're not going to involve her."

"She *is* involved. Ras—I mean R has been hiding her for nearly a year. And as soon as she has the baby, he moves her out."

"Which means he has plans for the baby and not for her."

Weezy gave him an arch look. "Oh, really? Let's think about that. He didn't just kick her out, he moved her into her own place, and guess where that place is."

"I was concerned about that before I knew who Osala was," Veilleur said. "Now that I know . . ."

"There are no coincidences here," the Lady said.

That was old news, but the words never failed to send a chill through Jack.

He turned to Weezy. "Okay, maybe he does have plans for her. But where do you fit in? You were a threat to his plans for the *Fhinntmanchca*, but that's over and done. So why would he be interested in you now?"

"It somehow involves the baby," she said. "I'll bet my life on it."

Veilleur's expression was grim. "Not a wager to take lightly where the One is concerned."

Weezy swallowed and nodded. "Oh, right."

Veilleur leaned forward. "Did Dawn mention anything to you about the infant's 'deformities'?"

Weezy's hand flew to her mouth. "Ohmygod! In all the clamor about the anagram, I forgot."

He raised his eyebrows. "Well?"

"She said it had black hair all over its body, little clawed hands, and . . . a tentacle coming out of each arm-pit."

Jack would have said simply that it looked like what a q'qr was supposed to look like, but Weezy was obviously letting Veilleur draw his own conclusion. And he did—with a bang.

He slammed his hands on the table and straightened from his seat.

"What?"

Even the Lady seemed shocked. "Please tell me you're joking."

Weezy shook her head. "That's what she told us."

Veilleur dropped back into his seat. "This shouldn't be. And yet it makes a strange sort of sense."

"Does it? Dawn giving birth to a quasi q'qr?" He glanced at Weezy. "We figure there's still some human in that baby."

"Correct," said Veilleur. "It's not one hundred percent what you call oDNA. But obviously it has enough to take on the appearance of a q'qr."

"That's what I thought," Weezy said. "A hybrid dis-playing the q'qr phenotype."

"Whatever," Jack said. "The big question, as I see it, is why is a baby q'qr so important? I mean, important enough for R himself to keep Dawn as a houseguest all through her pregnancy and for the Order's doctors to guide her through labor and then whisk the baby away as soon as he's born?"

"I don't have the answer to that," Veilleur said. "Let me tell you what I know about the baby's genesis. For that we have to go back to the First Age."

"That's fifteen thousand years," Jack said. "The baby's only two days old."

"But the Taint that fills him is ancient. You know about the q'qr race."

Weezy said, "Genetically altered humans created by the Otherness to fight its battles—its own private Mongol horde."

"Exactly. They multiplied like bacteria and overran everything in their path. A weapon designed to wipe them out misfired and killed only their females. So they mated with human women but human DNA trumped oDNA every time. Their offspring carried the Taint, but no new q'qrs were born. Their line was at a dead end. When the last one was killed, the q'qr race was extinct."

Weezy said, "I think the last q'qr died in 1983."

Veilleur gave her a strange look.

"One used to live on your property in the Pines. *Mister Foster*. Jack and I ran into it—the last one I'm sure—when we were teens. We're pretty sure it drowned."

He frowned. "You're quite sure?"

"Quite."

"How odd. But not impossible. A q'qr can be killed, but if left alone, it lives on and on."

"Immortal?" Weezy said.

"In a sense, yes."

Jack didn't care much about that q'qr. Dawn's was the one that mattered.

"Can we get back on topic? Why do the One and the Order want this quasi-q'qr baby?"

"Again, I can't even hazard a guess. Though I doubt

the One is personally changing diapers, he does seem to have taken the child under his wing."

"Or the Order has. Dawn mentioned that her OB man had the Order's sigil on his watch."

Weezy frowned. "You don't think they're going to worship him or anything like that, do you?"

Veilleur barked a laugh. "Oh, I doubt that very much. The Septimus Order has its roots in the First Age. Its leaders took orders from the Seven and marshaled the q'qr armies. They had nothing but contempt for their filthy, ignorant, brutal charges. In fact, when the Order executed one of its own for treachery or a high crime, they q'qred them."

"Meaning?"

"Meaning they would cut off his forearms at the elbows and shove them into his armpits as a show of contempt."

Jack stiffened and glanced at Weezy, only to find her staring at him.

"Mister Boruff!" she said, her voice barely above a whisper.

"Who?" Veilleur said.

Jack turned back to him. "A corpse we stumbled on in the Pine Barrens when we were kids—on your property, in fact—turned out to be a member of the Order, and he'd been killed that way."

"To mimic the form of a q'qr," Weezy added. "We never dreamed . . . no one had ever seen the Kicker Man back then."

"Speaking of which," Jack said, "if the q'qrs were fashioned by the seven-crazy Otherness, why do they have only six limbs instead of seven?"

Instead of answering, Veilleur turned to Weezy and pointed to the *Compendium*. "Do you think you could find the Order's sigil in there and trace it for me?"

"I'll try." She opened the book and began flipping through it. "With the way the pages shift around, finding anything in here is a real challenge." But only a few seconds later she stopped. "Well, I'll be. Got one."

She grabbed a pen and began tracing, then handed the sheet to him. Veilleur held it up for Jack to see.

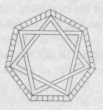

"Now," Veilleur said to Weezy, "may I have one of your markers?"

Weezy handed him one of her ever-present Sharpies and he went to work on the tracing.

"It's true that q'qrs do not have seven limbs, but their symbol, the one they left behind wherever they pillaged and slaughtered, the one Hank Thompson has misinterpreted as the Kicker Man, has seven points."

He held up his handiwork.

"And so, the rule of seven holds."

Jack shook his head in wonder. "It fits right into the sigil. I never saw it, never guessed."

"Everything is connected," Veilleur said. "Everything."

"But we still don't know why the One is protecting this baby instead of disposing of it. Because if he wanted it gone, he wouldn't have waited for its birth; he'd have killed Dawn last year and been done with it. Someone's got plans for that baby."

"Then those plans must include me," Weezy said. "Else why would he install the baby's mother across the hall?"

Jack had been thinking along those same lines.

Veilleur said, "What puzzles me more is the obviousness of the move. The One is devious. He's practiced at the art of misdirection. A blind man could see through this."

"Maybe that's the point," Weezy said. "Maybe we're supposed to see through it. Maybe its real purpose is to cause us to spin our wheels in confusion while the plan to bring down the Internet"—she glanced at the Lady—"and you, goes forward."

Jack shook his head. "Well, he's confusing me. Does he want us looking for Dawn's baby or not?"

"Maybe he doesn't care," Weezy said. "Maybe he's so confident the Internet will fall that he feels we're irrelevant now, and he's just playing with our heads."

Veilleur pushed himself up from the chair. "Weezy is right. If the assault on the Internet succeeds, these questions will be irrelevant. We must find a way to save the Internet."

If I'd been allowed to find and take out Rasalom, Jack thought, this conversation would never have happened, because *it* would be irrelevant.

"Yes, please," the Lady said. "I like it here. I don't want to leave you. I don't want you to suffer what will befall you if I am taken away."

Veilleur stared at her a moment, seemingly appraising her, then turned to Jack.

"May I ask you a couple of favors, Jack?"

"Sure."

"Would you drive me out to Queens tonight?"

"Sure. When?"

"Around midnight or so?"

Jack frowned. "Where do you want to go at midnight?"

"A graveyard. Would you be so kind as to bring along a two-gallon container of gasoline?"

"Um . . . okay. Can I ask what you need it for?"

"I'm going to help someone start a fire."

"Well, as I always say, set a fire for a man and he's warm for a day; set him on fire and he's warm for the rest of his life."

Weezy punched his arm. "Jack!"

But Veilleur's expression was stricken. "How did you know?"

SATURDAY

I. "Bayside?" Jack said as he headed for the Queens-boro Bridge. "What's over there?"

He'd pulled up in front of Veilleur's building in his big black Crown Vic at about 12:10 and found him waiting at the curb. The old guy had given him the destination as he'd settled into the roomy front seat.

"A cemetery."

Jack felt his gut clench. "That wouldn't be Saint Ann's, would it?"

"Yes. How did you know?"

"I'm familiar with it. My . . . daughter is buried there."

"Oh, yes. You mentioned her. Emma, correct?"

Jack nodded, his throat thick. She'd never been born, never officially lived, but she was far enough along in gestation and might have survived if not for the trauma Gia had suffered.

"I'm sorry," Veilleur said. "Had I known, I would have asked someone else."

He found his voice. "No, it's fine. Gia and I go out there every so often and visit her grave."

Veilleur shook his head. "Terrible thing to have to bury a child."

"Have you—? Never mind. Of course you have."

Over the span of the millennia he'd lived, Veilleur must have buried many children. Then Jack realized with a start that he'd lived long enough to bury *all* his children.

"Too many times. It wasn't so hard with the old ones—the sons and daughters who had lived a full life and eventually became sickly and decrepit with age. But the children who die as little ones . . . no matter how often you go through it, that ordeal does not get a bit easier."

They drove in silence for a while, with Jack wondering how many children Veilleur had sired through the ages.

"Do you remember them? All of them?"

A sigh. "All of them. They ran the gamut from the saintly to the downright evil."

"Evil? You had an evil child?"

He nodded. "A number of them. Some people are simply born bad. They grow up bad. There's no accounting for it. A couple of them, well, I had to end their lives myself."

Jack swallowed. "Kill your own child?"

"Twice, yes. They weren't children, they were grown men, and they were killers. This was in times without much in the way of civilization, no 'authorities' who could arrest them, no medications to treat them, no jails to lock them up. But they had to be stopped. They couldn't be allowed to go on raping and killing whenever they felt an urge in their loins or became angry. So it fell to their father to stop them."

Jack tried to imagine . . .

"There was no one else?"

"How could I let someone else kill one of my sons? I'd brought him into the world. He was my responsibility." He rolled his shoulders. "Can we talk about something else?"

"Yeah. Sure."

Gladly.

Jack said nothing for a while, too dazed by the thought of having to kill your own child. What kind of world had it been between civilizations? Rule by brute force . . . survival of the fittest . . .

Veilleur—Glaeken—had survived all that. The stories this man could tell . . .

In an effort to break the silence and change the subject, he said, "I'm pretty sure you won't be able to get in Saint Ann's at this hour."

"I won't need to."

He remembered the two-gallon can sitting behind his seat.

"I brought the gas."

"I know. I can smell it. Thank you."

"Mind telling me what this trip is all about?"

"I'd be glad to if I could, but I'm not sure myself. All I can say is that someone does not rest easy in the soil of Saint Ann's."

" 'Not easy' . . . we're not talking a vampire or anything like that, are we?"

Veilleur made an amused sound, not quite a laugh. "No, nothing so prosaic, I'm afraid. The inhabitant of this unmarked grave is human, or was, but somehow, in some way, it has been infused with the Otherness."

"You mean oDNA?"

"No. It's something from without. This is the One's doing."

Remembering something from one of his trips to St. Ann's, Jack said, "There's a patch of ground there where nothing will grow. I got that from a very frustrated grounds-keeper. No matter what he does, nothing will germinate or survive on this oblong patch."

Veilleur was nodding. "That's the grave. I visit it every so often, trying to decipher its purpose, what it means."

"And . . . ?"

"I remain baffled. But I have a feeling a few of my questions may be answered tonight."

"How do these 'feelings' work?"

He shrugged. "I'm not sure. After millennia of being connected to the Ally and fighting the One, I suppose I became sensitized. No doubt I lost some of that sensitivity along with my immortality, but enough remains to sense singularities and incongruities, and sometimes a coalescing and intersecting of forces. That's what I sense happening at Saint Ann's."

"You think the One's got a plan going?"

"I'm certain he has a number of plans running congruently. That's been the pattern of our struggle down the millennia: We both adhered to the practice of having a backup plan already in motion in case the current strategy fails. But I have a feeling—and I can't say why—that this has nothing to do with opening the way for the Otherness. I sense this is somehow personal."

Jack remembered something Mack had said.

"Guy I talked to yesterday says the One's been involved in something 'down south,' but didn't know much beyond that." He glanced at Veilleur. "What's your plan B?"

"I don't even have plan A. I'm out of this, Jack. I'm old and I'm tired. I can no longer lead. I can serve only in an advisory capacity."

Swell. But Jack had known that.

"And what do you advise?"

"Stay away from that baby. Other than that . . ." He shrugged.

Jack pounded his fist on the steering wheel. "What? How do we fight back without going after the One or the Order? It's like punching smoke."

Especially frustrating since Rasalom was no longer smoke. The realization that he had been living for the last ten months—at least—right across Central Park from Rasalom had gnawed at Jack since he'd seen that name on the tenants list. He'd been *right there*. And if he could be located, he could be followed. And if he could be followed, a routine could be established. And if a routine could be established, a trap could be set. And if a trap could be set, one with a big enough payload . . .

The One becomes the None.

And then it's: Okay, Otherness . . . now what?

They drove the rest of the way in silence.

Eventually Jack stopped before the cemetery's locked gates. He expected to wait with Veilleur but the old guy surprised him by opening his door and getting out.

"Wait. Where are you going?"

"They should be along soon."

"Who?"

"That's what I'm here to find out. May I have the gasoline?"

A cold breeze sliced at Jack as he got out and retrieved the can from behind his seat.

"You're gonna freeze your butt off."

Veilleur took the can. "I'll be fine. I've endured much colder."

Jack noted his heavy topcoat, scarf, homburg, and leather gloves. Yeah, he'd come prepared.

"You're sure you don't want me to wait?"

"Positive. I think this will work better if I am alone. Can I call you if I need a ride back?"

"Sure."

Veilleur waved with his cane and walked off, following the sidewalk that ran along the cemetery's high wall. Jack watched him for a moment, then slid back into the car and headed back to the city.

He turned on the radio and the Stones' "Miss You" was playing. Loved this song. Usually when it came on he'd empty his head and just follow the bass line. But tonight it made him think of Gia. He wished he was heading to her place instead of his.

2. What are the chances? Kewan wondered as he spliced the wires from the garage door opener receiver to the wires from the two blasting caps. Had to be one in a zillion, but still a chance.

He'd spent the past two days hooking up receivers to the Semtex and C4 he'd positioned earlier in the week. Kewan would have preferred using cell phones, but the high-ups were expecting transmissions to be iffy when kablooie time came, so these were better. Better for the high-ups maybe. Kewan didn't want to be anywhere near this stuff when it went off. Not that the explosions would cause much damage above ground—maybe a little flying pavement, maybe the world's worst potholes—but someone might see him and connect him. The cell would be so much easier and safer. He could sit in a bar on the other side of the world and trigger these things.

At least it was only moderately cold down here. Not like topside where the wind screamed across the fields and scoured the pavement.

Okay. The wires were all twisted up inside their splice caps. Now the weird part—powering up the receiver.

Yeah-yeah-yeah. He knew it was crazy, but what if someone driving nearby just happened to press his garage door opener transmitter at the very moment Kewan installed the batteries, and that transmitter just happened to send the same signal programmed into this receiver?

Kablooie.

But he'd done a shitload of these and it hadn't happened yet. So he took a breath and powered it up. Still holding that breath, he duct-taped the receiver to the fiber optic cable, then headed for the manhole.

Only a couple more left, then he'd go on standby, waiting for the signal to start activating these receivers.

He stuck his little periscope through one of the holes

in the manhole cover. All clear, so he pushed up and crawled out.

As he trotted for the shadows where the car hid, his heart rate kicked up. Not from exertion but excitement. Not long now before everything started falling apart. And he'd be partly responsible for the breakdown.

As he drove away he fought the temptation to shove some batteries into the transmitter and press the button. That would guarantee him the honor of firing the first shot. But it also guaranteed him a shitload of trouble if it tipped off the cops and ATF and all the powers that be that trouble was coming.

No, he'd be patient.

3. The phone woke Jack.

As he thumbed the TALK button he realized with a start that it was morning and he hadn't heard from Veilleur about a ride back from the cemetery. Had he caught a cab? Not an easy task in Bayside in the wee hours of the morning. He hoped the old guy hadn't frozen out there. Maybe this was him.

"Yeah?"

"Jack, this is Munir."

Uh-oh.

"Trouble?"

"Yes. But not personal. I think I know what the Jihad virus intends to do."

"What?"

"I will need to show you. Can you come over?"

"Sure. On my way."

Great, he thought as he pulled on some clothes. The first step toward stopping it is figuring out what it's gonna do.

He hurried out into the cold, grabbed a coffee from a

cart on Amsterdam, and hopped into a cab for Munir's. On the way to Turtle Bay he called Veilleur.

"Yes, I'm fine, Jack. Thanks for your concern. I met two fellows who gave me a ride home. In fact they're here right now. I'm making them breakfast. Care to join us?"

"Gotta see Munir. He might have figured out something on the virus."

"Interesting. Keep me informed."

Met two guys . . . brought them home . . . making them breakfast? Was Veilleur losing a few marbles?

At the Habib apartment, Munir pressed a finger to his lips as he opened the door.

"Barbara and Robby are still asleep."

He led Jack to his study with the multiple computers and monitors, then began tapping on one of the keyboards.

"I've isolated the stolen game code in the virus."

"So they're going to make everyone play *World of Warcraft*? Or maybe World of Jihadcraft?"

He said it facetiously but the humor—scant and dubious, he'd admit—was lost on Munir.

"I told you, I do not believe followers of Islam would countenance what was done to me. It must be someone else."

Might as well tell him.

"It is. The Septimus Order is behind it."

He frowned. "Septimus Order . . . I've heard of them. Aren't they like the Elks or the Moose Lodge? Or Masons?"

"They love you to think that."

The frown edged into a faint smile. "Are you going to tell me that they're a globe-spanning secret society like the Illuminati, plotting to take over the world?"

"If only."

Munir stared at him. "You're serious."

"Deadly—as in Russ, as in Valez. As you said: Well organized, well financed."

Munir sat silent for a while, then, "I dismissed you when you said they wanted to bring down the Internet. I thought they wanted to use it for their own purposes, control it rather than destroy it. Mainly because I didn't think it possible to bring down the Internet. Now . . ."

This was what Jack had come for.

"Now what?"

He shrugged. "If the botnet created by Jihad four/twenty is anywhere near as extensive as theorized, I think they can do it. As a matter of fact, I'm sure they can do it."

Jack had suspected this had been the purpose of the virus all along, but to hear it confirmed by a man whose stolen code had been spliced into it . . . chilling.

"How?"

"I've been baffled from the start as to how an online gaming enhancement program could be of use to hackers. Then I realized they'd utilized only my video transfer protocol and scrapped the rest."

"I'm not sure what that means."

"I developed a way of rapidly transferring video between a player's computer and an online game server. It uses a lot of bandwidth while running, but the beauty of it is it doesn't run for long. Russ loved it, called it the 'primo feature' of the package. Thinking about it now, I'm sure that was what he must have talked about to his fellow hackers. The wrong person overheard, and now . . . he's dead and my family's life is changed forever."

Jack saw Munir's throat work as he blinked a few times. He gave him a moment. Jack felt bad about Russ too. A sweet, harmless guy.

"Okay," he said finally, "how does this bring down the Internet?"

Munir cleared his throat. "By overloading it. I'm not

saying this is what the virus intends, but considering that it's created a billion-unit botnet that has high-bandwidth video transfer capability, that capability could be used to send video back and forth between all the computers on the botnet."

"I can see how that would jam up the computers, but how would that affect the Internet?"

"Imagine all the computers in the botnet simultaneously spewing tons of network traffic. Imagine computers all across the world overloading their ISPs. Not only is each ISP inundated with network traffic, but they keep trying to communicate with servers and Web sites across the world, over and over again, all at the same time. They have tremendous capacity, but they have their limits. Eventually, the whole Net grinds to a halt. Look what happened when Michael Jackson died. There were so many posts and searches about him that Google and Twitter slowed to a crawl. And those were just text, which is nothing compared to video. Even so, they thought they were under a DDoS attack."

"That denial of service you told me about?"

"Yes. A distributed denial of service attack. That's when hackers stream enormous amounts of data from a botnet at a specific target in an attempt to crash its servers."

"Why?"

"Because they can, I suppose. It's happened to the social networking sites numerous times; back in 2008 a group called 'Anonymous' crashed the Scientology site with a DDoS. If you overload a Web site with too much traffic, eventually it cannot keep up. All the users' connections to the site time out, and the site appears dead. This Jihad botnet could use my protocol to inundate servers all over the world."

"You're sure?"

"I'm positive. Since the nineties, experts have worried about demand for bandwidth exceeding the Internet's capacity. Video transfer demands large amounts and the explosion of video on the Internet has generated no little anxiety. It's enough of a concern to cause ISPs like AT&T and others to talk about charging extra for high-bandwidth users. So far, the Internet has always been able to expand its capacity to meet growing demand, but I don't think it's prepared for what Jihad four/twenty can throw at it."

Jack was having a hard time wrapping his mind around this.

"You're talking about using something like YouTube to crash the Internet?"

"I'm talking about bigger, longer, fatter videos than the clips on YouTube. What happens if you miss an episode of your favorite TV show? Used to be you'd have to wait for a rerun. No more. You simply go online and watch it. The days of the movie DVD are numbered. Online film rental services no longer have to ship you a disk, they simply download the film to your computer, or cell phone or iPod. That uses bandwidth—lots of it. Imagine a billion or more devices uploading and downloading video back and forth to each other, over and over."

There had to be more to it than that.

"That will crash the Internet?"

"If the Jihad botnet encompasses a billion computers—and I believe it has more—that will do it. But I have examined the code and I believe they may have more specific targets—like the root name servers."

"The what?"

"They're the heart of the Web. When you type in 'microsoft.com' or 'twitter.com,' those texts need to be translated into numerical IP addresses that computers can read. Knock out those specific servers and the Internet becomes terminally dyslexic. Back in oh-seven a botnet in Southeast Asia mounted a DoS attack on the name servers and managed to damage two. The Jihad botnet is incalculably bigger. It could succeed."

"But using video ... it's so ... simple, so obvious. Why hasn't some nut tried this before?"

"It only seems simple and obvious when someone points it out, but the execution is anything but. It took a cadre of expert hackers working in concert to come up with a virus that could slip past the best firewalls and create a botnet of sufficient size to make this feasible. And it took a new approach to video transfer—mine, unfortunately—to make it work."

"I'd have thought some terrorists—"

"Terrorists love the Internet. They can't communicate without it."

"Could this have been done without you?"

Munir nodded. "I think so. But the extra bandwidth my protocol demands makes it irresistible. That was why they came after me." He shook his head. "I wish to God I'd never learned how to program. If I'd returned home after college as my father had wished, Robby would still have ten fingers."

Jack had gone through his share of if-onlies about Emma, and he knew Munir wasn't seeing this from all angles.

"If you'd gone back to Saudi Arabia after college, there'd be no Robby."

Munir gave him a strange look. "Yes, that's true. I didn't think of that."

"Is a nine-fingered Robby better than no Robby?"

Munir nodded. "Most certainly."

Jack stared at the monitor and shook his head. Bring the Internet down just by swapping videos. Who'd have thought?

"Okay," he said. "Now that we know what they're going to do, how do we stop them?"

"*Do* we know that they're going to do this? Everything points to that as their purpose but . . ." Munir shrugged. "Why? This Septimus Order must use the Internet itself—to keep in touch with its membership, to . . . it must use it in many, many ways. Everyone does. Why cripple its own operations by bringing it down?"

Jack couldn't tell him about the noosphere and the Lady. Munir would think him crazy.

"Remember the reason you gave for the denial of service attacks? 'Because they can'? I believe that holds here."

Munir kept shaking his head. "But a DoS harms only the target servers. It doesn't inconvenience the attacker. This does. This . . ." He shot to his feet and began pacing. "Do you realize how much the everyday operations of civilization are tied into the Internet?"

"Well, there's email—"

"Email!" He began flailing his arms. "Email is nothing! Business will slow to a crawl. Companies have gradually been moving their transactions, their databases, their software online, into the cloud. Without the Internet there is no cloud. The computers that run banking, stock trading, transit systems, and traffic control systems communicate and route parts of their operations through the Internet. Communication networks depend on the Internet. We're not talking about losing eBay and Facebook. We're talking about commerce and finance and communication and even street traffic grinding to a halt. The result will be chaos."

And worse than all that, Jack thought, we'll lose the Lady.

"So—" Jack began, but Munir was still rolling.

"But what makes no sense is that this will all be temporary. Chaos at first, yes, but then a mad scramble to repair the servers and routers and get them back online as soon as possible. Everything is backed up—or should be—and many systems are redundant, so it won't be terribly long before things are back to normal. The white hats will figure a way to block the botnet and the antivirus companies will release software to disinfect our computers. People will be enormously inconvenienced for days, perhaps weeks, but the status quo will return before very long."

Don't count on it, Jack thought. Not if they're able to start the Change during the interval. A crashed Internet will be the least of your worries when you find yourself facing the Otherness.

"You're sure of that?"

"No one can say exactly how long. It's unprecedented. Of course, the botnet will still be out there, ready to do it again. But not for long, I think. A Jihad four/twenty killer will be developed very quickly." He shrugged. "So what's the point? Profit? Mischief? To go down in history?"

No, Jack thought. To *end* history.

He said, "We still need to do what we can to stop it, right?"

"Of course."

"Well, that brings us back to the same old question: Do what?"

"You and I?" Munir frowned. "Nothing by ourselves. But I'm going to call ICANN and NRO and anyone else I can think of and tell them what I know."

Jack wondered if he realized what he was getting himself into.

He held up a hand. "They're going to want to know how you know what you know. They're going to suspect you're part of the plot."

Munir stopped his pacing. "They will? Why would they do that?"

"Hey, you're an Arab and the virus is named 'Jihad' and your code is part of it. That makes you suspecto numero uno in anybody's book."

Munir stood silent in the center of the room with a stricken expression.

Jack felt for him. "You could do it anonymously."

He shook his head. "No. That would be just another crank call. I'll need a face and a name if I am to be credible. I'll go in person if I have to, but I must raise the alarm. This cannot be allowed to happen."

"Do you think anyone can stop it?"

"With enough time . . ." He looked at Jack. "Four/twenty is the Prophet's birthday. Do we have that long?"

Jack shook his head. "Not a chance."

Murnir dropped into a chair and began banging away on his keyboard.

"Then I've no time to waste. I must find the numbers to call."

"Think you'll find anyone on a weekend?"

He looked up. "What day it is it?"

"Saturday."

"Is it? With all that's happened, I've lost track." He shook his head. "I'll try anyway, but I might not reach anyone of consequence until Monday, because no one sees any danger but me."

Jack turned to go. "Well, good luck. And don't forget our deal: I don't exist."

"Monday . . ." Munir said softly, as if he hadn't heard. Maybe he hadn't.

"Munir . . . our deal?"

But Munir's eyes looked out of focus and his thoughts seemed far away. "Monday . . ."

"What about Monday?"

"No one of consequence around until Monday. That makes me think that if I were going to try to bring down the Internet, I would do it on a Saturday or a Sunday."

A thought hit Jack like a gut punch.

"What'll a crash do to the airlines?"

"Short term?" Munir said without looking up.

"Complete chaos for a while. Reservations, scheduling—all heavily Internet based. It might even affect air traffic control."

Gia . . . Vicky . . .

"Oh, crap."

"The FAA may have its own closed system, just like much of the military, but I don't know for sure."

"If you had to pick Saturday or Sunday, which would you pick?"

"Sunday, but I doubt it matters much."

Gia and Vicky were due to fly back tomorrow . . . Sunday.

"I'll let myself out," Jack said. "I've got a couple of important calls to make myself."

4.   As soon as he hit the street, Jack speed dialed Gia. Cell phone technology had been in common use since the nineties and he'd been using it since the turn of the millennium, but he still marveled at the ability to reach Gia anywhere at any time. Didn't matter if she was over on Sutton Square or in Ottumwa, Iowa—he dialed the same number and she answered.

As he listened to the rings, he wondered what to tell her. Get on an earlier flight? Cancel her flight and stay there?

The sound of her voice when she picked up and her obvious delight at hearing from him dissipated the enveloping chill. He wanted to jump right into the reason he'd called but forced himself to engage in some brief, obligatory small talk. Then . . .

"I think trouble may be coming."

"What sort?"

"Big sort. An Internet crash."

He knew this was a cell conversation and vulnerable as

all hell to eavesdropping, but he was in too much of a rush for circumlocution.

"The whole Net? I didn't think that could happen."

"It can . . . and it will."

A pause, then she said, *"Is this another one of Abe's theories?"*

"You mean like the one he drove us all crazy with for years about how the economy was heading for a meltdown?"

"Um, yeah. Okay. Touché."

Right. After the banking, brokerage, and stock market debacles, Abe had spent most of 2009 saying, *I told you so.* Not so much to Jack, who by necessity kept most of his net worth in gold, but he hadn't let anyone else he knew forget that he should henceforth be addressed as Nostradamus.

"It's not Abe. It's the Order."

Jack tried to keep Gia out of the loop as much as possible—and she was fine with that. He figured the less she knew, the better for her and Vicky. They were non-combatants and he didn't want them mistaken for anything else.

But last year he'd had to tell her something about the Order to explain why Weezy had had to move in with him for a while.

"They told you?"

"No. They're behind it."

"I know you said they were global, but do they really have that kind of power?"

"You've been hearing about that Jihad virus?"

"Of course. It's all over the news."

"Right. Well, that's theirs. And come to think of it, your home computer may be one of the few in the city that's uninfected."

"Why's that?"

"Because you haven't been around to open any contaminated emails."

"Lucky me."

"But here's the thing . . . I suspect—it's more of a gut reaction than anything based on hard evidence—that to-day or tomorrow could be it. And that's got me worried about your flight."

Gia was silent for a while, then, *"I see. If you're right, that could cause major problems."*

He was glad he didn't have to convince her of the con-sequences. She'd grasped them on her own right away.

"Question is: Should you risk it? I'd like you back here—for the usual selfish reasons, of course, but also because I want you where I can protect you."

"Will we need protection?"

"Well, things could get a little . . . disorderly."

Chaotic might be more like it. He didn't want to get all Armageddonish about it, but with communications crip-pled, or simply hampered, police response times would be lengthened. That might encourage certain elements of the urban population—particularly those with a little seven-pointed figure tattooed on a hand—to get frisky and reckless.

"For how long?"

"Days, weeks. No one can say."

If Munir didn't know, Jack wasn't going to guess.

"Do you think we'd be safer here?"

She was thinking about Vicky, he knew, and how Iowa might experience fewer repercussions if the Net went down. But it wasn't like the Midwest was crime free. Ed Gein and Jeffrey Dahmer had hung out there. Iowa wasn't all that dif-ferent from Kansas, and Kansas had produced Perry Smith and Dick Hickock. There had to be more of them, and if they learned no one was patrolling the hallways . . .

"Not necessarily. You could get an earlier flight—like switch to today and arrive before the virus starts doing its thing—"

"If it starts doing anything."

"Right. Or you could stay there. I'm going to leave it up to you."

Without hesitation, she said, *"I'll try for the earlier flight."*

"Miss me?"

"Terribly."

"And your folks are on your nerves?"

She laughed. He missed that sound. *"That too."* She lowered her voice. *"Somehow, whenever I visit, I'm suddenly twelve again. I love them, but they make me crazy after a while."*

"That's a parent's job with grown children."

His father had made him crazy, but he'd give an awful lot to have him back.

"I'll call you and let you know if I'm able to reschedule and when we're due in."

"Do that. And hurry. I don't know how much time we have."

He hung up and wished he'd never let them go.

5. Veilleur opened the door at Jack's knock.

"Jack. You made good time. I didn't expect you quite so soon." He glanced back into his apartment. "Perhaps we should talk in the Lady's quarters."

Jack glanced over his shoulder and saw three strangers in the front room. A tall guy with a grayish ponytail, a sixty-ish woman, and a thin, fidgety guy who had cop written all over him.

He stepped back, saying, "Those the ones who drove you back from Saint Ann's?"

"The men, yes. The woman just arrived. I'll meet you downstairs in a minute."

Jack took the two flights down and knocked on the Lady's door.

"Mister Veilleur will be down in a minute," he said as he entered. "I've got reason to believe—"

"That the assault will begin soon."

That stopped him. "How did you know?"

She looked tired. How could that be? She never slept.

"Certain . . ." She waved her hand. "I'm not sure how to express it. If I fix my attention I can sense a gathering of possibilities and probabilities."

That rang a bell from the past.

"Like that time back home when I was a kid and you told Weird Walt to stop drinking because he might be needed."

She nodded. "Exactly." She sighed. "Poor Walter. He carried that burden as best he could. He's dead, you know."

"Yeah. Read the obit last summer. Shame. Sweet guy." As much as he felt sorry for Walt Erskine, the Jihad virus was a more immediate concern. "But these gathering possibilities and probabilities you mentioned . . . do they point to this weekend?"

"I wish I could say more than 'soon.'"

"So do I," Jack muttered, thinking of Gia and Vicky.

Veilleur entered then.

"Sorry for the delay. Magda is asleep so I have a little free time." He looked at Jack. "What did you want to tell me?"

"The computer guy I told you about—he says the Jihad virus is going to use some of the code stolen from him to overload the Internet with video. Enough to bring it down."

Veilleur, his expression grim, glanced at the Lady, then back to Jack. "And they can succeed?"

"He seems pretty damn sure."

"And there's nothing we can do?"

"He's going to alert the military and the committees and groups and whatever in charge of the Internet, but doubts he'll get far because it's the weekend. And because of that, he thinks the weekend is the best time to trigger the virus."

Veilleur's eyebrows lifted. "You think it might be *this* weekend?"

"If you were the One, would you want to wait any longer than you had to?"

"Knowing that I would most likely get only one shot at this, I would want to maximize my chances of success. I would want to wait until the virus has spread as far as it can, until this botnet you speak of has reached maximum penetration."

That made sense, but . . .

"Doesn't this go against what you said about his impatience?"

Veilleur rubbed his beard. "It does, doesn't it. But there might be another reason he'll give it a little more time."

"Such as?"

"Remember how I told you that he never forgets a slight, never lets go of a grudge? Well, that's what 'Mister Osala' has been up to during his trips to the South: petty revenge."

"For what?"

He waved a hand. "Much too complicated to go into. But that long-haired man upstairs is involved. I've decided to head back to North Carolina with him to see if I can help him stymie the One."

Something about that sounded a warning note.

"You think that's wise? What if he sees you?"

"I'll stay well out of sight."

Jack shook his head. "I don't like it."

Veilleur stepped closer and put a big hand on Jack's shoulder.

"How frustrated are you that you can't strike back at the One?"

"You know all about that."

"Exactly. Imagine how I feel. I battled him for millennia. I frustrated his every move and finally trapped him and locked him away for what should have been forever." His eyes flashed. "Damn Nazis." He shook his head. "But now I'm enfeebled and mortal and I keep telling myself I'm out of the fight, that it's somebody else's worry."

Jack nodded. "So you've said. Most recently on the way to Saint Ann's. You've been pretty convincing."

"Well, I mean it when I say it, but inaction grinds at me." He balled his other hand into a meaty fist as his lips retreated into a snarl. "I long to lash out at him, crush him, strip his hide, grind his bones to dust."

Jack watched and listened, amazed. Here was a side of Veilleur he'd never seen. Here was the hidden warrior . . . Glaeken.

And just as quickly it faded.

"Alas, I cannot. So I must take my little victories wherever I can find them. And I believe just such an opportunity has presented itself. It's not pure ego. It has a practical purpose. If he can be frustrated and delayed in his revenge plot, perhaps that will give the computer specialists enough time to come up with a cure for this Jihad virus. And then a small victory will become a major victory, and we'll have bought more time."

More time for what? Jack thought. More sitting around and waiting for Rasalom's next move?

But he didn't voice it. They'd been over this ground before.

"Think it's worth the risk?"

Veilleur nodded. "I do. I'm going to arrange for round-the-clock nursing for Magda, but would you mind checking in once in a while?"

"Not at all."

"Good. The four of us will travel separately—the two men together, and Mrs. Treece with me."

Jack had a sudden inkling . . .

"This Mrs. Treece wouldn't happen to be the One's mother?"

He smiled. "Very good. Yes, she wants to come along and . . ." He shrugged. "She might prove useful. We're scheduling flights now. Leaving as soon as possible."

Didn't seem like he had a chance of changing Veilleur's mind, so . . .

"Need a ride to the airport?"

"Thanks, no. The men have a car."

"How long do you think you'll be gone?"

"The longer, the better, wouldn't you say?" He smiled and rubbed his hands together. "I'm really looking forward to this."

After he left, Jack turned to the Lady.

"He seems pretty energized. I guess that's good. What do you think? Any gathering possibilities and probabilities about this trip of his?"

She shrugged. "I wish I could say. As I've told you, there are times I can sense what the One is doing—because he is human—and others when I cannot—because he is something other than human as well. As a result, the possibilities and probabilities do not gather about him as with others."

"So you think this trip is okay?"

Her expression and voice remained flat. "No, I do not."

"Neither do I, damn it. Think we can talk him out of it?"

She shook her head. "Remember what he told you yesterday about the One?"

"You mean about how he's still human?"

"Yes. With all the foibles of a human, driven to certain actions by that human nature."

"Yeah. So?"

"He may not have realized it at the time, but he was talking about himself as well."

6. Eddie said, "Well, anything's better than that garage, I guess."

Jack joined him at the window in the rear of the apartment that revealed other windows looking out onto a brick-walled air shaft.

"Nice view."

"Hey," Weezy said from behind them. "It's the best I could do on such short notice. Craigslist wasn't exactly crammed with furnished, immediate-occupancy sublets. And I think it's not bad."

Jack agreed. Not bad at all. A third-floor walk-up in the West Village. Small, yes, but comfortable looking. The owner was connected to NYU in some way and off to Europe for a year.

"No one's complaining," Eddie said, turning to face her. "It's just . . ."

He looked worn and haggard. Well, who wouldn't after spending two days living in a van parked in a drafty garage? But it went deeper than that. He looked lost.

Jack said, "You miss your stuff."

He nodded, swallowing hard. "I miss my life." He looked at Jack. "Think I'll ever get it back?"

As far as Jack could see, the odds were stacked high against that.

Maybe if Veilleur delayed Rasalom long enough for an anti-Jihad program to be developed and released, Drexler would be demoted or sacked or might even be eliminated—Valez was proof that the Order wasn't shy about deep-sixing members who didn't live up to expectations. If that happened, the pressure on Eddie would lessen.

If, on the other hand, Veilleur failed and the Lady vanished, well, his old life would be the least of Eddie's worries.

But Jack looked around and understood how he felt. He couldn't rob him of all hope.

"Yeah, it's possible. But until it is, you've got to stay away from there. Count on them watching the place twenty-four/seven."

"Yes, Eddie," Weezy said, stepping closer to him. "If—"

He leaned back. "Don't get too close. I need a shower something awful."

"You've got a stall shower here and I bought you a change of clothes."

Jack said, "Listen, Eddie. If the virus works, or even only partially works, there's going to be one pissed-off world out there, and the Order doesn't want anyone— especially one of its own members—pointing a finger at it. They'll do anything to silence you."

Eddie nodded. "Okay, okay. I'm not stupid." Then he raised his hands. "All right, maybe I am for mentioning the virus to the wrong person. But I've learned my lesson about underestimating the Order."

"You've got to put distance between you and your money too," Weezy added.

"But the rent—"

"I've got that covered."

"I've got cash—"

"Which will set off all sorts of alarms if you try to use it to pay rent. We can straighten all that out later. Meanwhile I'll show you how to use ATMs without being tracked."

"Where'd you learn that?" He raised a hand as he glanced at Jack. "Never mind."

Jack's phone rang then. He checked the ID in the window.

"Hey, Gia. How'd you do?"

"I got us on the 3:45 out of Des Moines."

"Great."

At least he hoped it was great. And hoped Veilleur was right about Rasalom waiting until the botnet was maxed.

"That's the good news."

"Uh-oh. What's the bad?"

"A long layover in Chicago.We won't get in till eleven."

Jack did the math: Subtracting an hour for the time-zone change, that meant more than six hours in transit. Lots of time for things to go wrong.

"Not sure I like that. Nothing earlier?"

"Not a thing. Believe me, I tried. Something wrong?"

"Maybe you should stay."

"No, Jack. I already switched the flights and we're coming back. It's in my head now—both of our heads: We want to be home."

"And I want you home, but—"

"We're coming. Flight three-forty-six, American. You'll pick us up?"

He could see he wasn't going to talk her out of it. "Of course."

They chatted a bit longer, then ended the call. He snapped the phone closed with a gnawing foreboding.

Veilleur, he thought, you'd damn well better delay that virus. At least until tomorrow.

After that, his ladies would be home where he could watch over them.

7.   "Looks like they might pull it off," Jack said.

Abe swallowed a bite of the hot pastrami on rye Jack had brought him. Jack wasn't eating. Not hungry.

"Pull? Who? What?"

"The Order. Looks like they may be bringing down the Net. Munir thinks they can do it."

"When?"

"Maybe this weekend."

"Oy. So soon? What can I expect?"

"According to Munir, a real mess. Business—"

"Business, schmizzness. What about social order and such?"

Jack and he had had long discussions about civilization. Abe thought it was a veneer, easily stripped away. Jack disagreed, believing there were lots of civilized people about. Trouble was, those folks had no clue how to handle the wolves among them.

"Depends on how badly communications are hit, I suppose. I think things will hold together."

"But not your friend, the Lady."

Jack felt a wave of sadness. "No, I'm afraid not. She'll be dead."

"Well, she's not really alive, is she?"

True, but . . .

"She is to me. I first knew her as Mrs. Clevenger, and Mrs. Clevenger was a real person as far as I was concerned. And now that she's been stuck in this grandmotherly mode instead of switching her looks, she's more of a person than ever."

"I'm sorry for your coming loss."

Silence settled between them. Finally Abe broke it.

"So . . . we should maybe head for the hills?"

"We? I've got Gia and Vicky coming back from the middle of nowhere tonight."

"After you gather them to your bosom, then—the hills?"

The hills . . . Abe's code name for his hideaway in the wilds of Pennsylvania. He'd been predicting an economic holocaust and subsequent social and civic meltdown for as long as Jack had known him. The economy had crashed, though inflation hadn't achieved the Weimar levels Abe had envisioned. Civilization, such as it was, had managed to remain intact.

"I don't think that will be necessary . . . yet."

" 'Yet'? What's this 'yet' already?"

"Well, there's the Change."

"Ah . . . the Change. This is where you lose me. This

is where you start to sound a little *farblondjet* in the head."

"You accept the Lady but not the rest?"

"The Lady, well, I can buy the noosphere—that's rational and makes a certain amount of sense—but this Otherness-Ally business . . . maybe you're buying into some *narishkeit*."

Jack frowned. He'd listened to Abe talk for so many years that he understood most of his expressions. This was a new one.

"You got me on that one."

"It means nonsense, foolishness."

"Yeah, well, a couple of years ago, I'd have said the same. But I've seen too much. I mean even the rakoshi could have a rational explanation—like mutants, or something. But even if I'd had any doubts left, the *Fhinntman-chca* blew them away."

"Let me keep my doubts, already. I'll sleep better." He looked around. "Speaking of sleeping, maybe I'll sleep here tonight."

"Downstairs?"

"Where else?"

Jack had seen the bunk Abe kept in the armory downstairs. It looked a little small for him, but he didn't mention that.

"Yeah, well, short of a fire, I guess you'll be safe down there."

"Even with a fire, I'll be safe. You want some ammo while you're here? You may need it if things fall apart for a while."

Jack hesitated, then, "What the hell. Might as well stock up."

"They say you can have too much of a good thing. They're wrong. Ammo is a good thing and there's no such thing as too much ammo."

Jack couldn't argue with that.

8. Ernst Drexler's caller ID showed nothing but he took the call anyway. You never knew . . .

"Hello?"

"She's dead."

No greeting was necessary. He recognized the One's voice, and he sounded . . . happy.

"Who, sir? The Lady?"

"If only that were so. No, no one you know. She was what one might call an innocent victim. But those are the best kind, are they not? And after all, no one is really innocent."

"I don't understand."

"Of course you don't. No need for you to understand any of this. She died just a little while ago, and it was tasty."

"Tasty . . ."

"But she was merely an aperitif. The main course comes from the effect of her death on those closest to her . . . especially a certain someone. It will send him spinning out of control again, and just when he thinks life can do no worse to him, the Change will be upon us." The One paused—savoring his anticipation? *"This will be wholly delicious."*

"Yes, sir."

Ernst had no idea what he was talking about.

"When exactly is it due to begin this evening?"

He could mean only one thing: the virus.

"Eight o'clock Eastern Time."

"Perfect."

The One broke the connection without another word.

Ernst noticed that his hand was shaking as he laid his phone on the table.

Eight o'clock . . .

Six hours away . . . after all this time, all this preparation, the plan—his plan—was about to come to fruition.

And he was terrified.

Terrified it would fail.

Terrified it would work.

If it failed, the One would be furious. He might vent his murderous rage on Ernst, and he would never see the Change.

But did he want to see the Change?

The possibility of success terrified as well.

If bringing down the Internet diminished the already damaged noosphere to the point where it could no longer support the Lady, she would vanish, and with her, the last obstacle to the Change would be removed.

The Change . . . it fascinated and frightened him.

The end of the world as we know it.

An old and overused expression, and even the title of a once-popular song. But that was what the Change would mean. And he, among all of humanity, would be most responsible for making it possible. For which he would be rewarded.

Humanity consisted of the Moved and the Movers. He would ascend to Mover status—*Master* status.

But master of what?

What would the world be like after the Change? A different place, to be sure. But in what way? The Order's lore was vague about that. It did say that those who served the One before the change would become his overseers in the aftermath.

Overseeing what?

Those who fought the Otherness swore it would be a place of horror, but who could believe them? They were simply trying to frighten their followers into compliance, just as Christians tried to keep their faithful in line with tales of hell and damnation if they strayed from Church doctrine.

But could they be right?

Ernst had never had the nerve to ask the One what he

could expect. Could the Otherness be as inimical to humanity as the enemies said? That didn't seem likely. Else why would the One have spent millennia working to usher it in? Some of the Order's lore spoke of the One transforming with the Change, and his chosen transforming as well so that they could thrive in the new, Otherness-ruled world.

Ernst wasn't so sure now that he wanted the world or himself changed.

All fine and good when it was simply lore, something to expect in a nebulous future. But it was nebulous no more. He stood before the door to that future, waiting for it to swing open . . .

. . . terrified of what might step through.

9.   After settling Eddie in his new digs—which didn't take much since he had little more than the clothes on his back—and letting him shower and change into the sweatshirt and jeans Weezy had bought him this morning, they hit the streets.

He hadn't been able to empty his bank accounts entirely, but he'd walked away with a load of cash. Jack wanted him to use his remaining credit to confuse anyone who might be tracking him.

So they all hopped the A train at West 4th and took it to 207th Street in the Bronx—the end of the line. There Eddie used an ATM to withdraw some of the cash he'd left in the account. He did some quick shopping and charged some essential clothing, then trained back to the Village.

"I get it," Eddie said as they dropped off his purchases. "Next time I train to Brooklyn and buy stuff. And maybe Staten Island after that. Drive them crazy if they're tracking me."

Jack shook his head. "Maybe so, but they'll know

you're somewhere in the five boroughs. You've only got a few hundred left in the accounts, and we can put that to better use."

"How?"

"Grab some of your cash and I'll show you."

They hopped a cab uptown to Ernie's place. The folding sign set on the sidewalk before his narrow storefront said it all.

Ernie's I-D
All Kinds
Passport
Taxi
Drivers License

Cheap metal and pewter castings of the Empire State Building and the Statue of Liberty shared the front window display with snow globes of the Manhattan skyline and other souvenirs. A buzzer sounded as they opened the front door. Jack led the way toward the rear of the tiny store, passing a display of DVDs. Eddie stopped, pointing to one of the titles.

"Didn't that just open yesterday?"

Jack didn't bother looking. A Pakistani bootlegger down on 32nd Street kept Ernie supplied with the latest titles.

"Wouldn't be surprised. They're okay, I guess, if you don't mind people standing up and moving about in front of the movie."

Eddie pointed to a display of Spade, Vuitton, Gucci, and Prada accessories.

"Bootleg too?"

"Not just bootlegs—bootlegs of bootlegs."

Ernie took pride in never selling anything but knock-offs.

The man himself waited by the rear counter, whippet thin with thick, longish black hair and a nervous tongue that flicked in and out between Sten-gun sentences. His eyes lit when he saw Jack wasn't alone. He knew that often meant a payday.

"Hey, Jacko. How y'doin, how y'doin?"

"Good, good. Ernie, meet Eddie, Eddie, meet Ernie. You alone?"

"Just me and my dreams of winning Powerball. The pot's up to seventy mil. Need some tickets?"

"No." He'd probably printed them in the back this morning. "But Eddie needs to disappear and reappear."

Ernie didn't hesitate. "Not a problem. We can help."

He'd supplied all of Jack's many identities through the years. And he knew anyone Jack brought in would be stand-up.

He hurried to the front of the store where he flipped the OPEN sign to CLOSED.

When he returned he said, "We'll take some pics and pick out a nice new name. I don't know if Jack's told you, but I recommend keeping the first letter of your first name. Saves awkward moments when you sign something. May I suggest Ernest?"

"He also needs to be in two places at once."

Eddie looked at him. "What?"

"You'll see."

Ernie glanced at Jack. "Money in the accounts?"

"Some."

"Good, good."

"What are we talking about here?" Eddie said.

"Ernie's going to clone your card and give it to someone—where this time, Ern?"

"Got someone in Tennessee."

"Perfect."

"I don't get it," Eddie said.

"He's going to give all the info off your debit card, plus your PIN to someone in Tennessee who is going to make a new card."

"*What?*"

"Then they'll use that new card all over the state to buy whatever they want till the money runs out."

The light dawned in Eddie's eyes and he smiled. "I get it. Whoever's tracking me will think I've run to Tennessee."

"Exactly."

"Works beautiful," Ernie said, neglecting to mention that he'd be collecting a fee on both ends.

"He did the same for Weezy last year. Where was that?"

Ernie thought a moment. "Wyoming, wasn't it?"

"Yeah, I think so. But hang on to this till Monday, okay?"

"Not a problem. Come on into the back so I can steal your soul."

Eddie gave Jack a bewildered look.

"Photos, Eddie. He's going to take your picture."

As they disappeared behind a curtained doorway, Jack wandered to the front and stared through the glass door at the traffic on Tenth Avenue.

Should he have waited? If the Jihad virus worked and brought down the Net this would be an empty exercise.

Nah. Wrong mind-set. Play it like victory was a sure thing, otherwise you've already lost.

But wasn't that the case?

10.   "Who's that?" Jack said as a new tune started thumping from Weezy's iPod. He liked it.

"Moby." She began swaying to the beat. "From *The Bourne Identity*."

"Moby's awesome," Dawn said.

Weezy had invited her over. She seemed channeled into mother mode with the teen.

Eddie had opted out. He'd been fragged. He hadn't slept well the past few nights so they let him crash and returned to Weezy's.

Weezy opened her refrigerator door and checked out the shelves within.

"Hungry."

He knew from his own inspection a few minutes ago that they were bare. He glanced at the clock on her kitchen wall.

"Almost eight. We forgot to eat."

Almost eight . . . that meant Gia and Vicky were on their way. She'd called from O'Hare to say they were in safe and their flight to LaGuardia was on time.

Almost home free . . . almost.

"And I didn't have lunch," she said.

"You only eat veggies anyway."

Though Jack had to admit her diet was working.

"I'm feeling decadent tonight," she said. "Like Chinese takeout."

"My treat," Dawn said.

Weezy smiled. "Not necessary."

"I have money," she said. "And I need to contribute something here. You've both been so good to me."

Jack glanced at Weezy. How could they tell her what they knew about her baby? They'd discussed it earlier and decided it was better to leave some things unsaid.

"No, I totally insist," Dawn said, misinterpreting the look. She turned to Jack. "I mean, you went over there and checked out his place."

Jack shrugged. "No biggie."

He was glad he did. It had been a revelation.

"I still can't believe they're gone . . . just up and left. You think Mister Osala has the baby?"

He shrugged again. "Who can say? But you've got to admit, the timing is suspicious. He keeps you there until you have the baby, then the baby disappears and so does he."

"But Mack told you he never saw a baby."

"No. But I'm going to talk to him again and get the name of that moving company. This Osala guy has got to be somewhere."

"See?" Dawn said, tearing up a little. "That's what I mean. You're going to all this effort for me."

Not just for you, Jack thought. For me.

He hadn't thought to ask Mack for the name of the moving company yesterday—realizing Osala's true identity had blown everything else out of his mind—but he'd remedy that tomorrow. He wanted to know where Rasalom was setting up shop next. He'd promised Veilleur to keep his distance, but as far as Jack was concerned, that promise was voided if the Lady went down.

Then it was war . . . all-out war.

But right now, a change of subject was in order.

"Like I said: No biggie. But we can talk about this later. Right now we've got food to order. Shrimp egg foo yung for me, and maybe—"

"That's not a real Chinese dish, you know," Weezy said.

"If it's served in Chinese restaurants, that's Chinese enough for me."

"It's served in Chinese-American restaurants, but you can't get it in a *real* Chinese restaurant—i.e., those in China—because they've never heard of it. In Shanghai they have fuyung egg slices, but it's not the same dish."

Where did she dig this stuff up?

"Fascinating, Weez. Absolutely fascinating. But I still want egg foo yung—*shrimp* egg foo yung, if you don't mind—and an egg roll. Or are you going to tell me egg rolls were invented in Peoria?"

"Were you two ever married?" Dawn said.

"*No!*" they replied in unison, perhaps a tad too loudly.

"Oh, because—"

"We go back a long way," Jack said. "A real long—"

"Wait," Weezy said, holding up a hand. "Do you hear something?"

Jack listened and heard a voice coming from the spare bedroom. Sounded like a woman.

He looked at Weezy. "Someone here?"

She looked baffled, and a little worried. "No way."

Jack stepped up to the darkened doorway and peered within. The computer was running, with a black-and-white film playing on the monitor. It looked familiar.

Weezy came up behind him and peered over his shoulder.

"What the . . . ?" She squeezed past and flicked on the light. "I turned that off before I left to go to Eddie's place. And what's playing?"

"*Dark Victory.*"

"You think?"

He pointed to the actress speaking. "She's got Bette Davis eyes."

Weezy looked at him. "But I don't have any movies on my—" Her hand shot to her mouth. "Oh no!"

Jack's gut clenched as Munir's theory flashed through his brain.

"Video . . . it's downloading a video. It's started."

Dawn joined them. "What's started?"

"The Jihad virus," Weezy said as she leaped to her keyboard and began tapping madly. "I can't stop it. And it won't shut down." She leaned over and pressed the power button on the tower. The screen went blank. "There—" The screen came to life again. "It turned itself on!"

"Just unplug it," Jack said.

Instead she hit the lighted off switch on her power strip. As the screen went dark again, she looked at him with wide eyes.

"If this is happening all over the world . . ."

Jack said, "But it'll happen in a wave, right? As all the computer clocks hit the trigger time?"

"Not necessarily. Not if the virus is set to Greenwich Mean Time. If it was set for three P.M. GMT, then computers on the U.S. East Coast would trigger at eight local time. In the Central Time Zone they'd go at seven local, and in the Pacific Zone at five local."

"So they'd all start at once?"

She nodded. "That's the way I'd do it. That's the way to get the most bang out of the virus. Don't give anyone a chance to mount a defense. Hit them with an all-out frontal assault."

Jack envisioned a billion-plus computers across the globe turning themselves on and beginning to download video from the Internet. And as the data is recorded onto the hard drive, the computer begins to upload it to other computers in the botnet which in turn upload video back to it, back and forth and back and forth until their bandwidth is maxed out. All the computers in empty offices in every country, unattended but busily enslaved to Jihad4/20, trading video throughout their networks and beyond. Servers and routers all over the world crashing with the overload.

Gia . . . Vicky.

"How long . . ." His mouth had gone dry. "How long do you think it will take?"

She shrugged. "I'm no expert, not even close, but I imagine it depends on the size of the Jihad botnet. If it's as extensive as they say, could be just a matter of minutes, certainly no more than a few hours."

Jack pulled his phone from a pocket and speed dialed Gia. Her voice mail came up almost immediately. That meant she had her cell turned off. Of course she would. The airlines made you turn them off.

What flight had she said—346, right?

He dialed 411, got the number, and called American Airlines. After navigating a voice tree and punching in the flight number, a robotic female voice told him flight 346 had taken off on time and was due in at 10:50.

"Well," he said, turning to Weezy and Dawn, "at least that computer is still working."

Weezy said, "They're in the air?"

She kept her expression neutral but he could tell from her eyes that she didn't like that idea.

"They'll make it."

Dawn was shaking her head, her expression baffled. "What's happening? I've heard about the virus on the news, but what's that got to do with computer video and planes?"

As Weezy began to explain, Jack wandered back into the front room. His hands balled into fists. He jammed them into his pockets and squeezed his eyes shut as he fought to control the frustration boiling within.

Everywhere he turned lately he found himself facing situations he couldn't control, couldn't do anything about. Rasalom, the Jihad virus, and now Gia and Vicky in the air, in possible danger, and he could do nothing to bring them down safely. Had to depend on someone else . . . always someone else . . .

He needed to break something, hurt someone.

But he wouldn't. Instead he'd do the thing he hated, but the only thing he could do.

He'd wait.

11. *". . . again, if you're just tuning in, the message from the Department of Homeland Security is to unplug your computer and disconnect it from the Internet. In other words, if you have dial-up service, unplug the phone connector; if you have high-speed cable, disconnect from the cable; if you have Wi-Fi, disconnect and power* *off your router. Do this even if you have an uninfected computer. Where the Internet is working at all, transmission has slowed to a crawl. Many servers and routers are down and the ones still working are jammed."*

Dawn hugged herself as she leaned forward on the couch and stared at the TV.

"This is totally scary."

Weezy sat beside her. Jack hung back at the dining area table, listening with growing alarm as news heads from the local stations kept breaking into the regular programming with bulletins from the city and the feds.

The botnet had been active for only an hour or so but was already sending seismic shock waves through cyberspace.

"This just in from the mayor's office: Unless it is absolutely necessary to be elsewhere, please stay in your homes. Traffic signals have malfunctioned and traffic is snarled. We have the mother of all traffic jams out there, folks."

"Oh, hell."

Jack jumped up and stepped to the window. Saturday night traffic on the Upper West Side was always snarled, but what he could see below wasn't moving at all.

"What's wrong?" Weezy said.

"I've got to head for the airport."

"But it's only nine-thirty. They're not due in till eleven."

Right. Less than a ten-mile trip. New York City traffic could be a hassle any time, especially on a Saturday night. But this was New York City traffic on a Saturday night in the middle of a cyber meltdown.

"From the way things look, it could take me that long."

She came up beside him and stared down at the traffic.

"I see what you mean." She put a hand on his shoulder. "Be careful out there. And stay in touch, okay?"

"Will do. You stay put."

She shook her head. "I'm going over to sit with the Lady. She may need some company."

The Lady—in his worries about Gia and Vicky he'd forgotten about her.

"Think she's feeling the effects?"

Concern tightened her features. "I don't know. Nobody's ever been here before. She could have a slow weakening, or might not feel a thing till the whole Net crashes."

He looked past her at where Dawn stared at the TV screen. "What about her?"

"I'll have to leave her."

"Yeah. The truth might be hard to explain."

"Too hard."

Jack smiled. "Momma Weezy."

"She needs someone, Jack. She's all alone in the world."

Jack hadn't realized how true that was. Parents dead, baby stolen, cut off from whatever friends she'd had . . . the kid had no one.

"Going to leave her here?"

She shook her head. "She'll be safe in her place."

"Okay. Give the Lady my best. I'll stay in touch as best I can."

He grabbed his coat and headed for the door. He took the stairs down and hit the sidewalk at a trot, heading west toward where he garaged the Crown Vic. Traffic on the side street was stopped dead. As he loped past a taxi he saw a young couple get out and start to walk, leaving behind an angry-looking driver.

"It's cold," the girl said, tightening her coat around her neck.

The guy laid a protective arm over her shoulders. "Yeah, but at least we'll get there before it's over."

When Jack reached Amsterdam, he stopped. Always a

jam here, but at least with *some* sense of movement, even if only inches at a time. Right now—nothing.

He looked up and saw why: The traffic lights were blinking yellow in both directions. In this city a yellow caution light translated as *Hit the gas*. Yellow both ways meant everybody had the right of way. Yielding was for pussies. No surprise at the ironclad gridlock.

A traffic cop might have helped—if one could get here—but as Jack fought his way uptown along the crammed Broadway sidewalk, he doubted it. Every intersection was the same. This called for a cop on every corner and even that wouldn't work. There didn't seem anywhere left to go. It looked like every car in the five boroughs had been plunked down on the streets. The only solution Jack could see was to pave them over and start anew.

He passed an angry crowd outside the Beacon Theater, complaining about the inability to buy tickets for the Allman Brothers because the theater's computers were down. A waiter was taping a CASH ONLY sign to the window of a bistro. The subtitle read: "Can't run credit cards."

The faces around him showed a mixture of anger, frustration, bemusement, and bewilderment. At least no one looked bored.

It dawned on him that his car was useless.

Okay, he'd go subway. Catch a train down to Times Square and switch to the 7 out to Queens. It would drop him off with a good walk to the airport, but maybe he could grab a cab out there. Traffic couldn't be as bad as here.

He found a subway entrance and was halfway down the stairs when a haggard-looking suit coming up said, "Don't bother."

Jack stopped. He'd had a niggling worry about this.

"Not running?"

He shook his head. "Got a 1 just sitting in the station

with its doors open. Conductor says he doesn't know what's up. They got the word to sit tight. Something about switching or signal problems, he thinks."

Yeah, that made sense. They were controlled by computers, right?

Jack slammed a fist against the railing.

"I know how you feel," the guy said. "Well, there's always a cab."

"Not always."

Jack turned and followed him back up to the surface.

"Christ!" the guy said, stopping short as he saw the traffic. "What the fuck?"

Jack slipped past him and headed for Julio's.

12.   "Where's the remote?" Weezy said.

The Lady sat at the big table and pointed to the empty shelves built into the wall of the front room of her apartment. "Up there."

She didn't look so hot. Not as pale and frail as she'd been after the *Fhinntmanchca* assault, but not as good as she'd looked just yesterday. Weezy was worried about her.

But at least she was still here.

She found the remote where the Lady had indicated— and also found a thick coating of dust on it. She blew it off and coughed.

"I take it you don't watch much TV."

"I don't watch any."

"Not even news?"

"Of human events, the state of the world? I know whatever I wish to know."

Of course she did. Stupid questions. She was the product of the collective human consciousness.

"And the rest?"

She shrugged. "The fictions—the dramas, the comedies, the commentaries hold no interest for me."

"They do for me." Weezy pressed the ON button. "Especially now."

"*—appears that preventive measures are failing,*" said the channel seven newsreader.

"Too little too late," Weezy muttered.

"*Servers and routers all over the world are failing as they are inundated with a tsunami of video feeds that is overwhelming the bandwidth of the entire Internet. Here in the city . . .*"

Weezy heard a groan behind her and turned to find the Lady slumped forward on the table. She dropped the remote and hurried over to her.

"Are you all right?"

Another stupid question—of course she wasn't all right. She looked anything but all right.

"So weak." Her voice was thin, husky, fragile, as if it might dissolve to dust if she spoke too loud.

Weezy's heart clenched. This was it. They were losing her.

"You need to lie down. Which way's your bedroom?"

"I don't have a bedroom."

"You don't—?"

"I don't sleep."

"Okay. Fair enough. We'll find you a bed."

Glaeken had given her a furnished apartment. One of the rooms down the hall had to have a bed.

She put one of the Lady's arms over her shoulder and one of her own around her back, then lifted. She'd expected near dead weight, but the Lady came right off the chair.

So light . . . *too* light . . . much too light.

Was this how she was going to go? Lose her substance bit by bit and fade away?

She walked her down the hall. The first room on the right had a queen-size bed. Weezy stretched her out on it.

"Should I get you a blanket?"

"I don't feel cold. Or warmth. Temperature doesn't affect me. But I do feel terribly weak." She raised an arm and let it fall. "Weaker and weaker by the moment . . . as if the life is draining out of me."

Weezy felt her throat constrict. "Don't leave us."

"I will not go willingly. I will fight this." She waved a hand. "Let me lie here alone. I need to conserve my strength."

Weezy left her and returned to the front room. She sat before the TV and stared at the screen. It was running feeds from street cams, showing massive traffic jams.

How was Jack ever going to reach LaGuardia?

13. "Don't know what's taking him so long," Julio said. "He's only coming from Harlem."

Jack glanced at the St. Pauli Girl clock over the bar. Almost ten after ten.

Damn. Forty minutes till they landed.

He'd remembered that Julio's younger brother Juan was into motorcycles. Julio had called him and prevailed upon him to drive down to the bar and lend one of his bikes to Jack.

"If he's dealing with this traffic, it's going to take him a while—even weaving through it."

With all the arteries out of the city clogged, the only solution was something with the ability to slip between the clots. A motorcycle seemed perfect.

One problem, though. Jack hadn't ridden one in a while. He'd used two wheels pedaling around Burlington County as a kid, so when he was old enough for motorvating, he'd seen no reason to move up to four. His folks had hated his Harley, and his sister Kate, the doctor, repeatedly warned him about the motorcycle drivers she'd seen wheeled into the ER, brain dead from a dust-up with a car or truck. She'd called his Harley a "donorcycle."

Jack wouldn't listen, and owned a succession of Harleys through college. He loved motorcycles—he'd used Arlo Guthrie's pronunciation, rhyming with *pickle*—reveling in the anarchic freedom they offered. Plus, the helmet conferred anonymity.

Of course, he'd felt immortal then.

He'd brought one with him when he'd disappeared into the city, and rode it until a potentially fatal crash drove home how vulnerable he was on two wheels—like a turtle living outside its shell, roadkill waiting to happen at the hands of anyone who was fiddling with the radio or cell phone when traffic was coming to a sudden stop. What might be a simple fender bender in a car-to-car scenario escalated to bug-against-the-windshield potential when a motorcycle was involved. And when being chased by a gang of psychos in cars . . .

That was when he'd bought Ralph. And when the Corvair became too conspicuous, he'd graduated to the Crown Vic.

If he was going to be involved in any vehicle-to-vehicle mishap, Jack wanted to be the one to walk away.

He looked around the unusually crowded bar.

"You running a two-for-one special or something?"

Julio made a face. "Yeah, right." He jerked a thumb toward the street. "They're from out there. Traffic ain't movin' so they come in to kill time."

"I see you opened up the back tables."

He looked sheepish. "They need a place to go. Gotta put 'em somewhere."

This was mucho unJulio. He didn't like random patrons. If he had his way, his bar would be a private club that required a membership card, with him as sole arbiter of the suitability of who could be served.

"How civicly responsible."

He grinned. "Community service—my middle name, meng."

"And that ringing cash register has nothing to do with it."

"Like Abe says: Ain't nothin' better'n doing well while doing good."

Then the door banged open and a young Latino who resembled Julio—minus ten years and a lot of muscle—pushed a stripped-down motocross bike into the bar.

"Ay, Juanito. You can't bring that in here."

"Ain't leavin' it outside. Be gone in a beat."

Julio stepped forward and shot his hand toward Juan's face. For a second Jack thought he was going to hit him, but instead he grabbed his chin and turned his head.

"What happen to you?"

Jack could see it now—a good-size bruise on his chin, bleeding a little.

"Guy tried to steal my bike. It's getting crazy out there."

So soon?

Jack had figured it would take longer for the idea to filter to the synapses of the wolves that the shepherds had lost some of their eyes and ears and the sheeple were largely unguarded.

"Hey, I'm sorry about that," Jack said. "I owe you."

Juan shrugged. "S'okay. You don't owe this family nothing."

Jack looked at Julio. "What's he talking about?"

"Rosa." Julio gave Jack a backhand slap across an arm. "What? You forget?"

It took Jack a couple of seconds to realize he was talking about his sister. Rosa had been having some nasty trouble with her ex-husband. Jack had fixed it. And yeah, he'd kind of forgotten about it.

"Long time ago."

"This family, we got long memories. You know that."

"And nobody else was supposed to know."

Julio's deprecatory shrug could not quite hide his pride in his younger brother. "Juanito figured it out."

"Good for him." Jack held the door and nodded toward the street. "Back her out onto the sidewalk and you can show me how it works."

Juan rolled his eyes. "Aw, you ain't gonna tell me you never been on a bike before."

"Course I have. Just been a while is all. Be with you in a minute." As the door closed behind Juan and the bike, Jack turned to Julio. "Got anything I can use if I run into trouble?"

Julio's eyebrows lifted. "You ain't carrying?"

Jack cocked his head and gave him a stare.

"Silly me," Julio said with a twisted grin.

"Silence would be golden."

Julio ducked behind the bar and returned with something held tight against his outer thigh, shielding it from the room. When he reached Jack he slipped him a leather slapper. Jack gave it a surreptitious heft.

"Isn't this—?"

"Yeah, the one you got me."

Jack had bought it years ago from Abe as a gift for Julio. Basically a foot-long blackjack—fourteen ounces of lead in a flattened leather sleeve with a wrist strap. A fight ender.

"What if you need it?"

"I still got the bat and my little fren."

Little fren . . . Julio's borrowed name for the double-ought, sawed-off ten-gauge he kept under the bar.

Jack pocketed the sap and headed for the door.

Out on the sidewalk, the night had quieted some. Only an occasional echoing blare. Drivers seemed to have realized the futility of leaning on the horn. In fact some of the cars were empty, temporarily abandoned while their owners found something better to do—like hang out in Julio's.

Jack turned his attention to the bike. It looked like it had seen better days.

"Kind of old."

Juan puffed his chest. "Vintage Yamaha, man. Custom seat, titanium—"

"Great. I need a quick tour so I can get on the road."

"What you use to ride?"

"Harleys."

"Cool. But these ride different."

Juan quickly ran through the gearshift, the clutch, and the throttle. Pretty standard, except Jack hadn't driven anything with a clutch in ages.

Maybe this wasn't such a good idea. Get into an accident and break something major or, worse, wind up dead—what good would he be to Gia and Vicky then?

But it was the only idea left.

He thought of them landing and walking into an airport in chaos. Could they rent a car? Maybe, maybe not. Depended on whether the rental companies' computers were up and running. And then where could they drive? Not into the city. Maybe just catch a shuttle to an airport hotel. Yeah, that might work, but Jack wanted to be with them when they did it.

So it was Easy Rider time.

"Remember, this ain't no Harley. You gotta keep your weight forward on these models. The front wheel comes up easy if you don't. Keep your feet on the pegs and hug that gas tank with your knees."

"Got it."

"Yeah?" Juanito looked a little uncertain. "Let's see you ride."

Jack looked at the dead-still traffic on the street. "Where?"

"Yeah. You gotta point."

"I'll take her over to the museum," Jack said. "Run her around the lot to get used to her."

"Good idea. Want me to come?"

"Nah. You stay here and hang with your brother. Don't wait for me though. I don't know when I'll be able to return this thing."

Truth was, he wasn't sure what he was going to do with the bike once he got to the airport. No way he could ride Gia and Vicky back on it. If anything happened to it, he'd buy Juan a new one—the bike of his choice.

"You leave it anywhere, you chain it good." He touched the pouch behind the seat. "Chain and lock's in here. Key's with the ignition."

"Got it."

He swung his leg over and revved the engine as he got comfortable on the seat. He could half walk, half ride to the museum, only a few blocks from here. Use the sidewalks if he had to.

"Take this," Juan said, holding out the helmet.

Jack looked at his bruised, cut chin. "You say it's rough out there?"

"Guy tried to jump me when I slowed down."

Jack waved off the helmet. "You hang on to it."

"It's the law."

"Somehow I don't think the law's gonna be worrying about biker helmets tonight."

Besides, if things were heading south out there, he didn't want anything interfering with his peripheral vision.

14.   The Museum of Natural History's lot was deserted and in just a few minutes Jack felt like he'd never stopped riding. On the way to Julio's earlier he'd picked up an oversize gray Nets hoodie as an extra layer against the cold. He'd slipped it over his jacket. Now he pulled up the hood, tied it tight to give him a full view, and got moving.

The traffic on Central Park West . . . could he call it traffic? The word implied movement. No movement here. More like a parking lot. And little or no space between bumpers. People had inched forward until they were all practically touching. A lot of drivers had turned off their engines and sat, huddled lumps of frustration behind their steering wheels, staring out at the tableau, despairing of ever moving again.

Jack rode uptown on the downtown-bound side until he found a small pod of cars with enough space between their bumpers to let him through to the park side.

Now at least he was heading in the direction the traffic was pointing. He found narrow riding room on the shoulder. The sidewalk to his right separated him from the park, and was less crowded than those he'd seen farther west. Beyond a low stone-and-concrete wall, the trees loomed large and leafless against the night sky, the closer ones lit by the sodium streetlights, those farther in little more than dark smudges.

The park tempted him. He was sure the traverses were as jammed as every other street in the city, but he'd have better off-road opportunities there. A no-brainer if the sun was up. But on this night, in the dark . . . uh-uh. Odds of running into a wolf pack were a little too high. Be a different story in a few months when he'd start the Annual Park-a-Thon to raise money for the local Little League team. Then he'd dress in appropriate tourist gear and wander off the paths, *looking* to get jumped so he could mug the muggers for donations. But he couldn't afford any trouble tonight. No time for it.

So he'd have to settle for ten or so miles per hour along the CPW shoulder. He could have gone faster, but limited his speed for fear of someone opening a car door in front of him. Even so, he felt like he was whizzing by.

He'd reached the Nineties, closer to the uptown end of the park, and was passing the twin-towered mass of the Eldorado—one of his favorite Manhattan buildings— when a man's voice called out behind him.

"Young man! On the cycle! Wait!"

If the guy had called out, *Ay, yo!*, Jack would have kept going, but the cultured tone made him look back. An older gent was standing by the open door of a limo two cars back, waving.

"Please stop!"

Jack stopped and waited as the man hurried toward him. He looked maybe sixty, with dyed hair, wearing what looked like a cashmere coat. His jaw barely moved when he spoke.

"Can you give me a ride? I must get to Columbus and Ninety-sixth. I'll pay you—handsomely, I assure you."

That was the West Side. Jack was headed east.

He shook his head. "Out of my way."

As he started to kick off, the guy grabbed his arm.

"No, wait! I'll *buy* the bike from you. The whole bike. How much do you want for it? Name your price."

"Sorry. Not for sale."

As he began to move off, the guy grabbed him in a bear hug and tried to pull him off the bike.

"I've got to meet someone!"

Jack drove an elbow into his solar plexus—hard. The guy stumbled back and landed against the passenger door of a nearby car. A faint "Hey!" filtered from within. People on the sidewalk had stopped to watch. Slow night on Central Park West.

"So do I," Jack said.

"Mister Ausler?"

Jack looked around and saw a big guy in a black suit get out of the driver seat of the limo and start moving his way.

"Kevin!" the man who'd been called Ausler shouted, his voice thick with fury. "I need that bike! Get me that bike!"

Now he was moving his jaw.

Kevin? Bruno or Jeeves would have been more in keeping with the scene.

Jack gave Kevin a hard look and shook his head. "You don't want to start something you can't finish." Kevin stopped uncertainly by the front bumper.

Jack then looked at Ausler. "Didn't your mommy ever say no?"

"I offered to buy it!"

Jack twisted the throttle and roared off, passing more limos and junkers and even a pickup truck or two—hedge fund managers, secretaries, laborers, all frozen in position. A traffic jam was an equal-opportunity pain in the ass.

Riding along the park's western flank, the only cross traffic he'd had to deal with was at the rare traverses. They hadn't been too bad, but the gridlock at the 110th Street circle stopped him dead. So he turned east and ran along the top of the park. He made good time there until he reached the northeast corner at Fifth. Crossing that took some doing. He turned uptown again on Madison but had to stop and thread his way past every cross street until he reached 125th.

Harlem's main drag was a whole different kind of chaos. Almost a party vibe here. It looked like people had abandoned their cars either to walk to their destination or hit whatever bars or food joints they could find. If you couldn't drive, might as well get comfortable and hoist a few till the jam eased. A bonanza for the street vendors too—people were lined up for shish kebab and falafel and anything else edible. He spotted a couple of places advertising "soul food." Up ahead he noticed that the rear door of a Budweiser truck had been rolled up and folks were helping themselves to cases of beer and passing out the cans to anyone who wanted one. The driver was nowhere in sight.

The result was an impassable vehicular thicket. He could walk his bike along the crowded sidewalks but time was running out.

Jack needed 125th Street. It led directly to the Triboro Bridge. Only a few more blocks and he'd hit its ramp. The Triboro, true to its name, was actually a series of three bridges linking the Bronx, Manhattan, and, most important, Queens, where it led to the Grand Central Parkway, which in turn led to LaGuardia Airport. The bridges were linked by a long, high viaduct with no lights to slow the flow. Traffic should—*should*—open up there.

Well, he could try a parallel approach. He turned around and headed back down Madison against the traffic, then turned east on 124th.

Much better. Not good, but at least he was able to find a path through the cars. At Second Avenue he saw a sign to the Robert F. Kennedy Bridge. What the—?

Oh, yeah. They'd renamed the bridge back in '08, but nobody called it the Kennedy or the RFK. It was the Triboro and would always be the Triboro. Even the traffic guys on the radio still called it the Triboro.

Jack angled left onto the ramp and ran into real trouble.

15. "Lady?" Weezy said, edging into the darkened bedroom.

She'd never had to address her before by name and "Lady" sounded kind of awkward. But awkwardness be damned, she wasn't answering.

"Lady?"

Still no response.

Weezy stopped at the bedside and turned on the lamp. The Lady lay stretched out in her housedress, her arms at her side, her expression peaceful. She said she didn't sleep but her eyes were closed and—

She wasn't breathing.

Weezy dropped to her knees beside the bed and shook her. Her whole body moved. She seemed to be hollow, made of papier-mâché.

"Lady!"

A breath, then a barely audible, "Yes."

"I thought you were dead!"

Her eyes remained closed as she spoke. "So weak."

Too weak to open her eyes?

"You weren't breathing."

"I don't need air to exist, only to speak."

"Anything I can do?"

A thin smile. "Just go on being you. Now . . . I must conserve my strength."

"Sure. Of course." Weezy rose and backed away. "Conserve it. Every ounce. I'll be outside if you need me."

Need me? For what? What could she do?

She reached for the lamp. "Do you want the light out?"

"It doesn't matter."

Weezy left it on and returned to the front room.

"She's fading away," she whispered to no one. A sob broke free. "We're losing her."

16. The Triboro ramp was at a complete standstill. The tollbooths were bad enough. Each of the narrow lanes between them was blocked by a car that couldn't move forward or backward. Jack inched his bike past a Mini Cooper only to face the worst jam yet. Cars feeding toward the first bridge were packed so close they couldn't open their doors. Certainly no room for his bike.

He spotted open space far to the left—the exit to Randall's Island. Nobody seemed interested in that. Well, why not give that a try? Maybe he could find a way back up to the viaduct that would put him past this logjam.

A real rush to be able to feed the bike some gas down the empty ramp. After what he'd been through, thirty miles an hour felt like ninety.

He'd been here once or twice since moving to New York. Mostly a sports park with tennis courts, soccer and football fields, a couple of baseball diamonds, but also home to an FDNY fire academy and some sort of mental hospital.

Down on solid ground again, he followed a road paralleling the phalanx of huge columns that supported the viaduct looming a good hundred feet overhead. The light was poor down here and he had to depend on his headlight. He was rolling along, looking for a way back upstairs when the light picked up a hint of movement up ahead on the right near one of the columns. Could be nothing, could be bad news, like someone ducking out of sight. His headlight would have been visible for a while now, allowing time to set a trap.

As he sped through his options, he pulled the sap from his jacket and looped the thong around his wrist. He could have gone for the Glock nestled in the nylon holster in the small of his back, but he was going to need two hands to handle the bike. Still . . .

Thick brush lined the left side of the road, creating a gauntlet of sorts. He could stop and go back and look for another route, but there might not be one. He needed a way through here that would avoid trouble without slowing his progress.

As he closed in on the column, he made up his mind. Leaning low over the handlebars, he maxed the throttle and veered left, away from the column. The bike leaped ahead—

—and someone jumped from behind the column, swinging what looked like a two-by-four. It passed through the space where Jack's head would have been had he remained upright, but now it missed both high and wide.

As Jack glanced right to see if his would-be attacker was alone, something hit him from the left. He felt an arm go around his waist in a partially missed tackle. He slipped free but the impact was enough to unbalance him. He squeezed the brakes for all they were worth as the bike tipped. It went over, but he had his arms and legs tucked as metal scraped pavement. He was into a roll as he hit the ground, minimizing the impact. Still it knocked some of the wind out of him, and pain knifed through his right hip as it caught on the rim of a pothole.

Damn. Same leg that Valez had gouged.

The failed tackler was on him before he could regain his feet. In the glow of the bike's headlamp, he saw a boot flashing toward his face. He managed to block it and keep rolling. The move caused a stab of agony from his hip, and then a second kick caught him in the ribs—a glancing blow because of his roll, but it still hurt like hell.

Continuing to roll, he spotted the Buford Pusser wannabe approaching, two-by-four raised. He found the handle to the slapper—still attached by its thong—and took a wild swing, putting as much arm and wrist into it as he could manage from the ground. Nearly a pound of whipping lead connected with the tackler's knee. The guy let loose a cry of pain as his leg gave out. He pitched forward, landing next to Jack. With a howl of rage he made a gouge move at Jack's face, going for the eyes. Jack grabbed his wrist and rolled him atop him just as his buddy took a fence-buster swing at Jack's head. The board caught the tackler across the back; ribs cracked like twigs as the air went out of him in a strangled whoosh.

Jack took another wild swing with the slapper and caught

the batter's ankle. With a surprised yelp he hopped backward, grabbing at his lower leg. Jack lashed out with a kick from his uninjured leg, hooking the good ankle and unbalancing him. He landed hard on his ass with a pained, stunned look.

Jack rolled the grunting, gasping tackler off him, struggled to his feet, and hobbled over to the batter before he could recover. The guy took a wild swing at Jack's legs with the board but missed. Jack stepped in and backfisted him in the nose, snapping his head back, then dropped on him, planting a knee in his ample gut. The guy gave out an agonized grunt. He rolled back and forth, groaning and writhing as he clutched his belly. He bent a knee and as Jack saw it rise he swung the slapper, putting his back, arm, and wrist into the blow. The lead weight caught the kneecap dead center. He was pretty sure he heard it shatter before the guy's echoing scream blotted out all other sounds.

After making a quick full turn to see if the immediate area held any more surprises, Jack limped back to where the tackler lay on his side, trying to catch his breath as he struggled to rise. Jack flipped him over onto his back and disabled him the same way—another scream, another shattered knee.

He straightened and stared at the two writhing, groaning figures. He wanted to say something to them but his hip hurt like hell and his brain was stuck in a nonverbal gear that wanted to kill instead of speak.

He pulled the Glock and worked the slide to chamber a round. The tackler looked up at him, fear widening his eyes.

Not for you, Jack thought. Just insurance.

No need for something so final. No threat to him now—or to anyone else. Chaos might reign in the city over the next few days, but these two oxygen wasters would not be part of it.

He put the pistol away and turned to where the bike lay on its side. On the other hand, if the bike was disabled and he wouldn't be able to get to LaGuardia tonight, he might revisit the kill option.

The bike had stalled after the fall. He righted it, and in the backwash of the headlight, checked it out as best he could. No major structural damage he could see, no odor of leaking gas. He got on, put her in neutral, kicked the starter, and felt a flood of relief as she sputtered to life.

Before he got rolling again, he checked his watch: ten after eleven. Already late and these jerks had slowed him even more. He called Gia's cell with little hope of hearing her voice.

Yep. No answer. No surprise. If she'd landed she'd be calling him as soon as allowed.

He found the American Airlines number in his call history from earlier and hit that. Went all the way through the damn voice tree again only to be told that no flight information was available. He thumbed 0 until he reached a living, breathing human being who told him what he'd already guessed: The airline's computers were down.

"So, you don't know if the plane landed or is still in the air or crashed?"

"No, sir."

"Do you know the gate number?"

"I would need the system up for that, sir."

He noticed the batter rolling onto his belly.

"Well then, how about calling one of your gates at the airport and asking them to check if three forty-six is in?"

"I can't do that, sir."

"Even if I say 'Please'?"

"I'm sorry, sir."

He noticed Buford trying to rise onto his good knee.

"Uh-uh!" Jack told him.

The guy ignored him and kept rising.

"I'm sorry, sir?"

"You've got two knees. Nature deplores asymmetry. Want me to even them out?"

Buford blasted him a look of pure hatred and lowered himself to the ground.

"Sir?"

"Sorry. Talking to someone else. Look, how about giving me the number and I'll call."

"Sorry, sir."

Jack felt steam rising. She couldn't help the computer snafu, but she could do something about this.

"Hey, look—"

The phone went dead. Had she hung up on him?

He checked the cell's display: no bars . . . no service. But just a moment ago he'd had a strong signal. That could only mean—

Shit. Ripples from the botnet were seeping into the communications systems.

He resisted an urge to fling the phone and pocketed it instead. Service would be back up sooner or later. Probably later. But this meant no contact with Gia until he reached the airport.

If then.

He realized with a start that her flight might have been diverted. Well, that didn't change anything. Until he learned otherwise, he had to assume she was landing at LaGuardia, and so that was where he had to be.

He gunned the engine and got rolling again. He followed the Triboro viaduct above onto Ward's Island, which used to be separate but had been joined to Randall's by landfill. He rode across a soccer field and found a path that dead-ended near a baseball diamond at the water's edge. At no point had he seen an access ramp back onto the roadway that coursed directly above.

Jack sat on the bike and cursed as he stared across the water at the lights of Astoria . . . the northwest corner of

Queens. And along Astoria's eastern border lay LaGuardia Airport.

Narrow here. Not a thousand feet across. The far shore looked close enough to swim to, but not here, not even in summer. This strait, a branch of the East River known as Hell Gate, was famous for its treacherous currents and occasional whirlpools. Jack didn't know how much of that was real and how much myth, but even if it were all myth, here and now he'd never make it across that frigid water.

Still cursing he began to turn the bike. He was halfway around when he saw lights in the sky to the east . . . a plane . . . coming in for a landing.

All right. The airport was still functioning. Gia could be waiting there now, wondering where he was. Trouble was, she'd have to go on wondering for a while. Because Jack was going to have to go back and find a way past that pile-up—even if he had to pick up the bike and carry it over those jammed cars.

He glanced left and saw another bridge. He gunned in that direction and stopped under it. Above, silhouetted against the light pollution from the city, were what looked like slats.

Then he realized what they were.

Train tracks.

A train trestle. Couldn't belong to any of the mass transit lines. None of them ran this way. So it had to be a freight line. Of course. Trains ran all the way from New England into Queens across the Hell Gate trestle. If he could find a way onto those tracks, he had a route across the river.

He just had to hope the tracks stayed empty.

He raced back toward the on-ramp to the viaduct. As he was approaching the spot where he'd been jumped he noticed a sign that brought him to a skidding halt.

Queens Pedestrian Ramp

A closer look revealed a covered walkway running up to the viaduct. How had he missed that? He guessed his attackers had distracted him. More they had to answer for.

He gunned the bike. The pedestrian ramp was about to become a motocross ramp.

17. Kewan sat in the borrowed car, sipping luke-warm coffee and listening to the news while he waited for word. He'd parked on a little-used stretch of asphalt off the rural county road that led to the IXP. He'd tuned in to a Cleveland station and couldn't help grinning as he listened to news of the chaos. The city was paralyzed. Nobody could get anywhere.

He pumped a fist at the windshield. They'd done it— they brought down the system.

He checked his watch and a tingle ran through his chest. Less than a minute to go. He checked his cell phone. He'd been told to keep it handy in case Bridger called to tell him plans had changed, but that wasn't going to happen. The phone's window read *No Service*. Fine with Kewan. He didn't want to hear from Bridger. Didn't care much for the guy and got the impression the feeling was mutual. But he didn't have to like the guy. What mattered was with no service, there'd be no message telling him to walk away. No message meant it was Go for *blow!*

Timing was important. No sense in breaking up the infrastructure before the Net was down because that would actually save some routers. No, they wanted everything fried before the charges added icing to the cake.

He started the car and pulled up to the four-lane black-top of the county road. He paused there and sorted through his collection of seventeen garage door transmitters on the passenger seat. Each had a piece of white labeling tape on its cover, and each tape was labeled with a number. He found number 1 and opened the battery compartment. He slipped in two AA Energizers, then turned onto the empty road. Keeping an eye on his rearview mirror, he pressed the button.

A column of flame exploded from the center of the pavement, sending the manhole cover into orbit.

He laughed and pounded the wheel as he drove on. One down, sixteen more to go. Much as he liked to watch them blow, being there was risking getting his ass caught, the last thing he needed. He wanted to be out and about when everything fell apart, not in a jail cell.

But these transmitters didn't have much range, so he had no choice.

Maybe that was for the best. No worry then about someone passing a spot when it exploded. He was an evolutionary, not a revolutionary—a Kicker, not a killer. He didn't want innocent blood on his hands. Guilty blood, okay, but he wasn't no goddamn Arab. Anybody who got in the way of the evolution had to go down, but a mom driving home to her kids from a late shift . . . no way.

He kept to the speed limit as he drove toward the next spot.

18. "Hey, you gotta come with us," the guy said for what seemed like the thousandth time. "Jake'll be here any minute—lives like a mile from here—and then it's party time."

Gia kept a tight grip on Vicky's hand and stared straight ahead at the empty baggage carousel. After the nightmare plane ride, why did she have to be saddled with these two low-rent Lotharios?

For a while up there she'd been afraid the plane would never land. The pilot had announced that computer problems were slowing landings at all the New York airports and they'd been directed into a holding pattern. As they'd flown round and round, she'd wondered how much fuel the tanks held in reserve. Then, finally, they'd been cleared to land.

But upon leaving the plane, these two had attached themselves to her on the jetway. They'd obviously been drinking. Probably had a few at O'Hare before the flight and then more on board.

Gia had been about to say something back there, but then she'd emerged into chaos. The gates and aisles of Concourse D were jammed with angry-looking people. As she moved through the crowd she gathered that the same computer problems that had delayed their landing had delayed all departures, with no hint of when they might resume.

As she'd woven through the crowds, the two remoras stayed close behind, oblivious to their surroundings, focused solely on what they repeatedly referred to as her "fine ass." She finally stopped and confronted them and threatened to report them. A mistake. They'd only laughed and escalated the trash talk, becoming bolder and bolder as they moved from the concourse to the equally chaotic Central Terminal.

"Why are they following us, Mommy?" Vicky said.

"Just hang on. We'll be out of here soon."

"I don't like them."

She'd tried to lose them in the terminal, but they'd stayed close. They seemed to be traveling light and she'd prayed they wouldn't stick with her all the way to baggage.

They did.

Along the way she'd learned that the taller one was named Gabe and the shorter was Angelo. Gabe had bleached his hair a stark white but had left his eyebrows black. Angelo simply tied his long, dirty locks into a greasy ponytail. Both had Kicker Man tattoos on their hands.

Gabe was the mouthier of the pair. He leaned close now—close enough to share the whiskey on his breath as he spoke over her shoulder.

"You're one fine MILF, y'know that?"

Gia said nothing.

"You know what MILF means, don't you."

She did, but she ignored him. Too late she realized that was a mistake.

"It means you're a Mom I'd Like to Fuck."

Fury ignited within Gia. She spun to face him and shoved him away.

"If you've no respect for me, at least have some for this little girl!"

He looked at Vicky and grinned. "Hey, a couple more years on her and she'll be a TILF—a Tween I'd Like to Fuck."

This cracked up Angelo and the two of them bumped fists. Gia's hand started into motion to give his face a bump of her own, but she pulled it back. No telling what that would spark in these two.

"That does it. I'm getting a cop."

He laughed and made a dramatic show of looking around. "Yeah? Where?"

She made her own search. Her heart sank. Not a uniform of any kind in sight. No TSA. Nothing.

Two liquored-up creeps and her with a child. Jack had pushed her for years to carry a pistol but the very idea terrified her. To pacify him, she had agreed to a little spray can of Mace. She'd never had to use it, but she was ready now. Too bad it was on her dresser at home—no way to check it through onto the plane in her carry-on.

Where was Jack? She couldn't raise him on her cell phone—couldn't call anyone, in fact, including 911.

Then she felt a pair of hands grab her hips as Gabe began thrusting his pelvis against her buttocks.

Angelo laughed. "Ride her, cowboy!"

Gia tried to twist away but Gabe held her fast. Other people around her turned to look but no one moved to help. Maybe they thought they were a couple just fooling around, or maybe they simply didn't want to get involved.

Vicky's terrified expression fueled a burst of strength that allowed her to pull free. She whirled, fingers bent into claws. She remembered Jack telling her that if she was ever in a situation like this to go for the eyes. No matter how big or mean an attacker, they'd drop whatever they were doing to defend their eyes. A gouged cornea monopolized anyone's attention. She'd never thought she could do something like that, but this creep had crossed the line.

She lashed out and raked her nails across his face. He ducked back but not before she made contact, scraping his forehead and the bridge of his nose, but missing his eyes.

She grabbed Vicky and began to hurry her away when a hand clamped on the back of her neck.

"You fucking little—*ungh!*"

The hand suddenly released her. She looked over her shoulder and saw Gabe down on one knee, his face a mask of pain as a man twisted his ear. The man wore a Nets sweatshirt with the hood up. His face was partially hidden but her heart leaped as she recognized what she saw of it.

"Jack!" Vicky cried.

Jack didn't react to her. He had his eyes fixed on Angelo.

"Not another inch unless you want a present," he told him.

Gia knew that tone. She'd heard it only a few times and each of those had ended in terrible mayhem. It was the voice of the other Jack, the one he kept hidden. The Hyde

Jack. She knew she'd hesitate to strike at someone's eyes, even someone like Gabe. And that hesitation had given Gabe a chance to duck away. Hesitation was alien to Jack, especially the Hyde Jack. She didn't understand his thought processes in that sort of situation, or even if thought was involved. Jack *acted*.

She used to be afraid of the Hyde, worrying that he'd take over and not let go. But over the years she'd come to see that he was but a small part of Jack, and if she loved Jack, she'd have to love the Hyde Jack as well. Hyde was part of the package. And strangely enough, with time she realized that the seeming danger Hyde represented attracted her to Jack all the more.

Angelo looked baffled as he tried to make sense of Jack's comment. Gia was baffled as well.

"Present? What the f—?"

"Your buddy's ear." Jack gave it a vicious twist, eliciting a howl from Gabe as he touched his other knee to the floor and further lowered his head. "Another inch closer and I'll make you a present of it."

Angelo backed off a step.

Everybody around the carousel was watching now. But, as before, no one moved to interfere.

Jack turned his attention to Gabe. His voice shook as he spoke.

"What . . . what did you think you were just doing? What made you think you could do that to her? What-what-what-what-WHAT!" The last word was a barely decipherable roar.

Against all reason, Gia suddenly feared what might happen to the creep. Not for the creep's sake. For Jack's. He looked ready to lose it. And if he did he could end up in terrible trouble.

"Jack? Don't."

He didn't look up.

"Don't what?"

"Whatever it is you feel like doing to him, please don't."

"You can't imagine what I feel like doing to him."

"I won't even try."

She was about to say, *For your sake, don't*, but realized he might be in a place where that wouldn't matter. She did know something that wouldn't fail to reach him.

"Vicky's watching."

He glanced over at Vicky and her worried expression. He paused, then lowered his head toward Gabe's ear and said something. Gia couldn't make out the words, but she was pretty sure they weren't sweet nothings.

Finally he released Gabe and stepped back. The creep jumped up and covered his ear with a hand.

"You all right, Gabe?" Angelo said.

Instead of answering, Gabe pointed a finger at Jack.

"You're fucking dead! Angelo here is my witness, motherfucker. You are so fucking—!"

The word ended in a cry of pain and Gia realized that somehow Jack had gotten hold of his finger and bent it back at an impossible angle—impossible without breaking or dislocating it.

Again . . . without the slightest hint of hesitation.

Cradling his damaged hand in his good one, Gabe bent and hobbled away.

"You're dead!" he screamed. "DEAD!"

Jack watched them go, then turned and walked toward her—with a limp. What had happened? But as he approached, he smiled and Gia saw Hyde fade away.

19. "I want to go home," Vicky whined from her mother's lap.

So did Jack. And he knew Gia did too. But even if he could fit them on the back of the bike—and he couldn't—passage to the city was impossible unless he went back the way he came in. And that was out of the question. Riding the Triboro walkway into Astoria hadn't been bad, but he'd had to leave the highway and travel local streets to get here. Twice along the way guys tried to jump him, but he managed to scoot out of trouble by inches. He'd almost lost control of the bike once, coming *that* close to going over. And that had been solo. Taking the same route back with one passenger, let alone two, was out of the question.

Gia closed her phone with a frustrated snap.

"Still dead. How long is this going to last?"

Jack shrugged. "Could be a long time." He took her hand. "Sorry about this."

"This is hardly your fault."

"Your being here is. If I'd kept my mouth shut, you wouldn't have changed your flight. Right now you'd be in Iowa, sound asleep in your folks' place."

She squeezed his hand. "You hardly twisted my arm. I wanted to get home." She stared at his hood. "Are you going to keep that up all night?"

"Yeah. This is an airport. Cameras everywhere."

"But you're just sitting."

"I wasn't just sitting when I had my little run-in with your admirers."

"I'm sorry you had to wind up in the baggage area. I had it all planned to meet you out front so you wouldn't have to—"

"It's okay."

Whatever pain he might have felt revisiting the site of his father's murder had vanished in a blast of rage when he spotted that animal dry-humping Gia. It had taken every nanoparticle of restraint he possessed to keep from tearing off his ear and shoving it down his throat. He could feel the memory of it pulling his lips back from his teeth . . .

Shaking it off, he scanned the mobbed Central Terminal and sensed impending disaster. The place was a pressure cooker building toward an explosion. People with canceled flights could not go back home because the Grand Central Parkway outside and all the roads around it were at a standstill. Taxis and buses and limos filled the ramps to and from the terminals with nowhere to go.

At least the traffic was keeping new departing passengers from reaching the airport, but planes were still landing. And the debarking passengers had nowhere to go but the terminal and the baggage claim area.

As soon as they'd retrieved Gia's bag, Jack had found two seats at a table in the food court and installed Vicky and her there. They were lucky. Not an open seat left in the entire airport now. Then he'd hit the food stands, stocking up on whatever was ready for immediate consumption: bottles of water, bags of nuts, candy bars, big soft pretzels, hot dogs, and a couple of slices of pizza. Gia had passed on a dog, opting for pizza instead, while he and Vicky enjoyed theirs. They squirreled away the nuts and pretzels for later.

Good thing too. The concessions and restaurants, even though they were operating on a cash-only basis, soon ran out of food and drink. Bare display cases in the Italian specialty shop, empty ovens at the pizza place. Beer and liquor still remained in a good supply at a big, open bar at the center of the food court. That seemed a good thing right now, but what happened when they ran out?

More people kept pressing in from the arrival gates, but at a slower rate. With airports all over the country shutting down departures as well, fewer planes were in the air. All those passengers were on the ground, but they couldn't go home. How many more bodies could the terminals accommodate before someone blew a fuse and the place went nuts? Mass hysteria here could leave a lot of people dead, crushed in the panic.

"Should we stay?" Gia said with a worried look, obviously getting the same powder-keg vibe.

"Well, at least we're warm. It's pretty damn cold outside, and I don't see frostbite as a viable option. The hotels are full, so—"

"You're sure of that?"

"More than one source said so."

After picking up the food, he'd made his way to the drop-off area—somewhat difficult then, a major challenge now—and spoken to the skycaps. They said guys had walked to the hotels for a room and returned saying they were all sold out and people were camping in the lobbies.

He'd considered making the trip himself to verify it but hadn't wanted to leave his ladies alone that long. He couldn't see any reason for the skycaps to make that up.

"How long do we stay here?"

"We can try heading back to the city in the morning. It will be warmer then and, well, most likely we'll have to walk."

Her eyebrows lifted. "You really think so?"

"I do. Maybe not all the way. Your place is less than ten miles from here. Maybe some of the traffic will thin out overnight. Maybe we can cover some of the distance in a cab. It'll be cold, but we'll make it. And then we'll all be back home and feeling like we've won the lottery."

She leaned against him. "I'd give anything to be there now." She straightened and looked around. "Any sign of . . . ?"

"Your fans?"

Jack too took a quick look and saw nothing. Not that he could see very far. Every square foot of floor seemed occupied—those not standing were sitting on their suitcases. No one looked happy.

"Nah. Been watching. Didn't you say they had a friend nearby?"

She nodded. "They said their buddy Jake lives a mile from here and it was going to be 'party time.'"

"How could you turn down an offer like that?"

"Well, it wasn't easy, and under normal circumstances I'd jump at the chance—you know me, right?"

"World's number-one partay babe."

"You got it. But I know how cranky you get when I run off to partay with complete strangers."

"Yeah, well, but I'm in therapy for that—deep into multiple twelve-step programs—so you could've gone."

"Really? If only I'd known. I—" She looked around again and shook her head. "Sorry. Nothing funny about those two."

"No argument. But they're probably at their friend's place getting loaded. And even if they're still here, they aren't armed—"

"How can you be sure?"

"Well, they were on the flight with you." He lowered his voice. "You can sneak certain types of weapons aboard a plane these days"—he'd done it—"but neither of them struck me as having the wattage to pull it off."

"Well . . . I hope you're right."

He shrugged. "Even if I'm not, doesn't matter. I didn't have to go through security."

She lowered her own voice as she looked at him. "So you're . . ."

"Of course."

She snuggled against him again. "I can't believe how much comfort I'm taking from that."

"Ms. No-guns sees the light?"

"I was never antigun. My father has shotguns for hunting pheasant. And though I'm not crazy about the idea of going out and shooting harmless birds, it's part of life out there. But he stored them in a loft in the garage. Guns around the house, especially handguns, make me uncomfortable. Own all the guns you want, just not near me."

Jack smiled. "But I gather you'll admit to an occasional exception?"

"Don't rub it in."

Vicky twisted in her lap. "I'm hungry."

"I'm Mommy," Gia said. "Pleased to meet you, Hungry."

Vicky rolled her eyes. They went through this all the time. "Can I *pleeeease* have something to eat?"

"Sure you're not just bored?"

She clutched her throat and spoke in a strangled voice. "I'm *staaaarving!*"

Gia fished in her bag and came up with one of the big soft pretzels Jack had bought earlier. She gave Vicky half and tucked the rest away.

"Can't I have the whole thing?"

"If you finish that and you're still hungry, we'll see. We've got a long night ahead of us."

Jack watched her shrug and take a hefty bite. He saw Gia squirm under Vicky. She didn't weigh much, but she'd been perched on her mother's lap for a good hour.

"Want me to take her?"

"That's okay. I—"

"Hey!" Vicky cried.

Jack looked up and saw Gabe taking a big bite out of Vicky's pretzel. His left ear was red and swollen, and someone—the first aid station?—had taped his damaged pointer to its neighbor. Three welted scrapes ran across his forehead and the bridge of his nose—Gia's work. Angelo stood behind him, smirking. They'd squeezed through the crowd to wind up in front of them.

He spit out the bite and made a face.

"These things taste like shit without mustard."

Then he dropped the remainder and ground it under his sneaker.

Vicky began to cry. The sound hurled Jack to the brink. He felt the door to where he kept the darkness penned explode off its hinges. His muscles tensed, readying to leap at Gabe and rip out his throat, when he felt slim fingers grip his thigh.

"Don't," Gia said in a low voice. "He's goading you."

"Ya think?" His voice sounded far away, the words like croaks.

But she was right. A fight here could trigger a panic, endangering Gia and Vicky.

He let the darkness flow through him, saturating him without controlling him.

He locked eyes with Gabe and saw him flinch. Some of the confidence seemed to drain from him.

"We need to talk."

Gabe blinked. "Talk?"

"Yeah. Someplace private."

Gabe grinned, his cockiness back. "Oh, I getcha. Yeah. Private. I know just the place."

"I'll bet you do."

"Jack, don't," Gia said, increasing the pressure on his thigh.

"It's okay," he said, rising. He lifted the sobbing Vicky from Gia's lap and put her in his seat. "We're just going to talk." He glanced at Gabe. "Right?"

The grin widened. "Right."

She grabbed his hand. "Please, Jack. They've got something planned."

He looked down at her worried face and winked. Then pulled the hood farther forward to hide more of his face.

"We'll just talk. Like two civilized adults." He pulled free and turned to Gabe and Angelo. "Lead on."

"Jack, no!"

He waved but didn't look back. Gabe turned and began moving away. Angelo tried to fall in behind Jack.

"As if," Jack said, pointing to the spot behind his pal. "After you."

20. "You like making little girls cry?" Jack said as they forced their way through the crowd.

"Yeah," Gabe said over his shoulder. "I like making big girls cry even more. Like your GF. Oh, man, that bitch gonna cryyyyyyy for more when I do her."

Jack let the words roll off. Because they were only words. But this guy had assaulted Gia, and made Vicky cry. Actions . . . actions didn't roll off. Actions demanded reaction. And reaction was on the way.

He knew these guys—not these two in particular, but their type. He ran into them all the time. They weren't schooled, but they weren't dumb. They possessed a cunning lupine radar for when a situation could be turned to their advantage. They sensed the veneer of civilization thinning here and they were responding. They knew nothing about the Internet, but they knew this was no ordinary night. Opportunities were knocking and they were eager to answer the door.

Jack had been assessing the situation as he followed in their wake through the throng. They'd made sure to provoke him past the point where few men could remain passive. That meant they had a plan—and from the way Gabe had agreed to "someplace private," Jack figured getting him alone had been part of the plan all along. Too many witnesses and cell phone cameras in the Central Terminal.

This could go down a number of ways.

Get him alone and pound him to a pulp with some improvised weapon; Jack didn't see any sign of one on either of them, but they could have it waiting for them.

Or they could have a gun or a knife, delivered by their pal, Jake. Who knew? Jake himself might be waiting wherever they were leading him, ready to partake in the beat down.

They reached an EMPLOYEES ONLY door in a recess near some restrooms. People were huddled against the door, just as they huddled in every square foot of the terminal.

"Come on, move your asses," Gabe said. "I told you before, y'gotta keep this door clear."

Before . . . that meant he'd been through here recently.

"Yeah, clear," Angelo said.

Gabe pulled out a plastic card and swiped it through the reader.

"You work here?" Jack said.

"Nah. Got a friend who does."

Would his name be Jake, perhaps?

Gabe entered, Angelo close behind. Jack paused on the threshold, ostensibly concerned about the legality of all this . . .

"Are we allowed?"

. . . while he checked out both sides of the inner door-way.

Clear.

"Yeah," Gabe said. "We're cool."

Jack kept his head down as he stepped into a well-lit stairwell. He didn't bother to look around to check for cameras. He'd work on the assumption they were every-where. With all the chaos in the terminal, he doubted anyone was watching too closely, if at all. But he'd bet the ranch they were recording.

Keeping a careful watch behind and on all the shad-owed recesses along the way, he followed them down a series of flights of stairs. Gabe and Angelo hurried ahead but Jack refused to be rushed. Not that he had much choice. His injured hip complained bitterly about the stairs.

"You're slow as shit, y'know that?" Gabe said from below.

"I'm scared of heights."

"Pussy. I can beat the shit out of you, y'know."

"Maybe."

"Ain't no fuckin' maybe. You suckered me before. Got me from behind. Square on, man to man, I can kick your ass from here to the Bronx. Even with a broken finger I can take you."

As Gabe ranted, Jack sneaked a hand under his sweatshirt to make sure the Glock was loose in its nylon lowback holster. He'd chambered a round after the melee on Randall's Island, and it remained chambered, ready to fire. He had his slapper and his Spyderco Endura in his pockets, and his Kel-Tec backup in its ankle holster.

They kept going down until he was sure they had to be underground.

"Let me know if you spot a Morlock," Jack said.

Angelo glanced over his shoulder. "What?"

"Never mind."

They reached bottom where a heavy door stood open. A swipe-card reader jutted from the wall next to the frame. No Holmesian deduction needed to figure they'd been here before and prepared the space beyond. With what, he had no clue.

Gabe stopped on the threshold and gestured to the space beyond. A smile rippled his lips.

"Nice and private in here."

Still not sure of how he was going to play this, but getting an idea, Jack too gestured toward the doorway.

"About as private as you can get, from the look of it. Please—you two first."

As they stepped through, Jack grabbed the door and slammed it shut behind them. He wasn't sure how he was going to keep it closed, but that question became moot when he saw the big knife in the hand of the man who had been hiding behind the door. The only spot Jack hadn't been able—or had time—to check.

He leaped toward Jack, slashing with the eight-inch blade just as the door reopened and Gabe and Angelo came charging out.

Jack backpedaled, reaching behind him, but his hip slowed him and they were on him before he could grab the Glock. Gabe and Angelo each grabbed an arm while the newcomer held the point of his bowie knife's big, beveled blade against Jack's throat. The overhead fluorescents reflected off both the blade and his shaven skull.

"Real clown, this guy."

Jack didn't dare struggle too much. A heavy blade like that could open his throat with a flick of the wrist. He felt a little sweat gather in his armpits. He'd expected Jake to be waiting inside.

Okay, options-options-options. What did he have?

First off, play cool or scared? Cool might work better with these guys.

"You must be Jake," he said.

The guy's features went slack for a second as he glanced at Gabe. "How the fuck he know—?"

"Who gives a shit!" Gabe tugged Jack's arm and started him moving toward the doorway. "Get him inside!"

"I don't like him knowing my name, man."

"Fuhgeddaboudit. It ain't gonna matter."

That didn't sound good.

As they hauled him into the room, Jack put up enough of a struggle to work his hands behind his back. Jake closed the door, then took Jack's right arm and transferred the knife to Gabe. They slammed Jack back against the wall, but he managed to keep his hands behind him. They each hooked a leg around one of his, preventing any kicks on Jack's part. Seemed like they'd done this before.

"This isn't fair," he said.

"Ay, it's as fair as fair can be. I got a knife and you don't."

Jack lowered his head. "I guess I didn't plan well enough."

"I guess you didn't."

"Yeah, you know the old saying: If you find yourself in a fair fight it means you didn't plan well enough."

Gabe grinned. "Hey, I like that. And it looks like you didn't plan for shit." He twisted the blade back and forth. "Now it's playtime."

Jack writhed, as if trying to get as far as possible from the blade—which wasn't such a bad idea—but the move allowed him to slip his hand under his sweatshirt and find the grip of the Glock.

"Wh-what are you talking about?"

"I'm talkin 'bout you talkin big upstairs, talkin 'bout rippin off my ear and givin it to Angelo. Well, guess what? Guess who's gonna lose an ear? Maybe two?"

"Aw, you don't want to do that."

"That's just starters, asshole. The real fun will be when I gut you."

"G-gut me?"

Jack inched the Glock free of its holster as the tip of the bowie approached his abdomen.

"Yeah. Gonna slice you open and let your guts fall out."

Angelo laughed. "Yeah, like sausages."

Jake twisted his arm. "Maybe we'll feed you some. Like hot dogs."

Angelo guffawed. "Aw, man, we forgot the fuckin' rolls!"

This got laughs all around.

"B-b-but I'll die!"

"No shit!" Gabe shouted. "You're one smart asshole!"

More laughs. They all seemed to be getting a big kick out of this.

"Y-you can't get away with it! The security cameras! It'll all b-b-be on tape! They'll catch you!"

Gabe kept smiling. "All you need is a broom handle to tip them so they don't see nothin'."

Jack slipped his finger over the Glock's trigger. No

safety to worry about. Ready. Just needed to know one more thing.

"S-someone will hear!"

He laughed. "Not you, asshole, 'cause you won't have no ears. And besides, nobody up there can hear nothin' down here."

Just what he needed to hear.

"That's a relief."

Gabe gave him a puzzled look. "Wha—?"

"You didn't plan well enough."

He twisted to clear his right forearm, raised the Glock to hip level, and shot Gabe in the belly. The report was deafening in the small space. Angelo loosened his grip as he jumped and screamed like a girl, giving Jack a chance for a cross-body shot into his chest. Jake jumped on him and tried to take him down. Jack switched hands, slipped the pistol between his arm and his flank, and fired. Jake tumbled off, staggered back against the wall, and left a trail of blood as he slid to the floor.

Jack whirled and found Gabe on his side, hands clutched over his abdomen, kicking his legs as he made agonized, grunting noises. He'd taken a hardball round to the gut. Looked like it had exited via his back. Same with Jake, but his bullet must have hit something vital on its trip through his chest, because his wide, unblinking eyes said he was gone. As was Angelo. The second round in Jack's magazine tended to be a hollowpoint or a pre-frag. He'd used Hydra-Shoks this time. Not much useful left inside Angelo's rib cage.

He stepped over to Gabe and kicked the knife away. The guy's attention was centered on the pain in his belly, but why take a chance?

". . . hurts . . ." he grunted.

"So I've heard," Jack said. "But probably not as much as being gutted by a bowie knife."

Another grunt that sounded like ". . . doctor . . ."

"Don't think so."

". . . please . . ."

Jack rolled Gabe onto his back and pressed the muzzle of the Glock against his chest.

His eyes widened. "No!"

"You made a mistake. You thought you'd brought me into your world, but you wound up in mine. You threatened Gia and put your hands on her. You don't do that in my world. At the moment, life holds too many threats to me and mine that I can't seem to do anything about. You, I'm afraid, have the misfortune of being one that I can."

21. Jack waded back through the crowd until he reached a point where he had a line of sight to Gia. He waited till she looked his way, then waved. Her face lit when she saw him but he motioned her to stay seated.

"Meet me downstairs by the car rental booths," he called.

She gave him a questioning look.

"ASAP," he said.

She nodded and began buttoning Vicky's coat. He turned and squeezed through the crowd.

Far below, he'd left the three bodies where they'd fallen. He'd closed the door to the room and locked them in. No one without a swipe card could open it. After wiping down anything he'd touched, he'd made the long, painful climb back up to the ticketing level.

His hip was on fire now as he entered the crowded men's room and found he had to wait in line for a stall. When he finally reached one, he removed the sweatshirt and hung it on the hook on the back of the door. He waited a minute, then exited, leaving the hoodie behind.

He found a spot outside on the floor where he could watch the traffic in and out of the men's room. He thought it would take at least ten minutes, but it took only five before he spotted a tall, lanky kid exit the men's room with a gray sweatshirt rolled up under his arm. Could have been his own, but his swiveling head and furtive look meant he'd probably boosted it. When Jack spotted a piece of the Nets logo, he was sure.

Wear it in good health . . . but wear it.

Jack headed down to the baggage level and found his ladies waiting near the Hertz booth. Vicky smiled and waved. She seemed to have recovered from the loss of her pretzel. Gia's expression was more serious.

"Are you okay?"

He nodded as he took the handle of her rolling suit-case.

"Fine."

"What about—?"

"They're no longer interested in you."

She bit her upper lip. "Oh, Jack, I don't like the sound of that."

"It's okay."

"But what does that *mean*?"

"Just what it says: They won't be bothering you any-more."

"But . . ." She leaned close and whispered so Vicky couldn't hear. "Did they attack you?"

"As we both knew they would."

"Then why did you go?"

"To get them away from you."

"Did you . . . I mean, are they . . . ?"

He looked at her. "Do you really want to know the de-tails?"

She held his gaze, then looked away. "No. Not really. I have a good imagination."

"I hope Jack kicked their fucking asses."

Unwilling to believe Vicky had just said that, Jack turned and stared into her innocent blue eyes.

"What did you—?"

"Victoria Maria Westphalen!" Gia said, hands on hips in the classic shocked-and-angry mother pose.

It appeared to be dawning on Vicky that she'd crossed some sort of line, but she merely shrugged. "Well, he stole my pretzel."

"That's not the point. Have you ever heard me talk like that? Have you ever heard Jack talk like that? Where on Earth have you ever heard that kind of language?"

"On the bus. Everybody—"

"I don't care what everybody does, we do not use that kind of language, understand?"

"Okay, okay," she said in a my-mother-is-so-not-cool tone. "I hope he kicked their fucking heinies. Okay?"

Jack had to turn away. He could stifle—barely—the laugh that struggled to burst free, but he could not hide the grin. He shouldn't have bothered because, after a pregnant pause, Gia leaned against him and started laughing out loud. Jack joined her while Vicky looked at them like they were crazy.

When Gia finally composed herself she looked back at Vicky. "We don't drop f-bombs either."

"F-bombs?"

"The f-word."

Vicky rolled her eyes. "Okay, how about—?"

"How about we talk about something else?"

Vicky shrugged. "Okaaaaay."

Gia looked back at Jack. "What are we doing out here?"

"I thought we'd go for a walk."

"Back to the city? But—"

"No. One of the hotels. Whichever is closest."

"I thought you said they were full up."

"They are, so we'll camp in a lobby until morning."

"Why?"

"The airport might not be the best place to stay. Way too crowded in there. Something might set that mob off.

And if it does, you two might get hurt." He put an arm around her and pressed her against him. "Or worse."

That was one reason. But Jack had another. Since no one without the right swipe card could enter that room, the bodies had a decent chance of remaining undiscovered till morning. But he couldn't count on it. Someone might stumble on them five minutes from now. Word of a triple murder could panic the crowd. But even if word never reached the crowd, the cops and TSA people would be poring over the tapes. They might see a couple of the dead guys with someone in a gray Nets hoodie. Jack had spotted a good number of gray hoodies in the Central Terminal and, though it was highly unlikely in that packed throng, the tapes might link the hoodie with the dead guys to the hoodie who'd been with Gia and Vicky. That was the way his luck seemed to be running lately.

He lifted Vicky onto his shoulders. His hip protested but he ignored it. This was Vicky.

"Want to go for a ride?"

"Yes!"

He held out his arm to Gia. "Shall we?"

She hooked an arm around his elbow and they started walking. A couple of hotels waited not half a mile from the terminal. Any other night, it would be suicide to try to cross the Grand Central on foot. But tonight it would be like making their way through a crowded parking lot.

He looked up at the sparkling winter sky and thought of the Lady. With all the concern about Gia and Vicky, she'd slipped his mind.

He wondered how she was doing. It couldn't be good.

22. *"Well, it's official. A White House spokesperson has announced that the Internet, that globe-spanning conglomeration of computer networks for the sharing of information, has, for all intents and purposes, crashed. Internet data traffic has come to a virtual standstill. Uninfected intranets—self-contained computer networks with guarded Internet access—still remain functional, as do military and some government networks, but these form an infinitesimal fraction of what the Internet was. No World Wide Web, no Twitter, no Facebook, no chat rooms, no Usenet—it's all down. The Department of Defense is looking at this as a possible act of war. The Department of Homeland Security has raised the National Threat level to red or 'severe.'*

"In further comment, the White House announced—"

Weezy muted the TV.

She hadn't checked on the Lady for a while and was afraid to go see her now. She knew the end was near, maybe had passed.

She pushed herself up to her feet, and forced herself down the hall to the bedroom.

She stopped by the doorway, listening. Again, no breathing. She wasn't used to that, but she expected it. She stepped into the room. The bedside lamp still burned, illuminating the bed—

The *empty* bed!

No . . . no . . . someone there, under the covers. But she'd left the Lady lying atop the covers.

"Lady?"

Weezy gasped as she realized she was seeing the covers *through* the Lady. Her brain kept telling her to run, to flee this madness, but she put one foot in front of the other until she was standing at the bedside, looking down at what was left of the Lady.

Her body as well as her clothing had become transparent, or nearly so. What substance she retained had a faint, misty quality about it, just enough—barely enough—to provide a visible form. Weezy wondered at the transparency of her clothing until she realized that what appeared to be clothing on the Lady was really part of her, as malleable as her flesh—or rather, as malleable as it used to be.

Weezy stared at the two holes in that flesh. When Weezy had first met her last year, she'd shown her a tunnel carved front to back through her torso by a previous attempt to extinguish her. After the *Fhinntmanchca* attack, a second, larger tunnel had appeared on the other side of her navel.

She lay just as Weezy had left her, but . . . she'd been solid then. As before, her eyes were closed. Still conserving energy, or unable to open them?

She reached a hand toward her and noticed how it trembled. She pushed it toward the Lady's shoulder, finally touching it—

—and passing through.

She snatched it back. She'd felt something—the best she could describe it was a tepid liquid. The Lady's substance had sublimated to a semi-solid state. Was this how it would end? From solid to semisolid to . . . what? A vapor, her molecules dissipating into the air? Was that how she would end—a victim of Brownian motion?

And yet . . . why hadn't that already happened? If the Internet was down, why was she here at all? Weezy could only assume that the damaged noosphere was trying desperately to maintain her existence, and obviously losing the battle.

The mountain lake she'd described was draining dry.

"Lady?"

No motion, no response, not even a flutter of the eyelids. She seemed even less substantial than a moment ago.

Weezy felt a sob building in her chest. No need to suppress it, so she let it burst free. She'd come to love the Lady as a person. She knew she was simply a projection of the noosphere, but she seemed more than that. She seemed to have her own personality. Most likely that was merely a projection as well, but whatever it was, Weezy had come to love it.

She pulled a chair up beside the bed. She didn't want to look at what was left of the Lady, so she turned out the light. But even though the Lady wasn't human, she shouldn't have to die alone. Someone needed to be here to bear witness to her passing.

"I'll sit with you until . . ."

She couldn't bring herself to say it.

. . . *until there's no more of you to sit with.*

SUNDAY

1. Weezy awoke in the dark with a cold left hand. She remembered resting it on the bed next to the Lady's earlier. She must have fallen asleep. A cold weight rested on that hand.

Reaching across with her right, she turned on the light and gasped.

The Lady still lay on the bed as Weezy had last seen her, but she seemed more visible. No, she *was* more visible. She could no longer see the covers through her. The cold weight resting on Weezy's hand was the Lady's. It had substance now. Last night she'd been reduced to some sort of strange semiliquid, progressing toward vapor. Now she seemed to be gathering mass and moving in the other direction.

Weezy slipped her hand from under the Lady's and touched her arm. Definitely solid now.

But how could that be?

She shook her gently. "Lady? Lady, can you hear me?"

Nothing. No breath. No movement. But she was still here. And she must have moved sometime since Weezy dozed off, or else how would her hand have come to rest atop Weezy's?

She gave the Lady's arm a gentle squeeze. The flesh rebounded. How was this possible? The Internet was down, and yet she not only survived, she was rebounding.

Unless . . . had the Internet somehow rebounded just in time? It seemed too good to be true, but . . .

She looked around for a clock but couldn't find one. She dug out her cell phone and touched a key. The display lit to show no service and no time. She'd left the TV on in the front room and heard it now. She hurried out to see if she could learn anything from the tube.

The time was posted in the lower right corner of the screen: 2:32. A harried looking newsreader on one of the local stations sat at his desk, reading a press release.

". . . of Homeland Security says that Jihad-four-twenty, the virus responsible for the crash of the Internet, originated from a server in Tehran. In an unprecedented step, the intelligence services of the world are uniting to hunt down the hacker or cabal of hackers or the terrorist organization responsible."

He switched to another sheet of paper.

"The DHS has also revealed that shortly after the myriad servers and routers that feed the Internet crashed, terrorists launched a well-organized and widespread attack against the Internet's physical infrastructure. All across the globe, but mostly here in the United States, explosions ripped through the fiber-optic cables that crisscross the country and the oceans, linking data centers and nations. This will make rebuilding the Internet even more difficult. Not only will the countless crashed servers and routers need to be reprogrammed, but the damaged cables that link them will have to be repaired or replaced."

Weezy hit the mute button and stepped to the window. Clearly the Internet had not rebounded, and would not for some time. Below, the traffic was still snarled. Only a few headlights remained on. Nothing moved except a rare pedestrian.

The Internet crashed . . . the noosphere further weakened . . . the Lady should be gone. But she was hanging on.

No, more than hanging on—rallying.

How? Whence was she drawing strength?

2. The clock on the wall behind the Marriott's registration desk said it was a little after six-thirty. Jack looked out the front door. The sun hadn't yet cleared the horizon, but the sky had lightened enough to make travel feasible.

He'd spent the night trying to think of a way back to Gia's place that didn't involve a six- or seven-mile walk through the cold. Even if he could fit Gia and Vicky on the motocross bike, he couldn't guarantee their safety. He couldn't rent a car because the roads—at least all the roads he could see—were still jammed. The side streets here in Queens had probably eased up, but the problem was getting to them. Enough people had abandoned their cars, at least temporarily, to create a near-permanent snarl.

The fact that it was Sunday, without millions trying to get to work, would help, but it still might take all day to untangle this mess. They couldn't wait for that. The hotel coffee shop was out of everything but coffee, and that was in short supply. He'd managed to snag a couple of cups for Gia and himself, and an OJ for Vicky.

"Are we ready for this?" he said.

Gia and Vicky nodded. They were both well bundled up. Good thing they'd been returning from Iowa instead of Florida.

Gia looked at him. "How long do you think it will take?"

Jack had borrowed a map from the concierge during the night and checked out the shortest route to the Queensboro Bridge. Gia lived in its shadow.

"If we take the Grand Central to Northern Boulevard to the bridge, it's between six and a half and seven miles. It shouldn't be too hard to move at around three miles an hour—"

He caught Gia's glance at Vicky, then at his hip.

"I'm okay. The rest has helped." True enough. He'd

checked it in the men's room: big bruise, but much less painful. "And Vicks will be on my shoulders. I think we're talking two and a half hours, less if we're lucky."

Gia smiled. "Home by nine. You have no idea how good that sounds. I'll have scrambled eggs and coffee on the table by nine-thirty."

"You have no idea how good *that* sounds. Let's go. I'm starved."

Jack had paid the bell captain to check Gia's bag. So, unencumbered, they stepped out into the cold. Jack swung Vicky onto his shoulders and the three of them set off for Manhattan.

Vicky started singing "We're Off to See the Wizard" and Jack thought that was somehow appropriate. He would have sung along, but he feared that after last night, the Wizard's name was Rasalom.

3. "I . . . live?"

The Lady's voice was faint, hoarse, like a broom sweeping sand. She lay as she had before, but her eyes were open and she was conscious. Weezy had been watching her, talking to her, touching her. She'd seen her mouth move a few times, but these were the first words she'd heard her speak since last night.

She leaned closer. "Miraculously, yes. How?"

"Don't . . . know."

Speech seemed a war, each word a victory.

"Well, your enemies succeeded in bringing down the Net, but I guess the noosphere is stronger and more resilient than anyone imagined."

"No . . . not."

"But your continued survival is proof that it is."

"No . . . not."

"Not what?"

The Lady closed her eyes again. Weezy wanted to shake her—gently, of course—and ask her to explain, but she seemed to have slipped back into her sleep mode. The Lady had said she didn't sleep, but she was doing a convincing imitation. Except for the not-breathing part. Weezy couldn't get used to that.

She leaned back. *No . . . not.* What did she mean? That the noosphere was *not* sustaining her? How could that be? She was a creation of the noosphere, a projection of humanity's neuromass. Weezy had come to conceptualize her as a sort of hologram. But if the hologram's projector suffered a power failure, or its light source fizzled to a point where it could no longer sustain the projection, the hologram vanished.

The noosphere had suffered two crushing blows in less than a year. The nuclear strike from the *Fhinntmanchca* should have been a knockout punch. And would have been if not for the Internet. The Net had been swelling the noosphere with a massive, ongoing infusion of sentient interactions that had cushioned the blow, allowing it to continue supporting the Lady's existence. The *Fhinntmanchca* had knocked it down, but not out. It was regrouping but still had a long way to go before it regained its former depth and breadth. It needed the Internet input for recovery. Loss of that would put it on the critical list. It could never die—so long as humans existed and interacted, there would always be a noosphere—but what had happened last night should have reduced it to a shell of its former self, to Stone Age level, unable to maintain its avatar, its beacon, the Lady.

The Lady should have vanished. Yet she persisted.

And her persistence meant that this corner of reality was still perceived as sentient, and valuable—a worthy marble in the Ally's collection, and thus still under its protection.

Somehow, against all odds, Rasalom and the Order

had succeeded in bringing down the Internet yet failed to bring down the Lady.

Weezy wandered out to the front room. She wished Jack were here. Even more, she wished Mr. Veilleur were. He might be able to explain. But he hadn't returned from wherever he'd gone off to. She'd checked upstairs but the nurse he'd hired to watch over his wife said she hadn't heard from him.

She went to the window and looked out at the bright winter day.

"What's going *on*!"

4.　Hank Thompson couldn't sit still, so he left his office in the Lodge and strode down the hall toward Drexler's. Along the way he passed the grinning faces of his Kickers. They assumed their leader had been behind the fall of the Internet and they were digging it.

"Nice work, boss!" someone called.

"I didn't do anything. It was those crazy Muslims."

"Sure thing, boss." Then a laugh.

He stepped into Drexler's office without knocking because he knew it drove the uptight prick crazy.

"Well?" he said. "When does it start?"

Drexler sat behind his desk, hands steepled, tips of his index fingers against his lips. His tie was loose, and he looked uncharacteristically disheveled, as if he hadn't slept all night. Hank had slept like the proverbial baby.

As Drexler, seemingly lost in thought, looked up, his eyes focused. "What?"

He didn't even seem annoyed at Hank's intrusion. What was on his mind?

"The Change." Hank stepped to the window and gazed at the jammed traffic below. "Look at it out there. Chaos!

We've brought the whole damn city to a halt. We did our part, now your pal's got to do his."

Drexler gave him a long look. " '*Got* to'? You're going to tell the One what he's 'got' to do?"

"Well, not to his face. But the Net is down, and that means he's got a clear field to bring the Others back."

"Not unless the Lady is down as well."

"The Lady? Who's the Lady?"

Drexler looked like a kid who'd blurted something he shouldn't have.

"Nothing. Just a figure of speech."

"Yeah? Why don't I believe you?"

"What you believe is not my concern."

"You said all that was standing between the One and the Change was the Internet. Now you're talking about some lady. I think I got a right to know what gives."

"A figure of speech. Like the expression, 'It's not over until the fat lady sings.' There is no fat lady. It's just an expression."

"Like hell."

"Mister Thompson, I find you especially vexing today. Please leave. Now."

Hank was tempted to tell him to shove it, but he reminded himself, once again, that this building he and the Kickers occupied belonged to the Order, and Drexler was the Order's guy. Yeah, he'd leave, but not without a parting shot.

"Sure. I was leaving anyway. But you know what, I don't particularly care whether your fat lady sings or not. We killed the Internet. If that's all that happens, if it doesn't lead to the Change, fine. That's enough for me and Kickerdom." He'd come up with that word recently and loved it. "Because it pushes people one step closer to dissimilation. It forces them to realize that too much interconnectedness is a trap."

"Leave," Drexler said.

Hank left. He had things to do. Hadn't made any plans for cashing in on the Internet crash. The Change was supposed to follow close on its heels, but maybe it wouldn't. If not, he had to mobilize Kickerdom to get out and about and start securing converts.

Change or no Change, both presented opportunities, and Hank wasn't going to let them pass him by.

5. *We killed the Internet.*

What an idiot, Ernst thought as he watched the door swing closed behind Thompson.

Even though everything had gone according to plan, the Internet was not dead. He knew better than to think they could ever kill it. That would mean damaging it beyond repair, and that was not possible. It would be up and running in some limited form within a week or two, and soon after that would be back to near-normal activity.

Damaged and knocked unconscious, but not dead.

Questions swirled through his brain as he swiveled his chair to face the window. He put his feet up on the sill and leaned back. He was exhausted. He hadn't slept at all last night and he wasn't getting any younger.

How long must the Internet stay down to have the desired effect? How much time did the One require to begin the Change? How long would it take to restore the Lady after an inevitably revived Internet began pumping life again into the noosphere? And would it matter then? Would it be too late?

Only the One knew. Or did he? This was all terra incognita to him as well. Never before had the Change been so imminent. Perhaps he was as much in the dark as Ernst.

The Change . . .

Uncertainty, a novel emotion in his life, had plagued him since giving the word to unleash the virus. His life had been focused toward this moment. And now that it was here, he felt no triumph, only unease. He had to admit that he liked this life. He had power, position, privilege. He was privy to the forces that shaped history. And he was going to trade all that for . . . what?

The Change? Supposedly he would become one of the forces that would change the course of history—*end* history, in fact.

But what did that mean? Did anyone—even the One—know? The suspense was killing him. If only—

"You have failed me."

Ernst vaulted from his chair with a yelp of shock. He whirled to find the One standing on the far side of his desk, his expression grim, his eyes ebon eternities of fury. Fear deeper than Ernst had ever known glued his tongue to the roof of his mouth.

When he finally tore it free he managed a weak, "Failed?"

"She persists," he said, finishing with a prolonged hiss as he leaned over the desk.

Ernst repressed an urge to step back. "But the Internet is down. We succeeded—"

The One's voice remained low; Ernst almost wished he would shout.

"Was the end of the Internet the goal? No. It was elimination of the Lady. And the Lady persists. Therefore you have failed."

Ernst's heart began to pound.

"I did my part. We agreed that strangling the Internet's input was supposed to finish what the *Fhinntmanchca* began. I delivered on what I promised."

"And yet she endures. I have wasted months waiting for this scheme of yours to bear fruit. It has not. It has proved worthless. Just as you have proved worthless."

For a heartbeat, he feared the One was going to attack him—strangle him, snap his spine, hurl him through the window . . . a parade of agonizing possibilities marched through his mind.

But he did not. He simply trained his depthless black gaze on Ernst for what seemed like an eternity.

Suddenly, to Ernst's shock, he smiled.

"Fortunate for you, this meeting might have ended differently had not something *wonderful* happened yesterday."

Ernst found his voice. "Wonderful?"

"Yes!" The One became animated, almost giddy. "Something I should have suspected, but never dreamed possible!"

And then . . . he laughed. Ernst had never heard him laugh, never imagined he could.

"What—?"

"You wouldn't—couldn't understand, but it almost makes up for your failure. Yesterday I learned something that changes *evvvvvverything*."

And just as suddenly, his mood darkened. In a blindingly fast move, he reached across the desk and grabbed Ernst by the throat, lifting him off the ground as his fingers squeezed.

"But that does not mitigate your abject failure. You still might prove useful, otherwise . . ."

The last word hung in the air between them.

Ernst forced his words past the choking fingers.

"I've . . . dedicated . . . my life—"

The One's grip tightened, cutting him off.

"At last I can take direct action. I may call on you and your Order for minor logistical support, but now that I am free to act, I will take matters into my own hands. I will finish this myself."

With that he hurled Ernst across the office. The back

of his head struck the wall with brain-jarring force, blurring his vision. When it cleared, the One was gone.

At least he was alive. But what had just happened?

You still might prove useful . . .

Might? What did this mean? Would he not be elevated during the Change? Would he be left to suffer with the rabble?

And what "wonderful" occurrence had spurred such a drastic change in the One's tactics?

6. Hunger eased and bloodstream properly caffeinated, Jack arrived at Veilleur's front door shortly before ten-thirty. He'd cut a diagonal across the lower end of Central Park to shorten his walk from Gia's place. Traffic signals were still on the fritz but cops and cadets were directing at the major intersections, allowing cars to inch along. Still, he made better time walking.

Gia had whipped up breakfast while Jack had set some logs ablaze in the fireplace. None of them had thought they'd ever be warm again, but scrambled eggs and coffee—hot chocolate in Vicky's case—had worked wonders. He'd left his two ladies preparing to shower and, most likely, nap. No one had slept worth a damn last night.

Jack could have used a snooze himself, but he needed news more—news of the Lady. Neither his cell nor Gia's was working, and she'd canceled her landline last year after the accident. For all he knew, landlines were out too. The only solution left was to walk over and find out.

The doorman knew him by now and let him in. He took the elevator up to the next-to-top floor and stopped outside the Lady's door. He raised his hand to knock, but hesitated.

He'd put off thinking about this. Weezy had had to

face the Lady's death alone. He felt bad about dumping it on her, but Veilleur was off on some mission and Jack had had no choice—he loved Weezy like the sister he'd lost, but Gia and Vicky came first, and he was damn glad he'd made the trip to LaGuardia.

Now he had to deal with it: The Lady was gone. But *how* had she met her end? Poor Weezy . . .

He knocked. The door opened almost immediately and Weezy stood staring at him, her expression unreadable for a second. Then her eyes closed and her lips trembled and she fell into his arms, sobbing. He held her close, absorbing her sobs.

"I'm so sorry you had to—"

"She's alive!" she said, breaking free and wiping her eyes.

"What?"

"Somehow . . . she survived."

"Show me."

She led him to a bedroom in the rear of the apartment where daylight filtered through the closed blinds. In the dim light he could make out a shape lying on the bed. He stepped closer and recognized the Lady.

"She looks just the same," he whispered.

"You should have been here last night. She was transparent for a while. I thought—I was sure we were going to lose her then, but . . ."

With a jolt he noticed something. "She's not breathing."

"She doesn't have to. She's not a real person, and that's not a real human body."

Of course . . . obvious when he thought about it, but he'd never had to think about it until now.

"But—"

A noise from the front room cut him off. The sound of the door opening. They went to check and found Veilleur standing in the center of the room.

"It's true?" he said. "The Lady survived?"

Weezy nodded. "Yes. How did you know?"

"I would sense her absence. All the way home from North Carolina I waited to lose her, but she never left. She faded and I thought for sure that was it, but she's come back."

Jack said, "But how?"

"I think I know, but . . ."

He turned and slammed his fist on the big table. It shook the room.

"This means I'm an even bigger fool!"

Weezy stepped toward him. "What do you mean?"

"Rasalom—he knows."

"I thought we weren't supposed to say his name."

He turned toward them, eyes filled with pain. "Say it all you want now. It doesn't matter. He found me in North Carolina. He's seen me. He knows I'm old and powerless. He *knows*!"

7.

"It's a long story," Veilleur said. "Too long to tell right now."

The three of them had seated themselves at the big table. The Lady was conspicuous by her absence. Jack had recovered from his shock at the news, but not his ire. He resisted an I-told-you-so remark.

"All right, then. When? How long has he known?"

"Since yesterday morning. You said it was too risky and I should have listened. I never should have gone. It took the three of us nearly twenty-four hours to make it back here by car, and all the time—"

"Three?" Jack said. "I thought four of you were going."

Veilleur shook his head. "One of us didn't make it."

"His mother?" Jack said.

"No. She's . . ." He shook his head again. "Rasa-lom . . ."

Weezy said, "Maybe he knows about you, but if you keep saying his name, won't he find you and . . . ?"

"Kill me? He had ample opportunity yesterday, but didn't. That would send up a warning flare to the Ally. Besides, he wants me to see everything fall apart, see the Change well under way before he finishes me."

"Well, if we can use his name now, why don't we use yours as well . . . Glaeken?"

"Yeah," Jack said. "Let's let it all hang out."

"Very well." His expression remained grim. "Call me Glaeken."

"Okay, Glaeken," Jack said. "What change in tactics can we expect from Rasalom? He still can't start the Change—not with the Lady still around. The Ally won't let the Otherness in as long as our reality is listed in the 'sentient' category. So what can he do that he hasn't al-ready done?"

"He can be bolder, more aggressive. He no longer has to worry about the possibility of my lying in wait for him, baiting a trap. He's free to mount open assaults against the Lady."

"But he can't hurt her," Weezy said. "He's of this Earth and nothing of this Earth can hurt the Lady. So unless he's got another *Fhinntmanchca* lying about, he's out of luck."

Glaeken shook his head. "Don't be too sure. He's cun-ning and resourceful. She has been slain twice now. Re-member what she said about the third time."

Weezy nodded. "A third time, and Rasalom wins."

"Speaking of the Lady," Jack said, "you said you had a theory on why she's still with us. Care to share?"

"Yes," said a weak voice from behind him. "I should like an answer as well."

Jack turned and saw the Lady leaning in the arch to the

hallway. He leaped up and helped her to a seat at the table.

"Should you be up?" Weezy said, hovering.

She leaned heavily on the table. "I need to be with you." She looked at Glaeken. "I overheard. Rasalom knows?"

Glaeken nodded. "I'm afraid so."

"Tell me why I am here."

"First tell me this: Are you still connected to the noosphere?"

She nodded. "Still connected. I am still its avatar, still its beacon, but it does not support me. It cannot. It is too weak. I should not be here, yet I am. Why?"

"Because you refused to leave."

Her face reflected the shock Jack felt. "Refused? I cannot refuse."

"Hear me out. I began to suspect when the *Fhinntman-chca* didn't finish you. You winked out of existence for a few heartbeats."

"My second death."

"Yes, but then you returned—as an adult. You wouldn't have been an adult if the shocked and weakened noosphere had had to regenerate you. You would have returned as a child, am I right?"

She looked puzzled. "Yes . . . yes, I suppose that is true."

Jack wasn't following. "I don't get it."

Keeping her eyes on Glaeken, she said, "My ability to shape-shift to different ages and races is a function of the power of the noosphere. The noosphere should have been destroyed by the *Fhinntmanchca*. Instead, because of the Internet, it survived in a weakened state, thrown back to an earlier level of power when I could represent myself only as a young girl. I had no shape-shifting powers back then."

Jack said, "Why didn't you return as a young girl?"

Wonder lit her features. "I returned in the form I wore when the *Fhinntmanchca* attacked. I have been stuck in that form, unable to shift. And now, though still connected to the noosphere, I seem to be existing independent of it. How can that be?"

"Because, my dear, you have become a person."

Weezy gave her head an emphatic shake. "No. That's—"

"Impossible? Note I did not say 'human.' I said 'person.' There's a difference. The Lady has existed for so long that she's no longer a mere projection, she's developed a *self*—one with a real attachment to this world and the people who inhabit it. That self refused to leave us."

The Lady looked confused. "But if the noosphere isn't feeding me, how do I exist?"

Weezy's eyes lit. "Through us! You're being fed by humanity itself—directly."

Jack had an awful thought.

"Wait. Does this mean that Rasalom can hurt her now?"

Silence around the table until . . .

The Lady held out her hand to Jack. "Your knife, please?"

Jack pulled out his Endura, opened it, and gently pushed it across the table. The Lady took it, stared at the blade a moment, then stabbed it through the back of her other hand. Jack had known this was coming, but it still made him wince. Weezy had seen this demonstration before too, but she still let out a yelp.

They all watched as the Lady pulled the blade free. No blood on the steel, and as before, the wound sealed itself in an instant.

Jack released a breath he'd been holding. "Okay. At least we know that Rasalom can't hurt her."

Glaeken raised a finger. "Not by any means we know, but he's resourceful. He may find one. He will be relentless in seeking her third death. So our first priority must be to protect the Lady."

Jack balled his fists. "Defense again. Always defense."

Glaeken nodded. "Yes. Defend the Lady at all costs. But this latest development allows us a change in tactics."

Something in his voice . . . Jack leaned forward.

"What have you got in mind?"

Glaeken fixed him with his blue stare. "I'm releasing you from your promise, Jack. As you know, the only reason I've been holding you back was the fear that Rasalom would learn the truth about my condition. Well, thanks to a foolish old man, he now knows. So there's no further need for restraint. Go after him, Jack. Find him, kill him if you can."

Jack felt as if he'd been released from a cell.

"Open season? Anything goes?"

"Anything. You may well need anything and everything. He *can* die, but he is something more than human now, so he will be very hard to kill. Your first strike must be decisive. You may not get a second."

Weezy's expression turned fearful. "Better think this over, Jack. He's dangerous, and he's so powerful."

Jack knew. Did he ever. And that was why he wasn't going to let this rush of release take over. Yes, he was finally being allowed to do something, but he had to be careful and deliberate. When he made his moves, they'd matter.

"That's why I'll need your help," he told her. "Keep going through the *Compendium*. See if you can find a weakness, a vulnerability we can exploit."

She looked at Glaeken. "Isn't there anyone else?"

"You know there isn't. Jack is uniquely suited for this. And it makes you wonder, doesn't it, if perhaps his whole life has been steered toward this moment, this confrontation."

She turned back to Jack. "But first you've got to find him. He might not be calling himself Mister Osala anymore."

"I'd be surprised if he were."

But Jack had a good idea of where to start looking.

The rules of engagement had just changed, and Jack was going to take the war to Rasalom.

www.repairmanjack.com

THE SECRET HISTORY OF THE WORLD

The preponderance of my work deals with a history of the world that remains undiscovered, unexplored, and unknown to most of humanity. Some of this secret history has been revealed in the Adversary Cycle, some in the Repairman Jack novels, and bits and pieces in other, seemingly unconnected works. Taken together, even these millions of words barely scratch the surface of what has been going on behind the scenes, hidden from the workaday world. I've listed these works below in the chronological order in which the events in them occur.

Note: "Year Zero" is the end of civilization as we know it; "Year Zero Minus One" is the year preceding it, etc.

The Past
"Demonsong" (prehistory)
"Aryans and Absinthe" (1923–1924)**
Black Wind (1926–1945)
The Keep (1941)
Reborn (February–March 1968)
"Dat-tay-vao" (March 1968)***
Jack: Secret Histories (1983)
Jack: Secret Circles (1983)
Jack: Secret Vengeance (1983)

Year Zero Minus Three
Sibs (February)
"Faces" (early summer)*
The Tomb (summer)
"The Barrens" (ends in September)*
"A Day in the Life" (October)*

"The Long Way Home"
Legacies (December)

Year Zero Minus Two
"Interlude at Duane's" (April)**
Conspiracies (April) (includes "Home Repairs")
All the Rage (May) (includes "The Last Rakosh")
Hosts (June)
The Haunted Air (August)
Gateways (September)
Crisscross (November)
Infernal (December)

Year Zero Minus One
Harbingers (January)
Bloodline (April)
By the Sword (May)
Ground Zero (July)
The Touch (ends in August)
*The Peabody-Ozymandias Traveling Circus & Oddity
  Emporium* (ends in September)
"Tenants"*

Year Zero
"Pelts"*
Reprisal (ends in February)
Fatal Error (February)
The Dark at the End (March)
Nightworld (May)

---

*Available in *The Barrens and Others*.
**Available in *Aftershock & Others*.
***Available in the 2009 reissue of *The Touch*.

Read on for a preview of

THE DARK
AT THE END

F. PAUL WILSON

Available now
from Tom Doherty Associates

TOR®

1. "Sir!" the cabbie said in heavily accented English as Jack slammed the taxi door shut behind him. "Those people were—"

"Drive!"

"They were there first and—"

Jack slammed the plastic partition between them and shot him his best glare. "Drive, goddammit!"

The guy hesitated, then his dark features registered the truth that he wasn't going to win this one.

"Where?"

"There!" Jack pointed uptown, where the cab was facing. "Anywhere, just move!"

As the cab pulled into the bustling morning traffic on Central Park West, Jack twisted to peer through the rear window. The couple he'd shoved out of the way to commandeer the taxi stood at the curb, huddling against the March wind as they stared after him in openmouthed shock, but they seemed to be the only ones.

Good . . . as if anything about this could be called good.

He faced front again and checked his arm. His left deltoid hurt like hell. He noticed a bullet hole in the sleeve of his beloved beat-up bomber jacket. He reached inside, touched a *reeeally* tender spot. His fingers came out bloody.

Swell. Just swell. This was *not* how the day was supposed to go.

It had begun serenely enough: shower, coffee and kaisers with Gia, then a trip to Central Park West to drop in on the Lady. He knew certain forces wanted to rid the world of her, and had almost succeeded a couple of weeks ago. But he'd never expected an armed ambush.

After finding the Lady's apartment empty, he'd taken the stairs one floor up to Veilleur's floor.

Even though he could call him Glaeken now, he'd trained himself to think of him as Veilleur and Veilleur only for over a year, so shifting to his real name was going to take a little time.

He knocked on the steel door at the top step. "Hello?"

"Come in, Jack," said a voice from somewhere on the other side. "It's open."

Inside he found Glaeken slumped in an easy chair in the apartment's great room, sipping coffee as he stared out at the morning sky through the panoramic windows.

Jack slowed as he approached, struck by his appearance. He was as big as ever; his shoulders just as broad, his hair as gray, his eyes as blue. But he looked older today. Okay, the guy *was* old—he measured his age in millennia—but this morning, in this unguarded moment, he looked it. Jack hadn't been by since the Internet mess. Could Glaeken have aged so much since then?

"You okay?"

He straightened and smiled, and some—but not all—of the extra years dropped away. "Fine, fine. Just tired. Magda had a bad night."

His aged wife's memory had been slipping away for years and was little more than vapor now. Glaeken radiated devotion to her, and Jack knew he'd hoped they'd grow old together. The *old* part had worked out, but not the *together*. Glaeken was alone. Someone named Magda might be in a bedroom down the hall, but the mind of the woman he'd fallen in love with had left the building.

"Didn't the nurse—?"

"Yes, she did what she could, but sometimes I'm the only one who can calm her."

Jack shook his head. Like the old guy needed more stress in his life.

"Have you seen the Lady? I stopped in to check on how she's doing but her place is empty."

She occupied the apartment just below. Couldn't say she *lived* here, because the Lady wasn't alive in the conventional sense.

"You just missed her." Glaeken gestured to the window. "She went for her morning walk in the park."

"Really? When did she start that?"

"Almost a week now."

Jack stepped to the glass and stared down at Central Park, far below. A little to the left, ringed by winter-bare trees, the grass of the Sheep Meadow showed brown through patches of leftover snow.

"I take it she's recovering then?"

"Still weak but feeling a little stronger every day."

"Well, I guess after being wheelchair-bound and damn near dead a couple of weeks ago, that's not bad."

"Would that I had a fraction of her resilience."

Jack scanned the park but couldn't pick her out. Even though the park was relatively empty due to the cold, the strollers looked too small from up here. All his uncles looked like ants, as the joke went.

"Can you spot her?"

Glaeken rose and stood beside him, leaning into the sunlight as he squinted below. "My eyes aren't what they used to be."

"What's she wearing?"

"One of those house dresses she favors lately. It's yellow today."

"That's all? It's freezing—" He caught himself. "Never mind."

Glaeken shot him a quick glance but said nothing.

Right. He knew. The Lady didn't feel cold. Or heat. Or pain. And her clothes weren't really clothes, simply part of whatever look she was presenting to the world. She'd worn the form of Mrs. Clevenger before her near-death experience and seemed to be stuck in that form ever since.

Glaeken said, "You know how she likes to be out among her 'children.'"

Jack spotted a bright yellow someone strolling in the near half of the meadow.

"Got her." He turned away from the window. "I'll catch up to her."

"She'll be back soon."

Jack shook his head. "Got things to do. Today's the day I start looking for the R-Man."

"You can say his name now."

"I know. But it's geekier to have code names for him."

Glaeken looked at him. "Geekier?"

"Don't worry about it. Just me running at the mouth."

"I hope it doesn't indicate that you are in any way taking him lightly."

"Believe me, I'm not. I've seen what he can do."

Just my way of coping, he thought as he headed for the elevator.

Glaeken's elevator had two buttons—one for the top floor and one for the lobby. One of the perks of owning the building.

At street level, Jack waved to the doorman and stepped out onto the sidewalk. Central Park loomed just across the street. He strode to the corner of Sixty-fourth and waited for the light.

He'd developed enormous respect, maybe even a sort of love for the city's traffic signals after they'd gone down during the Internet crash. Days of pure hell followed.

They were back in working order now, though not all in sync yet. The Internet, however, still had a ways to go before it could call itself cured. The virus that had brought it down—and the city's traffic and transit systems along with it—was still replicating itself in unvaccinated regions of the Web. Cell phones were back up and running, much to everyone's relief, though local outages were still a problem.

He adjusted the curved bill of his Mets cap lower over his face. Working lights meant working traffic cams. Designed to catch red-light runners, they recorded tons of pedestrians every minute. Couldn't go anywhere these days without some goddamn camera sucking off a bit of your soul.

He crossed with the green and trotted a block uptown to one of the park entrances. He stopped at the edge of the fifteen-acre field known as the Sheep Meadow. In the old days it had lived up to its name, with a real shepherd and his flock housed in what was now Tavern on the Green. Nowadays, in warmer weather, hordes of sun worshippers littered the grass. None of those on this blustery March day, making the Lady's yellow dress easy to pick out.

He spotted her ambling along the tree line at the northern end. Gray-haired Mrs. Clevenger had been a fixture in his hometown when he was a kid, but she'd always worn black. To see her in any other color, especially yellow, was jarring.

As he started toward her, he noticed the stares she was attracting. People had to think she was a little off in the head, strolling around in this temperature wearing only a thin, sleeveless housedress.

He was about fifty yards away, and readying to call out, when four men stepped out of the trees, raised semiautomatic pistols, and began firing at her.

Jack froze for a shocked instant, thinking he had to be hallucinating, but no mistaking the loud cracks and muzzle flashes. He yanked the Glock 19 from the holster at the small of his back and broke into a run.

The Lady had stopped and was staring at the men firing nearly point-blank at her head and torso as they moved in on her. She didn't stagger, didn't even flinch. They couldn't be missing.

As he neared and got a better look, she seemed to be unharmed. No surprise. Her dress was undamaged as well. The bullets seemed to disappear before they reached her.

One of her assailants looked Jack's way. As their eyes locked the man shouted something in a foreign language and angled his pistol toward him. Jack swiveled his torso to reduce his exposure and veered left, popping three quick rounds at the gunman's center of mass. Two hit, staggering him, felling him. He landed on his back in a patch of old snow. The third bullet missed but winged his buddy behind him. Another of the attackers shouted something and fired just as Jack changed direction. He felt an impact and a stinging pain in his left upper arm. He dropped to a knee and began pulling the trigger, firing two-to-three rounds per second in a one-handed grip. This was going to run his mag in no time, but he had only one man down and couldn't allow any of the three still standing to get a bead on him.

Relief flooded him as they grabbed their wounded pal and ran back into the trees. He stopped firing and didn't follow. He'd counted thirteen rounds fired. That left two in his magazine and he wasn't carrying a spare—a firefight had not been on the morning's agenda. He did have his Kel-Tec backup in an ankle holster, but that was useful only at close range.

The Lady was staring at him. "They tried to kill me."

"Ya think?"

Jack looked at the downed attacker. His face matched the shade of the dirty snow cushioning his head. Ragged breaths bubbled the blood in his mouth. His pistol lay by his side. A Tokarev. Jack had seen a lot of Tokarevs lately—too many—and its presence pretty much nailed who'd sent him and his buddies.

The Order.

Drexler had sent out a hit team on the Lady. What was he thinking? Nothing of this Earth could harm her, and lead slugs were of this Earth. Drexler knew that. So why would he try? Unless he thought he'd come into some special super bullets.

As Jack holstered his Glock, he grabbed the Tokarev and felt a jab of pain in his left upper arm. Yeah, he'd been hit. Worry about that later. People were pointing their way, some already on cell phones. Too much to hope for one of the random phone outages here and now, he supposed. And even if they couldn't get their calls through, they could use the phones as cameras. None of the callers was too close but that could change. Cops would be here soon.

He shoved the Tokarev into his jacket and grabbed the Lady's arm.

"We've got to get you out of here."

In the good old days—as in, before last summer—she could simply change into someone else or disappear and reappear somewhere else. But nowadays she was stuck in old-woman mode and had to travel like a human.

She wasn't very spry but Jack moved her along as fast as she could go. He pulled his cap even lower and kept his head down, not exactly sure of where he was taking her— out of the park, definitely, but after that? Couldn't take her straight back to her apartment. Her damn yellow dress made her stick out like a canary at a crow convention. Needed to get her off the street, then figure out what to do.

As they reached the sidewalk he saw a taxi pull to a stop before a late-middle-aged couple—he wore an *Intrepid* cap and she carried a Hard Rock shopping bag.

Tourists. They stood a few feet ahead. He knew his next step . . .

The Lady sat beside him in the rear of the cab and stared at the blood on his hand.

"You're hurt."

"Yeah. Looks that way."

Jack wiped his fingers on his jeans and moved his left arm. Pain shot up and down when he flexed the elbow. He checked the sleeve and found the exit hole in the leather. He wondered how bad it was but wasn't about to remove the jacket here in the cab to find out.

The Lady gently touched his sleeve over the wound, her expression sad.

"Not so long ago I could have healed you."

"I know." What he hadn't known was that she no longer could. "You've lost that too?"

She nodded. "I have lost so much. But at least I am still here."

"Yeah, that's the important part. But there *is* something you could do that would help things."

"Tell me."

"Can you change into someone else?"

She shook her head. "I am not able. I am still fixed as Mrs. Clevenger."

"Well, how about switching that dress to something less noticeable?"

"That I can do." Suddenly she was wearing a drab cloth coat. "Better?"

"Much."

He marveled at how he'd come to take these things as a matter of course. The workaday world remained blissfully unaware of the secret lives and secret histories playing out around them. As he once had been. As no doubt their cabbie was.

He checked their driver. The Lady was seated directly behind him and he gave no sign that he'd witnessed the transformation. If and when he did notice the coat, he'd assume she'd carried it in with her.

Jack spotted Seventy-second Street approaching. The light was green. He rapped on the plastic partition.

"Take a right up here—into the park."

The cab turned into the traverse and headed across Central Park. Where to now? Couldn't head straight back to Glaeken's. He'd left a dead guy behind in the park. NYPD would be all over the area, collecting witness accounts, checking the traffic cams. They might end up talking to . . . he checked the operator license taped on the other side of the partition: *Abhra Rahman* . . . they might track down Abhra and want to know where he'd dropped them. Jack needed a diversionary stop.

He pictured the city. They were heading east. What was landmarky in this area of the East Side? Of course— Bloomie's down on Fifty-ninth and Lexington. Get out there, then downstairs to the subway station, hop a downtown N, R, or Q two stops to West Fifty-seventh, then cab back to Glaeken's.

Yeah. That would work.

He rapped gently on the partition. "Drop us at Bloomingdale's, please."

He'd make sure to give Mr. Rahman a good tip.

TOR

Award-winning authors
Compelling stories

Please join us at the website
below for more information
about this author and other great
Tor selections, and to sign up for
our monthly newsletter!